Praise for the Novels of Lynn Viehl

The Novels of the Kyndred

Dreamveil

"This urban fantasy is pure magic."   —The Best Reviews

"Followers of the series won't want to skip this one. . . . Rowan is a great heroine and, if you're a fan of the series, there are revelations that you won't want to miss."

—All About Romance

"Viehl's imaginative spin-off series continues as she once more explores the hazardous world of the genetically altered Kyndred. This story is rife with stunning secrets, treachery, and betrayal, [and is] guaranteed to keep readers guessing."

—*Romantic Times*

Shadowlight

"Hot enough to keep anyone warm on a cold winter's night. *Shadowlight* is an intense romantic thriller from the pen of Lynn Viehl, and readers will eagerly devour her latest in anticipation of the next installment!"

—Romance Reviews Today

"My love for Lynn Viehl's Darkyn series runs deep, and I'll admit to shedding a tear when I finished *Stay the Night*. [Then] I heard that she would be continuing to write in that world but with a new crop of characters. . . . *Shadowlight*, the first book in her Kyndred series, was everything I could ask for and more. Once again, Viehl delivers with a heroine who can stand on her own two feet, a devoted hero, and a cast of secondary characters who completely suck you into their world."

—Bitten by Books

"Expanding the world of the Darkyn . . . Lynn Viehl provides her fans with an even more complex realm in her latest enjoyable urban romantic fantasy. Fast-paced and filled with plenty of suspense."   native Worlds

continued . . .

D0251885

"Complex and engaging ... fans of Lynn Viehl will enjoy this book immensely, and hopefully a group of new fans will be brought into the fold after reading *Shadowlight*."

—Fallen Angel Reviews

The Novels of the Darkyn

Stay the Night

"Truly transfixing!"   —*Romantic Times*

"The best Darkyn novel to date."   —*The Romance Reader*

"Filled with romance, intrigue, and nonstop action, this book does not fail to satisfy."

—ParaNormal Romance
(A PNR Staff Recommended Read)

Twilight Fall

"[An] intelligent and breathtaking addition to the incomparable Darkyn series."   —Fresh Fiction

"An electrifying addition to this top-notch series ... a definite must-read."   —Romance Junkies

"A really good series ... excellent."   —*Affaire de Coeur*

Evermore

"[F]ull of exciting twists and turns.... Viehl tells a self-contained, page-turning story of medieval vampires."

—*Publishers Weekly*

"Dual cases of unexpressed love have kept two potential mates dancing around each other. Add in guilt and remorse and this is a recipe for emotional disaster. Thankfully, Viehl knows just how to liven things up: by adding danger, treachery, and betrayal to the mix. Things never run smoothly in the Darkyn world!"   —*Romantic Times*

"Lynn Viehl sure knows how to tell a hell of a story."

—Romance Reviews Today

"[O]ne of my favorites, if not *the* favorite, Darkyn book to date."   —Romance Reader at Heart

Night Lost

"Viehl continues to weave an intricate web of intrigue in this contribution to the amazing series. . . . I became completely engrossed in this compelling story. Lynn Viehl had me hooked from the first page. . . . Exceptional . . . I definitely recommend this marvelous book."
—Romance Junkies

"Fast-paced and fully packed. You won't regret spending time in this darkly dangerous and romantic world!"
—*Romantic Times*

"Fans of the series will agree that Lynn Viehl is at the top of her game."
—Alternative Worlds

Dark Need

"An exciting book and a must-read . . . frightening and creepy characters that will keep you awake late at night. Balancing the darkness is the searing heat and eroticism that is generated between Samantha and Lucan."
—Vampire Genre

Private Demon

"Lynn Viehl's vampire saga began spectacularly in *If Angels Burn*, and this second novel in the Darkyn series justifies the great beginning. Indeed, it is as splendid, if not more, than the first one."
—Curled Up with a Good Book

"Strong . . . a tense, multifaceted thriller. . . . Fans of Lori Handeland's Moon novels will want to read Lynn Viehl's delightful tale."
—*Midwest Book Review*

If Angels Burn

"Erotic, darker than sin, and better than good chocolate."
—Holly Lisle

"This exciting vampire romance is action-packed. . . . Lynn Viehl writes a fascinating paranormal tale."
—The Best Reviews

OTHER NOVELS BY LYNN VIEHL

Kyndred Series

Shadowlight
Dreamveil
Frostfire

Darkyn Series

If Angels Burn
Private Demon
Dark Need
Night Lost
Evermore
Twilight Fall
Stay the Night

NIGHTSHINE

A NOVEL OF THE KYNDRED

Lynn Viehl

A SIGNET SELECT BOOK

SIGNET SELECT
Published by New American Library, a division of
Penguin Group (USA) Inc., 375 Hudson Street,
New York, New York 10014, USA
Penguin Group (Canada), 90 Eglinton Avenue East, Suite 700, Toronto,
Ontario M4P 2Y3, Canada (a division of Pearson Penguin Canada Inc.)
Penguin Books Ltd., 80 Strand, London WC2R 0RL, England
Penguin Ireland, 25 St. Stephen's Green, Dublin 2,
Ireland (a division of Penguin Books Ltd.)
Penguin Group (Australia), 250 Camberwell Road, Camberwell, Victoria 3124,
Australia (a division of Pearson Australia Group Pty. Ltd.)
Penguin Books India Pvt. Ltd., 11 Community Centre, Panchsheel Park,
New Delhi - 110 017, India
Penguin Group (NZ), 67 Apollo Drive, Rosedale, Auckland 0632,
New Zealand (a division of Pearson New Zealand Ltd.)
Penguin Books (South Africa) (Pty.) Ltd., 24 Sturdee Avenue,
Rosebank, Johannesburg 2196, South Africa

Penguin Books Ltd., Registered Offices:
80 Strand, London WC2R 0RL, England

First published by Signet Select, an imprint of New American Library,
a division of Penguin Group (USA) Inc.

First Printing, November 2011
10 9 8 7 6 5 4 3 2 1

Copyright © Sheila Kelly, 2011
All rights reserved

SIGNET SELECT and logo are trademarks of Penguin Group (USA) Inc.

Printed in the United States of America

Without limiting the rights under copyright reserved above, no part of this pub-
lication may be reproduced, stored in or introduced into a retrieval system, or
transmitted, in any form, or by any means (electronic, mechanical, photocopying,
recording, or otherwise), without the prior written permission of both the copyright owner and the above publisher of this book.

PUBLISHER'S NOTE
This is a work of fiction. Names, characters, places, and incidents either are the
product of the author's imagination or are used fictitiously, and any resemblance
to actual persons, living or dead, business establishments, events, or locales is
entirely coincidental.
    The publisher does not have any control over and does not assume any re-
sponsibility for author or third-party Web sites or their content.

If you purchased this book without a cover you should be aware that this book
is stolen property. It was reported as "unsold and destroyed" to the publisher
and neither the author nor the publisher has received any payment for this
"stripped book."

The scanning, uploading, and distribution of this book via the Internet or via any
other means without the permission of the publisher is illegal and punishable by
law. Please purchase only authorized electronic editions, and do not participate
in or encourage electronic piracy of copyrighted materials. Your support of the
author's rights is appreciated.

DEDICATION
Por Isabelle, mi obstetriz.
Siempre que miro a mi hija,
pienso en usted.
Muchísimas gracias.

Beneath a night no longer May,
Where only cold stars shine,
One glimmering ocean spreads away
This haunted life of mine;
And, shattered on the frozen shore,
My harp can never wake—
When will this night of death be o'er?
When will the morning break?

—William Winter, "The Night Watch"

mu·ta·tion [myü-tā-shən]—noun

a. a sudden departure from the parent type in one or more heritable characteristics, caused by a change in a gene or a chromosome.

b. an individual, species, or the like, resulting from such a departure.[1]

"The results of the last 20 years of research on the genetic basis of adaptation has led us to a great Darwinian paradox. Those [genes] that are obviously variable within natural populations do not seem to lie at the basis of many major adaptive changes, while those [genes] that seemingly do constitute the foundation of many, if not most, major adaptive changes apparently are not variable within natural populations."[2]

—John McDonald, geneticist, University of Georgia

[1] Based on the Random House Dictionary, © Random House, Inc. 2010.

[2] Michael J. Behe. *Darwin's Black Box.* New York: The Free Press, 1996.

PART ONE

Golden Gate

The lord of deception and fate stared out at Sokojot-sin from the invaders' eyes. He recognized the great deceiver by how he had cloaked himself in that blackness, the color of the north, the color of death. He had lured the stinking, filthy dogs over the great waters and across the marshes and maize fields to surround the twin jewels in the center of the world. The serpent wall had not kept them out; nor had all the warriors of the House of Eagles.

They had not, for Sokojotsin had himself opened the city to them. He had welcomed them, these foul creatures, and demonstrated his superiority by bestowing many gifts on them, and permitted them to dwell among the people so that he might know them as he had known the others who had come before them. But their priests had deceived him, and he soon discovered that none of them had ever walked the path of the beautiful death. In his anger Sokojotsin had released the thousand blades to kill many of them, and drive out the rest.

That rage had been his greatest mistake of all.

The dogs had run away in fear, but their greed soon overcame their cowardice. So they made treaty with and gathered his enemies, and with them marched on the city, and conquered it in the name of their faceless God. For all of seventeen days they had drenched that indifferent altar with the blood of those they had butchered. The rest they imprisoned so that they could be questioned . . . and questioned they had been, until they died of it.

Sokojotsin was one of the last left alive. Soon they would come for him, he knew. They would come and pierce him with their ugly blades, or separate his head from his neck. His heart would die in his chest. His death would have no meaning.

He had railed at them through their smiling, cringing priests, roaring of his magnificence, of his splendor. He who had been bathed every fourth hour, who had never donned the same garment again, who had never fucked the same woman twice in a year, the sun god, the ruler of the universe, son of the silent death, the warlord and the rain, beloved of highest clouds and coldest air, the light of war, the skinner of souls.

No more. The dark metal of the gods had cast him down cruelly before the invaders, and he was undone. Now there would be no coming forth of flowers for him, no dances in his memory, no offerings of jade and serpentine. He would be tossed into one of their pits and left to rot among the peasants, without so much as a few grains of maize placed on his tongue.

He glanced at the pile of bread sitting beside the gap in the bars through which they pushed it each day. Green-gray mold covered it now. Dust and dead insects floated on the untouched water in the pail. They did not understand why he would not eat or drink, but they would not enter the cell to force it on him. Cowards, all of them.

"Sinner."

Although the scribe was one of the few dogs that spoke his tongue, Sokojotsin did not look upon his squat, robed figure hovering outside the bars. He would not pollute his eyes with the scribe's meekness.

"Sinner, I have been sent by the captain to ask you

one last time," the scribe said in his pompous fashion. "Give me the secret of the thousand blades, and your death will be quick and merciful."

Sokojotsin caught one of the beetles burrowing happily into the heap of moldy bread and held the squirming bug between two of his broken fingers. "That I could be as you, little glutton, crawling the stones and cowering in shadows so that I might eat of the shit of these dogs." He crushed the beetle and tossed it to the scribe, who scuttled away.

"You have transgressed against the one and only God," the scribe ranted. "You are cursed for all eternity. This is your last chance to save your soul."

Sokojotsin closed his eyes against the burning light streaming into his cell and waited. They would next bring one of his nineteen children before him, or perhaps one of his wives. His beloved ones would not beg, but the dogs would threaten to rape the women before his eyes or cut the throats of his sons unless he confessed. That was their way.

"Majesty."

The deep, soothing voice of his ambassador seemed to come from within Sokojotsin's dreaming, and he smiled a little until he smelled his blood. He opened his eyes to see his most trusted one standing on the other side of the bars.

Beads of blood welled on Tendile's cracked lips as he spoke. "I am brought to beg you, Majesty; do as they will of you. Could I bite the tongue from my mouth, I would, but . . ." He smiled, showing his torn, empty gums. "This kindness I would show myself, they have taken from me."

With some difficulty Sokojotsin rose and hobbled over to the bars. He could no longer stand straight, but neither could Tendile; nor would his most trusted one meet his gaze. "Look upon me, *pipiltin*."

His ambassador's bloodshot, pain-clouded eyes shifted with such reluctance that compassion filled Sokojotsin's heart. "Sire, I am the rot of the temple before you."

"Not so, my child." Sokojotsin fit his hand through the bars and graced his most trusted one with a touch to his swollen face. "It is I who sent you, and I who have failed you. You and all my people."

Tears trembled on the other man's lashes. "Majesty, we have brought this disgrace. In our shamed eyes you are as the sun."

"Your strong heart could never fail me," he assured him. "So I would see you end as beautiful as it is."

Too overcome to speak, Tendile nodded.

The scribe appeared beside his ambassador. "Enough of this nonsense," he said to Tendile. "Tell him—" His words dissolved into a girlish scream as blood sprayed into his face.

Sokojotsin jerked his hand out of his most trusted one's chest, bringing with it Tendile's heart, which pulsed once more before it went still. He lifted it up to the sunlight, praising the warrior's soul before he brought it to his mouth and drank.

The bars opened, and spiked cudgels struck Sokojotsin over and over before the dogs dragged him out. Tendile's offering had given him enough strength to lash out at them, but he did not resist or strike back. He would not give *them* the dignity of death.

They hauled him through the prison they had made of his palace to the temple, where their captain stood and watched over Sokojotsin's metalworkers. The scribe spoke quickly in their graceless tongue while he pointed and capered around the bloody prisoner.

The captain jerked up Sokojotsin's head by his hair and spit out a handful of words.

"You have committed the mortal sin of murder," the scribe translated out loud. "You will burn for it and all your other transgressions unless you tell us now. Tell us the secret of the thousand blades."

Sokojotsin kept his eyes closed as he licked the last of the blood from his lips.

"So be it. May God have mercy on your evil soul."

They dragged him to the pounding stones, where they used dark metal to lash him in place. He would die on his knees, but in a few moments he would join those who had gone before on the star path, the most beautiful path of all.

"Give it to me."

Sokojotsin felt the heat against his face, and opened his eyes to see the captain standing before him, his heavy gauntlets wrapped around the shaft of the vat dipper. Inside the deep bowl yellow-white molten ore bubbled, so hot that tiny flames danced around the edges.

"Open his mouth."

Chapter 1

June 1, 2010

"She says I don't understand women. Right before she gets up and walks out of the restaurant," Vincent O'Hara said as he reached out the driver's window to empty the last inch of cold coffee from his thermal mug. "Just like that. So I get to spend our first date sitting there by myself and eating seventy bucks' worth of lobster and prime rib."

"You don't understand women." Charlotte Marena yawned as she flipped through the completed incident reports on her clipboard and signed the bottom of each. "Why didn't you ask for a take-home box and go after her?"

"I was hungry." Vince scowled at the sound of her chuckle. "Well, I was, Charlie. Besides, if I'd gone after her, she'd have made a federal case out of whatever I did and starved me for a couple more hours."

"I warned you about dating a Botoxed bulimic," Charlie told him.

"She's not like that." Her partner sounded less certain now. "You're not always right about them."

She thought for a moment. "Let's see, the last one *was* separated, not single. The one before that *had* just gotten out of rehab, and the one before her *was* already pregnant. So, yes, I am always right about them."

"Yeah, yeah. So how could you tell this time?"

Informing her partner exactly how she knew his new flame was a botulism and binge junkie wasn't an option. "First two things I noticed about her." She pointed to the center of her forehead. "Needle marks." She brought her finger down and touched her lips. "Perpetual Listerine breath."

Vince grunted. "You could have mentioned it *after* I slept with her. Which also didn't happen." He checked his watch before he moved into the turn lane. "Time to pack it in. By the way, I did stop by her place on the way home to make sure she was okay. She wouldn't answer the door or her phone."

"Probably too busy gorging on whatever she planned to puke up." She covered a yawn with her hand. "You should date someone on the job. We're too tired to be neurotic."

He scoffed. "*You* keep turning me down."

"I'm waiting for Taylor Lautner to be legal." She reached for the radio mike on the console. "Dispatch, this is Echo one-M-seven." After the dispatcher at EMSC responded by repeating their rig's call sign, she added, "Ten ninety-eight to switch Adam, en route SFGH."

After a short pause the dispatcher replied with, "Echo one-M-seven, advise your twenty."

Surprised, Charlie glanced at the GPS. "Dispatch, we're about two miles southwest of Doyle Drive bayside."

The call came back at once. "Echo one-M-seven, respond code one to GGB viaduct, report of multivehicle collision with injuries, eleven eighty-one, CHP on scene."

GGB. Charlie's blood ran cold.

"Ah, great." Vince groaned as he rolled the steering wheel to make a U-turn and head toward the enormous, orange-red suspension bridge that could be seen from virtually any spot in the city. "Fucking East Bay commuters couldn't wait another fifteen minutes to get to work."

"Ten-four, Dispatch." Charlotte flipped on the lights to avoid looking at the bridge. "Echo one-M-seven en route, ETA two minutes." She couldn't let her phobia get the better of her, so she retrieved a war story for her partner. "Be grateful. Last time Tom and I took an eleven eighty-one, we had to evac a pregnant woman with a fractured tibia from a bad fall. I had to push her gurney all the way from the end of the pier."

"Big deal," Vince said. "I could jog that in my sleep with two gurneys."

"She weighed four hundred pounds, screamed for her mama the entire time, and nearly ripped the restraints off," Charlie told him. "Oh, did I mention she was in hard labor, and the baby crowned by the time I got her streetside for the chopper?"

"You get all the best calls, Marena." Vince yelped as she punched his shoulder. "You do."

As Vince sped toward the Golden Gate Bridge, Charlie removed their handhelds from the console charger and clipped them to their belts. After their last call, she'd stowed their carry-ins in the back to swap out at shift change, and they were both running low on dressings. Fortunately she and Vince were both religious about checking and restocking their supply bins before shift start. "I'll grab some more packing; anything else you need for your bag?"

"I used my last collar on that HNR." Her partner swerved around a slow-moving semi and blew through a red light. "Traffic had better be on point. I don't feel like dodging rubberneckers or lane hoppers."

Providing quality EMS care to the citizens of any busy, overcrowded metropolitan city always presented major challenges, but since Governor Schwarzenegger had signed Assembly Bill 2917, the county's emergency medical services authority had been required to overhaul most of their existing licensing and response systems. The bill, which had been enacted to assure that all paramedics and EMTs were properly certified, licensed,

and subject to criminal background checks, had put
nearly half of the city's private ambulance services on
probation for failure to comply with the new law. Many
EMTs who had been concealing unsavory pasts had
been fired, but others who felt outraged at the prospect
of being fingerprinted and otherwise treated like crimi-
nals had simply quit, resulting in a severe shortage of
qualified techs.

The fire department, the primary provider of the
city's 911 medical services for the past fourteen years,
had already been wrestling with call-management and
response-time problems in every district. Unfortunately
the state's response to its economic troubles was to institute a hiring freeze at the same time, which resulted in
Charlie and her coworkers pulling mandatory double
shifts every week. They were also coping with the department's new "dynamic deployment" policy, which
required ambulances to be stationed at different grid
points around the city versus waiting at their district stations for calls. It had improved their initial response
time, but if a second incident call came in for the same
area while they were responding to the first, then other
rigs had to be diverted from their assigned points, which
created instant gaps in the deployment grid.

It didn't help that one-third of the calls the department received every year were for nonemergency situa-
tions. Most of those callers turned out to simply need a
ride to the hospital, and thought the fire department
should provide free taxi service. Some days Charlie felt
more like a bus driver than a medic.

The windshield turned white as the dense fog rolling
in from the bay swamped them, erasing the bridge entrance road and making the two bridge towers appear as
if they were nothing more than a couple of bright red
clips sticking out of an old lady giant's fluffy white hair.

Vince flipped on the fog lamps before he peered
ahead. "You see the HP?"

Charlie spotted the muted red and blue lights flashing through the fog. "Looks like he's up by the pylon." She ignored the tightening in her chest and picked up the mike. "Echo one-M-seven, dispatch, please advise traffic response to eleven eighty-one GGB city-side."

"Echo one-M-seven, Marin County Sheriff currently diverting southbound at tollbooth," the dispatcher told her. "CHP backup en route, ETA four minutes."

Marin County had shut down the tollbooths, which would keep commuters coming from the opposite direction toward San Francisco off the bridge, but the accident was located on the south end, where there were no tollbooths, and Highway Patrol was two minutes behind them. While northbound traffic was lighter in the mornings, rush hour still attracted thousands of drivers. Low visibility due to the fog added another dangerous obstacle, one that had the potential to turn a simple fender bender into a massive pileup.

"What the hell is that trooper doing, just sitting up there instead of setting up the barricades?" Vince grumbled. "How much you want to bet he's some rookie tossing his last coffee and doughnut over the railing?"

"I don't bet against the Highway Patrol," she told him as she gnawed at one side of her bottom lip before she called in again. "Dispatch, Echo one-M-seven, ten forty officer on scene?" They didn't usually radio the patrolmen directly, but the northbound lanes needed to be blocked off now.

"Echo one-M-seven, OS is code six, not responding."

"Told you," her partner said. "He's puking his guts out."

"Or he's performing CPR." Charlie frowned. Even the greenest rookies knew to carry their handhelds with them when they left their vehicles. Something wasn't right.

"What else would keep him so busy that he couldn't respond to dispatch?" Vince demanded.

Charlie knew. "Jumper."

The Golden Gate Bridge held one grisly honor, in that it was the most popular place in the world to commit suicide. Roughly twice a month someone leapt from the deck and dropped two hundred and forty-five feet to the water below, where they almost always died on impact. Those few who survived hitting the water's surface, which at the height and speed of the jump was equal to crashing into a concrete wall at seventy-five mph, would then either drown or succumb to hypothermia.

A few years back Charlie had been disgusted to learn that a documentary maker had been given permission by the bridge authority to film the bridge as a monument, only to use the permit to secretly capture footage of twenty-three of the twenty-four suicides that had occurred that year.

Vince, one of the few people aware that Charlie actively avoided the bridge—no one knew why—was giving her the quick glances of a man trying to drive too fast and see whether his partner was going to lose it at the same time.

"I'll call for another rig," he said, reaching for the mike.

"No." She put her hand on his to stop him. "Odds were that it would happen sometime."

"Charlie, we gotta go *on* the bridge, and you've got fucking bridge-a-phobia," he said. "You sure?"

"It's okay. I'm fine." No; she wasn't, but as much as she wanted to dump the call on someone else, she couldn't dodge her responsibility. Nor could she ask Vince to drop her off at the next corner and let him handle it alone. She would do her job, no matter how many ghosts were waiting for her at the scene.

"You've never told the powers that be about this thing of yours, have you?" Vince asked.

"Not something you put on the résumé, partner." She rubbed her eyes. "You know, I won't even drive across the goddamn thing. I always take the ferry."

"Good day to get over this shit, then," Vince said, giving her shoulder a gentle cuff. "Ferry's too fucking slow."

To keep from screaming, Charlie focused on the call

and what possibly could have gone wrong. Highway Patrol responded to jumper calls, and often talked down the suicidal before they took the fatal leap. If the officer on scene was actively engaging the jumper, he might have temporarily turned down his radio to keep from spooking them.

But as they approached the S1 pylon, Charlie didn't spot anyone on the walkway or the deck railing. In fact, she could see the black Highway Patrol car with its distinctive white door and golden star emblem, and the trooper still sitting in it. He'd parked it in front of a blue compact, a silver SUV, and what appeared to be a long black limousine. From the damage to both vehicles Charlie could see that the SUV had rear-ended the compact, crushing the trunk as well as crumpling its own hood. The limo sat facing the compact as if the driver had been driving in the opposite direction and had swerved over and stopped to render assistance.

Or the rich asshole told his driver to make a U-turn on the bridge and caused the accident, Charlie thought. *That would be more logical.*

She needed to learn what she could before the sun rose, so she closed her eyes and listened. The blare of the rig's sirens and her own fluttering heartbeat dwindled away and a different sound filled her thoughts.

The thought stream came roaring through her. *Can't give in can't let her be shot he won't die she will the pain I can't stand it damn it let me think.*

The agony he was feeling came along with his thoughts, and racked her with such intense pain that she almost doubled over. She managed to shut off the stream and looked at the CHP vehicle, but she couldn't tell whether the thoughts were coming from the trooper.

As Vince drove up behind the trooper's car, Charlie's eyes went into snapshot mode, taking in the scene with brief, intense glances. Car doors left hanging open. The flash of an orange taillight. Two bodies sprawled in the middle lane. A third lay half in, half out of the compact's driver-side door. She focused on the most important elements at the scene—the victims—and began to assess. Bloodied clothes, slack faces, awkward positions. None of them moved.

Death. Once more, the bridge was covered in it.

"Shit." Vince reversed, turning the rig so that they faced oncoming traffic, and switched on their front and side flashers. "You ready for this?"

She nodded. "Go."

Charlie jumped out, running behind to yank open the doors and grab their carry-ins. She paused only long enough to stuff two handfuls of bandages into a side pocket before she trotted around and tossed Vince's bag to him. Her partner ran to the two victims in the road while she went to the officer.

"Officer, why are you . . ." She stopped as she saw the telltale spiderweb of cracks around the small hole in the patrolman's front windshield, and the corresponding hole in the officer's forehead. She reached in to check for a pulse that no longer beat before she grabbed her handheld. "Dispatch, Echo one-M-seven, EMP Charlie Marena, ten ninety-seven S-one pylon, ten one-oh-eight, officer down, GSW to the head, request immediate assistance—"

Something cracked sharply, then whined in her ear as her radio unit exploded in her hand. At the same time a man's voice shouted, *"Get down."*

Charlie wrenched open the trooper's door and crouched behind it, looking out at Vince, who was trying to shield the victims with his own body.

Another disjointed thought stream began jabbering inside her head: *Golden giant midnight girl all here now master I see I can do this I can take them bring them have my reward live forever yes live forever at his side his forever always eternity yes I can do this forever and ever and ever.*

"Charlie." Vince grabbed both bodies by the collars of their clothes and began dragging them toward her. *"Shooter."*

Staying crouched over as far as she could, she met her partner halfway and seized one of the bodies under the arms.

"The cop?" Vince demanded.

"Dead." She saw her patient's chest move and the blood oozing from the head wound of Vince's vic. "But these two aren't. Let's move it."

They managed to drag the two victims behind the patrolman's unit and grab Charlie's bag before another shot rang out. This time it shattered the back window of the limo.

As they went to work on the victims, Vince popped his head up to look around. "Did you see where he is?"

There were no other vehicles at the scene, and hardly anyplace on the bridge where a gunman could hide. But the morning fog had effectively blanketed the bridge deck all the way past the south tower, so for all Charlie knew he could be standing out in the open on one of the walkways, or even atop the safety railing.

As the gunman fired again, she grabbed Vince's shoulder and jerked him down. *"Careful."*

"Always . . . right." Her partner swayed and then slumped over, blood streaking down his face from a long, deep gash in his scalp.

"Vince."

She eased him down and straddled him, working quickly to probe and then dress the wound as she tried to rouse him. "O'Hara? Come on, partner. No sleeping on the job."

His eyelids fluttered, and he groaned. "Fucker . . . caught me." He squinted at her. "How . . . bad?"

She checked his pupils with her penlight, and felt a surge of relief when they reacted normally. "I think you're going to be parting your hair differently from now on."

"Charlotte, are you hurt?"

Hearing her name being called out by the man from the limo made Charlie frown. "We're fine." He must have heard her using her radio and assumed Charlie was short for Charlotte. "Stay where you are. Are you injured?"

"No. My driver was shot in the chest," he called back. "He's lost a great deal of blood."

The driver had to be the one whose thoughts and pain she'd picked up. Or this driver might not exist and Limo Guy was the shooter, trying to lure her out in the open. Until she got closer to them she wouldn't know. "Sir, do you know where the gunman is?"

"South tower," he answered. "Left side."

Charlie glanced over the edge of the vehicle at the tower, but at first saw only fog and shadows. Then the first rays of the sun pierced the fog, and a tiny glint of light flashed from the base of the tower. A second later another window blew out on the limo.

Charlie's relief was short-lived. Limo Guy wasn't trying to make her victim number seven, but the man by the south tower would, and to be able to do this much damage from that distance meant he had the skills and accuracy of a highly trained sniper. Hearing the wail of approaching sirens didn't improve the situation; if the gunman had enough ammunition, he could shoot anyone who set foot on the bridge.

Somehow Charlie had to warn the cops.

Quickly she searched through the clothing of the two victims to look for a mobile phone, but found nothing. "Sir," she called out toward the limo. "Do you have a phone with you?"

"There are two in the car," he said, "but I can't leave James."

"That's okay. Stay right there with him." She slung the strap of her carry-in over her neck and cinched it so that it pressed against her chest. She lowered herself to the ground on her forearms and knees, letting the fog waft over her before she began crawling toward the limo.

It seemed to take forever, and the roughness of the

asphalt scraped through her sleeves and trousers. Charlie held her breath as she moved across each open gap, praying silently that the fog was concealing her movements as much as she hoped. By the time she reached the shiny front bumper of the big car she was shaking all over.

As soon as there was enough limo between her and the sniper, Charlie yanked the strap over her head and rose in a half-crouched position, moving quickly to the two men taking cover behind the rear wheel well of the limo. One was a slim, dark-haired man wearing a chauffeur's uniform with blood blooming on the right side of his jacket; the other man was a golden-haired, bearded hulk in a black trench coat. The hulk had the chauffeur cradled against his arm, and held a folded, red-splotched white silk scarf pressed against the wound in his chest.

He looked up at her with narrow black eyes that were all wrong for his Nordic golden hair and gorgeous mocha skin.

Something like déjà vu came over her. Charlie would have sworn on a stack of Bibles that she had never seen the man before this moment. He was too big, too odd, too unforgettable, and yet . . . she knew him.

The jolt of familiarity had to be some kind of fluke, she thought, shrugging it off. She'd seen someone like him once; that was all.

"He can barely breathe," the man told her.

She glanced at the blue tinge around the driver's lips and the distended veins in his neck, and her focus abruptly shifted back to her job.

"Were you shot?" she asked him as she tore open the chauffeur's jacket and used her stethoscope to check his heart and lung sounds.

"I'm fine," he said. "What's wrong with James?"

"His lung has collapsed." She reached into her case and pulled out her pneumothorax pack. "I have to bleed out the air trapped in his chest or his heart will fail. What's your name?"

"I'm Samuel, and you are Charlotte." He said her name precisely, and with a certain amount of satisfaction.

"Actually, I go by Charlie." She smiled to remove the sting. "Now, let's put James here down on his back."

Once they had carefully lowered the driver onto the ground, Charlie pulled his clothing out of the way and took out the scalpel from the pack.

Samuel frowned. "You're not thinking of operating on him. Not here."

"No, I'm simply going to make a small incision so I can put in a tube to remove the air." As she lined up what she needed on the driver's chest, she saw Samuel's expression. "I know this sounds scary, but I've done it a hundred times and I haven't lost anyone yet. So don't freak out on me, okay?"

He nodded.

"Here we go." She made the incision, cutting through the skin and the underlying tissue, and then fed the decompression catheter into his body just above the cephalad border of the rib to avoid the intercostal vessels. Within a few seconds the driver's breathing became less labored, and his lips began to turn pink.

"That's more like it." She taped the catheter in place and checked his breathing sounds again before she turned her attention to the blood-soaked scarf. "Sam, I need you to move your hand now. When James was shot, did you see any blood spurting from his gunshot wound? Like a little geyser or fountain?"

"It was more of a small stream. A pulsing stream." As she reached for the edge of the scarf, he reluctantly took his hand away. "Is it his heart?"

She carefully lifted the side of the makeshift bandage and inspected the wound, noting the position of the small, neat hole and the seepage from it. "Doesn't look that way. I think the bullet might have just nicked the lung. We'll know better when we get him to the hospital." She began dressing the chest wound. "Where exactly are the phones in the car?"

"One is in the front console by the driver's seat," he said, nodding in that direction, "and the other is on the right side of the rear-facing seats in the back."

Neither would be easy to reach unless she opened the limo's doors and crawled inside. "Dispatch doesn't know about the sniper. I have to call this in before backup arrives." She cringed as a shot pinged off the roof of the limo. "Son of a bitch. How much ammo has he got?"

"The backseats are in his direct line of fire," Samuel told her as he moved to the other side of James's still form. "I'll retrieve the phone from the front."

He was already moving toward the driver's door before she could argue with him. "Keep your head down," she called after him.

The sniper fired three more times before Samuel returned with the cordless receiver. As glass shattered over their heads, he ducked, lost his balance, and nearly fell over.

"Whoa." Charlie grabbed his sleeve and righted him. "I thought you said you weren't hurt."

"I'm only a bit awkward." He leaned on his left side and rubbed his hand over his thigh. "Normally I use a cane to walk."

She saw the cane in question several feet away by the deck railing. The gold handle had been cast in the shape of a lion's head. "You'll have to do without it for now." She put the receiver on speaker and dialed the emergency number for dispatch, which the shift supervisor answered immediately. "This is Echo one-M-seven, EMP Marena. We have five GSW casualties on the bridge with an active sniper at the base of the south tower, left side." She rapidly related the details of the wounded before she added, "My partner has been shot and I'm taking cover with two of the vics."

"Stand by." The supervisor repeated the details she'd

given him over the police emergency band before issuing terse orders to reroute other rigs to the scene. Finally he said, "Echo, we can't get to you until SWAT
responds and secures the scene. Keep this line open and
use your MCI protocols."

"Acknowledged, dispatch." Another window blew
out over their heads, pelting them with broken glass.
"You want to tell SWAT to move their asses, please?"

"They're on the way," the supervisor promised.
"Hang in, Echo."

"What are MCI protocols?" Samuel asked as she
started an IV on the driver.

She tore off a strip of tape and rolled it over the gauze
she'd placed over the needle. "It's how we respond to a
mass casualty incident."

"You consider this a mass casualty situation?"

"Any incident that has more patients than the on-scene
responders can treat or transport is an MCI," she told
him. "The protocol we use is called START, for simple
triage and rapid treatment, which includes tagging everyone." She pulled her tags out of her bag. "James here gets
a red tag, which means he's salvable but he needs immediate treatment." She taped the oversize tag onto the driver's sleeve and then clipped another onto Samuel's lapel.
"You're walking wounded, so you get one of these."

He glanced down at the green tag. "I'm not wounded."

"We don't have a tag for 'nothing happened to this
guy,' so it's the next-best thing." She shoved the rest of
the tags in her pocket, where she could easily reach
them, and slung her carry-in strap over her neck. "I have
to get back and tag the others. You keep your head
down, and yell for me if James starts having trouble
again."

One of his huge hands clamped around her wrist.
"You're not going anywhere."

Samuel Taske was not accustomed to trying to restrain a
woman with physical force. Aside from his size and

strength, both of which bordered on superhuman, he had been taught virtually from birth to treat all females with gentleness and respect.

He didn't consider it a hardship in the slightest. He adored everything about women: their scents and smiles, their instincts and intelligence. He often watched them with the wistful longing of a man who had already accepted that he would live out his life alone, thanks to the additional psychic gift that allowed him to see individual time lines as they stretched out far into the future. He had used it to examine his own future, which followed a solitary path that would never be crossed or entwined with that of a wife or children.

That he was prepared to break Charlotte Marena's wrist to keep her from leaving him had nothing to do with his feelings about women. He had come to this place, to this bridge, solely for the purpose of keeping her alive. If he had to put her in a cast to do so, he would.

"Sam, I have to do this," she was saying in a careful, gentle tone she probably used with people suffering some sort of mental crisis. "I need to check on the other patients and make sure they're doing okay. It's my job."

"You can't do anything for them if you're dead, Charlotte." He didn't release her. "The police will be here soon. I can hear the sirens."

"They might have a hostage negotiator try to talk him down first," she said. "That kind of thing usually takes time."

"Then I'll have to entertain you with stories from my last trip overseas." He had to stop staring at her big dark eyes; he felt as if he were about to tumble into them. "Have you ever been to Paris? Very old and stately. Amazing cuisine. Dreadful waiters."

"Can't say I have." Instead of lightening, her expression turned grim. "Much as I'd love to hear all about your jaunts around the globe—"

"*Oye, cabrón.*"

The high-pitched shout came from the tower beyond, and Charlotte's eyes narrowed.

"I know you hear me, *pendejo*." A short laugh followed the shout, and then, "Hey, *hermana, ese tipo tiene mucha lana*, eh? Maybe after, he give you a big reward, eh?"

Samuel frowned. "I don't speak much Spanish."

"I do. He says you have a lot of money," Charlotte said, her mouth tight. "You know this jackass?"

"Not at all." Half the truth was better than none. "Do you think you can persuade him to cease fire?"

Charlotte rubbed her eyes and sighed before she called out, *"Señor, deje lo que estás haciendo y escúchame."*

From that point Charlotte spoke too rapidly for Taske to follow, but he took advantage of her focus on the sniper to remove one glove and ease his hand inside his coat. Dragging James out of the car had torn some of the stitches in his side, but thanks to his body heat the blood-soaked linen of his shirt had partially dried and was beginning to stanch the old wound. He'd thought he might have to use it as an excuse to keep Charlotte with him, but now that she had engaged the sniper, there was no need to mention it.

Not that he wished to. Charlotte would want to know how he had sustained the injury, and he couldn't tell her the truth. She would never believe that he had been attacked by werewolves and wild animals, all of whom had been under the mind control of Lilah Devereaux, a powerful Kyndred friend whom Taske believed also held the key to a cure for his own condition. He'd stalked Lilah, hiring detectives to hunt her down for him, but his foolish actions had nearly gotten them both killed. In the end Lilah had forgiven him, but Taske had yet to overcome his own shame.

The mellow contralto of Charlotte's voice felt soothing to his ears, and he allowed himself to rest against the side of the car and watch her. For the first time since his

ability had manifested it had been maddeningly short on
details; unlike the other people he had rescued over the
years, this woman's time line had been shrouded in
darkness. He'd been unable to discern who she was,
where she lived and worked, her surname, or any clue of
what her destiny was, although he sensed it to be of crit-
ical importance to humanity. In the end he had been
forced to act on the only thing he did know: that unless
he saved her, a woman named Charlotte would be murdered on the Golden Gate Bridge by a suicidal man.

Until she had crawled out of the fog, Taske hadn't
even known exactly what Charlotte would look like, another first for him. For some reason he had expected her
to be a dark, petite angel with a beguiling smile, not a
fierce-eyed Amazon with as many muscles as she had
curves. No doubt her statuesque proportions had drawn
some criticism from those who kissed the bony, wasted
feet of current fashion, but she made him think of the
glory of forgotten eras, when towering warrior queens
had been worshiped as goddesses.

Acolytes of Apollo would have made her their high
priestess; sunlight had scattered golden streaks through
her dark brown hair and kissed her brown eyes with amber flecks. Her tanned skin had a delicious bloom to it,
like the rose flush of a ripe peach. He had never met a
woman who looked more vital and alive than Charlotte
Marena, which made his mission all the more imperative. Something inside her made her glow like a beacon
of hope; her mysterious destiny must be directly linked
to hundreds if not thousands of other lives.

After she repeated the same question three times,
Charlotte fell silent and listened. After a minute and no
response from the gunman she shook her head and
glanced at Taske. "This guy isn't a Chicano—a Mexican-
American," she tacked on as an explanation of the term.
"I can't place his accent, either. He's trying to talk like a
street thug but he's using formal Spanish. He's also slur-
ring his words."

"How is that significant?"

"It could be caused by drug use or psychosis." She hesitated before she said, "Sometimes these guys go off because they're sick. Whitman, the guy who shot all those people from that tower in Texas back in the sixties, had an aggressive brain tumor."

Taske heard equal parts of frustration and regret in her voice, and saw the way she kept glancing toward the east. "You can't negotiate with a diseased mind, Charlotte."

"I know. Neither can the cops." She picked up the phone. "Dispatch, Echo one-M-seven, come back."

"Go ahead, Echo."

"Please advise SFPD and CHP—"

The high-pitched voice from the tower interrupted her as the sniper shouted at them.

"Stand by, dispatch." She listened, frowning.

"What is he saying?" Taske prompted.

"I don't know. Something about white willows." She turned her head. " 'The time has come for us to go, by day or by night, down into the mysteries of death. I make my tribute,' or maybe 'my offering. . . .' "

A shout came from the tower. *"¡La Raza Cósmica!"*

Her expression grew alarmed. "Oh, God, he's going to jump." She shot to her feet. *"Señor, por favor, escúchame ahora—"*

Charlotte stood too far away for him to pull down, and Taske forgot about the burning, twisting snake wrapped around his own spine as he shot up and staggered forward to shield her with his body. He had his arms around her when she cried out, but not because she had been shot.

A man's limp body fell from the tower. At first Taske couldn't make sense of it, until he saw the blood streaking the slack face. An instant later the body slammed into the walkway railing before it flipped and disappeared over the side.

It seemed that the gunman had taken one final life—his own.

Charlotte closed her eyes and turned her face against his chest. She didn't speak, but her whole body shook violently.

He stroked her back as he stared at the now-empty tower. Although the pain searing his back and side had yet to abate, he felt a sense of overwhelming relief along with a terrible pity.

"I need to check the others," Charlotte said as she stepped away from him, her voice still raw with emotion. "Can you give me a hand and get the gurney from my rig?"

He wanted to do nothing more than slide to the ground and stay wherever he landed, but he nodded and limped over with her to where her partner and the other victims lay. Every step sent a new jolt of misery along his spine and tore at the edges of the wound in his side. As she pulled her tags from her jacket he hobbled past her to open the back doors of the ambulance. He had to pause for a moment to catch his breath before he unbuckled the strap holding the gurney in place. Pulling it out of the back of the rig almost caused him to fall atop it, and he braced his hands against the side rail as he fought back the pain.

She has enough to deal with now, Taske thought, staring down at his whitened knuckles. *I can wait until more help arrives.*

Years of stringent self-discipline allowed him to move through the pain until it subsided enough for him to breathe again. With some difficulty he reached down to lock in place the wheels on the extending frame.

Charlotte appeared on the other side of the gurney. If anything, she looked even paler than before. "Sam."

"Where do you—" He stopped as he saw the man behind her, and the rifle he held pointed at the back of her head. He was the same man who had been shooting from the tower. Taske was so shocked to see him he said exactly what he thought. "You threw someone else off the bridge."

"Shut up." The man jerked his chin at the open back of the ambulance. "Inside."

Before Taske could reply Charlotte said, "Do what he says."

He pushed the gurney inside and used the open door to hoist himself into the back of the rig. The effort sent him to his knees, but he recovered quickly.

Charlotte followed, turning around at once to face the gunman. "Please stop this. Leave us here; we won't try to stop you. You can still get away."

"No one escapes the master." The gunman's lips parted, showing beautiful white teeth that had been filed down to sharp points in a shark's grin. He slammed the doors shut.

Charlotte grabbed the inside handle, jerking on it. "He's jammed it," she said to Taske as she spun around, scanning the interior. She went still as the door to the front cab opened and closed and the engine started. "No, he can't— Damn it." She pushed past Taske and went to the sliding window, pounding on it with one fist. "Hey, listen to me. You can't do this; those people out there are in—"

Something hissed, and she coughed and fell back against Taske.

He looked down at her chest, expecting to see blood and a bullet wound, not smoke pouring from a small metal canister in her lap. He held his breath and bent over, trying to grab it, but it rolled off her leg and disappeared under the gurney.

Taske's eyes burned as he dragged Charlotte to the back of the rig, where he heaved himself against the doors. Metal dented and groaned, but they remained locked. He slammed his shoulder into them until white fire enveloped his spine, felling him as it forced out the breath he was holding.

Taske coughed uncontrollably, but somehow managed to hold on to Charlotte's limp form. He dragged her close, trying to focus his bleary gaze on her still features. Even if the gunman didn't kill them both, Samuel knew from the warm wetness he now felt seeping from his side how unlikely it was that he would ever see her face again.

His last thought was of how utterly he had failed her. *I wish I had been stronger, Charlotte. Then I might have saved both of us. . . .*

Chapter 2

The CEO of the most powerful biotech corporation in the world looked down the length of the conference table at the faces of his department heads. None were fool enough to avoid Jonah Genaro's gaze or show their emotions, but he could smell the fear hovering, an invisible, quivering cloud over their heads.

"I have reviewed all the reports regarding the incidents in Denver and New York." He let the stack of files in his hands drop onto the table. "All they tell me is that this company has now failed three times to secure acquisitions vital to the successful development of the transerum."

One of his attorneys discreetly adjusted the knot in his tie. "Mr. Genaro, it's becoming increasingly difficult to divert unwanted attention from the media and the federal authorities. I strongly advise that we consider a fresh approach to ... acquiring ... these particular assets for the project."

"I agree," Eliot Kirchner, Genaro's chief geneticist, said. "We've known for some time that a select group is somehow communicating with one another, and we've seen evidence of cooperative behavior. They could be organizing."

"I disagree. The last thing these people want is for anyone to know what they are," Don Delaporte, Genaro's security chief, said. "They're not going to start a members-only club."

"Then how do you explain the losses here in Atlanta?" Kirchner demanded. "Bellamy had help escaping capture. So did the female shifter in New York."

"We know Andrew Riordan interfered in the Bellamy case," Delaporte said, referring to Genaro's former technical supervisor. "We were unable to uncover any connection between him and Gerald King, who enabled the shifter to escape capture in New York."

"Excuse me," Evan Shores, the head of accounting, said.

Delaporte ignored him. "Nor was Riordan in any way involved with Tina Segreta's operation in Denver. You're seeing conspiracies everywhere, Doctor."

"Excuse me." Shores used a too-loud voice, and cringed a little as everyone turned to stare at him. "I'm sorry, but there is someone who was peripherally involved in two of the incidents."

Genaro sat down. "Who is it?"

"Uh, an antiques dealer named Samuel Taske, sir." The accountant sat up a little straighter. "Before he died, Gerald King appointed him executor of his estate, as well as the legal guardian of his teenage daughter."

"King's daughter was already cleared," Kirchner snapped. "She's too young to fit the profile."

"It's not that, sir," Shores assured him. "Samuel Taske also flew to Denver the day after you and Ms. Segreta arrived there." He pulled a sheet from his file. "I have the hotel records."

"What do we know about Taske?" Genaro asked.

"We ran a standard background check on him when he assumed custody of the King girl," Delaporte said. "He's the son of Davis Taske, the discount-supermarket-chain mogul. As the sole heir, Samuel Taske inherited fifteen billion dollars from his family's estate, which he has since doubled, mainly through the acquisition and sale of rare art and antiquities. He maintains a controlling interest in Taskecorp, but continues to work as an antiques dealer out of Boston. Tax records show that over the years Taske sold several works of art to King. Taske also gave the eulogy at King's funeral and called him his 'good friend.'"

Genaro turned to the accountant. "Why was Taske in Denver?"

"I can't say, sir," Shores admitted, "but his financial records show that he travels frequently around the country."

"That's not unusual for a man who buys and sells antiques," Delaporte said. "Taske is well-known in his business, and he's never tried to avoid publicity. Quite the contrary; we were able to access dozens of photos of him from newspapers and trade magazines."

Genaro, who knew the value of hiding in plain sight, wasn't convinced. "Can you tell me where he was when the New York operation fell apart?"

Shores consulted his records. "He flew to New York a week before Gerald King died."

"No doubt to find the daughter," his security chief said. "She ran away from home just after King was diagnosed with terminal cancer. After the old man died, Taske was the one who found her."

"And this good friend of Gerald King's just happened to go to Denver at the exact same time we lost two of our acquisitions." Genaro sat down. "Mr. Delaporte, I want a complete investigation performed on Samuel Taske. Find out everything about him they don't print in antiques magazines. Mr. Shores, I want to see a complete breakdown on his personal and business financial records."

Shores nodded eagerly. "How far should I go back, sir?"

"Birth, Mr. Shores." He regarded the rest of his supervisors. "The rest of you gather the peripheral data. I want to see lists of known associates, employee rosters, medical records, school transcripts, every single thing

this man has done since he was removed from the womb.
I expect prelim reports by close of business today. Now
get out."

All of his employees except one quickly left the conference room. Kirchner lingered by the door and, once
the last supervisor passed him, closed it.

Genaro didn't glance at him. "I am not in the mood
for one of your tantrums, Eliot."

"Then it's fortunate that I'm not planning to have
one." He walked over and placed a slim jewel case on
the table in front of Genaro. "I received this last night
from the lab in Denver. It's all the data they were able to
recover from Segreta's laptop."

Genaro frowned. "Give it to technical for analysis."

"I don't think you'll want them to analyze her final
video phone conversation with you." He sat down in the
chair beside him. "You had her sedate me and search me
on the plane. Why?"

Of course Tina had recorded everything; she hadn't
been in the business of selling merely herself. "She led
me to believe that you were working for outside inter-
ests."

Kirchner removed his jacket and began rolling up his
sleeves.

"What are you doing?"

"You've forgotten why I do this." Once he had bared
his forearms, he turned his wrists out so that the old,
dark lines marring his skin were visible. "You remember the conditions of my last employment. They kept
me locked in that lab for years. They deliberately ad-
dicted me to heroin to keep me motivated. The only
reason I'm alive is because you purchased me. You
took me out of there, cleaned me up, and gave me back
my freedom." He extended one arm. "This is what's
waiting for me out there. The abyss. Now, why the hell
would you think I'd repay you by voluntarily jumping
back into it?"

"Of all my people, you are the one I depend on most,"

Genaro told him. "Lately you've become temperamental and paranoid. I have to know the reason for it."

Kirchner drew his arm back. "I am not experimenting on rats or monkeys, Jonah. For the sake of creating a successful transerum, I have sanctioned the kidnapping, torture, murder, and dissection of human beings. If we fail, all I have to look forward to are a few miserable years on death row before I'm given a lethal injection. Or it's back to the abyss."

"We are not going to fail." He looked over as the conference room door opened and Delaporte stepped inside. "What is it?"

"Taske," his security chief said, crossing over to the wall monitor and accessing the public broadcasting feed. "He's just been taken hostage in California."

Genaro watched the special news report on the Golden Gate Bridge sniper, who shot half a dozen motorists and killed a state trooper before abducting the antiques dealer and a paramedic from the scene.

"The first patrolmen responding to the scene did not attempt to stop the sniper, who used the paramedic's ambulance as his getaway vehicle," the news anchor said. "Authorities have issued an all-points bulletin for the stolen rig and the alleged gunman, who is said to be a Hispanic male in his mid-fifties. Police advise that the suspect is armed and should be considered extremely dangerous. Anyone with information as to his whereabouts should contact their local police, the California Highway Patrol, or the Crimebusters toll-free tip hotline."

Delaporte switched off the monitor. "I've contacted our San Francisco office. The shooter isn't one of ours."

"I should hope not." Kirchner looked appalled.

"They're monitoring the situation," the security chief continued, "but the consensus is that this was a random act of violence."

"The sniper shot everyone but Taske and the paramedic. There is nothing at all random about that." Genaro checked his watch. "Contact the flight crew and have them prepare the jet to fly to San Francisco in one hour."

Delaporte frowned. "Sir, our office out there has an excellent team of investigators and operatives."

"No doubt they do." Genaro stood. "This time I will be able to personally assess their performance in the field."

Sirens wailed in Charlie's ears, sending invisible ice picks into her brain. Her lungs felt as if she'd inhaled fire, and her heart thudded dully under her ribs. Something had been wrapped around her head—a sack or a pillowcase. A sudden screech of brakes sent her sliding into something big, hard, and immovable; she felt soft hair brush across her face.

Hands yanked her away by the ankles and grabbed her waist to sling her over a strong shoulder. She heard and smelled seawater and gasoline before something stabbed into her hip. The burn spreading across her buttocks told her she was being injected with drugs; the subsequent sensation of nauseating euphoria and numbing paralysis made her heart flutter with panic.

Morphine . . . and some kind of sedative . . .

Blackness.

Charlotte felt the cocoon of softness around her falling away, and hot breath touched her cheek. She opened her eyes to see an enormous black cat staring at her behind silver bars scored with deep scratches. The big cat yawned and began licking its paw.

A man's voice spoke in a strange language, and was answered by a deeper, unearthly tone. Charlotte turned her head and saw two shadows, big and small, looming over a golden-haired giant's bloodied, unmoving body.

The big shadow dropped down, lifting the golden head and pressing a goblet of red wine to the giant's lips. Some of the wine trickled down the sides of his face.

A third shadow merged with the smaller one, and in English Charlotte heard a woman's sulky voice ask,

"Why does he try again? You know it will only kill the male."

"He does as he wishes," the man snapped. "This one was not on the list anyway."

"On the bridge Tacal sensed he was Chosen." The woman sighed. "He was very good at that."

"Not anymore."

Charlotte heard a choking sound, and the thud of the giant's body as it dropped back to the floor.

"We should keep him here until he dies," the woman said. "The children will only bury him, and then we will have to dig him back up."

"The master says he stays with the female."

The woman laughed. "Then perhaps she will save us the trouble and burn him."

When Charlie woke the next time, she found herself sitting in a chair. She looked down at the cheetah-patterned drape covering her from her neck to her knees before she glanced at the large mirror in front of her. She was in a beauty salon. Someone had taken her hair out of the braid and put it up in a fancy 'do with strands of golden pearls woven through the elaborate coils. She was also wearing dark red lipstick with a golden sheen, dark purple eye shadow, and enough black eyeliner and mascara to polish a pair of shoes.

She tried to grab the drape and pull it off, which was when she discovered that she was completely paralyzed.

In the chair next to hers the giant—no, the Limo Guy . . . *Sam,* she remembered at last—sat with his eyes closed and his chin tucked against his leopard-patterned drape. The elderly Latina trimming the back of his hair noticed Charlie watching and smiled.

"Big and virile, isn't he?" She came around and gently tipped Sam's head back. "He's a good match for you."

It took Charlie two tries to get the words out of her dry throat. "Where are we?"

The woman began carefully trimming away the big man's beard. "You're safe now, *hija*."

"I'm not your daughter."

"I wish you were. I would be so proud to give him a girl child." She let the golden hair fall onto the shroud until she had cropped his beard close to his skin, and then reached for an electric razor. "Men do such foolish things. Why does he cover such a handsome face?"

"Who are you?" Charlie demanded. "What are we doing here? Why can't I move?"

"So impatient." The Latina made a clucking sound with her tongue. "All will be explained to you when you wake up."

"I'm not asleep." Everything that had happened on the bridge came rushing back into her head. "I've been drugged. I've been kidnapped."

"You've been saved," the hairdresser insisted. "You should be grateful. You will have a beautiful life with this one. If he lives. I think he will. He is stronger than the others."

Charlie wanted to scream "Lady, I don't even *know* that man."

The Latina gave her a knowing glance. "You will."

Charlie saw the syringe in her hand and heard herself beg. "Please. No more drugs."

"This is the last dose, *chica*. I promise." The hairdresser stabbed the needle into Charlie's upper arm.

The drape rose up and wrapped itself around her head, smothering her into unconsciousness. For a long time she drifted, lost and aimless, until a beautiful warmth surrounded her. While she still couldn't see anything, she no longer felt as if she were alone.

What is going to happen to me?

Be careful what you ask, a deep voice whispered. *You may not care for the answers.*

Lines began stretching out through the darkness, radiating around her like a web made of amber light. In the center of them stood the big blond man from the bridge.

Samuel?

He turned toward her, his eyes closed but his mouth smiling. *There you are.* He held out his hand, and she saw her own reaching for it.

As soon as they touched she knew the warmth had come from him, for a deeper, richer wave of it swept up her arm. *Are you doing this, or am I hallucinating?*

A little of both, I think. He drew her closer. *Charlotte, whatever happens, you must live. Fight for your life. Everything depends on it.*

Everything? She felt bemused. *Like what?*

I can't see it yet, he admitted, caressing her cheek with the backs of his fingers. *It's like you. I can only feel it. But it's very important that you live.*

We all die, Sam. She didn't want to think about it. *This is a great dream, though.* She admired the shifting patterns of the lines. *I could stay here with you forever.*

That's not your destiny. He sounded tired now. *Or mine.*

I thought you couldn't see anything, she chided.

I know that I'm dying, he said gently. *I thought I'd accepted it, but now ... Why couldn't I have met you years ago?*

We have. She didn't know how she knew that, only that it was the truth. *On the bridge, I felt it. I'd never seen you before in my life, but I swear I recognized you.*

It was the same for me. He lifted his head and then put his arms around her. *I don't know if I'll survive this, but when you wake up, look for me. Find me.*

I will. The darkness was dragging at her, pulling her out of his arms. *Samuel.*

Don't be afraid, Charlotte. The light and the warmth dwindled, and the last thing she heard was his voice. *Here or in the real world, I'll be watching for you.*

Time passed unnoticed. The sound of the sea finally roused Charlie, but the sunlight on her skin and the decadent comfort of the fine linens swaddling her tried to lure her back to sleep. The fragrance of some exotic fruit rose from the pillow under her cheek, as if the sinfully soft bedsheets had been washed with pineapples or mangoes. She turned her nose into the delicious scent, and a firm, smooth texture brushed across her lips.

Skin. Naked skin.

She opened one eye and looked at the chest she was nuzzling. The golden eye of a bird tattoo stared back at her, and for a moment she thought she saw its scarlet-tipped black wings flutter where they had been inked over strong collarbones. She glanced down and saw its lower body had been fashioned out of curling flames.

Not a bird, Charlie thought as she idly traced the blaze of fire and feathers with one fingertip. *A phoenix.*

A phoenix tattoo.

She pushed herself away from the chest. The man beside her lay sprawled over two-thirds of the enormous bed, his clean-shaven face still, his chest barely moving as he slept on.

It was Sam, the man from the bridge. But why was she in bed with him?

Charlie jerked off the scarlet cotton sheet twisted around her and saw only naked skin. She crawled away backward, not stopping until she went over the side of the bed and fell to her knees. Softness cushioned her shins, and she looked down at the black fur throw spread out over a floor made of clear blue water, coral, and tiny tropical fish. Only when she saw the ghostly image of her own wide-eyed face staring back at her did she realize the water was under a layer of crystal-clear glass.

Slowly Charlie lifted her head. If she was in a hotel room, it was the largest she'd ever seen: at least two thousand square feet, with a cathedral ceiling supported by innumerable lengths of smoothly polished bamboo. Primitive-looking motifs and murals covered the walls in bright primary colors, all of which darkened into an azure-purple ombré at the base, giving the impression that the entire room was melting into the gigantic aquarium of the floor. Irregular flat plates of multicolored stone had been stacked to form treelike columns that supported light fixtures of green glass blown in long, graceful curves that suggested palm fronds. Bowls woven from twigs and set on carved wooden pedestals held mounds of fresh fruit.

An odd dragging sensation on her scalp made her reach up and touch her hair, which had been taken out of the braid she wore for work and curled. She felt a long strand of beads woven through the curls and pulled it out, wincing as some hairs came with it. The beads turned out to be pearls, and as she remembered the dream she threw it away from her.

"Who's here?" she called out, angry now. "Where am I?"

Through the three-story glass panels of the exterior wall Charlie could see an extended patio deck, and beyond that real palm trees, fanlike palmettos, and clustered thatches of towering bamboo. A slate-lined path led down from the deck and through the tropical landscaping to a golden sand beach, where ivory-edged turquoise waves lapped lazily over long, scrolling bands of seashells.

Charlie had seen pictures of places like this. They were called resorts instead of hotels. There would be butlers instead of bellboys, personal chefs instead of vending machines, and if you had to ask how much the room cost per night, you couldn't afford it.

There was one person in the room who could, however, and she kept her eye on him as she looked around for some clothes. She found a pair of thick, soft, gold velour robes draped across the foot of a lounge chair and jerked one on as she came around the bed.

"Sam. Wake up."

"Buenos días, Señorita Marena."

Charlie whirled around, but no one else had entered

the room. "Who's there? Come out here where I can see you."

"Welcome to Séptima Casa," the man's voice said, and this time she spotted the intercom panel set into the wall beside a mural of dolphins leaping from the waves. "This is your new home. We will see to it that you and Señor Taske live in complete comfort and happiness. As long as you abide by two simple rules, you will want for nothing."

Charlie exploded. "Who the hell do you think you are?" She turned toward the bed. "Is this your idea of a practical joke? Because I don't think it's funny. Get up." She strode over and shook Sam's shoulder, but he remained limp.

"The first rule is that you must not try to escape," the man continued smoothly, as if she'd said nothing. "Any attempt at escape will result in immediate punishment."

"Samuel." She shook him harder. "Wake up."

The faintly snide voice went on. "The second rule is that you and your partner will have sexual intercourse at least once each day. If you fail to do so for any reason, again, you will be punished."

Charlie stopped listening to the man as she felt something damp on her forearm, and turned it to see a fresh bloodstain. She pulled away the sodden sheet from a wide, bleeding gash in Samuel's side.

"Christ." Now she saw the ashen tone of his skin and felt the cool moistness of it as she checked his pulse, which was weak and fluttered rapidly under her fingertips. She saw no swelling or bruising across his abdomen, and when she thumbed up his eyelids his pupils appeared enlarged.

Quickly she dragged down one of the pillows and elevated his legs before she tore a dry section away from the bottom of the sheet. Once she had folded and pressed it against the wound, she turned her head toward the speaker. "This man is wounded and in shock," she shouted. "He needs to be taken to a hospital. Immediately."

"Buenos días, Señorita Marena," the man's voice said, exactly as he had before. "Welcome to Séptima Casa. This is your new home. We will see to it that you and Señor Taske live in complete comfort and happiness. . . ."

The voice was a looped recording, Charlie realized, and swore under her breath as she quickly inspected the wound. She saw no indication of internal injuries or serious bleeders, which was the only good news. She had no way to measure how much blood he'd lost or how long he'd been in shock.

Under her arm, Samuel's chest fell and didn't rise again.

"Sam." She couldn't find a pulse anymore, and tilted his head back, putting her ear down by his nose and mouth to listen and feel for a breath that never came. She opened his mouth to check his airway and found two fresh puncture wounds in his upper palate. She ignored them as she tipped his head back, pinched his nostrils shut, sealed her lips over his, and forced her breath into his lungs.

He didn't start breathing.

Charlie centered her hands on his chest and began compressions, counting under her breath until she reached thirty before giving him another breath. The muddy gray of his skin made her swear as she began the second set of compressions.

"Come on, Sam," she told him as she worked his chest. "You're not dying on me, not here. Are you listening?"

His body heaved under her hands as violent tremors racked his limbs. Just as quickly he fell still and coughed several times before he began breathing on his own. His features remained ashen in color, and against her skin she could feel his body temperature dropping.

Charlie kept her fingers pressed against his throat; feeling his sluggish pulse throb dully, she watched a little color return to his face. "Okay, Sam, that's better. You just keep those lungs working." She glanced down at the wound in his side to check the bleeding, which had slowed dramatically.

She didn't know whether he'd had a seizure or a stroke, but she couldn't be concerned with that now. The wound probably wasn't going to kill him, but the blood loss would.

She used the belt from the other robe to bind her makeshift bandage in place, and then ran across the glass floor to the arched open doorway opposite the exterior glass wall. She hurried out into a corridor filled with doors.

Judging by the vast interior dimensions and artful decor, they'd been brought to someone's private mansion. As she hurried down the hall she began jerking open doors and glancing inside, but found the other rooms just as empty.

"Is anyone here? I have a wounded man who needs a doctor," she called out several times, but the only thing that answered her was the echo of her own voice. At the end of the hall she opened the last door and then stopped, aghast to see that the interior had been outfitted to serve as a medical treatment room. Someone had installed an exam table, lab equipment, and glass-fronted cabinets filled with supplies. Her own carry-in bag sat on a rolling cart next to the table.

Charlie went to the refrigerated storage unit and opened the door. Inside were several vials of insulin, antibiotics, and other perishable drugs, along with enough units of blood to stock a small blood bank.

Sam's desperate need for a transfusion made her reach for the blood. The packaging looked unfamiliar, and none of the units had been labeled or typed, although different symbols had been drawn in black marker on each of the bags. She had no way to tell what sort of blood it was, nor the time to test it to see whether it was safe.

There was only one thing she could do.

She replaced the bag in the storage unit and slammed the door shut, turning to the cabinets to pull what she needed. After she stuffed the supplies in her bag she grabbed it and ran back down the hall.

"Sam," she said as she pulled on a pair of gloves and began to set up. "Can you hear me? I need you to wake up now. I'm going to take care of you, but I have to know what happened."

She had to repeat herself several times before he stirred, and then at last his eyes opened. "Charlotte." His voice barely registered above a whisper, and he grimaced as if it hurt to speak. "Safe?"

"For now," she lied. "Do you remember how you got this wound in your side? Did someone stab you?"

He shook his head. "Accident. In Denver. Weeks ago." His eyelids began to droop. "So tired . . ."

"You can't go to sleep yet, Sam," she said, putting her hand on his cheek. "Look at me. That's it. Can you tell me what your blood type is?"

"O. Negative."

They were both universal donors with the same blood type; relief made her feel a little dizzy. "Then I think it's your lucky day."

She prepped a pressure bag and filled half of it with isotonic saline, which would dilute her own blood but give his body the extra fluid it needed. Once she tied off his upper arm with a tourniquet, she inserted an eighteen-gauge needle into one prominent, distended subcutaneous vein. As soon as she saw the dark red flashback that confirmed the needle was in place, she taped it down and attached the tubing before starting on her own arm.

"Okay, Sam, here we go," she said as she inflated the pressure bag, hanging it from one of the knobs along the top of the headboard and releasing the clamp. Blood flowed from her arm through the tube into the bag, where it mixed with the saline and began to descend.

Charlie watched the drip chamber closely. The flow had to be continuous, but if she used too much pressure, the bag seams would split or the blood cells would lyse. Once she felt good about the flow rate, she took out her stethoscope and checked his heart and lung sounds. His pulse, while still slow, had grown stronger.

"Still beating," he murmured. His face appeared less gray now, and his voice was a little stronger.

"So I hear. I like that a lot. Keep doing it." She didn't hear any arrhythmias that would indicate an allergic reaction to the transfusion. "Can you feel this?" She took her hand and squeezed the fingers on his right hand and then his left. Both times he nodded and moved his fingers. "Is there any numbness on either side of your body?"

"No. Just . . . tired."

"You're entitled. Now, open up for me." When he did, she tilted his head back to inspect his palate, and saw the two wounds were much smaller than they'd looked at first glance, and weren't punctures, as she had originally assumed. "Do you remember how you hurt your mouth?"

"No." He looked confused.

"It's okay," she assured him. "You've just got a couple abrasions on the roof of your mouth, that's all."

The urgency involved in providing medical care to a male patient always neutralized any normal interest Charlie might have felt toward him; whenever she worked on a man he was simply the patient. She took that distance for granted, as she was usually too busy trying to keep her patients alive to notice how attractive they were or what kind of body they had.

That wasn't happening this time, not with Samuel. Her eyes kept straying back to his face, but not to check his color or watch for signs of reaction. Without the beard masking the lower half of his face, his strong features were almost savagely handsome, from the high-def cheekbones down to the squared jaw. The mixed bag of his genetics had saved him from a thin line of a mouth and instead gifted him with the kind of full, sensual lips that made a woman think instantly of kissing.

As heart-stopping as Samuel's face was, his body proved even harder to ignore. His perfectly tanned skin looked sprayed on, it seemed so flawless, and the development of his upper body was nothing short of superb. She'd known guys who spent half their lives gulping protein shakes and pumping iron who never achieved such beautiful muscles or physical symmetry.

It won't matter what he looks like if he codes on me again.

Charlie forced herself to focus on her job. She couldn't afford to give him too much of her own blood, but she pushed it to the limit before she finished the transfusion and took out the suture kit.

"Hey, Sam, I've got to stitch you up. Bad news is that I didn't find any local anesthetic I can give you for the pain. Good news is that I'm really fast with a needle, but I need you to hold still." When he didn't answer her she glanced down and saw he'd slipped back into unconsciousness. "All right, that'll work, too."

Chapter 3

Andrew Riordan parked his rental car on the street across from the marina and watched the cops taping off the access turn to the parking lot. A forensics team surrounded the abandoned ambulance, working silently as they removed plastic bags of evidence and dusted the surfaces for prints.

Earlier that day Drew had been sitting in his apartment in a small northern California town, sipping instant coffee and checking news reports, when he'd caught the live coverage of the shooting on the Golden Gate Bridge. The moment he'd learned that Samuel Taske had been taken hostage by the gunman, he'd dressed, grabbed his go bag, and left, making the necessary calls from his car as he drove south toward San Francisco.

Samuel Taske was ranked by *Forbes* as the seventh-richest man in America, something that made him a very attractive prospect for kidnapping. What the public didn't know about the antiques dealer was that he was part of the Takyn, a very private, select group of people who had been genetically altered in infancy to become superhumans with extraordinary psychic abilities. Samuel, known by most of the Takyn as Paracelsus, was the second-oldest and probably the wealthiest member of the group, and had the ability to read the history of objects simply by touching them with his bare hands.

At first Drew had known Samuel only through the
Internet site the Takyn used to communicate with one
another, but over the past winter they had become close
friends. The antiques dealer had spared no expense in
helping Drew track down Rowan Dietrich, another
member of the Takyn, after a motorcycle accident had
left her stranded in New York City.

Now Samuel was in trouble, and Drew would do
whatever it took to get him back safely.

He put on his wireless mike and speed-dialed a
number in Tennessee on his encrypted satellite phone.
"It's Drew," he said as soon the man on the other end
answered. "I'm in Monterey. They've recovered the
ambulance, but there is no sign of the shooter or the
hostages."

"We have received no word yet from Paracelsus,"
Matthias told him. "Zephyr is at the hospital watching
over the driver, but he is still in surgery. We will move
him as soon as he is stable enough for transport."

"Why the rush?" Drew asked.

"Genaro left Atlanta by private jet this morning,"
Matthias told him. "His pilot filed a flight plan for San
Francisco."

"Great." Drew took a penny from the change niche
in the dash and rubbed it between his fingers. "This
doesn't feel like a GenHance operation, boss. For one
thing, they'd never want this kind of publicity." The
penny in his hand rose in the air above his palm and
spun in a slow circle. "What about the EMT?"

"We know a little, mostly from the news," Matthias
said. "Her name is Charlotte Marena, twenty-nine, the
daughter of Mexican immigrants. She is single, a gradu-
ate of UCLA, a licensed emergency care practitioner,
and employed by the city fire department."

"So she was simply in the wrong place at the wrong
time." Drew didn't believe it for a second. "Ask your
lady if she would take a good look at Ms. Marena."

"Jessa has already begun the background investigation."

"Excellent. I'll contact you when I have news."

After ending the call, Drew reached under his seat and took out a large zippered case from which he removed a folded tie, a gun and shoulder holster, and forged credentials identifying him as an FBI special agent. Once he had switched out his fake IDs and strapped on the weapon, he turned and grabbed the jacket he kept on the backseat and got out, sliding on his sunglasses before donning the jacket and heading toward the patrolman manning the barricade.

"Officer." Drew showed him the phony ID. "Agent Frasier from San Francisco. Who's in charge of the scene?"

"Detective Goldberg." He pointed to a short, dark-haired man talking to one of the forensic techs. "He's coordinating with SFPD over the phone. How'd you get here so quick?"

"I was on vacation in the area and got pulled." Drew glanced at the dock. "Any sign of the hostages?"

"They found some blood inside the rig," the patrolman said. "No cars have been reported stolen, so it might have been a prearranged drop."

"Thanks." Drew walked in the general direction of the detective, but once the patrolman had turned back to watch the road, he headed for the dock.

Most of the vessels docked at the pier were big, expensive, and fitted with canvas toppers, suggesting they were the weekend toys of suburb sailors. Drew spotted one elderly man sitting on a deck chair on an old but beautifully preserved sloop; he puffed on a cigar while he watched the cops in the parking lot. Every now and then he would shake his head a little.

Drew stopped by the stern of the sloop. "Afternoon. Mind if I come on board and ask you a couple questions?"

"What's in it for me?" the old man demanded.

"I don't take you downtown, hold you as a material witness to a kidnapping, or question you for hours," Drew countered.

"That'll work." The old man gestured for him to approach.

He stepped over the starboard railing onto the deck and looked out at the parking lot before taking out a notepad. "Did you see that ambulance when it arrived here?"

"I heard the lead-footed ass driving it when he laid on the brakes. Sounded like he ran over a cat." He squinted up at Drew. "You're not local."

"I'm with FBI's San Francisco office." Drew looked down the row of boats and noted the empty slip at the very end. "About what time did you hear the noise?"

"Might have been two, two thirty. I came up to see what all the commotion was." He drew on the end of the cigar and let the smoke waft slowly from his mouth into his nostrils. "Mexican fella pushed a cart covered with a mound of bloodstained sheets on it down to Wass's slip. Howie said he'd gotten chartered to take some sportfishermen down to Mexico, but more likely he was hired to take the bodies out a few miles and dump them."

Drew stopped pretending to take notes. "What happened then?"

"The Mexican and Howie carried what looked like two stiffs on board and stowed them below. I didn't see Howie again after that. Greedy bastard probably got his throat cut." The old man carefully snuffed out his cigar. "The Mexican came up a bit later, cast off the lines, and headed out."

"Can you describe the people they carried on board?"

He shrugged. "They had sacks over their heads. One was big, and the other had to be a woman. Even with the sheet wrapped around her, I could see she had a beautiful rack."

"They were both unconscious?"

The old man nodded. "The big one was bleeding from the side. It was all over the sheet."

Drew knew a little about Samuel's condition, which had been slowly crippling him for years. Although the Takyn all had the ability to heal faster than normal humans, Samuel's weakened state combined with an open wound might prove too much for the big man to survive. "Was that when you called the police?"

"Oh, I didn't call them, son."

Drew eyed him. "Why not?"

"No phone," the old man said, gesturing below. "No desire to get my throat cut, either."

Drew glanced out at the bay. "Did you see what direction he took the boat?"

"He'll be heading south for Manzanillo, Mexico." The old-timer grinned at him. "Howie stopped by last night to borrow some maps. He's never been down that far south, so I plotted the course for him."

Drew jotted down the name of the city. "Is there anything else you can think of?"

"You'd best get out of here before the real cops see you talking to me," the old-timer said. "Or you'll end up going downtown. I hope you find your friends."

"So do I." Drew smiled a little. "What gave me away?"

"Something only an old shoemaker like me would notice." The old man nodded at the deck. "No FBI agent wears green sneakers, son."

No drug, treatment, or therapy had ever succeeded in completely relieving the pain caused by Samuel Taske's deteriorating spine. He had spent years learning how to rest through meditation and napping for an hour or two, usually in an upright position in one of his custom-built ergonomic chairs. To wake from a deep, satisfying sleep and find himself flat on his back in a real bed was not only a novelty but something of a precious gift.

One he would begin paying for immediately, he

thought as he lay as still as possible. As soon as he moved he would likely be in agony. At least Morehouse would arrive shortly with his morning tea and paper, and after administering his injection he would help him get up and into the whirlpool. . . .

Two fingers pressed against a bone in his wrist while a warm hand settled on his brow. None of them belonged to his house manager.

"No fever, no rash, no arrhythmias," a woman murmured. "So why don't you wake up, *mío*?"

"It usually requires a pot of tea and the *Wall Street Journal*." He looked up at Charlotte Marena's face. Beyond her he could see bright colors and beautiful furnishings. "Hello again."

"Hey." Her smile lit up her tired face. "Welcome back. How are you feeling?"

"Puzzled." Taske turned his head to the right and left to take in as much as he could, and made another discovery as he felt the smoothness of the linen pillowcase against his cheek. "Someone shaved off my beard."

She nodded. "Wasn't me."

He didn't see any medical equipment around the bed. "We're not at a hospital, are we?"

"I don't know where we are, Sam," Charlotte admitted. "I was kind of hoping that you did."

"I'll have to disappoint you." Luxurious and unique as it was, he didn't recognize the room. "How did we come to be here?"

"The last thing I remember was passing out in the back of my rig." She straightened. "Yesterday I woke up here with you. That's all I know."

"Yesterday." He frowned. "I've been unconscious that long?"

"At least a day." She made a helpless gesture. "Maybe two or three, or even a week." She looked as if she wanted to say more, and then subsided.

"But you woke before me." A vague memory of Charlotte's urgent voice came back to him, and without thinking he reached across his abdomen to touch the wound in his side.

"It's okay. It's already healed." She pulled down the sheet covering him to expose the unmarked skin over his ribs. "The stitches I put in popped out during the night, There isn't even a scar. Maybe you can explain that to me?"

"I'll try." Taske had not enjoyed such a rapid recovery from a serious wound in years, but that was not the only revelation that stunned him. When he had moved, he had felt nothing.

"Problem?"

He frowned as he carefully drew his arm back and then moved his legs just enough to shift the lower half of his spine. "I don't feel anything."

Charlotte turned and touched his thigh. "You can't feel my hand?"

"No, I have feeling in my legs." Still not trusting his body, he bent his arm to prop his weight on his elbow and roll onto his side. His muscles felt stiff, but the searing coil of nerves around his spine didn't offer even the slightest twinge. "Charlotte." He stared at her. "I need you to tell me precisely what happened to me."

"When I woke up yesterday I found you in shock from the blood loss. You were left here bleeding from a reopened wound." She ducked her head. "Your heart stopped, and I had to perform CPR, but I got you back. I had to give you a vein-to-vein blood transfusion. Fortunately we have the same type. I'm also tested regularly for my job, so don't worry about it. I know I'm clean."

"I remember your asking me about my blood type." She had given him her own blood; no wonder she looked so drawn and pale. "What did you do to my back?"

"Nothing." She put her hand on his arm. "You probably wrenched it on the bridge. I'll see if I can find something for the pain."

"Pain. That is the problem. I'm not *in* pain. Any

pain." He laughed a little. "Charlotte, somehow you've healed me."

"Jesus healed the lame, Sam. I just gave you some blood." She looked uncertain. "You're sure you don't feel any pain at all? Maybe you're just riding an adrenaline high."

"After fifteen years of enduring it every day—lately every hour of every day—I know pain," he assured her. "Not feeling it is incredible." He frowned. "And impossible."

"Sam, while I was working on you, you had some kind of seizure," she told him. "It could have been a small stroke, and that can cause nerve damage."

"Then I would have some paralysis as well, which I don't." He looked down at himself. "Everything seems to be working very well."

"Yeah, but you were in shock, too. Sometimes a combination of these things can do some weird stuff to the body." When he would have sat up the rest of the way she pressed his arm. "Take it slow. If you fall, I don't think I'm going to be able to pick you up without help." She put her arm around his back. "Anytime you want to stop, just tell me."

As he moved into a sitting position, Taske's head remained as clear as his sight. He felt no discomfort, numbness, or any sensation other than that of his muscles coiling and uncoiling to accommodate his movements. As Charlotte stood up and watched him he eased his legs over the side of the bed, and then slowly rose. Expecting his knees to buckle, he put a hand on her shoulder, but his legs remained strong and steady.

"I've walked with a limp since I was a teenager." He took one step, and then another, and suddenly, effortlessly, he was moving across the room. It had been so long since he'd walked without using a cane that his hand and arm felt odd, but not once did he lose his balance or stagger. Joy rushed through him, a genie re-

leased after a thousand years bottled up who had
granted his dearest wish without even asking him. He
turned around and strode to Charlotte, seizing her by
the waist and lifting her off her feet to twirl her around.

"Look at me." He laughed. "Charlotte, I can *walk*. My
God, I think I can even run."

"That's terrific, Sam." Her hands clamped on his
shoulders. "Would you put me down now?"

"Forgive me." He laughed again as he lowered her
back to her feet and pulled her against him in an affec-
tionate hug. "You can't know what this means." He cradled her face between his hands. "I thought I was a dead
man—no, I knew I was—and now I wake up and I can
walk." He stroked a hand over her tousled hair before
he kissed her pretty mouth.

The delight pouring through him grew heated as he
tasted the sweetness of her lips, and suddenly his excitement became urgent and dark. He filled his hands with
her hair and nudged her lips apart, inhaling her startled
breath and tasting her with his tongue. Her hands slid up
his chest, pressing for a moment before they curved
around his neck. He wanted to laugh again as he splayed
his hands over her back and worked them down to the
luscious curves of her hips. Before this he could only
look at her and wish, but now that he was healed, now
that he was strong, he could be like any other man, and
take her to his bed, and give her hours and hours of
pleasure. . . .

His bed was in Tannerbridge, not here.

Taske lifted his mouth from hers. Charlotte stood
very still, her eyes wide and fixed on his face, her cheeks
rosy. She appeared as appalled as he was astonished. He
intended to apologize, instantly and profusely, but the
words he spoke had nothing to do with regret.

"I know you." He lifted a length of her hair to his
nose, breathing in before he let the gold-shot strands
fall back into place. "Your scent, the feel of your skin,

everything about you is new to me. We've never met before I saw you on the bridge; I'd swear to it. But . . . I know you."

"I'm pretty sure I would remember meeting a guy your size." She eased out of his arms and turned her face away. "Maybe in another life."

"Reincarnation is a fantasy. This life is the only one we have." He didn't understand why she wouldn't look at him, until he glanced down at his body. Not only was he stark naked; he sported a monumental erection. He pulled the sheet from the bed and wrapped it around his hips. "I do beg your pardon, Charlotte." He wouldn't apologize for kissing her, not with the taste of her still on his mouth.

"Not a problem. In my line of work, I see plenty of naked guys," she advised him. "But if you really want my forgiveness, stop calling me Charlotte."

"I'll try." By this time he couldn't think of her as anything else, but he had no wish to antagonize her. "Charlotte is a lovely name. Why do you prefer Charlie?"

"Charlotte is too old-fashioned. Here." She brought him a large gold velour robe. "I found a supply of men's and women's clothes. Mostly casual stuff, like this." She tugged at the edge of the cloth wrapped around her breasts.

He studied the vivid orange sarong under the lacy white shrug she was wearing. Both made her look like a present waiting to be unwrapped, he thought, until the reason why she was wearing it dawned on him. "He took our clothes from us? He left us both here naked?" When she nodded, he felt a surge of violent anger. "Did he touch you?"

"I don't think so." She wrapped her arms around herself. "I checked myself thoroughly, and I didn't find any bruises or other signs of an assault."

What she didn't say was that she still felt violated. Taske wanted to find their abductor and beat him senseless. Even better, now that his back had been healed, he could. "Where is this bastard?"

"I wish I knew." Her expression turned grim. "I've looked through the entire place, and there's no one here but us." She pointed to a speaker set into the wall. "A man spoke to me through that yesterday, after I woke up. What he said repeated a couple of times, so it had to be a recording. He said this was our new home." Again she looked as if she wanted to say more, but lapsed into silence.

Taske looked around the room. "Did you recognize any of the surrounding area outside the house?"

"I didn't go out," she admitted. "By the time I finished going through the house it was dark, and I really didn't want to leave you alone for long."

She averted her eyes, and a slight change in her stance suggested she wasn't being entirely honest with him. "My dear, surely you know you can trust me."

"Of course I do." Now she turned around and brought her hand up to her chest, pointing with one finger to one side of the ceiling and then the other. "If you're feeling all right, maybe we can take a walk down to the beach."

Taske glanced up discreetly and saw the two security cameras mounted on swivel bases; she had turned her back on them to conceal her hand movements. As he deliberately walked back to the glass wall, he heard the faint whir of gears and confirmed with another glance that one of the cameras had followed his movements. Now he understood her odd silences; they were being actively monitored.

Taske hoped whoever was spying on them was close by. The fury streaming through his veins needed an outlet. "I'll need to dress first."

"The clothes are in here." She gestured for him to follow her into a walk-in closet. Once they were both inside, she leaned close to whisper, "There are cameras in all the rooms and hallways. I don't know if he can hear us, but still, watch what you say." She reached for some clothes hangers and in a normal voice said, "These look like they'll fit you."

He pulled on the denim cutoff shorts and the thin, bright blue tank top, and surveyed himself. "I look like a Beach Boy."

"Sorry there aren't any Valentino suits." She took the robe and hung it from a hook. "Ready?"

He nodded and followed her out. She picked up a short length of polished, carved teak propped beside the arched doorway and held it like a club. "Where did you find that?"

"It used to be part of a chair downstairs." She gave it a test swing. In a lower voice she added, "I played softball in college. If he comes at us, just give me some room."

"If he comes at us," he countered, "hand it to me."

She gave him a skeptical look. "You ever mix it up with anyone, rich man?"

"One can use a cane for more than walking, honey," he assured her.

Charlotte guided him to a narrow, spiral staircase made of tiled steps and sided in glass panels suspended between bamboo supports. As they descended he noted the display of primitive animal masks inlaid with turquoise, gold, and bone.

"Mesoamerican," he murmured, pausing beside one likeness of a snarling jaguar. "Not a relic, however. Quite new." He reached out to touch it before he stopped and glanced at his bare hand. He had been bare-handed since waking up and somehow had not noticed. That discovery shook him down to his heels. "Charlotte, please lend me your bat for a moment, if you would?"

She handed it over, and Taske closed his eyes as he curled his fingers around it. Since childhood he'd never had to consciously use his ability; it manifested the moment he touched anything. Upon contact he could see the entire history of any object, from the moment it was created until the present date, no matter how old it was.

His ability had enabled him to become one of the foremost experts on antiques in the world, but it had come with a heavy price. Just as King Midas had been cursed to turn anything he handled into gold, Taske saw the history of literally everything he touched.

Gradually an image came to him of Charlotte lifting a small chair and repeatedly striking it against a stone pillar until one of the legs snapped off. Beyond that he saw nothing, no image from the past, no vision of who had brought the chair to this place, or who had purchased it, upholstered it, carved or assembled it.

Taske opened his eyes, unsure of what to think as he handed it back to her. "Thank you."

"Nice artwork," she said, her eyes briefly shifting to the camera overhead watching them. "I can't wait to see what's outside."

Another glassed-over water floor, this one stocked with circular green leaves and pale white lilies, led them to a wide entrance hall with towering walls. Taske noted the display of odd-looking weapons, hung far out of reach, which had the same ancient design yet new appearance as the masks by the staircase.

Charlotte inspected the teak door before she tried the ornate brass latch and slowly opened it. An exterior stepped platform led down to a walkway of shell-studded polished coral, which wound around through tumbleweed-shaped agaves and billowing mounds of white sweet alyssum before it disappeared.

The area beyond the house stood lush, green, and entirely deserted.

Taske heard the sound of the sea clearly now. "Perhaps we're somewhere on the coast."

"This isn't California."

"How do you know that?"

"I just do." She turned around, and for a moment the glory of her sun-gilded features took his breath away. "None of it rings a bell with you? Maybe it's someplace you went to work on your tan?"

"I fear our whereabouts are a mystery," he said, "and alas, the tan is congenital."

"'Alas'?" She shook her head. "No one says 'alas' anymore, Sam. Not for at least the last hundred years."

"Another thing about the deterioration of the English language to mourn." Again he detected the note of scorn in her tone. He wondered what he had done to earn it, and how quickly he might dispel it. For some reason Charlotte didn't like him, and that would not do at all. "Let's have a look at the beach. We might be able to see something from there."

Charlotte silently accompanied him down the coral path and along a grassy trail through a dense thicket of banana trees. As they passed one ripe bunch she stopped and inspected them.

"These look okay." She snapped off two, handing one to him, and proceeded to devour hers in a couple of bites before taking another and doing the same.

Her show of hunger worried him. "Isn't there any food at the house?"

"Enough to feed an army, but after the way they drugged us, I'm not touching it." She sighed and tossed the peels away. "Come on."

Chapter 4

The two bananas helped settle Charlie's empty, churning stomach, but every step she took away from the mansion made her anger burn brighter. Although Sam seemed as surprised as she was at waking up in this tropical paradise, she still couldn't get rid of the suspicion that he knew more than he was telling her. He'd told her he was handicapped, which he was anything but, and then there was that business on the stairs with the mask and her club.

By the time they reached the edge of the walkway leading down to the empty pier she felt ready to explode. She took a moment to look for surveillance equipment before she turned on him. "Okay. I need to know exactly what this is about. For real."

"So do I." He studied her face. "I see. You still have some doubts about me."

"Some?" she snapped. "I'm kidnapped, drugged, and dumped at a Club Med for millionaires. I wake up naked, with pearls in my hair, next to a cripple who is in shock from blood loss and nearly dies on me. Twelve hours later his wound disappears, and suddenly he's not a cripple anymore. In fact, he looks like he can run the hundred in five flat and tosses me around like I'm a rag doll. So yeah, Sam, I have doubts. Not some; many." She moved her hand horizontally from left to right. "Imagine a mountain range of doubts."

"Let's walk down to the water," he suggested. "The sound of the waves should cover our voices."

The pristine, powdery amber sand spoiled her attempt to stalk down the beach, and that annoyed her almost as much as Sam's neutral expression. Once they were standing in the sea up to their ankles, she glanced back and went still.

Only the tiered, flat rooftop of the mansion was visible from the shore, but the beach itself curved away from them on both sides, hugging the landmass in an irregular circle before it vanished behind it. The only other structure in sight was the long wooden dock. The coast and roadways she had expected to see didn't exist, and over the very tops of the trees to the left she saw a distant green blur swaddled by ocean.

Suddenly it made sense why she hadn't been able to pick up any thought streams last night. "We're on an island."

"That would explain why he didn't secure us in the house." Sam made a slow three-sixty turn. "No boats, no way for us to leave, and no way to call for help."

Now she noticed just how pristine the empty beach was: no litter, no lifeguard, not even a discarded cigarette butt. "Who kidnaps two strangers and dumps them in a mansion on a deserted island? And why?"

"I wish I knew." Sam glanced back at the house. "You said you heard a recording over the speaker in the bedroom. Was it the sniper?"

"No, the voice was different. Educated, more polite. He also spoke Spanish and English, but his accent was strange." She wished she could erase what he'd said from her mind, but his words still needled her. "He knew my name and yours. He called the house Séptima Casa. He said it was our new home."

Samuel knew just enough Spanish to translate the name of the villa. "The Seventh House."

"That's not all he said." Her voice went flat as she told him the rest.

"So if we follow the rules, become lovers, and don't attempt to escape, we will want for nothing." Sam seemed bemused by the bizarre demands. "May I ask you a personal question?"

She folded her arms. "I don't care what the jerk said or how many pearls he puts in my hair; I'm not sleeping with you."

"I never presumed that you would." He glanced down at her arms. "Charlotte, by any chance were you adopted as a child?"

Of all the things he could have asked her. "This is not the time to play 'Let's Get to Know Each Other.' "

He gave her a direct look. "Answer me, please. It's rather important."

"No, I wasn't adopted." Honesty made her add, "Not legally, anyway. I was abandoned when I was little. An older couple found me and took me in."

"I know this is none of my business," he said carefully, "but can you tell me how you came to be with your new family?"

She didn't have to tell him what had happened before she'd met the Marenas. "I was hungry, and my parents caught me in their backyard stealing tomatoes and peppers from their little vegetable garden. They didn't have any family or kids, so they took me in and pretended I was theirs. They'd just moved to San Francisco, so none of the neighbors questioned it."

He nodded. "Why didn't they turn you over to the police?"

"At the time, INS was having one of their crackdown sweeps through the city. Mama thought I might be a migrant kid, and was afraid I'd be deported and end up in a Mexican border orphanage." She looked down and nudged a piece of conch shell with her toe. "They didn't have much, but they spent every penny they had to get me papers and stuff so I could stay with them and go to school."

"Where are they now?"

"Planting tomatoes and peppers in heaven, I hope.

Papa died of a massive stroke my second year of college." She took in a deep breath. "Mama's heart gave out a few months later."

"I'm so sorry." His hand moved up to her shoulder. "I have one last question, and then I'll stop prying, all right?"

When she nodded, he asked, "When your parents found you in their garden, you had been tattooed, hadn't you?"

She felt sick. "Yeah."

"May I see it?"

She stepped back until she broke the contact between them and looked at the body ink curling over his collarbones. "It's not as pretty as yours." She shrugged off the white lace wrap and turned her back on him, showing him the dark purple oval and the six blunt triangles inked on her shoulder. "Most people think it's a lopsided sun."

"It's a turtle." He traced the center oval with his fingertip. "It's actually quite adorable."

"Glad you like it." She pulled on her shirt and faced him. "Now tell me how you knew that I've had it since I was a kid."

"We are not random strangers abducted purely by chance," he said. "I believe we were deliberately targeted, although I don't know how he could have known where we would be." He saw her confusion. "My parents also adopted me, Charlotte."

"And when your parents got you, you had that bird tattoo on your chest." Suddenly it all made sense. "Oh, no."

"Don't be afraid." He tried to put his arm around her shoulders.

She shook her head, backing away from him. "He knew what we are." Wildly she looked around. "They'll be coming for us. We have to find a place to hide." Her stomach surged, and she stumbled away, falling to her knees as she heaved.

Sam knelt beside her and pulled back her hair, bracing her with his other arm as she emptied her stomach into the water. When the last of her heaving subsided, he dampened the hem of his shirt and used it to wipe her mouth. "It's all right, my dear."

"No, it's not." She staggered to her feet, breathing in deeply. "There's a biotech company that hunts people like us for our DNA. Sam, they'll kill us for it."

"I know very well what GenHance has been doing," he told her. "But if they had abducted us, I believe we'd already be dead and dissected."

Another shock wave went through her. "How do you know that?"

"I belong to a very private online group. People like us who have been sharing information about our unusual talents." His eyes narrowed. "As, I suspect, you do."

"Your hands." She glanced at them and then his face. "Jesus. You're Paracelsus."

Colotl watched as the two newcomers rose from the sand and walked back to their villa. When they passed by his position, he did not breathe or move. The woman, as dark as the man was fair, appeared bigger and stronger than their women. She resembled one of the master's concubines, but she didn't move or speak like one. He found the moments when she had shown her anger to the man and then vomited into the sea particularly intriguing.

So was their body art. *Phoenix and turtle*. Colotl had never seen such markings, but he sensed the power radiating from both of them.

Once he heard them enter the house, he drew back into the green shadows and made his way to the cave, where the other men waited. Gathering like this was dangerous at any time, but the master's unknown sentinel seemed to be less vigilant during the day.

"Why did you not bring him?" Ihiyo, always impatient, asked as soon as he joined them.

"He is an American." He knelt down to drink from

the spring, but the reflection rippling on the surface of the water made him sit back on his haunches. He could hide from everything but his own face. "So is the woman. They speak like the steward."

"Their scents are strong in the air. The woman has been bled." Tzinacan dropped a pebble into the spring. "And the man smells of the master's blood."

Ihiyo and the other four men all began to talk at once. When their voices grew too loud, Colotl stood and lifted his hands for silence.

"They have only just arrived. For now, we will watch them." He glanced at Liniz. "What did you see last night?"

"She was afraid at first, but she composed herself quickly. She gave the man her blood by tube, and then sewed up a wound in his side." When Ihiyo made a rude remark, Liniz scowled at him. "She saved his life."

"That is what they want us to think," Ihiyo snapped. "Pici's time is coming. What will this woman do to her when it begins? What if she comes after your Xochi?"

"If she tries to do anything," Liniz said flatly, "I will slit her throat."

"Brothers." Colotl rose and touched Liniz's shoulder briefly before he addressed the others. "For now, we will watch. Each of us, in three-hour shifts. The next boat will come tomorrow. Ihiyo, you are the closest; you will go first. Report to Tlemi before sunset. I need to know everything they do."

Ihiyo's expression darkened. "What if no boat arrives?"

"Then we will know a little more about them." Colotl gestured toward the narrow entrance to the cave. "Go now."

Each of the men picked up his bundles, shouldering them before he filed out. Only Liniz lingered, and when they were alone he took a small black stone blade from his pocket and offered it to Colotl. The stone's beveled edge reflected the light with tiny prisms.

"I know what you are going to say," Liniz told him. "But as soon as I saw him stand, I had to make it. He is almost as big as the master."

Colotl tested the edge of the stone weapon, which sliced into his fingertip the moment he touched it. "You take too many chances, my friend."

"Ihiyo forgets that I would do whatever I must to protect what is mine." He held out his left hand and splayed the stumps of two missing fingers. "Do not make the same mistake, brother." He removed a string of fish from the water and strode out.

Colotl used one of the hidden paths to make his way back to the other side of the island. He heard the sound of splashing as he emerged from the forest, and changed direction to walk into the water garden.

Tlemi's long red hair blazed in the sunlight as she stood naked in the center of the saltwater pool and fed bits of seaweed and fish to the baby sea turtles she kept there. The freckles that covered every inch of her resembled golden lace hugging her skin.

"You were a long time," she said without looking at him.

"The mangoes by the stream were not yet ripe." He dropped his bundle on the grass and stripped off his shirt and shorts before he stepped into the pool. Immediately a swarm of the small green-and-black reptiles surrounded him, bumping their bullet-shaped heads against his thighs. "They are growing fast."

"I think we should release them next week." She scattered the last of the food before turning to him. "The man is awake, and healed. The woman is weary. She did not sleep or eat." She rubbed her temple. "Her mind is powerful. During the day it sleeps, but it becomes like a beacon after dark. If she suspects . . ."

"I will see to it that she does not," he promised. He cupped her cheek. "You are flushed."

"I have been hot this morning."

Her smile didn't reach her eyes, and he understood

the warning. "Then I will have to keep you wet." He lowered his head.

Her fingernails dug into his arms as he kissed her, signaling a frustration he shared. Since Colotl was a boy he had known Tlemi was for him—those choices had been made soon after they came to the master—but unlike the others he had not resisted his duty. Not until they had come to the island.

She tasted of coconut and mint, and her warmth sank into him until he could feel her in his bones. Every time he touched her he wanted to be inside her, a need that he'd assumed would dwindle over time. It hadn't; in the years since their first night he had grown obsessed with having her as often as he could.

She broke the kiss first, her breath rapid and unsteady. "You make me forget myself."

The passion should have been a gift. Instead it had become a burden they both carried.

"You make me burn," he murmured against her lips. He eased his hand between her taut thighs and stroked her, watching her eyelids droop and her lips part. "Do you need me now?"

Sadness tinged her laugh. "I need you always."

He picked her up in his strong arms and carried her out of the pool.

"Señor Frasier?"

Drew looked up from the newspaper he couldn't read to see a woman he couldn't stop staring at. His eyes shifted from the top of her glossy black hair down to the open toes of her ivory pumps, and then traveled back up again to her heart-shaped face. Her irises didn't match—one was the color of sand, the other as jet-black as her hair—but the effect made it seem as if some unseen beam of light had caught her eye.

She appeared as immaculate as if she'd just come from a photo shoot for a high-end fashion magazine. The cream color of her silk suit set off the tawny smoothness of her skin, and had been cleverly tailored to complement her petite proportions without overemphasizing them. The jewelry she wore was made from narrow, hammered gold and glinted discreetly from her ears, throat, and wrists. Dark red gloss accentuated her full lips, but if she wore any other makeup, he couldn't see a trace of it.

Somehow he got to his feet. "I'm Agent Martin Frasier." The gray-bearded Mexican detective who had left him to wait in the empty office had said something in broken English about a translator. "Are you the interpreter?" *Please say yes.*

"No, but I do speak English." She put down the portfolio she carried and held out her hand. "My name is Agraciana Flores. I'm an agent with La Procuraduría Federal de Protección al Ambiente."

Drew resisted the urge to rub his hand against the side of his trousers before taking hers. "I'm sorry, but I don't understand all that," he said as soon as he forced himself to let go. "Does that mean you're with the police department?"

"PROFEPA is in charge of governing and protecting Mexico's natural resources," she explained. "I have been called in to consult on this case."

He frowned. "Why?"

"Part of the investigation involves Las Islas Revillagigedo, a group of islands off the coast that are under federal protection as a priority biosphere reserve," she told him. "Under our laws, no one is permitted within six nautical miles of the archipelago. My agency has been tasked to oversee any operation that takes place in their vicinity."

She wasn't a cop; she was some sort of government conservationist. "I'm sorry; I don't understand. What do these islands have to do with my case?"

"It is somewhat complicated." She glanced down at the cup in her hand. "Detective Ortega suggested I bring you some coffee from the squad room, but I like Americans." She offered him the cup. "I bring this from home for myself. It is a little like, ah, hot chocolate?"

Drew accepted the cup and took a sip. The thick, hot drink tasted dark and smoky, and was only slightly sweet. The tingle it left behind after he swallowed was unexpected but oddly satisfying. "It's very good. Thank you for not hating me and my countrymen."

She didn't smile, but a delicate pink color appeared on her cheekbones. "I hope you feel the same after we have discussed the case." She pulled out a chair and gestured to his. "Please, sit down. Is this your first visit to Manzanillo?"

"Yes." Drew wasn't sure what to think of it, either. Down by the water the Mexican seaside town had reminded him of the more expensive parts of the Caribbean, all palm trees and white palatial hotels. But turning east he had left behind the glitz and glimmer and followed the narrow streets up the surprisingly steep hills into the heart of the city, where he expected the powerful sunlight to bring out every detail of the poverty and urban decay the tourists never saw. Instead he found a town as clean and charming as any theme-park resort. "What's with that gigantic blue fish statue down at the oceanfront?"

"El Monumento al Pez Vela." She smiled a little. "Sportfishing is very important to the local economy. We call it *el camarón*—the shrimp—because of the way it is curled up. Are you staying in Obregón Garden?"

"No, I haven't gotten a room yet." Drew had driven past some dazzling hotels by the twin bays, and stopped to stare at one that had been built as a replica of a massive Mayan temple, but they were too high-profile for his needs. "I'll take care of that later."

From her briefcase she removed several slim files and some sketches, which she set between them in two neat piles.

Drew tried not to stare at the top sketch, which bore a striking resemblance to the photos of Samuel that he had pulled off the Internet. "You've found the victims?"

"Unfortunately, we have not." She opened one file and produced a photograph of a boat. "This vessel was found abandoned at the public docks." She gave him the registration. "Is this the boat that was stolen from Monterey?"

He took out his notepad and compared the numbers. "Yes. Did you recover the victims?"

"There was only one victim." She showed him another photo, this one of a dead man on his back, his face covered in blood.

Drew almost snatched the picture from her, but relaxed when he saw the man's black hair and small stature. "This isn't Samuel Taske."

"We have already identified him. His name is Pedro Tacal." She regarded him steadily. "He left Mexico City last week to visit a sister in Sacramento. We assume he was traveling back home when he was attacked and abducted."

"I'm sorry to hear that." Drew put down the ghastly picture. "I'd like to help with your investigation, but my priority is to find the Americans who were kidnapped."

"You have not heard. . . . Of course, you have been traveling." She put away the photos. "Last night Señor Tacal was killed in front of dozens of people on the public docks, not far from where the boat was abandoned."

So that was the connection. "Do you think he was killed because he saw the sniper and his victims?"

"I cannot say why he was murdered." She hesitated before adding, "But the descriptions of Tacal's killers match those of the man and woman whom you claim were kidnapped in San Francisco." She checked her own notepad. "Samuel Taske and Charlotte Marena. We have issued warrants under those names for their arrest."

Drew felt as if he'd been kicked in the stomach. "These people were kidnapped, Agent Flores. If they killed anyone, it was in self-defense, probably while trying to escape. This Tacal must have been the sniper who abducted them."

She shook her head. "According to our witnesses, Tacal was unarmed and begged for mercy. The American male—presumably Taske—bludgeoned him until Tacal lost consciousness, at which time his female companion shot him in the head. They then stole another boat."

"This is bullshit." Drew shoved out of his chair and began pacing the length of the room. "Samuel Taske can barely walk, much less beat a man unconscious. Charlotte Marena is a paramedic and the first responder to reach the victims on the bridge." He turned and looked at her. "Neither of them would harm anyone."

"Perhaps not until last night." Agent Flores averted her eyes as her tone became brisk. "You can examine the sketches made by our artist; they are based on the descriptions of the witnesses and match the photos that were sent to us from the San Francisco police. I will also arrange for you to see the statements collected by the police. They, too, are very detailed."

"I'm sure they are, but I don't read Spanish any better than I speak it." Drew dragged a hand through his hair. "What are your people doing to find Taske and Marena?"

"My agency has sent two of our patrol boats to search the islands and the waters surrounding the archipelago," she said. "We have also radioed all the ships in the area and asked them to report any sighting of the stolen vessel."

"How long will this take?"

She shrugged. "Days, perhaps weeks. Assuming the suspects remain in the search area."

"Two kidnap victims don't turn into murderers overnight," Drew said finally. "I'll need to talk to these witnesses myself. In person, Gracie."

She eyed him. "Then it is regrettable that you don't speak Spanish, *Marty*."

Before Drew could reply, Detective Ortega lumbered in and spoke sharply to Agent Flores, who said very little in return. Drew noted how the older cop's eyes kept drifting south toward Gracie's sternum, and the casual way he reached down to adjust his package.

As soon as Ortega left, Gracie turned her attention back to him. "I am instructed to tell you that Chief Ruiz has personally taken over the investigation." Her voice remained calm, but anger simmered in her eyes. "Our assistance, while appreciated, is no longer required by the department."

"They're kicking both of us off the case?"

"So it would seem." She gathered up her files and re-placed them in her suitcase. She glanced at him, hesi-tated, and then added, "I can recommend a reasonably priced hotel down by the water if you would like to rest for a day before returning to the United States."

He took hold of her wrist. "What I would really like, Gracie, is to find out what the hell is going on here. To do that, I need your help."

His touch seemed to shock her into stillness, and she stared at his hand as her face turned pink again. "I am sorry, Agent Frasier, but I am in no position to disregard the expressed orders of my superiors." She started to say something else, and then pressed her lips together and tugged her wrist free. "I hope you have a pleasant jour-ney back to the States."

"Wait." He got to his feet. "I think I will stay a day or two. You've got your own car here, right?" She nodded. "Great, then can I follow you to this hotel you recom-mend?" Before she could refuse, he added, "I get lost pretty easy, even in my own country."

"Very well, Agent Frasier," she said after a long, silent look. "Come with me."

Chapter 5

Watching Andrew Riordan while his former employee charmed Agraciana Flores was almost as tedious for Jonah Genaro as the time and effort required to have the PROFEPA agent removed from the case. It would have taken even more time to acquire the kind of leverage needed to bring Flores under his control, however, and Genaro already had the chief of police and most of his men to do his bidding. As for Riordan, after being exposed as a spy he never should have walked out of GenHance headquarters alive, but he'd preplanned his escape. That, combined with the extensive sabotage he'd committed just before escaping, had allowed him to do the impossible.

Now Andrew was here in Mexico, unaware that he would never leave it alive.

It had taken too much time to trace the stolen ambulance to Monterey, where the sniper had escaped capture again by charter boat. Genaro had replaced the only witness at the marina with one of his own men, primarily to stall the police and the media. Fortunately his operative had spotted and recognized Andrew Riordan before he had come to question him, and had called Genaro directly for instructions.

"He's talking to one of the cops in the parking lot," the operative had said after snapping a shot of Riordan on his phone and forwarding it to Genaro. "Should I take care of him, sir?"

Another man would have told the operative to kill the traitor, but Genaro was more interested in why Riordan would risk exposing himself in order to find Samuel Taske and Charlotte Marena. After spying on GenHance for years, Riordan had destroyed valuable equipment and caused irreparable damage to their database before successfully fleeing Atlanta and disappearing completely off the grid.

"No," Genaro had replied. "Tell him exactly what the old man said. Be convincing."

Giving Riordan just enough information to send him to Mexico had created the bait. Now that he was here Genaro expected to reel in more than one catch.

"He sounds like a federal agent," Manzanillo Chief of Police Manuel Carasegas said as he watched Riordan through the two-way mirror. "I think you may have the wrong man."

"No," Genaro told him. "I don't."

"I did have his credentials checked, señor." Chief Carasegas shifted his weight from one foot to the other. "Agent Frasier is on active duty, and works for the FBI in Sacramento."

"I have no doubt there is an agent named Frasier in Sacramento, but this man is not him." As Agent Flores accompanied Drew Riordan out of the interview room, Genaro turned away from the mirror. "My team is not yet in place. Send two of your men to keep them both under surveillance."

The chief's bushy brows rose. "You do not wish me to arrest this man for impersonating a federal officer?"

"Not yet."

Carasegas used the phone on the wall to call down to the squad room and dispatch two men. As he did, Genaro checked the time. He had brought with him several disposable cell phones, the purchase and use of which could not be traced back to him or GenHance, but the call he needed to make in five minutes also had to come from inside the police department, to add to the chain of evidence Genaro would use against Carasegas should the Mexican ever decide to run his mouth or otherwise renege on their agreement. "Do you have a secure line in this building?" he asked when the chief hung up the wall phone.

Carasegas nodded. "You may use the private line in my office."

Genaro knew Carasegas probably kept the line tapped so he could acquire whatever blackmail he used to stay in power. A quaint tactic, one that had been obsolete for forty years on the other side of the border, but that, too, would serve Genaro's purposes.

"Very well." He picked up the only bag he had brought with him from the States. "I'll need the line and your office for the next thirty minutes."

"I should tell you that this additional surveillance will be expensive," the chief warned, his expression more calculated now. "For such sensitive work, I can use only certain men, and they expect to be paid well."

"Here is five thousand U.S." Genaro removed two bundles of bills from his jacket and dropped them into the chief's hands. "I will provide another five thousand when Taske and Marena have been recovered, and the final ten thousand when you place them and the man claiming to be Agent Frasier in my custody."

"You are very generous, Señor Genaro." The money vanished into the chief's jacket. "Come, I will show you to my office so you can make your call."

Charlie's legs didn't want to stay vertical anymore, so she walked up to where the sand was dry and sat down, hugging her knees with her arms. After a moment Sam came to sit beside her, and they both watched the waves as they rolled in.

"How long have you known who I am?" she heard herself ask.

"I don't know who you are." When he saw her face, he added, "Until a few moments ago, I thought you were an ordinary woman caught up in a scheme to abduct me, or that you had been brought along only to provide me with whatever medical attention I needed."

A surge of bitterness made her smile. Of course he thought of her existing only to serve his needs. He probably thought the rest of the world did, too. "What changed your mind?"

"The shooting on the bridge, being brought to this island, and the manner in which we're being treated now suggest that we were both deliberately targeted for reasons other than my wealth and your skills," he said. "This man knew we were Takyn."

"How could he have known that?" Charlie demanded. "And if he doesn't work for GenHance, then what possible reason could he have for snatching us?"

"I don't know." He picked up a shell and tossed it at the water. "But until we have those answers, we will have to be cautious."

Samuel knew more than he was telling her. Charlie had spent years treating patients who deliberately concealed things out of embarrassment or fear; she knew when someone was holding out on her. At least she wouldn't have to play friends to coax it out of him. As soon as the sun set she was going to find out exactly what Samuel Taske was thinking, and there was no way on earth he could stop her.

"I've already met Aphrodite, Vulcan, and Delilah in real life," Samuel said tentatively. "I doubt you're Sapphira; I believe she lives somewhere in Canada." He leaned forward, trying to catch her eye. "Are you going to keep me in suspense?"

She wanted to put him in traction for the next six months. "You were right about that new Melissa Etheridge CD." She studied his face. "I loved it."

At last he looked as stricken as she felt. "You're Magdalene." Unbelievably his expression went from shocked to amused. "You're nothing like I imagined you'd be."

Her shoulders stiffened. "I expected you to be a little

bald guy with horn-rimmed glasses and a pocket calculator."

"Well, in my mind you were a freckled, ponytailed, much younger version of Julia Child." He tried to charm her with another of his slow smiles. "You are a remarkable cook. I could happily live on nothing more than your dessert recipes."

"You'd just become a type-two diabetic." To keep from punching him in the face, she turned her head back to watch the waves.

"Have you met any of the others?"

"In real life?" She shook her head. "You're the first, and if we get out of this, you'll be the last." Disgusted with herself and him, she got up and dusted off her legs.

"You're upset," Sam said as he followed her up to the stone path. "Am I such a disappointment in person?"

"Not at all. You don't have to impress me, Sam. Just help me get back home, and I'll adore you forever." She stopped outside the front entrance to the villa. "Maybe we should try walking the beach, see if we can spot any boats out there."

"I think we should first try to establish communications with our captor," he said as he reached for the door latch. "I may also be able to pick up some information from the interior."

"May?" She glanced down at his hands. "On the Internet you said you had to wear gloves to keep from picking up everything about everything." *Or did you lie about that, too?*

"My ability isn't working as it has in the past. Here it seems to be limited, or perhaps muted. I'm not sure." He didn't sound concerned. "If it is fading, I certainly won't complain, but I should use what I have left to see what I can learn about the man who brought us here."

She heard the unasked question in his voice, but there was no way in hell she was confiding in him now. "My ability isn't going to help us." She walked inside.

He closed the door behind her. "I don't wish to pry, Charlotte. I know how personal our talents are. But if there is anything you can do to improve our situation—"

"There's nothing." It wasn't her fault she got stuck with the one ability that had absolutely no value on a deserted island, so why did she feel guilty? "Come on; I'll give you a tour of the place."

Inside the villa she took him to the large, well-equipped kitchen and showed him the generous quantities of food that had been stored for them. "No freezer, and no prepackaged or canned stuff in the pantry, but there's a tank over there with live lobsters and maybe some oysters or clams."

He sorted through the vegetables and fruit in the refrigerator bins. "Garlic, asparagus, gingerroot, avocados, peppers, carrots, peppers, pineapples, strawberries. Odd assortment."

"The bins in the cabinets are filled with root vegetables," she told him as he removed a gallon-size plastic container filled with an amber liquid and opened the lid. "What's that? Apple juice?"

He sniffed the contents. "Honey." He frowned. "This doesn't make any sense. What other foods have you found?"

"I haven't found any sugar or flour or baking stuff, but there's a cabinet filled with spices over here." She opened the cabinet. "They're not labeled, but looks like lots of seeds, some dried herbs, different types of pepper." She took out a plastic bag packed with what looked like long black bean pods and another filled with purple and reddish brown beans. "Either of these look familiar to you?"

"The long pods are vanilla bean, I believe." He eyed the other bag. "The other might be cocoa." When he put the container back in the fridge he took a black fig from the bin and began to break it open.

"No," she said, taking it away from him and dropping it back in the bin. "We don't know what's in this stuff."

He frowned. "It looked like a fig to me."

"A fig that this wacko could have injected with more sedatives, or some kind of hallucinogen." She closed the door to the fridge.

"I'm sure it hasn't been tampered with," he assured her, showing her his hands, and then looked up at the four large glass dome light fixtures. "Charlotte, are all the lights in the house electric?"

"Everything I've seen is." She caught on to what he meant. "How do you have power on a deserted island?"

"If there were generators, I think we would have heard them when we were outside." He studied the primitive pottery displayed in the glass-fronted niches above the cabinetry, and then the empty counters below them. "You didn't find any cookware, did you?"

"No. All the dishes and utensils are plastic or foam, so cleanup will be easy." She wanted to ask him what he was thinking, but even a whisper might be picked up by hidden mics or the security camera in the corner of the ceiling. "Come on; you've got to see the living room in this place."

Charlie led him out of the kitchen and across the hall to the large room she had mentally dubbed "the pit." Bright orange, purple, and blue wall murals imitated a tropical sunset, and made a dramatic backdrop for three different pit groups in matching colored velvet, suede, and raw silk. Swags of metallic ribbons and silk flowers hung down over wide windows offering different views of the greenery outside.

"If it were any brighter in here, I'd probably develop instantaneous cataracts." Charlie picked up one of the intricately embroidered pillows that had been scattered around the cushions. "How are you supposed to take a nap in a room like this?"

"I don't think napping was the decorator's intention." Sam reached out and ran his hand over the purple velvet before turning his head to look back through the door at the kitchen. "Are the other rooms like this?"

"Some variations on the theme, but basically, yes. Nice furniture, bright colors, lots of fancy fabrics. No televisions, stereos, or other electronic gadgets that could tell us where the hell we are, but art on all the walls and plenty of color-coordinated fruit." She eyed the basket of pomegranates, tangerines, and plums on the low table in the center of one pit group. Something about the fruit nagged at her, but she didn't know why.

"Let's have a look at that speaker in the bedroom," Sam suggested.

Before they went into the bedroom upstairs, Charlie showed Sam the exam room.

"It's got everything you'd find in a treatment room in any trauma center," she said as she sat on the end of the exam table. "I could even run labs in here."

"Indeed." Sam peered into one cabinet. "Why would you need to?"

"I don't know, but this is the weirdest thing." She showed him the blood in cold storage. "Twenty-eight pints—enough to transfuse a dozen patients—but not a mark on one of them. I can't even tell if it's human blood unless I run some tests."

Sam walked around the exam table. "What are these?" he asked, touching one of the corner universal socket clamps.

"We use them to attach add-ons and extensions to the table, like arm boards, IV pools, stirrups, that kind of thing." She bent over to open one of the drawers under the table. "He stowed the extensions under here."

His expression turned bleak as he turned his back on the security camera and took her hand. "I could use a hug," he said, shifting his eyes up. As soon as she gave him a decidedly reluctant embrace, he put his mouth next to her ear and murmured, "Any surgical equipment?" Quickly she shook her head. "Good."

She didn't know whether she agreed, especially since

the nearest hospital might as well have been on the surface of the moon. "Just don't burst an appendix anytime soon, okay?" she muttered back.

He kept one arm around her as they left the treatment room and went down the hall to the master bedroom suite. Once inside Samuel went directly to the wall speaker to inspect it, giving Charlie a moment to compose herself.

The stress of the last twenty-four hours combined with discovering that the rich, handsome stranger whose life she'd saved was someone she had considered her closest friend in the world had begun to grind on her. Her EMT training was the only reason she hadn't dissolved into a puddle of helpless feminine goo, and now that Sam had miraculously recovered she wasn't too sure how much longer that would keep her from going all girly on him.

Some of it was on him, Charlie decided. He'd kept far too much from her. Although the group had agreed that concealing their identities and locations was an important safeguard, she and Paracelsus had grown close enough to share more than a few intimate details of their lives. He'd always listened whenever she'd needed to vent, and had given her advice on how to handle the loneliness and depression that came with being Takyn. She'd even trusted him enough to tell him about her last disastrous attempt at a relationship.

He told me he wanted to go to the nightclub so we could dance, she'd typed one night via IM. *But he only took me there because he had a bad day, and he wanted to get loaded and flirt with everything in a skirt. You know what he had planned? A threesome. Me, him, and some waitress he wanted more than me.*

At least he showed you his real character before you got serious about him, Paracelsus had replied. *Imagine how you'd feel if you were living with him and he'd brought that waitress home.*

You're right, I know, and it's better that I found out

before I got too involved. She hesitated before she added, *Don't you get tired of it? Always being by yourself, never having anyone to love?*

Of course I do, he admitted. *Everyone does. When I feel lonely, I remind myself of how fortunate I am to have friends like you. I may live the rest of my life without a partner, but I never have to be alone. I carry you and the others with me in my heart, Magdalene.*

Sure he does, she thought, pushing the memory out of her head as she went back to watching him examine the speaker. *Right next to his platinum credit cards.*

"This is wired to a radio receiver behind it in the wall." He gestured to the perforated plate. "It was not set up to transmit."

"Maybe he didn't need it to." As a warning, she glanced up at the cameras.

"It's more than that." He took her over to the glass wall, turning her so that they both stood with their backs to the cameras. "When I touched the speaker, I saw the technician who installed the equipment. The cameras transmit only a video feed, and there are no other monitoring devices in the villa."

"So the son of a bitch is watching us, but he can't hear us. I guess when you're making homemade porn you don't need the audio." She leaned forward to press her forehead against the cool glass and closed her eyes. "God, I hate this."

"You must be exhausted." His hand cupped the back of her neck. "You should rest for a few hours."

"No, I'm fine." She straightened at once. "He could come back in a few hours. What we need to do is —"

"Buenas tardes, Señor Taske, Señorita Marena," the man's voice said from the speaker. "We are happy to see you becoming familiar with your new home. As you have now discovered, you have everything you need to live comfortably at Séptima Casa. Since Señor Taske has completely recovered from his injury, you may now begin your new life together."

"Our new life." Charlie wanted to throw something at the camera. "You don't decide how we live, you jack-ass. You hear me?"

"Señor Taske, if your companion has not yet informed you of this, there are two rules you both must obey," the man continued. "The first is that you must never attempt to escape the island. The second is that you and Señorita Marena are to have sexual intercourse at least once each day."

Charlie felt like screaming. "What's the matter, you pervert? Can't you get off unless you watch someone else doing it? Why don't you just go buy some dirty movies?"

"Charlotte." Sam gestured for her to be quiet.

". . . ignore these rules," the man was saying, "you will be punished."

Samuel waved his hands at the camera, and then said very slowly, "We must speak with you. Why are we here? What is the punishment for breaking the rules?"

"You said he can't hear us," she reminded him.

"He may be able to read my lips," Samuel replied.

Several moments of silence passed, and then the man's voice spoke again. "*Buenas tardes, Señor Taske, Señorita Marena.* We are happy to see you becoming familiar with your new home. . . ."

"It's a recording, just like yesterday." Charlie sat on the floor, propping her elbows on her knees as she pressed the heels of her hands to her eyes. "How can he punish us when we're stranded alone on an island?"

"You're assuming we're alone."

"If the pervert or anyone else was around, I'd have sensed them last night." Aware that she'd just given her-self away, she got up, opened the sliding door, and walked out onto the patio.

Samuel joined her at the railing. "Either your hearing is exceptional, or you're some sort of a telepath."

"Telepaths can communicate back and forth. I'm more like a satellite dish. All I can do is pick up thoughts."

She rubbed her tired eyes. "Don't waste any time thinking of your favorite color, either, because it only works at night. During the day I'm as oblivious as any other ordinary woman."

Her sarcasm seemed to elude him. "A nocturnal empath." He sounded thoughtful. "Does your ability have any other limitations? Range, for example?"

Her mouth twisted. "Not many." Sunlight pierced the foliage beyond the patio, revealing something she hadn't noticed before. From the position of the sun, Charlie knew it would be setting soon. She glanced around until she spied the cover fitted over the large hot tub, and took his hand. "Come on. Let's see if that Jacuzzi over there works."

He frowned. "Charlotte, you really should try to get some sleep."

"Oh, I plan to." She threaded her fingers through his. "After we have sex."

PART TWO

Seventh House

Chapter 6

"The attorney called." Brent Collins handed his wife a snifter, his hand shaking so badly that the inch of dark Calvados at the bottom threatened to slosh over the rim. "There is nothing more he can do for us."

"Not since he's run through the retainer. Bastard." Randa Collins drank half the brandy before cradling the delicate crystal bowl between her manicured hands. She thought of the List, her mental tally of their wealthy, influential, and elite friends. Too many names had been crossed off in the past week, but there was always someone left. Someone in need of her personal attention . . . "I'll get in touch with Howard. Under the circumstances, certainly he can arrange a reasonable loan—"

"Howard's dead, darling. He ate a bottle of pills last night." Brent put a hand on the top of her head briefly before wandering over to the deck window. "Ron's gone to hide in Barbados; Carl's already filed and intends to move in with his parents."

Randa refused to believe it was this bad, and set aside the drink. "What about Jerry? He was your best friend at Yale."

"He's testifying before Congress next week." Brent

tucked his hands into his pockets. "One of the many conditions attached to his plea agreement."

"Mommy?"

The low, sweet voice grated against Randa's ears, and she had to take a moment to compose her expression before she turned to look at her daughter. "Emily, you're supposed to be asleep by now." A resentful corner of her heart added, *And you weren't supposed to be so big, or dark, or whiny.*

"I know." The six-year-old hung her head. "But no one came to kiss me good night."

"Daddy and I have been busy." Randa rose, absently smoothing down the folds of her dress before she picked up the house phone and pressed nine. When Emily's nanny answered, she said, "Mary, Miss Collins has come downstairs. She needs to be taken back to the nursery." She ignored the nanny's hurried apology and replaced the receiver.

Brent walked over to crouch down in front of their daughter. "We didn't mean to forget you, sweetheart. Mommy and I just . . . needed to talk about things." She slipped into his arms and buried her face against his neck. "Did you have another bad dream?"

Under his chin, her untidy black mop moved from side to side. "Miss Mary is upset. She's going away in the morning."

"What did you say?" Randa's heels made sharp sounds as she strode across the imported marble and grabbed Emily by the arm. "Did she tell you she was leaving?"

"No, Mommy." Her daughter cringed. "It was the fairies again. They told me she was."

"For God's sake." She let go of Emily with a contemptuous fling of her hand. "I've told you a dozen times, there are no such things as fairies."

"Randie." Brent looked up and shook his head a little. To Emily, he said, "You just stop listening to those fairies and go to sleep like a good girl, all right?"

"Yes, Daddy."

The disheveled nanny came through the doors and hurried over to take Emily's hand. "I'm so sorry, Mrs. Collins. I thought she was already asleep. I did check on her before I went to bed, and—"

"I'm sure you did. That will be all." Randa gave the door a direct look.

When the nanny began walking Emily out, the little girl dragged against her arm and looked back at her parents. "You'll come up to tuck me in, Daddy?"

Brent smiled. "In a few minutes, sweetheart." As soon as the child and the nanny left, his expression faded into bleakness. "We'll have to call Chicago first thing in the morning."

"I already did," Randa told him. "They won't take her back, not now. They've destroyed the paperwork, but we have to deal with getting rid of her." She might as well tell him the rest. "I called an adoption attorney, and he's been looking for a girl her age. He says he can place her with a wealthy couple in Mexico."

"My God." Brent whitened. "Randa, she's just a little girl. None of this is her fault."

Randa knew her husband. Brent, an only child, had been worshiped by his parents since the moment he'd been yanked from between his mother's legs, and after they died he'd gone looking for new groupies. She'd been happy to cater to him for the duration of their courtship, but she'd never been interested in wasting her life playing his adoring fan. A child had been the logical answer, but rather than destroy her body she'd arranged Emily's adoption.

Randa didn't care what happened to Emily now, but she had to think about her future. "Darling, it's better this way. I'm sure she'll be well treated by these Mexicans. After all, they're probably her people."

Brent began to pace. "We'll turn her over to the authorities. They'll put her in foster care here in the States."

"You mean, drop her off at the nearest police station?" Randa felt a surge of bitter amusement. "I think they'll want to know who you are and where you found her. Are you going to tell them how we bought her, or why you can't take care of her anymore?"

His expression turned stubborn. "It doesn't have to be me. I'll pay Mary to take her to them after we leave in the morning."

She rested her head against her hand. "Where do you think we're going, lover? The money's gone. Our friends are wiped out. At least Howard only swindled you. If you'd been in bed with him, they'd be coming after you now." She saw his expression and shot to her feet. "Oh, for God's sake, Brent. How could you be so fucking stupid?"

He hung his head. "Howard needed more investors, and I had the connections. He made me a partner and tripled my percentage. It shouldn't have fallen apart so quickly. He swore to me—"

"Swore to you?" she shouted. "Don't you see, you idiot? Howard is dead, and Ron is testifying. That leaves you to be the fall guy. They're going to come after you for all this now. You'll be the one they splash all over the papers and parade on television and drag off to prison."

Brent wouldn't look at her. "It doesn't have to be like that for us."

Time to cut her losses. "It won't be for *me*." She looked around. "Where is my purse?"

"I was wrong." Brent strode over to her. "You aren't leaving me and Emily now. We're a family, and whatever it takes, we're going to stay together. We need you. We love you."

Randa closed her eyes briefly before she smiled at him. "Darling, this may come as something of a shock, but I don't need you. Or your shit. Or that little monkey-faced bitch."

He hit her, his open palm slamming into her face, and Randa stumbled away as she pressed her hand to her burning cheek.

"I'm your husband. Emily is your daughter," he told her as he took hold of her arms. A strange calmness seemed to settle over him, erasing the lines of strain from his face and most of the emotion from his eyes. "You can't abandon us."

She had never loved him, but now she hated him. "If you try to stop me, I'll testify against you."

"You're still my wife." Brent's eyes grew sad. "Emily needs her mother."

Randa would have laughed at that, but her husband's slim hands encircled her throat, choking off her voice and then her breath.

"You can't leave us," he whispered again into her ear. "We're a family. We have to go together."

Chapter 7

Charlotte's distrust had been difficult enough for Samuel to manage, but her brisk decision to go to bed with him was nothing short of utterly confounding.

"I don't wish to upset you," he said as she led him across the deck to the hot tub. "But I believe the stress of our situation has affected your judgment."

"Alas, *mío*, you believe wrong." She knelt down to unfasten the cover and glanced up at him. "Will you get the other side, please?"

Automatically he walked around and bent to pick up the edge of the canvas cover, folding it back onto itself before he shifted it away from the Jacuzzi. The water inside the tub was clean and clear and, when Charlotte pressed a button on the tub's console, began to bubble rapidly.

"I don't think we'll need the heat." She slipped her legs over the edge and lowered herself into the tub until the water reached her waist. "Nice and cool. For now, anyway. Get in."

He tried not to look at how her sarong soaked up the water. "I should go and collect something for us to eat. You must be hungry."

"You can't be shy." She held out her hand. "Come on. I won't bite. Unless you want me to."

Samuel sat down on the edge of the tub, intent only on persuading her out of it. He didn't expect her to pull him into the water, or to wrap herself around him as soon as he planted his feet.

"There," she said, linking her hands behind his neck. "Feels good, doesn't it?"

"It feels amazingly good." So did she, and he gave himself a moment to enjoy the sensation of her voluptuous body pressed to his. "You've a generous soul, Charlotte, and I am beyond flattered, but—"

"You are gorgeous, but you talk too much." She leaned close to kiss his cheek, and whispered, "There's a man hiding in the brush about thirty yards off the deck to your right. Don't turn your head when you look."

Samuel spotted the shadowy figure at once. "I see."

"The sun will set in a few minutes, and then I'll be able to do my thing," she said. "The closer he is, the easier it'll be for me to read him. So let's give him a reason to stay there, all right?"

Taske should have felt relieved, but he was too furious with himself and their captor. "I could go and have a few words with him."

"He could be armed, and I don't have any more blood to spare." She drew him back to the wide bench seat under the water, reversing their positions and pushing him down so that his back was to the man watching them. "Take off my top," she murmured, "and throw it on the deck."

Taske did as she directed, his anger making him tear the lacy fabric in the process. "Forgive me."

"No, that's good. Very convincing." As she straddled him, she brought her face close to his, keeping their lips only a whisper apart, but looked to the left of him. "He's moving closer," she breathed against his mouth. "Now pretend I'm a skinny little heiress and tell me how much you want me."

"Why would I do that?" He put his hands on either side of her waist, both to steady her and to keep her from rubbing against the erection straining under his shorts.

Her smile tightened. "With how I look I know it's a stretch, but try."

"I meant, why would I pretend you were someone else?" He threaded his fingers through her thick hair as he looked all over her face. "Seeing you, I understand why some men invaded countries and defeated armies and conquered emperors to have one woman. Helen of Troy must have been as strong and fierce and desirable as you."

"Oh, she was?" Her expression turned ironic. "In all the movies I've seen about Troy, Helen is a gorgeous little blonde."

"Helen's legend was born in the Mediterranean," he told her. "Even today, most of the natives of that region are black haired and have dark complexions. In the art of her era, Helen is portrayed as a statuesque brunette. It was only much later that artists began painting her as a petite woman with fair hair and white skin."

She seemed amused. "That's what most men want."

"Most men are fools," he assured her.

She ran her hands over his shoulders. "At least guys never have to worry about it. The bigger, the better."

"On the contrary." It infuriated him to think the men in her past had made her feel unattractive. "Despite the strapping heroic figures that regularly grace the covers of romance novels, in reality most women find men built like me quite intimidating."

"Then most women are idiots, *mío*." She glanced past him and said in a louder voice, "I'm glad you don't mind my size. Even big girls like me need love."

He knew she was only playing to their voyeur, but the fact that she considered herself unattractive infuriated him. "How could I mind having you in my arms? Since the first moment I saw you, I've thought of little else." He stroked his hand down her arm. "Seeing you makes me believe in things I know to be impossible. Answered prayers. Granted wishes." He traced the outline of her lips with his fingertips. "Wildest dreams."

"Keep talking like that, *mío*," she said, her voice shaking a little, "and you'll break my heart."

He dragged her hand from his shoulder to his chest, pressing it over the heavy throb beneath his skin. "Then you can have mine, *mía*."

She closed her eyes as she took in a sharp breath, and Taske brought her parted lips to his. He felt her jerk beneath his kiss, but she didn't pull back, and then she was opening for him, her mouth sweet and hot. Suddenly he didn't care about the man watching them or what he thought. Putting on a show didn't matter, and merely tasting Charlotte wasn't enough. Taske wanted more, he needed more, and she gave it to him, caressing him with her lips and gliding her tongue against his.

Far too soon she tugged her mouth free of his, and Taske saw she was frowning. "Charlotte, what is it?"

"Nothing." She closed her eyes briefly before she murmured, "I'm not getting anything from him."

Although the sun no longer appeared in the reflection on the glass wall of the villa, Taske could see some light on the horizon. "Give it a few minutes."

"Let me try something." She rested her hand against his neck. "Think of your favorite color."

"Done." Taske watched her eyes widen as she brought her fingers to her lips, and knew she had heard his thoughts. "What is it?"

"'Kissed by a Rose' is the name of a song," she told him, "not a color."

The blush that darkened her cheeks, he decided, would be his second-favorite color. "But that's what your mouth feels like."

She looked as if she meant to argue, and then she glanced to the right and sighed. "Looks like our voyeur took off."

"Did you pick up any thoughts from him?"

"Not one," she said. "I don't understand it. I can read anyone, but that man . . . Sam, it was like he wasn't even there."

"But you're certain that he's gone." When she nodded, he cradled her face between his hands. "Kiss me again, Charlotte."

She bit her lower lip. "He's gone. Show's over."

"I know." He pressed his thumb against her mouth, taking the place of her lip between the edges of her teeth. "Kiss me again anyway."

"You don't understand. I don't just read someone's thoughts." She drew in an uneven breath. "I also get the emotions."

"Then you know how I feel about you." He was glad; he didn't want to hide how much he wanted her anymore.

"It's more than that." She swallowed. "I feel what you feel, Sam. The physical sensations that go with the emotions. And right now, you're very . . ." Her eyelashes swept down as she shuddered. "Hot and bothered."

"See how this feels," he said, bringing her mouth to his.

As Taske kissed her again, she groaned and plastered herself against him. Always in the past he had been forced to hold back, to temper his hunger along with his strength for fear of taking too much too fast. But nothing about Charlotte was flimsy or fragile, and she responded with equal passion, demanding as much as he wanted from her.

How long they kissed, Taske didn't know or care; he couldn't think beyond the fusion of their mouths and bodies. The strip of fabric binding her breasts floated away, and he pulled her in to feel the luxurious weight on his chest. The soft vise of her thighs settled her sex against him, and there she rocked gently, working with tormenting friction against the swollen ache of his shaft. His muscles bunched as he lifted her, lust blinding him as he suckled at one breast and then the other, scoring her with the edge of his teeth.

He released her when he felt her snarl her fists in his hair, but by that moment reason had vanished. All he could think of was putting his mouth on her.

"Sam."

He brought her down so he could feel his name on her lips. "I'm here." He dropped one hand beneath the water to clasp the top of her leg, gripping the taut muscle and smiling as she trembled with reaction. "Whatever you want, whatever you need, Charlotte, let me give it to you. Please."

"Samuel." She panted against his mouth, her body shuddering as he followed the curve of her inner thigh up to the soft, full flower of her sex. "I don't know if . . ." She trailed off with a groan as he used his fingers to stroke her. "God, that feels . . . Oh, that's good."

He took his hand from her, but only long enough to release the front of his shorts. He splayed his hand across her bottom, urging her closer so he could settle her against his shaft. "There you are." It had been so long, too long, and the feel of her silkiness on him was almost too much. He clenched his teeth as he ignored the burning ache in his balls. "Look at me."

"This is crazy." Her dazed eyes met his. "We don't know each other."

"Yes, we do." He shifted his hips so that his shaft parted her folds and dragged along her inner tissues. He could feel the small protrusion of her clit as his cock head nudged over it, and shifted again. He moved just enough so that the heavy ridge of his glans slid over the little knot before he went still. "Go ahead, Charlotte. Use me however you like. Let me feel your pleasure." He cupped her buttocks as her thighs tightened against his hips. "It's only fair."

"No, it's not, you wicked man." Her hands clutched his shoulders as she moved, rocking herself slowly against him. "But, God, you feel so good."

Taske braced himself, watching her face as she rubbed herself over him. Her sweet lips parted as her breath quickened and the water churned around them. The delicious glide of her sex tugged at his foreskin, pushing his own needs to the brink, but he held back, unwilling to find his own release until he saw hers.

When she came, it was with a long, graceful roll of her hips, her folds engulfing the straining head of his penis. It took every last shred of his control not to push in and pump himself deep. He drew his hips back, just enough to position the tip against her clit, and then with a groan that came from his heels let his climax jet against her.

"Sam." She came again, this time with a cry, writhing under his hands as the tremors racked her a second time.

Taske tucked her face against his neck and held her, soothing her through the aftershocks by stroking his hands along her spine. Her breathing slowed and her body gradually went limp, and when he murmured her name, she barely stirred.

Like an exhausted child, she'd fallen asleep.

Taske shifted her so that he could support her legs, and carefully stepped up and out of the pool. Water streamed down his legs as he stood for a moment and realized what he didn't feel. Yesterday lifting something as insignificant as a briefcase had been impossible for him. Now he held Charlotte without difficulty, without even thinking about it. He barely felt her weight at all.

As a boy Taske had been as healthy and active as any other child, and had spent every moment he could out-doors. When he'd joined in games with other children, his size had given him some advantages, but his physical strength had never been anything out of the ordinary. Now something was changing him on the physical level, and from the surges of energy he felt, he suspected the process was continuing. As if whatever had healed him hadn't finished with him yet. He could almost feel the power growing inside him.

Taske looked at the villa, and then at the woman sleeping in his arms. Twenty-four hours ago he had thought only of saving one more life before he ended his own. Now, because of her, everything had changed.

Now it was time to find out why.

*   *   *

Drew stood on the whitewashed steps outside the hill-side home of the fifth witness to Tacal's murder and watched as Agent Flores spoke to the old woman who had answered the door. After being unable to speak to four of the witnesses, he was convinced they were only wasting their time, but his companion had insisted on trying one more address.

Drew didn't mind letting her take the lead, not when she spoke the language and knew every street in Manzanillo. He'd left his rental in the guest lot at the small but scrupulously clean hotel Gracie had recommended, and from there had let her drive them around town in her old but well-maintained Subaru, both out of deference to her and to have time to think over the situation.

Someone had set up Samuel Taske and the paramedic for Tacal's murder; of that Drew had absolutely no doubt. Even if somehow Taske had been physically capable of beating a man unconscious, he was too intelligent and fastidious to do so in front of a crowd in a strange country. There was always the possibility that his friend had been drugged or had suffered some kind of psychotic break as a result of being abducted, but if that were the case, why would he stop and let the EMT finish the job?

At first the old lady seemed only a little suspicious, until Gracie asked a question and gestured toward the bay. A few sharp words, a shake of the head, and the elderly woman scurried back inside.

"Let me guess," Drew said as the door slammed shut. "The witness left this morning on an extended trip and won't be back until sometime near Christmas. Again."

Gracie closed her notepad and tucked it away. "I do not understand this. How could every witness to this one murder leave the city at the same time?"

"By not leaving and telling their families to say they did." He glanced out at the horizon, where the sky was darkening from deep purple to black. "It's getting late. We might as well call it a night."

"Of course." She gave him a perplexed look. "What else would we call it?"

"That's American slang for 'it's time to quit,'" he explained. "Or 'it's time to go and have a drink with me.'"

She started down the steps toward the narrow street at the base of the hill, her heels clicking against the stone. "Well, which is it?"

He grinned as he followed. "I'll leave the interpretation up to you, Agent Flores."

"I have to work in the morning." She stopped to unlock the passenger door before she went around to the driver's side. She glanced across the car roof at him. "And you are returning to the U.S. tomorrow, no?"

He couldn't lie to the only person interested in helping him. "I'm not leaving until I find out what really happened to these people. I'd also like to know why you were taken off this case, and why you decided to help me anyway."

For a moment she looked as if she wanted to turn and walk off. "*Bueno.* One drink."

Gracie drove back toward the police station, but parked on the next block over in front of a small café. As soon as Drew stepped out he smelled coffee and burned sugar, and saw two women wearing colorful aprons removing trays of pastries from the glass cases inside. "It looks like they're closing for the night."

"Not yet." Gracie gestured toward a small garden courtyard beside the building. "Go, sit down." She went inside, and one of the women came out from behind the counter to hug her.

Drew watched them chat for a moment before he walked back to the courtyard and sat down at a table in one shadowed corner. A few minutes later Gracie joined him, a small tray in her hands.

He eyed a plate heaped with tiny pastries and two steaming mugs. "More hot chocolate?"

"*Café de olla y conchas.*" She unloaded the tray before setting it aside and sitting down next to him. "Mexican coffee and pastries."

He tested the drink, which was dark, flavored with cinnamon, and came with a powerful kick. "That's not just coffee. I thought you had to work in the morning."

"That is why I bought the *conchas*." She selected one, nibbling at the edge of the shell-shaped pastry before she licked the crumbs it left on her lips. "You're staring at me, Agent Frasier."

"You're more interesting than the garden, Agent Flores." He reached over to rub his thumb over some sugar she'd missed. "So why are you helping me?"

She cleared her throat. "It is only a professional courtesy. You would do the same if I were in your country."

"Oh, I'd do a lot more." Drew grinned. "You're blushing again. Admit it. You like me."

"If I were a man," she countered, "we'd be in a cantina, drinking and talking about women."

"If you were a man, I'd be too busy crying. But we can talk about women, if you like." He sat back. "What made you decide to become an environmental cop?"

"It was the right thing to do," she said slowly. "Mexico has not always been a poor country. When your ancestors were living in animal-skin tents and hunting with bows, mine were building temples to the gods."

"Actually my ancestors were probably drinking, poaching deer, and thieving from the British." He studied her expression. "You take your job very seriously, don't you?"

"How can I do anything else?" Idly she broke her pastry into small pieces. "The first invaders, the conquistadores, came here looking for gold. They burned our cities and butchered thousands trying to find it. Today the oil companies, the tourists, and the sportfishermen are not so brutal, perhaps, but they, too, have no conscience. If we let them do as they please, they will steal or destroy the few treasures we have left." Her lips twisted. "It would be easier if I were not a woman. Men in my country think we belong at home, cooking their meals and having their babies."

He glanced at the police station across the street. "Do you think that's why they took you off this case? Because you're a woman?"

"I did not—" A ring from her mobile phone interrupted her, and she retrieved it from her case. As soon as she looked at the display she rose to her feet. "Excuse me for a moment."

Drew watched her walk a short distance out to the curb, and then checked his own mobile. His signal status still stood at one-half bar; he'd have to ask her what service she used so he could piggyback a call to their tower once he returned to the hotel.

Gracie returned after a minute. "I am sorry to rush you, but that was the clerk from your hotel. He says a detective is there, waiting to see you."

Her back was to the streetlights, and her face shadowed, but Drew heard the tension in her voice and saw the rigid set of her slim shoulders. She wasn't looking at him, either.

His gaze shifted as a dark car pulled up to the front of the police station. Two men emerged and stood for a moment beside the car; one was the police chief.

The other was his old boss, Jonah Genaro.

Drew slid off his copper bracelet, holding it in his hand briefly before opening his fingers. His ability reshaped the dark metal cuff, straightening and elongating it before it blunted itself on one end and formed a point-tipped blade on the other.

He moved quickly around Gracie, clamping his free hand over her mouth as he hauled her out of sight. "Hold still and don't make a sound," he murmured against her hair as he watched Genaro shake hands with the police chief before he got into the back of the car.

She shook her head and gripped his arm with her hands, trying to free herself.

"I mean it, Gracie." Drew let her see the copper blade and felt her stiffen against him. Although he'd stab himself before he'd hurt her, he couldn't let Genaro see either of them.

Once the dark car left, the police chief went back inside the station. Drew waited another few seconds before he relaxed a little and removed his hand from Gracie's mouth, although he kept his arms around her.

"What are you doing?" she demanded, pulling at his arm again. "Have you gone crazy? Let go of me."

"I'm not crazy, and I'm not hallucinating, either." He turned her around to face him. "Why is Jonah Genaro here in Mexico?"

All the emotion left her face and her eyes went flat. "I don't know who you mean, Agent Frasier."

"You're a lovely woman, Gracie," he told her as he marched her back over to the table to retrieve the keys to her car. "But a lousy liar."

When they reached her car he put the keys in her hands. "Unlock the door." As soon as she did he opened it and hustled her inside, moving her over to the driver's seat as he climbed in after her.

"This is kidnapping," she said as he clipped her seat belt over her. "You will go to prison for many years, Martin. Our prisons are nothing like those in America."

"Compared to what Genaro has planned for me, trust me, it'd be a vacation." He pushed the key in the ignition. "And my name's not Martin. It's Andrew. Start the car."

She didn't move. "I will do nothing more for you."

"Then I'll lock you in the trunk," he told her. "Start the damn car, Gracie."

Reluctantly she turned the key. "I will take you to the airport. You can put me in the trunk there and leave on the next plane."

He chuckled. "I thought you weren't going to help me."

"I am not helping." She lifted her chin. "I am ridding myself of you."

"Genaro will have men at the airport waiting to take me," he assured her. "And the border, and the docks, and every other way out of this fucking country." He pointed toward the bay. "Drive toward the water."

She glared at him before she started down the road. "So what is your plan? Do you think you can steal a boat, too?"

"I'm not leaving Mexico until I find my friends." He was telling her too much, but he didn't care anymore. His seeing Genaro had completely changed the game. "How long has Jonah been in the city? Did he frame Taske and Marena for the murder?"

"I do not know this man," she said flatly. "Tonight was the first time I have ever seen him in Manzanillo."

Drew's instincts were never wrong, and they were telling him that she was speaking the truth. "Okay, I believe you."

"You say these people are your friends." She glanced at him. "Are you a criminal, too?"

"No." He watched the rearview mirror. "Actually I'm an unemployed computer geek. Turn left at the next intersection."

Gracie made the turn and looked ahead. "Do you even know where you are going, Andrew?"

"When I said I was lousy at following directions? I lied." He checked the GPS on his mobile as they drove down a row of beachside cottages, and then pointed at the next open parking spot. "Pull in there."

As soon as Gracie parked he switched off the engine and pocketed the keys. As he opened his door he latched onto her arm. "Come out this side."

Drew held on to her as he stepped up onto the sidewalk and glanced down both sides of the street. "Which one is yours?"

"I don't live here."

"Like I said, lady, you're a lousy liar." He glanced at her stubborn expression. "I can start waking up your neighbors, if you want."

"Wake them." She folded her arms. "They will be happy to call the police and have you arrested."

He saw the curtains in the window twitch and pulled her close. "Not after they see this."

Gracie stood frozen as Drew kissed her, and then she tried to hammer on his chest with her fists. He held on to her and used his tongue to muffle the outraged sounds she made. He retreated when she tried to bite him, and grabbed a handful of her silky hair as she turned her head away. Then she was kissing him back, with all the fire and passion he'd sensed seething under her all-business demeanor.

He eased back to look into her furious eyes. "You kiss like a wildcat fights."

Gracie slapped him. "You are a pig."

"Maybe so." He caught her wrist before she could hit him a second time and held it between them. "But do you really want me dead, Agraciana?"

"Yes," she snapped. Then, with visible resentment: "No, of course not. Unless you try to hurt me, and then I will kill you myself." She hesitated. "Why are you doing this? Why did this Genaro follow you here? Where does he want to take you?"

With Genaro now in Mexico and his men probably searching the streets of the city, Drew had no choice but to trust her. "Tell me which place is yours, and we'll go inside and talk."

She gave him a long, doubtful look before she gestured toward a small, pale blue cottage at the end of the row. "I will listen to what you have to say, as long as you do not try to kiss me again."

"I won't." Unlike her, Drew was an excellent liar.

Chapter 8

Genaro left downtown Manzanillo and directed his driver to take him up into the hills outside the city. The dirt roads they followed weren't on any map, but neither was the private estate they led to.

A flat-faced young Mexican woman driving a golf cart stopped on the other side of the compound gates. She wore a large red poppy in her hair, and smiled at him, displaying a slight gap between her teeth.

"Your driver will have to wait here, señor," she said as she used a remote to open the gates.

"That's fine." Genaro noted the ubiquitous black-and-white maid's uniform she wore as he walked through. He stopped as she produced a handheld metal detector. "I'm not armed."

"I am not concerned with weapons." She passed the device over the front and back of his body before she stepped back and held out a small rectangular basket. "Your watch, your wallet, and all of your electronic devices, please."

Impatiently he removed and placed the items in the basket. "Is that all?"

"For now." She gestured to the cart. "Please."

The girl said nothing, and held no interest for Genaro, so as she drove from the gates to the towering home they protected, he turned his attention to the surroundings. Enormous fires burned from tall braziers and cast flickering light over sprawling gardens and heavily laden fruit trees. The girl drove through a network of animal pens stocked with sheep, goats, and pigs before she circled around an artificial pond filled with waterfowl, and through a maze of flowering shrubs that perfumed the air with heavy sweetness.

It was what Genaro didn't see that held his interest. Thanks to the ongoing drug wars, the men who ran Mexico's enormous cartels were hypervigilant about their own protection, especially at home. Yet here there appeared to be no armed guards or any special security measures other than the fifteen-foot-high brick wall encompassing the property. Aside from a few old women working in the garden, he saw no people at all.

The girl stopped the cart at another gate, which stood open in front of a short stone path that led up to the main house.

"One moment, please." She got out of the cart and went to the gate, where a man emerged and escorted her back. Like the girl, he wore black and white, but instead of a uniform he wore a well-tailored suit. "Señor Genaro, this is Segundo. He will speak to Energúmeno for you."

He got out of the cart. "I can speak for myself, thank you."

"No one doubts that, sir," Segundo said, his voice as colorless as his appearance. "But can you do so in Nahautl?"

Genaro glanced up at the house. "Your employer doesn't speak English?"

"Energúmeno doesn't have to, Mr. Genaro." Segundo gestured toward the house. "If you will follow me, please."

The main house exceeded anything Genaro had seen since arriving in Mexico, and rivaled the size of his own estate in the States; the first floor had to be no less than thirty thousand square feet. From the first level unadorned adobe walls soared straight up, capped not by the ubiquitous terra-cotta tile but an enormous thatched *palapas* supported independently of the structure by pillars carved from whole tree trunks and inlaid with long rows of jasper and onyx spheres.

In Genaro's experience drug lords predictably built ornate, tasteless mansions and decorated them like brothels to compensate for their humble beginnings as dirt-poor peasants. Energúmeno had dispensed with the usual flashy show of wealth and had aspired to more palatial surroundings.

Segundo led him into a winding passage lit by small torches and into a main reception area made up of free-standing glass walls. Behind each pane of glass a pedestal displayed intricately painted pots; masks made of jade, silver, and onyx; and tall, delicate crystal vases filled with gilt-edged white feathers.

Somewhere a dark, sultry-scented incense burned, and water rushed and splashed. Genaro didn't mind the torches or the noticeable absence of air-conditioning, but the pungent smoke brought back memories he didn't care to recall.

The steward stopped by a pair of crooked arrows hammered out of pure gold. "May I offer a suggestion, señor?" When Genaro eyed him, Segundo lost his smile. "In his presence, speak only the truth."

"Why would I lie to your employer when I come here asking for his assistance?" Genaro countered.

The steward spread his hands. "Those who rely on deception often become incapable of honesty. Just as those who hold the truth sacred become intolerant of liars. Observe carefully, and you will see this for yourself."

Segundo led him through the treasure collection into a long, narrow room that curved around a crescent-shaped cage of gold. Inside the cage a black jaguar lay on its side and licked a paw. From the rounded distension of its black belly it was either overfed or a pregnant female. A mound of bones had been scattered around the floor of the cage, some shredded flesh still adhering to the gleaming white surfaces. Beyond the cage a wall of white, semitransparent silk formed a partition; the shadow of a large seated figure behind it flickered as if backlit by fire.

Segundo faced him. "You may speak to Energúmeno through me, Mr. Genaro."

"I appreciate the opportunity to speak with you personally." He waited for the steward to translate before he continued. "As I said on the phone, I have come to your city for two Americans who were brought here from California. I am willing to offer you the compensation of your choice for any assistance you can give me in locating them."

After Segundo repeated what he'd said in Nahautl, there was a long stretch of silence. Then from behind the silk curtain came an odd, resonant voice.

The steward eyed him. "Energúmeno has not yet decided what is to be done with these Americans. He wishes to know why you want them."

Genaro kept his expression bland. "The man has information about people involved in a genetic experiment that I wish to duplicate. What he knows may be of great value to my company."

Energúmeno spoke again, this time issuing only a few terse words.

"Why did you not send hired men to do this?" Segundo translated.

Genaro glanced at the remains of the jaguar's recent feast. One femur near the edge of the cage was too large to be from anything but a human being.

Those who rely on deception often become incapable of honesty. Just as those who hold the truth sacred become intolerant of liars.

"Samuel Taske, the man who was brought here, is wealthy and resourceful," Genaro said. "I was unwilling to depend on others to find and capture him. He's too important to my project."

Energúmeno spoke again.

"What will you do with this man when you are finished with him?" the steward asked.

"If I can't persuade him to work for me," Genaro said, "I will have him killed."

The shadow elongated against the silk curtain.

"If you are concerned about the American authorities, don't be," he added quickly. "Once I take these fugitives back to America, I will see to it that there is nothing to connect either of them to you."

Energúmeno spoke to the steward a final time before his shadow dwindled and then disappeared.

"Certain preparations must be made," Segundo said. "Energúmeno has ordered a meal prepared for you, señor. This way."

Genaro followed the steward out of the reception room and through a curving corridor into a formal dining area. Two places were set: one at the head of the long stone table and one to the right. Bountiful platters of food had been set out, and the girl who had driven the cart stood waiting with a bottle of wine.

Genaro had no desire to eat or drink, but sat down in the chair the steward drew out for him. "I'll just have water, thank you."

Segundo inclined his head, and then left the dining room with the girl.

Genaro drank down half of the water in his glass. As unnerving as the interview had been, it had been worth the risk; Energúmeno would be an invaluable ally.

The girl returned several minutes later to refresh his empty water glass. The gap in her teeth didn't seem as noticeable this time when she smiled at him, and the red poppy in her hair emphasized how dark and glossy it was. "Is the food not to your liking, señor?"

"I was waiting for your employer." He nodded at the empty place setting.

"Energúmeno prefers to dine alone." She sat down beside him and helped herself to a cluster of grapes.

"You should have tried the wine. It is very good. We make it ourselves."

Genaro's satisfaction abruptly vanished, leaving behind a cold knot in his belly. He was not being feted; he was being stalled. "Perhaps another time." He stood. "I have some business to attend to in the city. Will you take me to my car?"

"Of course."

She led him out of the house and to the waiting cart. As she started toward the gate Genaro felt his nausea fade, and realized he'd overreacted to the situation, and had behaved abominably toward his companion. "I apologize."

"To me?" She glanced at him, her lovely face amused. "Why would you do that, señor?"

"I was rude to you earlier," he admitted, his eyes drawn to the elegant way she handled the steering wheel of the cart. The girl had thin, delicate hands, one of which sported a tattoo he hadn't noticed before now. His penis stiffened as he imagined her clasping it in her pretty hands and stroking it. "That was unkind."

Her slim shoulders moved. "I am used to it, and it never lasts."

"What is your name?"

Her lips curved. "Quinequia."

Looking at the silver dove that had been inked onto the back of her hand made his erection grow harder. "Come back with me to the city." He had never begged a woman to do anything, but he knew he couldn't leave without her. He plucked the poppy from her hair and drew it down her cheek, caressing her with its soft petals. "Spend the night with me."

"Energúmeno does not allow us to leave the compound." Quinequia stopped the cart by the front gates, taking the poppy from his fingers and replacing it in her hair. "Here we are."

Genaro didn't see his car or driver, but ignored the police officer waiting for them. "If you won't come with me," he wheedled, "I'll stay here with you."

"That is also not permitted, señor." She nodded to the officer, who came over and took Genaro's arm, pulling it behind his back. "Energúmeno wishes you to go with this man. He will take you where you belong. As soon as you walk through the gates, you will forget me."

"Go," he heard himself say in a slurred, dull voice as the cop handcuffed his wrists behind his back. "Forget."

Quinequia smiled. "Very good, Jonah. You should do well where you are going." She patted his shoulder before taking out a handheld radio and speaking into it in Spanish.

As the cop helped Genaro out to the battered police car, he glanced backward at a young, flat-faced Mexican woman who stood watching them. "Who is that?"

The cop grinned. "Just some girl with bad teeth."

An insect buzzing in Charlie's ear made her frown and swat her hand. When the bug only got louder she opened her eyes and stared through the mesh of damp hair at sunlight-gilded bamboo. Her heavy limbs didn't want to move, not when the memory of nearly having sex with Samuel Taske came back to her. Even worse, she'd enjoyed it more than all the other times when she'd had real sex with the men she'd known. Which should have made her feel pathetic, and oddly didn't.

Samuel had stripped her out of her wet sarong but had wrapped her in one of the robes, a gesture she found curiously touching. *Always a gentleman, aren't you,* mío? She'd have preferred to see him sleeping on the other side of the bed, which lay empty, as did the rest of the room.

The buzzing sound distracted her again, but this time she realized it wasn't being made by an insect. The faint, high-pitched noise came from outside the sliding doors, which had been left open. She saw Samuel dressed only in a pair of cutoffs and standing with his back toward her, and got out of bed, belting the robe as she went out onto the deck.

"Why didn't you wake me?" she asked as she came to stand beside him.

"You needed the rest. You were exhausted." He glanced down at her. "How do you feel?"

"Rested and annoyed." She glanced back at the position of the sun, and estimated it was an hour after dawn. "How long have you been up?"

"I never went to sleep."

"So tonight it'll be your turn to crash." The buzzing sound grew annoyingly loud, and she peered out at the water. "That sound, is that—"

"It's a boat coming toward the island," he confirmed, turning her back toward the room. "You should get dressed."

"Okay." She watched him retrieve a shirt from the closet. "What are you going to do?"

He pulled the shirt over his head. "I have some preparations to make for our visitor."

The flatness of his voice both spooked and reassured her at the same time. "There's a pair of suture scissors in my bag, in the treatment room. The blades aren't very long, but they're sharp and made of surgical steel."

He nodded and went to the door, where he retrieved her teak chair-leg club. "Meet me in the kitchen."

Charlie went into the closet, ignoring the skimpy female clothing as she sorted through what had been stocked for Samuel. Most of the garments were far too big for her, but she found some black stretch swim trunks that covered her from waist to knees, and paired them with a red tank, the hem of which she stretched out and knotted over her right hip.

No shoes had been provided for them, so she went downstairs barefoot, and found Samuel pouring a pot of watery soup through a strainer into one of two clear plastic bottles.

The smell made her wrinkle her nose. "You're making soup, *mío*? At a time like this?"

"I don't recommend tasting it," he said as he strained

the rest of the liquid into the second bottle. Once he set the pot and the strainer aside, he screwed on the bottle tops.

Charlie couldn't hold back her laugh. "Sam, those are enema bottles."

"Yes, they are." He wrapped one with a cloth before he handed it to her. "Tuck it in your waistband behind your back. You'll have to be close to use it, but just go for the eyes." He saw her expression and smiled. "I made it by boiling together onions, lemon juice, and several types of chilies. Consider it a kind of homemade pepper spray."

Now she understood why he'd used enema bottles, which were made out of thin, very flexible plastic designed to administer the liquid contents with a gentle squeeze. "You're brilliant."

"I'm stupid. I should have spent last night fashioning spears and setting up pit traps." He also handed her the suture scissors. "You're an expert on where to inflict the maximum damage with these. I'll fare better with the club."

"Don't kill him," she warned as she pocketed the scissors. "He's the only one who can tell us where we are, and how to get back home."

"I believe we're somewhere off the coast of Mexico," Sam told her. "Everything I've touched thus far in the house was brought over from the mainland."

"Your ability is working again?"

"Now and then." He tucked his wrapped bottle into the back of his shorts before he picked up the club. He also handed her a length of tourniquet hose. "Once I have him pinned, bind his hands with this."

"All right." She looped the hose around her wrist and wove the ends in a loose knot. "But if he has a gun, we stay out of sight." When he started to argue she held up her hand. "You saw what he did on the bridge. He can take you out with one shot, and then I'll be alone with him."

"If that happens," he said flatly, "you'll have to kill him."

She had never imagined harming another person; it went against her calling to heal and everything she believed in. She had thought those beliefs had protected her, too, until that morning on the bridge. "Count on it."

They left the villa and went quickly down the walkway toward the water, stopping at the edge of the sand. Samuel led her behind a cluster of sea grape bushes and crouched down there with her, parting the branches to look down at the dock.

The boat, a large ocean cruiser, lay anchored several hundred yards away from the pier. A tall man stood at the helm, and another walked along the deck railing, a rifle parked on his shoulder. Neither of them was the gunman.

"He brought friends," she murmured. "Why are they just sitting out there?"

A metallic click answered her, and Charlie felt the rounded end of a gun pressed firmly against her nape.

"Don't move," a pleasant voice said in English. "Put your hands on top of your head."

Charlie glanced over at Samuel, who had a rifle pressed against his back, before she slowly lifted her hands into position.

"Very good. My name is Segundo, and I am in charge here. Mr. Taske, you may drop that chair leg. Very good." In Spanish, he said, "Take the bottles and the scissors."

Once they had been divested of their only weapons, Segundo told them to stand up. "Now, keep your hands on your head and walk down to the beach."

"This was my idea," Samuel said quickly. "Ms. Marena had nothing to do with it."

"So polite," Segundo said in a mocking tone. "Still, you're already protective of her, which is excellent. It is a pity that you didn't consider her welfare before we arrived, but I doubt it will happen again."

Without warning Samuel spun around and tried to snatch the rifle from the man behind him. A hard arm clamped around Charlie's neck as she was dragged back.

A third man shot Samuel in the chest with the prongs from a Taser.

"Sam." She fought wildly to free herself, until Segundo pressed a blade under her chin.

"Be very still now," he told her. "I don't want to slit your throat unless it's absolutely necessary."

Even while Samuel was being jolted by the shock device, he managed to wrench the rifle out of the guard's hands. A fourth man hurried up and shot him with another Taser, and the combined jolts sent Samuel to his knees. Although he was shaking helplessly now, the guards kept pumping more electricity into him.

"Please tell them to stop," Charlie begged. "We won't try anything else. I swear."

Segundo waited another moment before he called off the guards. Samuel wavered, almost falling over before they grabbed his arms and with difficulty dragged him along the path to the beach.

"Do you work for the man who brought us here?" Charlie asked.

"Tacal?" He chuckled. "No, dear girl. And you needn't worry about him; he's been dealt with and won't trouble you again."

"Then why are we here? What is this place?" When Segundo didn't answer, she added, "I don't know what you think you're doing, but you can't keep us. We're American citizens. We have rights."

"It always surprises me how Americans believe they are entitled to freedom," Segundo said as he forced her to follow them. His colorless voice took on a slight foreign accent. "Even when your lives depend on obedience and submission, you resist. You fight." He stopped halfway down the beach and gestured toward Samuel's sagging form. "And then you are shocked when you're made to suffer for it."

Finally Charlie placed his voice. "You're the man who made the recordings that have been playing over the speaker."

"You have an excellent ear, Ms. Marena. I hope your tolerance for pain is equally developed." To his men he said, *"Pare aquí."*

Samuel's head drooped as the guards forced him back down on his knees in the sand. One of them produced a bottle of water and poured the contents into Samuel's face, causing him to sputter and cough.

"He's had enough," Charlie said as Segundo maneuvered her to stand a foot in front of Samuel. "I'll take whatever punishment you had planned for him."

"Oh, we never punish the men, dear girl." Segundo beckoned to the largest of the guards. "We just make them watch."

"Watch what?"

"The consequences of your actions." He smiled. "You and Mr. Taske did put on a convincing performance last night, but you did not, in fact, have sexual intercourse. That is a violation of the rules, for which you will now be punished."

The big guard came over and grabbed her by the throat. Charlie lifted her leg, driving the side of her foot into the guard's knee at the same time she plowed her fist into his solar plexus, jerking her arm back quickly and hooking a third punch up to deliver a crunching blow to the nose. As he howled and clutched his face, she went for one of the guards holding a rifle, only to be tripped by Segundo.

"It seems you've taken some self-defense classes." He hauled her up from the sand and wrenched her arms behind her back, pinning them in the awkward position. "I'm afraid that will only make this worse for you."

Before she could get her weight balanced, a broad hand slapped her, the open palm cracking as it slammed into her cheek. Pain shot across her face, and she tasted blood.

"Charlotte." Samuel surged up, trying to get his feet under him.

"It's all right, Sam." She braced herself as she looked

at the guard she'd punched. In Spanish she said, "What's the matter, you coward? You afraid to fight a mere woman?"

"This isn't a fight, Ms. Marena." Segundo tightened his grip on her arms, pushing them up until Charlie thought the pressure would snap her bones. "This is simply an old-fashioned beating."

Samuel surged up, knocking the guards away from him as if they were rag dolls. "Touch her again and I'll put you in the ground."

Segundo took out a pistol and pointed it at Samuel. "You were both informed of the rules, Mr. Taske."

Samuel's eyes shifted as he measured the distance between them. "Do you believe you can kill me before I reach you?"

Charlie caught her breath. "Sam, no."

Sand shot up in a fountain as a bullet struck the ground beside Samuel's right foot. Charlie looked out and saw the man on the deck of the boat pointing a rifle at them.

"Perhaps I won't, but the marksman on our boat will." Segundo smiled. "Make no mistake, Mr. Taske. You are the expendable half of this equation. If you continue to interfere, we will remove you from it and give Ms. Marena to another partner."

Charlie met Sam's gaze. "Let them do what they want." When he started to speak, she shook her head. "I need you alive, *mío*. Don't leave me alone with them."

Samuel's big hands knotted into fists as he looked back at the boat and then at Segundo. "You'd better practice looking over your shoulder, because one day I will be there."

"No, old boy, I'm afraid you won't. The only way either of you will ever leave this island is in dismembered pieces in a biohazard shipping container." Segundo gave him an insulting smile before he nodded to the guard with the bloody nose.

Charlie had grown up in the barrio; she knew how to take a beating. She kept her chin tucked in and hunched her body over as much as her pinned arms would allow. The guard started in on her upper body with fast jabs of his fists, pummeling her shoulders, upper arms, and ribs. Knowing any cry she made might provoke Samuel into doing something foolish, Charlie bit down on her torn lip to keep anything but air from leaving her mouth.

Her eyes blurred as he suddenly switched to hitting her in the face, bruising her cheeks and drawing blood from her mouth and nose. After a dozen punches her vision blurred and her eyes began to swell shut. Still she refused to make a sound.

Some cold, clinical part of her kept a running inventory of the contusions and lacerations being inflicted on her, and gradually she realized something: The guard was deliberately avoiding hitting her breasts, her belly, or anyplace below her waist. He was also pulling his punches to keep from breaking bones or knocking out her teeth.

A guttural roaring sound swelled in her ears, punctuated by a dull thud and the sound of a body hitting the ground. Through the watery slits of her eyes she saw Samuel facedown in the sand, and that was the blow she couldn't take. The cry that burst from her lips rang out as she collapsed.

Sand, blood, tears, pain; that was her new world until she heard Sam's voice calling her name.

A shadow fell across her as Segundo bent down and turned her face toward him. "The next time you or your man break the rules, Ms. Marena, I will allow three guards to spend ten minutes with you to do whatever they like. I'm afraid they like many unpleasant, painful things. Mr. Taske will also be tied up and made to watch every moment of it. Please nod if you understand."

Charlie moved her head up and down.

"Very good." He released her and straightened.

"Charlotte." Samuel crawled up beside her, blood streaking his face. He wrapped his arms around her and drew her into him as he looked up. "She needs a doctor."

"Not this time."

"For God's sake, man—"

"There is no doctor here." Segundo slid his pistol into his waistband. "I suggest you take Ms. Marena up to the house and see to her wounds. The rules are still in effect, as they will be for the duration of your life on the island. You will not attempt to escape, and you have until dawn tomorrow to have sexual intercourse." He snapped his fingers, and the guards followed him up the beach.

Charlie pressed her hot, throbbing face against the coolness of Samuel's chest, and a string of wretched, horrible laughs came out of her. "Have sex. Like this." The laughter became sobs.

"Charlotte." He held her with one arm as she wept, and gently wiped the blood and tears from her face. "I have to get you up to the house."

"Wait." She forced her eyes open. "Where did they shoot you?"

"No one shot me. One of them clouted me with the end of his rifle." He reached up to touch his temple. "It's just a cut."

"Good. I'm in no shape to dig a slug out of your head." She struggled into a sitting position, moaning a little as her ribs and shoulders protested the movements. "I think I can walk. With some help, maybe."

Samuel carefully lifted her, holding her by the waist until she straightened, and then swept her up into his arms.

"You're hurt," she reminded him.

"It's not even bleeding now." He walked slowly across the sand with her, but when he reached the walkway he picked up the pace. "How well do you heal?"

"Takyn fast." She grimaced as she touched her lip. "By tomorrow I'll just have some bruises and scabs.

Sam, those men didn't bring us here to ransom us, or to chop us up and sell our parts to GenHance. But you already know that."

"I considered the possibilities." He looked down at her. "There's only one explanation that makes sense of this place, the rules, and some of things Segundo said."

"We're not hostages, and this isn't a prison." As much as she hurt, part of her had gone numb, just as it had that day long ago when she had crawled out of San Francisco Bay. "It's a menagerie."

Chapter 9

The sound of the tide mingled with birdsong as the sun rose over the bay and illuminated the row of cottages hemming the edge of the beach road. Drew Riordan's voice took on a slight rasp as he finished explaining to Agent Flores exactly why he'd impersonated a federal agent and come to Mexico to find Samuel Taske and Charlotte Marena.

Drew did hold back some details, like the exact nature of Takyn abilities, but to justify his actions he had to tell her about GenHance and why the biotech corporation was hunting them. Now that Genaro was in Mexico and had to know Drew was here, he needed Gracie's help more than ever.

As for what Gracie thought, he couldn't tell. She sat very still, wearing the perfect poker face as she listened to every word.

Once he had finished, he noticed that Gracie had turned to watch the sunrise through the back windows of the cottage. For the first time in hours Drew became aware of his surroundings. Gracie's front room, airy and spotless, all snow-white and dark blue. Everywhere he looked there was some reminder of the sea, from the watercolors of boats she had hung in long parallel rows along the walls to the sun-bleached fishing nets she had wound around her curtain rods. A curio cabinet displayed a collection of polished abalone shells: all perfect specimens. Misty hunks of sea glass occupied a beautiful bowl carved out of driftwood next to an old brass ship's compass, its needle still dutifully pointing north.

"You live here so you can be close to the water," he said as he sifted his fingers through the bits of wave-polished glass. "I wouldn't have guessed that about you."

"My *papi*—my father—is a fisherman. I grew up by the sea." She sounded wistful.

"You miss your home?"

"Of course. Sometimes I wish I could live there again. Life in the village is . . . not so complicated." Her mouth tightened. "But I can never go back."

"Are you on bad terms with your folks or something?"

"*Papi* understands what I do, and why. He only wished different for me." She forced a smile. "Do your parents know about how special you are?"

He nodded. "They found out when I was a kid."

Telling Gracie that he was the result of an illicit genetic experiment performed on him as an infant didn't bother Drew. Being made Takyn hadn't been his choice, and feeling shame over the gifts it had bestowed on him would be the same as regretting winning the lottery. But for a moment he wished he could be an ordinary guy who didn't bring along the kind of baggage that would scare the hell out of any woman.

"How did they treat you after they discovered what you were?" she asked.

"They were worried, and probably a little terrified, but they definitely wanted to protect me. I guess if anything, it brought us closer together." He thought of the last conversation he'd had with his mother, just before leaving Monterey. "I don't get home too often, but maybe after this is over I'll have a chance."

"If you are not caught, or arrested," she pointed out. "Or, if this Genaro is as vicious as you say, killed."

"Everything I've told you is real, Gracie." He leaned forward, holding her gaze. "It's happening right now. I'd love to walk away, especially now that I've seen Genaro here, but I can't. If I don't find Samuel before they do, my friend will end up on a dissection table. I can't allow that."

She gave him an odd look. "Even if it means sacrificing your own life for his?"

"If I do this right, nobody dies." He grinned. "Unless you still want me dead."

"Dead, you would be of no use to anyone." Abruptly she stood. "We have much to do. I will make us some breakfast."

"Is your amazing hot chocolate included?" he asked as he followed her into the tiny kitchen.

"If you like." She handed him a pan and a container of milk. "I will show you how to make it."

They worked side by side at her tiny stove, and while Drew stirred the hot chocolate to keep it from scalding he watched her set out eggs, black beans, chopped ham, and a small block of cheese. "Is that going to be an omelet?"

"Something better." She broke four eggs into a skillet, frying them before removing them to a plate and taking a jug from the fridge. She poured yellow batter from the jug into the pan, forming a large circle, which she flipped over until it was golden brown. She scooped two of the eggs to top the pancake, and then deftly added the rest of the ingredients.

"I didn't know you could make a pancake into a burrito," he told her as he hunted through her cabinets for two cups.

"This is not a pancake or burrito." She transferred the contents of the pan to a plate before she started on a second serving. "I'm making *huevos motuleños*."

"Does that mean 'Mexican Eggs Benedict'?"

She gave him a dry look. "It means eggs Motul-style."

As Gracie finished cooking, Drew set the little kitchen table and filled their cups with the hot chocolate. She brought the plates over and sat down beside him.

Drew breathed in the tantalizing aroma rising from the plate. "Oh, God. I'm never going to be able to eat Taco Bell again, am I?"

"Probably not," she advised him.

From the first bite of the spicy, eggy concoction, Drew fell in love, and wolfed down his portion at starving-man speed.

"We should go to my village," Gracie said unexpectedly. "It's not far from the city, and my father has a good boat. There is an English scientist who lives on a small island near the zone. He was given permission to put cameras in the protected areas to record the island birds that he studies. If your friends are hiding there, he may have seen them land."

"I'd like to talk to him," he said, "but what about your job here?"

"I am due some leave time." She didn't seem concerned.

When he noticed Gracie only picking at her meal he put down his fork. "What's wrong? Don't tell me you're dieting."

"I'm not very hungry. I should change and pack some things for the journey. Here." She pushed her plate toward him and got up to walk out of the kitchen.

"Gracie." As she stopped, Drew saw how she kept her back toward him, and the rigid set of her shoulders. As much as he needed her, he had disrupted her life and put her in an impossible situation. He had to give her an out. "If you're having second thoughts, it's okay. I'll take off on my own."

"You said this Jonah Genaro, he will do anything to catch you and kill you," she said. "My duty is to preserve life."

Drew frowned. "Gracie, you don't have to do anything. I'm not your responsibility."

She glanced back at him, her expression unreadable. "You are now, Andrew."

* * *

Knowing Charlotte would not suffer through days of pain as an ordinary human would provided little consolation for Samuel. By the time he carried her up to the treatment room, her bruises had appeared, and many of the dark, angry splotches shaped themselves into blurry copies of the guard's fingers, palms, and knuckles. Both of her eyes had been blackened, and her eyelids had swelled together, effectively blinding her.

He didn't waste time fumbling about with the medical supplies. Once he set her down gently on the table, he said, "Tell me what to do."

"You can start by getting out the scissors I have in the side pocket of my bag and cutting off this shirt." She held out her arms. "Start at the shoulder seams, then go straight down the middle."

Samuel found the scissors and carefully snipped through the fabric as she had instructed. It fell away from her in pieces, revealing so much bruising on both sides of her abdomen Samuel caught his breath.

"I know how bad it looks," she said, wincing as she felt along both sides. "Nothing's broken, though. Are there any tears in my skin or bulges under it?"

He circled around her. "None."

"Good." She extended her arms, turning her wrists and then flexing her elbows. "He got me a few times with his fingernails. Do you see the scratches?"

He was already counting them. "Yes."

"Get some gauze pads and the big brown bottle on the second shelf in the corner cabinet." When he brought them over, she felt the shape of the bottle and nodded. "Wet the pads with this and use them to scrub out the scratches."

He wanted to throw the bottle across the room, and had to force back his anger as he opened it. "How do you do this every day?"

"This? This is nothing, *mío*. Imagine finding a fifteen-year-old girl sitting in a puddle of her own blood after her boyfriend slices her open. While you're working on her, you have to listen to her beg you not to call the police. Her intestines are spilling into her lap, and forget the ER; you know she's going to bleed out before you can get her into the rig. You listen to her cry, not for herself, but for him. Because, of course, he loves her, and he didn't mean to do it." Her head drooped. "After your shift is over, you go to the gym and punch a bag until you can't feel your hands anymore. Or you find a bar and get drunk, or you pick up a stranger. Or you go to church and get on your knees and pray to the Holy Mother to give you the strength to go back to work the next day."

He tucked some loose hair back behind her ear. "Somehow I can't see you going to a bar or a gym."

"I like church." She sounded defensive. "It's quiet. Peaceful. People don't go there to hurt each other."

"That's probably why they call it a sanctuary, honey." He kissed her forehead. "Now let me finish these scratches."

Once he cleaned the last of the scrapes on her arms, Charlotte was able to open her eyes enough to view his handiwork. "Very good. That leaves my face, which must look like a Halloween mask." Gingerly she began palpating her chin, cheeks, and eyelids. "Feels like two black eyes, a swollen nose, a fat lip, and ear-to-ear bruises."

"That sums it up." He pulled her hand away from her face. "You're sure nothing is broken?"

She opened her mouth and closed it, and then felt the sides of her face. "He came close with that last punch, but no, everything still works. You just need to wash off the blood and make up a cold compress for my eyes and nose."

There was still sand mixed with the blood in her hair, he realized, from when she had fallen on the beach. "I have an idea." He picked her up in his arms. "Let's take a bath first."

"You just want to see the rest of me naked," she chided.

"Consider it fair play. After all, you've seen me in all

my glory, such as it is." He walked down the hall to the master suite and took her into the adjoining bathroom. Once he set her on her feet, he turned on the shower and adjusted the temperature to lukewarm before removing her shorts and stripping out of his own clothes.

After he guided her into the stall, which was just big enough for both of them, he turned her back toward the spray. "I'll wash out your hair first, and then your face."

Samuel shifted to one side to draw her hair back, and saw how rigidly she was holding herself. "Is the water too cold?" He glanced down at the dark pink–tinted streams emptying into the drain. "Or too warm?"

"It isn't the water." She reached out and groped for his chest, bracing her hand against it. "How did they know what we planned to do?"

He had hoped to hold off this conversation until Charlotte had rested and healed a little more. "We'll talk about it later."

"They knew everything. They found us as if they already knew exactly where we would be," she countered. "They even knew in which pocket I had put the scissors. Sam, the cameras aren't the only things watching us."

He had his own suspicions, but he didn't want to alarm her. "Perhaps it was the man by the deck."

"What if he's like us? Like me?" She tapped her temple. "That's the only way they could know what we didn't do in the hot tub."

He heard the fear and anger in her voice. "You don't have to be concerned about this now."

"Don't I?" She turned her face into the spray, rinsing off the blood to reveal her battered features. "Take a good look at me, Sam. Just one of them did this. Tomorrow it will be three. Do you know how much damage can be done to the human body in thirty minutes? I do."

"Sweetheart, listen to me." He put his hands on her waist. "We're not spending the rest of our lives on this island. We are going to escape, and we are going home.

But for now, the simplest solution— the safest one—is to take the path of least resistance."

Her shoulders slumped. "You mean we follow the rules."

"For now, Charlotte."

She pressed her forehead against his shoulder. "It's funny, isn't it? How hard this is."

"It's been some time since I've had the pleasure," he admitted, "but it's not something one forgets how to do."

"You're handsome, and any woman would want you, but that isn't making it easier for me." She looked down at the tiles. "I feel like doing this will break my heart."

"We're not zoo animals." He bent down and touched his mouth to the corner of hers. "We're not just going to have sex, Charlotte. We're going to be lovers, and that is no small thing for either of us."

"I know." She sounded bitter. "Men like you don't take women like me as lovers."

"Men like me . . ." He trailed off as the bruise beside her mouth lightened from reddish purple to a yellowish brown and then faded away altogether. "My God."

"What is it?"

"One of the bruises on your face just disappeared." He brought her fingers up to the spot. "Right here, where I kissed you. Just how quickly do you heal?"

She tested the skin. "Not this fast. Do it again." When he put his mouth to the same spot, she turned her face so that his lips trailed across her swollen cheek. "Tell me what you see."

Samuel watched the swelling sink down and the bruising fade everywhere his mouth had touched. This time he felt the surge in his blood: a kind of effervescent thrill that bewildered him. "You're healing in seconds. How are you doing that?"

"It's not me." Her hand moved across the surface of her cheek. "It's coming from you. You kissed me and made it better. How?"

"I don't know." He touched her face again. "I've never been able to do anything like this."

"You said your ability was fading. Maybe something else is happening to it." She lifted her face. "Try again."

He pressed his lips to one swollen eye and then the other, drawing back to watch as the purplish skin around them cleared and her eyelids returned to normal size. As her eyelashes parted and she gave him an astonished look, he saw splotches of blood that had hemorrhaged beneath her corneas seep away and vanish.

"Are you feeling any pain when I do that?" He still couldn't accept what he was seeing with his own eyes.

"It doesn't hurt. It feels only . . . warm." Her gaze shifted as she looked up. "Sam, the cut on your head is gone."

"Come here." He seized her hand and almost dragged her out into the bedroom, where he brought her to the bed. "Lie down on your back." When she did he knelt beside her, and felt her immediately tense. "I'm not trying to rush you into sex. There may be limits to this new ability, and I want to heal you everywhere you're hurt while I'm still able to use it. All right?"

"I trust you, *mío*," she said. "Just stop if you feel strange or weak."

Samuel brought her bruised knuckles to his lips, kissing each one before turning her hands over and brushing his mouth over the cuts her fingernails had made in her palms. Her hands went from battered to unmarked in less than a minute.

The first scratch he kissed, a thin but ugly gouge across the inside of her wrist, seemed to pull in on itself and submerge into her flesh. Hairline pink scars took their place, flattening and turning white before they, too, slowly erased themselves.

Charlotte held still as he worked his way up one arm and across her shoulder, but when he reached the bruises on her throat, she took a sharp breath.

Instantly he lifted his head. "Did that hurt you?"

"It doesn't hurt." She caught her bottom lip between her teeth for a moment. "Keep going."

He didn't touch her. "You are feeling something that you're not telling me." He glanced down and saw the tight pucker of her nipples, surrounded by a distinctive flush. "Charlotte."

"It's not just warm." She crossed her arms over her bare breasts. "What you're doing is making me hot. Understand?"

He bent down and kissed her bottom lip. "Should I stop?"

"If you do, *mío*," she said, her voice wry, "then I will be rushing *you* into sex."

He turned his head to put his tongue to her palm, and felt a dark satisfaction when she shivered. "Hold that thought for a little longer, honey."

Samuel turned her head to one side to have a better look at the uneven ring of contusions left by the guard's brutal hand. As he stroked his fingertips over them, they seemed to come apart, ugly beads falling from a broken necklace. He deliberately cupped her throat with his hand, and when he lifted his palm the bruises were gone.

"It seems I don't have to kiss you to make it better." He studied his hand. "Touching works just as well."

Charlotte looked up at him. "Can you do both?"

Her question made him go still. "That might not be wise."

Charlie knew healing wasn't supposed to be an erotic experience. She'd monitored enough patients to know that at best it was a tedious, pain-racked process. While she didn't understand how Sam had acquired an ability that bypassed all that, or why, she wanted more. In fact, she wanted everything she could get, and since they'd agreed to become lovers, he should have been happy to give it to her.

Unless he's been lying.

He'd told her that he found her attractive, and yet

now, when she asked for more, it had turned him off. Since they were both naked on a bed with nothing between them but a towel, it had to be something he was feeling, something she wouldn't be able to know for sure until after sunset.

Samuel was an educated, courteous man with exquisite manners. However he felt, he'd never insult her. And what had he called it, having sex with her?

The path of least resistance.

"It's not what you want. That's all you have to say." Charlotte sat up and reached for the sheet to cover herself. "We'll take a break now, and later—"

He yanked the sheet away from her, and was on top of her so fast she didn't have time to inhale.

"No breaks, Charlotte," he said in a low, rough tone she'd never before heard him use. "We have to finish this right now." He lowered his voice and his head, murmuring the rest against her ear. "Because the moment you're better, my beautiful darling, the very second you'll have me, I'm going to put myself inside you, and make love to you, and not stop until we're both too tired to move. *That* is what I want."

Oh, she liked him this way: so hungry for her that he forgot his pretty manners. He was gripping her wrists, so she nudged him with her shoulder until he lifted his head. She saw the frustration in his eyes, and recalled something he'd mentioned earlier. "How long has it been for you?"

"Years."

She smiled. "Then you should get a move on, *mío*."

His hand held her face as he covered her mouth with his, taking away the soreness and rawness as he healed the split in her bottom lip. From there he followed the curve of her lip and then the line of her jaw, soothing away the soreness and creating a deeper, more immediate ache.

There was so much of him to touch and explore that

Charlie couldn't wait for him to finish. As soon as he let go of her wrists she had her hands in his hair. It looked baby-soft but felt thick and heavy, a snare for her fingers. Each strand caught the light and held it captive, glittering like something spun by an enchanted fairy-tale creature.

He rubbed his head against her hand, a low sound rumbling from his chest as she worked her fingertips against his scalp. "That feels good."

"So do you." Charlie admired his eyes. The amber lashes framing them didn't curl, but spiked down over the darkness of his irises. This close she could see tiny starbursts around his pupils, so pale a silver they could be easily mistaken for reflected lights. "Finished yet?"

"Almost." He bent his head to her shoulder, first kissing away the pain and then following the curve up to her neck with the velvet stroke of his tongue.

Charlie worked her hands down his broad back, finding the edge of the towel he'd tucked around his hips and loosening it until she could tug it away. The last barrier gone, she pulled him over on top of her, arching up into him, wanting to feel him everywhere, from the wide vault of his chest rubbing against her aching breasts to the sculpted columns of his legs gliding against the tense muscles all along her thighs and calves.

"Charlotte." He pushed his fingers under her, lifting her bottom as he settled himself between her thighs. His hands were shaking now, and as soon as the rigid shaft of his penis touched her, he felt the liquid heat of her arousal and groaned. "I was going to try to take this slow."

"It's been years, right?" Was she breathless, digging her nails into his shoulders, and twisting under him like a shameless, greedy thing? It seemed she was. "Try slow next week."

Samuel lifted her again, reaching down between their bodies to position himself before tightening his buttocks. As she felt the delicious press of his cock head parting her folds, she braced her heels and moved with him, welcoming that first slow breach and the steady penetration that followed. He filled her until the stretching ache made her gasp, and then held himself inside her, his jaw tight and his breath warm on her lips.

He was asking her something, and she was so absorbed by the way they had melded together that she'd gone deaf. She looped an arm around his strong neck, bringing his mouth across that last inch separating their faces and nipping his bottom lip.

"Next week," he muttered, gathering her up as he answered her gentle bite with a hungry, soul-wrenching kiss.

Samuel's hips recoiled, and she clenched against the drag of his steady withdrawal, aching to hold on and savor the thrill of being completed by his flesh in hers. Last night she'd climaxed rubbing against him and only imagining how it would feel; now she knew and it was so much more, the incredible heat and power of him rolling through her as he stroked back in. And how amazing it felt, the taking and giving, the softness of her sex swelling around him as he worked his shaft deeper, the muscles of his back knotting and growing slick with sweat under her hands.

Charlie had her hands in his hair again when he took his lips from hers, and bowed her back, offering her breast. As he sucked at her he pushed in hard and fast, startling a cry from her; he added to the torment by cupping the flushed globe and kneading it in time to the tugging pull of his mouth. She bucked beneath him, shocked soundless by the sudden explosion of her orgasm, and then he was taking her like a wild man, driving into her as she shuddered and refusing to let her come down, his fingers gliding down over her belly to work her clit as he brought her over again.

The room spun and time blurred as she came a third time, his name spilling from her lips as she shuddered under him, and Samuel's big frame shook, but instead of coming he tried to draw out of her completely.

Instinctively Charlie knew what he meant to do. "No." She clamped her legs around him, pushing herself against him. "I need all of you."

That sent Samuel into a frenzy, and he clamped his hands on her buttocks, jerking her up and holding her there as he gave her the last hard, uneven strokes before he went deep and stilled. She felt his semen pulsing and spreading inside her body, warm and thick, and curled her arms around his shoulders to hold him as he buried his face in her hair.

They lay like that until Samuel murmured something and rolled onto his side, still keeping her pressed against him. Sweat streaked the sides of his face, and as she smoothed back his hair he trailed a line of kisses over her brow.

"I know why you grow your hair long." She made rings of it around her fingers. "Cutting it makes your barber feel like a butcher."

"Findley trims it for me every morning," he told her as he rolled onto his side to run his hand down her arm. "It grows very fast, sometimes as much as twelve inches in a day. So does my beard." He frowned as he touched his jaw, over which dark gold stubble was just beginning to show. "At least, it did before we were brought here."

"The beard was interesting, *mío*, but I like you better without it." A strange tenderness welled inside her as she rested a hand on his hip. "So what do you think of all this?"

He propped himself up on one elbow. "Trying slow actually may have to wait until next month. Possibly Christmas. And you?"

"I need to sleep with more cripples." She laughed as he scowled and tickled her. "All right, ex-cripples."

Samuel bent his head to hers, and Charlie's gaze wandered, coming to an abrupt stop at the glint of a lens.

Like all the others in the room, it was aimed directly at the bed.

They'd forgotten about the cameras.

As she closed her eyes to enjoy Samuel's kiss, Charlie lifted her hand from the back of his neck and extended her middle finger.

Chapter 10

In the kitchen of her home, Tlemi set out what she would prepare for their midday meal: mangoes, smoked fish, and some of the herbed flatbread Xochi had learned how to bake. After watching the Americans she had no appetite, but if she didn't feed Colotl, he would forget to eat, as he did so often now.

This place was making them all sick, not in body, but in spirit.

Living on the island had once made Tlemi feel as if she had come to paradise. Before they had been brought here, all they had ever known had been the darkness of the master's domain. Tlemi's oldest memories were of long, moonlit nights playing with Colotl and the other children in the gardens while the *abuelas* had tended the flowers or gathered fruit under the braziers. When the roosters crowed they were brought inside and sent to sleep in the cool, dark rooms in the lower levels.

As she began slicing the mango, Tlemi remembered the delighted laughter that had spilled from her lips when she and Colotl had risen from their bed to watch their first sunrise on the island.

In those early days after the master had sent them to live apart from him, they had been like little children again, running and playing and laughing with delight over each new discovery. It frightened some of the other women, but Tlemi felt she had been given all the gifts she could ever want: a beautiful home, good friends, and being Colotl's woman. Even the price she had to pay for their new home had not weighed on her, not at first.

That had been a precious time, one that had ended brutally when the master had sent Segundo to them to explain their duties, and Mocaya had been found out.

The steward had come with his brutes and a man they had never seen before, a doctor from America. As soon as it was Mocaya's turn to go to the seventh house and be examined, she had tried to flee. The men had run her down like a dog and dragged her back, and then the doctor sedated her, making her unable to keep her body changed as it was. That was when the secret she had been hiding had been revealed: she had been born with the body not of a woman, but of a man.

What Tlemi remembered most about that terrible day was how Segundo had smiled, just before he shot Mocaya in the head. He offered the same smile a week later when he brought Pici to Ihiyo.

Pici had cringed as Ihiyo exploded with rage, and then Segundo had pistol-whipped him into silence. As Ihiyo bled on the sands, the master's steward had leaned over him and advised him to close his eyes while he did his duty.

Fortunately Pici was a petite, helpless girl who cried easily, and had appealed to something in Ihiyo. Or perhaps Ihiyo wanted to live more than he wanted to be with another man. Tlemi knew he didn't close his eyes when he was with Pici, but every night, after she fell asleep, he wept for Mocaya.

Like many things she knew about their friends, Tlemi had never revealed it to them. Not even to Colotl, who had been Ihiyo's friend since they were boys. He would have understood, but he already blamed himself for not knowing Ihiyo and Mocaya's secret. It was why he had been so stubborn about the Americans.

"Tlemi?"

She looked over to see Colotl watching her from the doorway.

His long moonlight hair and silver eyes always seemed to glow against his brown skin, which was as dark as hers was pale. He had taken off his shirt and hung it around his neck, and from the sand still clinging to his ankles she knew he had been walking along his lines, not to check them but to think.

"You are back early." Then, because she knew exactly why he had come to speak to her, she added, "He has seen to her."

Some of the tension around his mouth eased. "Did she fight him?"

She shook her head, picking up the knife to finish slicing the mango. Knowing their lives depended on it, she had agreed to watch the Americans, but what she had witnessed troubled her. They were all well aware of why the master had sent them here, and if he discovered what the big man could do . . .

"Can you bring that down to the beach?" Colotl asked. "I need to check my lines."

She nodded. Once he left, she took out a basket, placing the fruit and smoked fish in smaller containers before adding them and two of the colorful napkins Delores had embroidered.

Colotl met her on the pathway outside, taking the basket from her and lifting the lid. His eyes narrowed as soon as he saw the red napkins covered with intricate designs in black thread. "It looks very good. I'm hungry."

"I think it will please you." She patted his shoulder twice before walking with him to the sand. Along the way she felt the air around them go completely still, although the trees overhead still swayed gently in the breeze.

A small crab scuttled toward her toes, his front claws snapping, only to encounter something that knocked him onto his back.

"What is it?" Colotl asked as soon as the barrier was in place.

"The American man." She shook out the big coverlet and placed it on the sand. "He has changed."

"Changed?"

"Not like Mocaya," she said quickly. "His gift has changed. He healed the woman's injuries."

Colotl stopped by one of the poles he had driven into the sand and knelt down, making a pretense of testing the fishing line knotted to it. Without looking at her, he muttered, "Did he use his blood?"

"No, he used kisses and touching. It is the gift, not the master's curse. He lives. He walks in the sunlight. He will not turn." Tlemi felt impatient. "You have to call the others together and tell them what he is."

His expression turned impassive. "Why would I do this?"

"Colotl, please." She dropped down beside him. "With the gifts he has been given, the American could help us."

He made a bitter sound. "Why would he do that?"

"He is still like us." When he gave her a narrow look, she sighed. "If the master had brought him into his domain, he would be our brother. What does it matter now, anyway? Here we are no different."

"No different? We don't even speak the same language." He stood and began reeling in the line. As it emerged from the surf, fish caught on the hooks knotted to it began flopping.

Tlemi knew exactly how they felt.

"Pici's time is coming. Soon," she reminded him. "She is too small and weak. You know what will happen if she dies. They will just bring another woman, and this time I think Ihiyo will go mad. *Colotl.*" His silence made her sit down on the sand and stare at the water. "Very well. Who will dig the grave for her? You, or me?"

"What would you have me do?" he demanded, taking

her by the shoulders and dragging her to her feet. "Kill you to save them? I don't *know* them. You are the other half of my soul. I can't live without you. I won't."

"How much time do you think we have left together?" She picked up a piece of seaweed and idly wound it around her wrist. "One season? Two?"

"What are you talking about?"

She eyed him. "The master will not wait forever."

He said nothing at first, and then his mouth flattened. "If it comes to that, we will give him what he wants."

Tlemi had been taught to be obedient. She loved Colotl, and she deferred to his judgment in all things. Except this. "No. Never."

"Do you think it is easy for me to say?" he demanded. "To even think? But if I have to choose—"

"Then Segundo will have to bring you another woman," she promised him, "because on that day I will go into the water, and I will swim out to where it is dark, and I will not come back."

"Tlemi." His voice broke on her name. "I cannot lose you."

"I will never do it," she said simply. "Not for him, and not for you. But you know your duty, Colotl. Tie me up. Lock me away. I still have fingernails, and teeth. My veins are not so deep."

He lifted his hand as if to strike her, but Tlemi didn't flinch. In all their years together, Colotl had never once touched her in anger.

His hand moved slower than it should have, not to slap her face but to caress her cheek. "If you go into the dark water, so do I."

All of the fight poured out of her as sobs tore at her throat. "Colotl. Please. This could be our only chance to live. To be *free.*"

He hauled her into his arms and held her as she wept. When Tlemi had no more tears, he used his shirt to dry her face.

"We cannot do this without the others," he said slowly. "I will speak to them about the American tomorrow. If they refuse—"

Tlemi thought of Pici's desperate eyes. "They will not."

As Samuel brought the tray into the master suite, Charlotte rolled onto her side and looked at him. Although she smiled, her eyes were once more guarded and watchful.

"I was wondering where you were." She glanced at the fruit salads he'd prepared. "Dinner in bed?"

"On the patio, I think," he said, scooping up her robe and handing it to her.

She muffled a yawn with the backs of her fingers. "You want to watch the sunset?"

"Not especially." He waited for her to rise before walking outside with her. "But if you stayed in bed, we probably wouldn't be dining until well after midnight."

"Or dawn." She sat on the edge of one lounge and tightened the robe's belt around her waist. "Are you a vegetarian?"

He sat across from her. "No."

"That makes two of us." She accepted the plate he offered and picked up a slice of mango. "You did notice that there's no protein in our convenient little pantry."

"That's why I'm planning to do a little fishing in the morning." He set his plate aside to watch her eat, which she did with delicate greed. She also kept her gaze averted from his face, which made him wonder what was going on in her head. "Are you having any second thoughts?"

"Why would I?" She bit into a strawberry and licked the red juice from her lips. "We're consenting adults, we agreed on this together, and having sex with you will save me a lot of pain and suffering. It's all good."

He wondered whether she would feel the same in nine months. "Whatever happens here, Charlotte, I want you to know that when we return to the States, I'll look after you."

"That's decent of you, *mío*, but I take care of myself." She stood. "We should look around outside for the source of the electricity. They may have some tools or other things stored in a utility building that we can use." She went back inside.

To give her some time for herself, Samuel ate and watched the sunset. He didn't want to think about the possibility of pregnancy, much less discuss it out loud, but he couldn't keep the speculation out of his head. They would be having sex at least once a day, and he had yet to find any form of protection they could use. If Charlotte had been on the pill for birth control, she no longer had access to it. That meant they could conceive a child together in as little time as a few weeks.

"No." Charlotte emerged, dressed in two sarongs she had folded and fashioned into an impromptu halter dress.

"I beg your pardon?"

"I know what's on your mind." Her smile was a masterpiece of irony as she took his hand in hers. "Don't worry." As she spoke, she used one fingertip to trace three letters on his palm: I, U, and D. "We're safe now."

The relief he'd expected didn't come over him; instead he felt a moment of stunning disappointment before he cleared his thoughts. "But you don't want this, do you?"

"I'm fine with you and the sex for the duration." She gestured around them. "I don't want to be here. I'm useless here."

He realized she was referring to their isolation. "Is it so different from being back in the States?" When her expression became incredulous, he added, "You told me once in chat that you hardly ever use your ability, although you never mentioned why."

"Aside from it being a complete violation of someone else's privacy," she countered, "it's too painful."

"Using your ability hurts them?"

She gave him a bitter smile. "Oh, they don't even know I'm in their heads, *mío*. It does a number on me. When I listen in, I not only hear everything someone thinks, but I feel what they feel. If they're pissed off and I'm tapped in, I'm flooded with their rage. If they're really upset, I start crying. If they're in pain, I suffer, too."

"There's always a price, isn't there?" he murmured. "It must be terribly unpleasant for you."

"Unpleasant?" Her cheeks darkened and her eyes flashed. "Do you know how many times ordinary people think about things like punching out their spouse, stabbing their boss in the chest, or ramming their car into the back of someone who cuts them off? Or how it feels to have the same urges pouring into you?" Before he could answer her, she waved a hand at him. "Of course you don't. People like you never have to deal with the real world."

"Wait." He understood her anger, but not her contempt. "What do you mean, 'people like you'?"

"People with limos and chauffeurs and no-limit credit cards," she said. "People who don't have to work, or worry about the bills, or live paycheck to paycheck. I figured you were pretty comfortable from some of the things you told me online, but you've got a lot more than that, don't you? How much are you worth, Sam? Do you even know?"

"At the moment I might as well be penniless," he countered, "and you'd be surprised to know what I've dealt with, Charlotte."

"You're not making me feel guilty," she snapped. "Not after the way you've been stringing me along all this time."

"Stringing you along?" Now he was completely lost.

"Didn't you think it was hilarious when I told you how you could save money by making your own tortillas?" Her upper lip curled. "What do you really do when you're hungry? Ring a bell? Have some maid bring you a gourmet meal on a silver tray with cloth napkins and a rose in a crystal vase? Before we were dumped here, you probably never stepped one foot in a kitchen."

"I do have someone who cooks for me," he informed her gravely. "Lately he's also had to bring my meals to me on a tray, but not because I choose to eat in bed. Until this morning, I've been so weak that when I wake I can't sit up without a shot of morphine and two men to help me."

"That's right; you're a cripple." She looked him over. "For some reason I keep forgetting that."

"I find it difficult to grasp as well," he told her. "But you saw me on the bridge. Did I look as if I could run the hundred in five flat?"

"No, but you were bleeding from an open wound. Something *else* you forgot to mention." She rubbed her temples as if her head ached. "Besides, whatever pain you were in was nothing compared to your driver's. That guy was in agony, but even then all he could think of was protecting some woman."

"You read James's mind?"

"I picked up his thoughts when we got to the scene," she said. "It was so bad I nearly passed out."

A shrewd look came into his eyes. "You can read someone's mind even when they're unconscious?"

"I don't do dreams or the subconscious," she said. "For me to read anyone, they have to be awake and alert."

"I see." His mouth hitched. "James was shot before you arrived. I'm afraid he never regained consciousness."

It took her a moment to put it together. "That was you?"

He inclined his head. "When the sniper opened fire on us, I had to drag James out of the car. At the time I was in no condition to do so."

She drew back, visibly appalled. "That didn't come

from your wound. What made you feel that kind of pain?"

"It doesn't—"

"Damn it, Sam, *tell* me."

"My back," he said reluctantly. "One side effect of my ability has been causing damage to my spine."

"But that should have healed."

All of the Takyn had accelerated immune systems that allowed them to recover from injury many times faster than ordinary human beings—all but Samuel.

"When I was younger, it did," he agreed. "I can't tell you why, but as I've aged my ability to heal like you and the others has been compromised. For some time now my health and mobility have been steadily declining. Last summer my doctors told me that the damage had begun to accelerate."

Her voice went low and husky. "How long did they give you to live?"

"Twelve months."

New anger flared in her eyes. "What the hell were you doing on that bridge? If you were in that much pain, you should have been in a hospital."

She wasn't ready to hear about the gift of his foresight, not yet. "I received information from an anonymous source that one of the Takyn named Charlie would be killed on the bridge that morning. I couldn't allow that to happen." When she started to speak he shook his head. "It was supposed to be my final act of courage." He thought of Lilah, and the utter stupidity with which he had behaved toward her, for which he could never atone. "Or perhaps one last attempt at redemption."

She looked sick. "Why didn't you ever tell me your condition was that bad?"

"There was nothing you could have done. I've investigated and tried every possible treatment; even one I should never have considered," he admitted. "Nothing slowed the deterioration."

"Then who healed you? And don't tell me you did it

yourself," she added. "When I woke up last night you'd almost bled out. I nearly lost you."

"I don't know who to thank—or blame—for that."

"Maybe I can run some blood tests later." She glanced through the window and quickly released his hand. "We should go before we lose the last of the light."

Samuel helped her collect the plates, carrying them downstairs to the kitchen. After he put them in the disposal bin under the sink, the lid closed with a snap and he heard the sound of suction. When the sound stopped, he lifted the lid and saw that the bin had been emptied.

"It seems we won't have to argue over who takes out the trash." He inspected the interior of the bin before he looked through the window over the sink, but saw nothing outside. The previous day he'd also noticed no cables or wires leading to the house. "They must have buried everything under the soil when they were building the house."

"It would protect against storm damage." She removed two candles from a drawer and turned on the stove, lighting the wicks in the gas flame. She sniffed, and then bent over and blew out the flame but left the dial on. "I have a gas stove at home. It doesn't smell like this."

Samuel went over and breathed in. "This isn't commercial-grade methane." He switched off the dial and looked again at the bin, this time crouching and thrusting his hand inside before he found the lid latch and pushed it down. Powerful suction yanked at his arm before he released the latch to shut it off. "The land surrounding the house elevates in the back, doesn't it?"

"From what I could see. There's a lot of landscaping back there." She peered up at him. "What are you thinking?"

"I've never cared for our dependency on foreign oil, so over the years I've invested in a number of ventures researching and inventing alternative fuel sources. Solar, wind, and water." He stood up. "And garbage."

"I don't understand."

"I have to see the generator to be sure, but I think I know what they're using for power." He checked the window again. "We're almost out of light. Come on."

Charlotte followed him from the house to the back, where the land rose in a gentle slope toward tiers of shrubs and small trees. Samuel went first, pushing his way through the stiff branches of the sea grapes and squeezing through the narrow gaps between palmettos, holding back as much as he could for Charlotte.

When they reached the top of the slope, he saw sharp-edged saw grass that appeared to have been heaped together atop a long, narrow mound. Beneath his feet he felt a faint vibration that told him he was in the right place.

"Stay here," he told her, before he waded into the grass, keeping his pace slow and holding his arms up over the thorny blades. In the center of the mound he found a depression, and when he pulled away the grass he uncovered a heavy door made out of teak with a combination lock on the latch.

He placed his hand on the lock, closing his eyes as he coaxed his flagging ability to show him the last combination used. Once he had the numbers, he also knew enough about the structure to support his theory, but opened it anyway.

A huge wave of sound blasted out, startling birds out of the trees overhead. Samuel squinted as a light inside snapped on, illuminating two enormous machines painted bright orange. Only one of the pair was running, but the sounds it made confirmed Samuel's suspicions. Both machines were powerful, gas-driven industrial generators, known in the States as "thunder pumpkins" for their appearance and distinctive roar.

A hand covered with bleeding scratches pushed the door closed, and he turned to find Charlotte beside him. "I told you to wait."

"I yelled, but you couldn't hear me over all the noise."

She pointed toward the house. "Our Peeping Tom is back."

Samuel swept her off her feet and carried her through the saw grass back to safer ground, and then scanned the area. "Where is he?"

"He went inside the house." She caught his wrist. "He wouldn't walk right in there for kicks. Maybe he wants to talk."

"The sun has set." He eyed the dark windows. "You still can't read his thoughts now?"

She shook her head. "It's like he's some kind of phantom."

Samuel didn't believe in ghosts. "Then it's time we find out why he's haunting us."

Chapter 11

Cold water flooding over his face hurtled Jonah Genaro back to consciousness.

"Get up."

The boot that collided with his ribs was neither vicious nor merciful; its owner used just enough force to inflict the maximum amount of pain without causing serious injury. Genaro felt no surprise when he looked up to see rusting bars and the bored features of the uniformed prison guard.

"Get up," the guard repeated. "*El jefe* wants to see you."

Genaro made a personal inventory as he stood; they'd taken his shoes, socks, belt, tie, and jacket. He'd also been stripped and re-dressed; his shirt remained crookedly buttoned. The air in the cell stank of old urine and despair; graffiti that ran the gamut from pathetic to obscene littered the cracked paint covering the cinderblock walls.

The last thing he remembered was drinking some water while he waited for Energúmeno in his dining room. Whatever drug they had used, it had been completely tasteless.

The guard kept one eye on him as he unlocked the cell door, and then stepped back to make a terse gesture for Genaro to go out first. He walked over the filthy concrete floor into the outside corridor. Wherever he was, it was a popular dumping ground; at least ten men occupied each of the other cells, all of which had been built to comfortably accommodate only two.

Every eye watched them as they walked down the corridor; not one of the inmates uttered a sound.

The guard escorted him through a maze of cell corridors, holding areas, and guard stations, using different keys to gain access whenever they came to another barrier. On his hip he wore a truncheon that needed cleaning and a .38 automatic in an old leather holster; the outlines of a backup clip bulged in his pocket.

The guard knocked on a door that had been painted more recently than the fifties, and waited until a voice called out something in Spanish. He opened the door and gave Genaro a push inside.

The office contained all the cheap trappings of desperate self-importance: framed official-looking documents and photos of minor politicians smiling stiffly at the cameras, their hands clasped in the big-knuckled grip of a pudgy, balding man in an ill-fitted suit. The Mexican flag stood proudly displayed next to a small shrine to the country's current president. A glass-fronted case held the curiosities of the confiscated: homemade tattoo machines, electrical wire garrotes, and blades fashioned from toothbrushes and utensil handles.

Behind the desk sat the pudgy man featured so prominently in the wall photos. Today he wore a slightly better suit, but his comb-over was disordered and a red welt marred his right, pockmarked cheek.

"I am Warden Delgado." The warden did not look up from the paperwork he was pretending to read. "Sit down."

Genaro glanced at the stained leather upholstery of the chair in front of the desk, and saw how many gouges had been left in the wooden arms. The guard shuffled forward to stand behind it, fingering the grip of his truncheon, and glare at Genaro.

"Do you know who I am?" Genaro asked the warden.

"You are a prisoner." Delgado sounded bored. "If

you do not sit down in the next five seconds, you will be a prisoner with a crack in his head, bleeding on my floor."

As soon as Genaro occupied the chair, the guard cuffed his right wrist to the chair and withdrew from the room. The warden continued his farce of busywork until the door opened again, this time admitting Carasegas.

"You remember our police chief?" The warden stood, stacking some papers that he tucked into a folder before he walked around the desk. To the chief, he said, "He is waiting for your call."

Genaro noted the shift in the warden's tone as he spoke to the chief. Delgado was trying to project machismo when in reality he was terrified—and not of Genaro or the chief.

Carasegas nodded. "I will contact him as soon as I've finished with the prisoner."

Genaro watched Delgado leave and the chief take his place behind the desk. "Why am I here?"

"You were arrested for murdering Pedro Tacal." Carasegas tucked his hands behind his neck and sat back, idly rocking in the executive chair. "With great remorse you confessed to me the details of your crime, and tomorrow you will plead guilty before a judge. You will be sentenced to life without parole and placed in solitary confinement."

"Why am I being framed for this murder?" Genaro asked.

"You will have no phone or legal privileges," the chief continued, as if Genaro hadn't spoken. "Any records pertaining to you and your incarceration will be destroyed. By next week no one, not even I, will know where you are."

Genaro inclined his head to acknowledge the chief's threat. "Is there some sort of financial arrangement we can make in order to divert this unhappy fate of mine?"

"You think your money can buy you anything, eh, *gabacho*?" Carasegas indulged in a big belly laugh. "Maybe it can in America, but you are in *my* country now." He snapped his fingers. "Like that you could be gone. Forever. They wouldn't even find your bones."

"If you intended to keep me incarcerated," Genaro said, "you would have taken my clothes and left me to rot. If you wanted to kill me, I'd already be dead. So tell me, who is your employer, and what does he really want from me?"

A flicker of unease passed over the chief's features before he leaned forward to put his folded hands on the desk. "You will give me the names and current locations of all the people you intended to use for this special project of yours."

Energúmeno must have arranged this, Genaro thought. No one else had the knowledge or the resources to pull it off. "Is that all?"

"You also have a scientist working for you." The chief took a folded note from his pocket and read from it. "Dr. Eliot Kirchner. You will call him and tell him to come to Manzanillo." He pushed the phone on the desk to the edge. "Now."

Genaro picked up the receiver with his free hand and dialed a number. "Eliot? There's been a complication. I need you to fly down to Manzanillo." He listened to the empty line for a moment. "It can't wait. Take the next flight out. I'll have someone meet you at the airport." He paused. "Good, then I'll see you tonight." He hung up the receiver and regarded the chief. "I'll need access to a computer to retrieve the data you want."

"There are no computers here." Carasegas frowned. "Call the doctor back. Tell him to bring it with him."

"Kirchner doesn't have access to my personal database. No one does except me." He twisted his cuffed wrist. "If you want the data, I need to use a computer with Internet access. Perhaps if we were to return to my hotel, I could—"

"I'll take you back to the station," Carasegas decided. "You'll use my computer, and if you try anything, anything at all . . ." He snapped his fingers.

The police chief made two calls while a guard arrived with Genaro's shoes and jacket. He was uncuffed only long enough to put them on, but as soon as he smoothed down his lapels he held out his wrists.

As Genaro suspected, the jail was some distance from the city, and it took Carasegas thirty minutes to make the drive back. Along the way he told Genaro how little his power, influence, and wealth meant south of the border.

"You Americans always come down here expecting movie Mexicans in their sombreros and ponchos, holding their dirty hands out for a few pesos." He snorted. "We are smarter than you thought, eh?"

"You're certainly more resourceful than I anticipated," Genaro conceded, keeping his eyes on the rearview mirror. "Does your employer plan to collect my targets himself, or send you after them?"

Carasegas's smug smile evaporated. "That is not for you to know, *gabacho*. As soon as you give me the list of names, you are leaving Mexico, and if you are smart, you will never return."

"I'm sure this will be my final visit." Genaro saw a white cargo van come up alongside the chief's car, where it paced him for a moment before dropping back and merging into the traffic behind it. "I think I'm having a reaction to the drugs you gave me. Would you pull over?"

"No."

He produced a liquid cough. "Then you have no objection to my vomiting on your seats?"

Carasegas swore as he veered off the road and came to a stop on the shoulder. He marched around to the back door, opening it to pull Genaro out.

"You Americans with your weak bellies," the chief started, only to stop and look back as the cargo van pulled up behind them. The driver climbed out and called something in Spanish, to which the chief answered casually. The distraction kept him from noticing the second van that pulled off the road in front of his car.

Genaro watched his men pour out of both vans; all of them were armed with automatic weapons. By the time Carasegas had gotten out his pistol he was surrounded.

The police chief eyed him. "How did you send for them? Did you use some code when you called the scientist?"

"I never actually called Eliot, and I believe it's my turn to ask the questions." He held out his wrists, and one of the men removed the handcuffs. "Who are you working for, and where is he?"

"That's for me to know." A sly look came into his eyes. "I can take you to Energúmeno. You could ask him."

"I'll be talking to him soon enough." Genaro stepped closer. "How did he learn about my project?"

The chief grinned. "You told him yourself, fool."

"So Energúmeno is your boss."

"Sure he is." The chief laughed. "Or maybe I do it for a favor for your mother, after I fucked her."

Genaro nodded to one of the men, who shoved the barrel of his weapon into the chief's neck. "I'll ask you one more time. Who told you to do this, and where can I find him?"

"Nowhere." Carasegas's face lost all expression. "Everywhere. He is God." He lifted the gun in his hand and pressed the end under his chin, pulling the trigger.

Genaro put up his arm to block the spray of blood and brain matter, lowering it to watch the chief's body tumble backward onto the grass. He removed his bloodstained jacket and handed it to one of the men. "Put the body in the van, and get rid of the car. Give me a phone."

Delaporte answered before the first ring ended. "Mr. Genaro? Are you secure?"

"For the moment." He walked up to the first van. "I need you to find out who paid off the drug lord and Carasegas to frame me for murder. Whoever it was knows about the transerum and the Kyndred."

*　　*　　*

As they approached the house, Charlotte began to sweat. Behind Samuel's watchful, handsome face a lot of unspoken rage seethed, and it was pouring into her like liquid fire.

At the door she touched his arm. "Let me go in and talk to him," she murmured.

He stared at her. "So he can attack you first? No."

"We need some answers, *mío*." She nodded at his knotted fists. "*Before* you beat the daylights out of him."

"We'll go in together." When she started to argue, he shook his head. "And if he attacks, you will step aside and let me deal with him."

"Don't kill him."

They slipped inside the villa, pausing as Samuel listened. No sound gave away the intruder's location, but Charlie felt an odd sensation crawl over her skin, something like the frigid air one felt when opening the door to a freezer, minus the actual chill.

She exhaled and watched with wide eyes as her breath briefly became a white mist before it dissipated. When she looked down, she saw the water in the floor had frozen in places, the ice shaped like footprints.

Samuel pointed in the direction they took toward the staircase, the steps of which were lightly coated in frost, and then looked up at the ceiling.

She nodded and followed him up the stairs. The patches of ice led down the hall to the master suite, where the door stood open.

Samuel moved quickly, taking a position to one side of the door and gesturing for Charlotte to stand opposite. Glancing inside, she saw the man walk out of the bathroom and cross over to the patio doors, where he stepped outside.

Without warning Samuel went after him, and reached him before Charlie could catch up. The man turned as Samuel reached out to grab him, and then stood still as Sam's hands passed through his body.

Samuel tried to seize him again, and then drew back

his hands, both of which were coated with ice. Impatiently he clapped his hands together, smashing the ice away before he eyed the apparition. "What are you?"

The man replied with a few sneering words.

When Samuel glanced at her, Charlie shook her head. "It's not Spanish. It sounds Indian." To the ghost, she said, "*¿Habla inglés? ¿Español?*"

The man eyed her, his body becoming more transparent. In mangled Spanish, he asked, "You woman doctor?"

Charlie doubted she could explain the difference between an EMP and an MD to a ghost, so she went with her instincts. "Yes, I am a doctor."

He came at her, passing through Samuel as if he weren't there. "Pici no die." He tried to touch her, but his arms began to disappear, and he uttered something in his own language before he stepped back. "You save."

Charlie nodded. "Where is Pici? How can I help her?"

"Go." The man pointed toward the back of the villa. "Tell Colotl." As soon as his arm dropped his body faded away into nothingness.

Charlie saw Sam sitting on the deck. "What happened? Are you all right?"

"At the moment, I'm defrosting." Samuel brushed at the ice crystals already melting on his chest. "Whatever that thing was, contact with it causes instant frostbite."

"Let me have a look." Charlie knelt down beside him, brushing away the slush on his chest to expose the stiff, dark skin beneath. As she palpated the area, Sam's flesh became more pliable. When she lifted her hand, it had already lightened to a deep pink, and then assumed its normal light caramel color. She checked the rest of his torso, finding the same process ongoing. After another minute passed, all the damaged skin had healed.

She extended one of his arms, putting her own beside it. Scratches from walking through the saw grass still made angry, crisscrossed slashes over her skin, while his didn't have a mark on it.

"You should have said something." Sam ran his hand down her arm, healing the scratches. "Better?"

"Scary. You not only can heal me; you're healing yourself." Charlie felt a tickling sensation at the base of her neck, and brushed at it. *"Niman achtopa yah in Ihiyo."*

"I'm sorry?"

"Ihiyo was the first to go." She felt a surge of impatience at having to translate it into English for him. "You shouldn't have tried to catch him. You should have just waited. He would come to you himself soon enough."

Samuel peered at her. "Who is Ihiyo?"

"No one of importance." He wanted to play, she could tell, and the hunger came into her, full and ripe. She fluttered her eyelashes at him. "Why don't we go to bed?"

"Perhaps a little later, after we talk." He looked into her eyes. "How are you feeling right now?"

"I feel like having you in me." She climbed over him, pushing him back against the deck. "But we can play here, too." She pulled her shirt up over her head, flinging it away before she drew his hands up to her aching breasts. *"Ahmo tläcacemeleh*. He is not pretty to look at. Not like you."

"Charlotte." He cradled her face between his hands. "Come back to me."

A different emotion streaked through her, leaching away the strange lust and making her crawl backward away from him. *"Ie ixqujch*. No more, please."

Samuel caught her before she could escape and brought her up onto her knees, shaking her a little. "Charlotte, can you hear me? Something is trying to take control. You have to shut them off. Get them out of your head. *Charlotte.*"

"I'm here." Charlie pushed her way through the alien emotions, panting as she emerged and slammed up her mental barriers behind her. "Jesus." She sagged against him.

"Who's doing this to you?" Samuel demanded as he helped her to her feet. "Is it Segundo?"

"I don't know. They're so strong. Coming at me from all directions." She huddled against him as echoes of the thought streams hammered all around the mental walls she had erected. "I don't know if I can . . ." She choked on bile as a tangle of fear, anger, and terror tried to push through. *"No."*

He brought her face close to his. "Don't panic. You know what you have to do. Look at me, yes, like that. I'm right here with you."

While Samuel talked to her, Charlie used him as her anchor, keeping her thoughts trained on him as she reinforced her mental barriers.

At last she felt secure enough to relax a little. "I'm clear of them. For now, anyway."

He kept his arm around her and lifted her chin to inspect her face. "Does it always do this to you?"

"I haven't been keeping my guard up the way I do at home. With just you and me here, I didn't think I had to." She exhaled slowly as the intense nausea receded. "Usually I feel people long before I can read them, but this time . . . it was like they just materialized out of nowhere."

"Do you think they're on the island?"

"I know they are. Where, I'm not sure exactly. They're together in a group, and they're close, but . . ." She shook her head and swiped at the tears clinging to her lashes. "There were too many voices to sort out at once, and all of them were speaking in that odd language. Maybe I can try to sweep for them a little later—"

"Not after what they just did to you," he told her. "You spoke to me in a language I've never before heard." He bent to pick up her shirt. "And you were definitely not yourself," he added as he helped her pull it on.

"I wanted to jump you. I did jump you." She looked down at her hands, which were clenched. "Part of it was me but not me. As if someone had helped themselves to my libido." Her lips twisted. "Then something shifted and I was terrified and . . . sick to my stomach."

"The second person you sensed was ill?"

She made an uncertain gesture. "You scared me, and all I could think about was getting away, throwing up, and soaking my feet. They were killing me."

He glanced at her toes. "Could one of these people be hurt?"

"I don't think so." She frowned as she tried to recall the emotions that had overrun her mind. "The first surge was really strong. Almost primitive. As if men and sex are all she thinks about. The second wave was the complete opposite. She wants to get away. Be left alone with . . ." The thought dissipated, and she shook her head.

"Did either of the women think about what they were doing on the island?"

"Sex Kitten just wanted you, or, for that matter, any guy with a pulse." She frowned as a fragment of imagery came back to her. "The girl who was sick and scared, she wasn't reacting to only you." She looked back at the villa. "It's this place. Seeing it was what made her feel sick. Something inside." She grabbed his hand. "Come with me."

Charlie led him through the master suite and down the hall, but stopped just outside the door to the assessment room. She looked in at the empty table, and then released his hand, walking slowly toward the end of the upholstered seat. She reached under and pulled up one stirrup and then the other, curling her fingers over the metal supports.

"Charlotte?"

"She was in here," she murmured as the images coalesced in her mind. "On the table, staring at the ceiling. An older man was giving her a pelvic exam. She was in so much pain." She pushed the table toward the wall, and glanced down. Dark reddish brown stains colored the grout between the white tiles in a two-foot area. "Oh, God. I think that's her blood."

Samuel knelt down and touched the grout. "There was a pool of it." He made a circling gesture. "About three feet in diameter. The doctor mopped it up."

Charlie stepped back. "She was hemorrhaging. Maybe from an illegal abortion." She winced as the thought streams outside her barriers became more intense and focused. "Sam? They're here."

"Here on the island?"

"No." She covered her face with her hands, pressing her fingers against her eyelids before she dropped her arms. "They're standing right outside the front door."

Samuel gave her a narrow look. "How do you know that?"

"I can feel them." She showed him the goose bumps covering her forearms.

He rested a hand on her shoulder. "I don't suppose you'd stay here while I go down to see what they want?"

"Not a chance."

Charlie saw the torches through the downstairs windows, but when she stepped outside with Samuel the group waiting for them shocked her into silence. Twelve men and women, dressed in ragged clothing, stood in two rows: the men in the front and the women behind them. She saw blondes, brunettes, and several redheads, with skin tones ranging from alabaster to ebony. From what she could make out of their features they were all of multiracial lineage, although it was obvious they all shared some Caucasian characteristics.

Not one of them, however, appeared to be Mexican.

One of the men with the darkest skin stepped forward and touched his chest as he said, "Colotl." He made a broad gesture encompassing the others. *"Amigos."* He pointed to Charlie and then Samuel. *"¿Ustedes?"*

"I'm Samuel Taske," Sam said. "This is Charlotte Marena. Do any of you speak English?"

Colotl uttered a few words to one of the other men before he spoke to Samuel again. *"¿Curandero?"*

"He's asking if you're a healer." To Colotl she said, *"Yo soy médica. ¿Alguien está lastimada?"*

The red-haired woman standing behind Colotl murmured something to him, and he raised both hands palms out toward Charlie before speaking to Samuel again. *"¿Manos curativas?"* He pointed at Samuel's hands.

"Charlotte," Sam said softly, "I believe they know about my newfound ability."

"Whether they do or not, we shouldn't volunteer anything just yet." She looked at Colotl, asking him the same question as before while pressing a hand to her chest and mimicking a pained expression. She then repeated the question in English. "Is someone hurt?"

"Hurt." Colotl glanced at the other men. "No."

She recalled what the apparition in the house had said. *"¿Pici está contigo?"*

Colotl beckoned to the smallest of the women, who shuffled over to stand beside him.

"That's what our visitor meant by 'woman doctor.' " Charlie's eyes shifted to the high, swollen mound of her abdomen. "A doctor for a woman. A pregnant woman." She moved toward Pici, who cringed and huddled against Colotl. "It's all right, sweetie. I won't hurt you."

"Momento." Colotl turned his head and spoke to the others, and one by one the other women began to step forward into the light from the torches.

"My God," Samuel muttered under his breath.

Charlie looked down the row of females, unwilling to accept what she was seeing but unable to deny the evidence. "Sam, we're not here to be displayed." Of the twelve women, eleven were in various stages of advanced pregnancy. "We're livestock."

PART THREE

Night of Tears

Chapter 12

September 29, 1978
Mexico City, Mexico

"You're sure what you saw was gold," Foster Stanton said as he hunched over to follow Chavez into the narrow shaft. "You could be wrong, you know. It might be copper, or pyrite inlay, or some sort of resin—"

"Not this," the electrician promised. "I know the difference."

Stanton knew he was betting his professional reputation—not to mention his personal liberty—on the word of an almost illiterate utility worker. But since Chavez had been a member of the original work crew that had accidentally unearthed an eight-ton stone disk carved with the relief of an ancient Aztec goddess, the archaeologist had no choice. No one from Mexico's National Institute of Anthropology and History allowed anyone but their own people to work the site, and their lack of funding and equipment had brought the dig practically to a standstill.

Fortunately the electricians who had been rerouting the city's power conduits were still permitted access, and Chavez had vouched for Stanton. Removing the artifact would be much more difficult, but first Stanton had to determine whether the find was even worth his trouble.

The electrician stopped, tucking his flashlight under

his chin as he grabbed a panel of particleboard and moved it aside.

"Through here, señor," Chavez said, holding up his flashlight to illuminate the low entrance he had uncovered.

Stanton saw the crumbling condition of the mud-covered walls and hesitated. "Has anyone been in here to reinforce the ceilings?" An odor wafted out and he almost choked. "What is that smell?"

"That's from the old sewer pipe. The ceiling will hold." Chavez gave him a disgusted look. "What are you, afraid? You want a priest to bless the place first?"

Stanton held a handkerchief over his nose and mouth as he bent over and ducked into the small chamber. The air inside smelled of decay, not human waste, but he forgot about the bile rising in his throat as soon as Chavez trained his light on the partially dug pit in the floor, and what gleamed through the disturbed earth. "My God."

The statue appeared to be a life-size sculpture of a Mesoamerican nobleman. Stanton fell to his knees, bruising them on the shells surrounding the edge of the pit, and reached in with a trembling hand to brush away more soil. He uncovered the leg of the statue from knee to hip, where he discovered the jagged edges of the top of the limb where it had separated from the torso.

He jerked up his head to glare at Chavez. "Did you hack off the leg?"

"No, señor. I found it just as you see." The electrician winced and rubbed the back of his neck. "It is too heavy for the two of us to carry out. We will need more men."

"Solid gold." Stanton felt exactly what Carter must have the first time he laid eyes on the riches contained in Tutankhamen's tomb. "It's impossible." He laughed as he started digging around the leg with his hands. "It's miraculous."

"We must go now." Chavez slapped a hand against his arm. "There are too many bugs down here. I can feel them biting me."

The archaeologist barely heard him as he finished uncovering the entire limb. Unlike other burial tributes, this one was incredibly lifelike, as if it had been cast directly from a living human leg. "You go up. I have to see more of it."

Carefully he stepped down into the pit and straddled the lower portion of the statue in order to uncover the head. Like the leg it had been raggedly detached from the torso, and the sculptor had not bothered to adorn it with precious gems or intricate inlay, but the spectacularly rendered features and minute detailing—even the closed eyelids had two rows of tiny, curling lashes—were breathtaking.

"Señor." The electrician yelped and dropped the flashlight. "Something is wrong. Something is—" His voice dissolved into a cry as he stumbled into one of the walls, and dirt rained down atop Stanton and the pit.

"Hold still, you idiot, before you bring the whole place down on our heads. Here, take this." He grabbed the flashlight and aimed the beam at the sound of Chavez's whining.

The beam illuminated bloody hands pressed over the electrician's face. When he dropped them, Stanton saw dozens of deep cuts crisscrossing the man's features, as if someone had slashed him repeatedly in the face. As more wounds appeared, as if his flesh were being cut from the inside, his eyes rolled back and he toppled over next to the pit.

Stanton pushed himself up, in the process dislodging a huge, round shell on the edge of the pit. The shell rolled in atop the statue, and when he turned the flashlight caught the three black holes bored in it and the two rows of teeth gleaming through a fringe of black.

Shells don't have teeth, Stanton thought. *Or mustaches.*

Stanton jerked back and his hand landed in something wet. He looked down to see a stream of blood flowing over his fingers, and followed it up to the electri-

cian's body. More poured from the wide gap in his throat
and ran over the edge of the pit. When he looked back
down he saw he was kneeling in a crimson pool.

Soil shifted, revealing more gold.

Pain sliced across Stanton's forehead as he scrambled
backward, trying to crawl out of the pit. The warm wetness that ran into his eyes blinded him, but he kept pis-
toning his legs and arms, splashing in the blood that now
ran down his chest and forearms and thighs, until he
slipped and fell backward, slamming his head against a
column of stone.

He brought up his numb hands, wiping his eyes clear
so he could see what was happening to him. He couldn't
be dying, not like this. Not in a dirt pit with more ancient
gold than he'd ever seen. No one would ever know that
he'd been the one to discover it.

"Help me," he pleaded, reaching up toward the
shadow hovering over him. *"Ayúdame, por favor."*

"Cämpa tihuällah? Tlein nonacayo?" a voice thun-
dered in his ears. *"Mä niquitta."*

*Where have you come from? What is my body? Let
me see it.*

Stanton's killer spoke as if he were the ancient Cë-
Acatl. Dredging up the proper response, he said in
stilted Nahautl, *"Nimitznottitïlïco in monacayo, To-
piltzin."* *I have come to show you your body, Our Beloved Lord.*

"Cämpa tihuällah?" *Where have you come from?*

"Ömpa nihuïtz in Nonohualcatepëtl ïtzintlan," Stanton lied. *I have come from the foot of the mountain
Nonoalcatepëtl.* *"Ca nimomäcëhual."* *I am your subject.*

Chapter 13

"I don't think your father likes me," Drew said as he cast off the last line tying the battered old fishing boat to the dock before waving to the elderly Mexican watching from the end of the pier. The old man didn't wave back. "Is it because I'm American?"

"No." Gracie used a frayed pull cord to start an outboard motor that was only slightly less ancient than the boat.

He joined her and ran a hand over his scalp. "Is red hair considered unlucky?"

"If red were an unlucky color, we would not have it on our national flag." She moved to the helm and steered the boat away from the dock.

As they moved out into the bay, Drew looked out over the bow, but all he saw was endless ocean. "How long will it take us to reach this Englishman's island?"

"A few hours." She nodded to the cramped recess leading belowdecks. "My father has a bunk down there. You should go and sleep while you can."

"And leave you to sail through stormy seas by yourself?" He grinned. "Not a chance, sweetheart."

She adjusted the controls before she turned to him. "The sea is calm, you are exhausted, and I am not your sweetheart."

"You didn't sleep last night, either," he reminded her, but his smile faded as he saw the whiteness of her knuckles as she gripped the wheel. "You don't have to do this, Gracie, not if it's going to cause trouble with your family. We can turn it around right now and go back. I'll hire one of the other fishermen to do this."

"No one will take you near the islands. They know the law. If we're stopped, I can use my credentials." She checked the navigational equipment before sitting down in the captain's chair. "*Papi* is not angry at you. It's me." She sighed. "It's always me."

"I noticed he didn't exactly break out the champagne when we showed up." Drew sat down beside her. "Is it because you left home?"

"My family never approved of my going to school and getting a job in the city," she admitted. "They wanted me to marry. *Papi* even had a husband picked out for me."

Longing and jealousy ricocheted inside him, two pin-balls covered with spikes. "Was this husband-to-be a fat, ugly old widower with six kids?"

"Eduardo? He was young, slim, and handsome. No children, but no desire for an educated, working wife." She sounded depressed, but when she looked at him her eyes twinkled. "Now he is older and a little fat."

"And he has six kids?"

She smiled. "Four."

It might have been the way the sun was gilding the tips of her eyelashes, or the sheen of sea spray on her cheeks, but in that moment Drew knew he had never seen and would never again see anyone as beautiful as Agraciana Flores. "You could have both, you know," he heard himself say. "The family and the career. Lots of women do it."

"Women in your country." She caught a piece of her hair that escaped from the colorful scarf she'd tied around her head and tucked it under the edge. "Here we are not so liberated."

"You should consider emigrating, then." He reached out to trace the curve of her cheek, and was startled when she whipped her head away. "Gracie?"

She stood up, gripping the wheel tightly. "There are some bottles of water in an ice chest below if you are thirsty."

Every time he got close to her, Drew realized, she pushed him away. "I'm not—"

"I am." She gave him a direct look. "Would you bring one for me, please?"

Drew gave up and went below to retrieve the water. The cramped space had been made into a tidy little living space, complete with a narrow bunk, an ancient but clean cookstove, and a tiny bathroom. It should have been hot and airless, but the old man had rigged some sort of ventilation system, and a steady stream of cool, salt-tinged air wafted in Drew's face.

He noticed a crate stashed in one corner that had been filled with magazines and books, all written in Spanish but obviously about sailing and fishing.

"So *Papi* likes to read." He picked up one paperback and thumbed through it before something fluttered out of the pages. He bent to pick up a small photograph of a petite, dark-haired child in a red dress standing with a younger version of *Papi* in front of the old boat.

"She's still your girl, isn't she, old man?" He noticed what he first assumed was a sleeve was actually a bandage on the child's right arm. "But who the hell hurt her?"

He knew he should have replaced the photo, but he gave in to the impulse and tucked it into his pocket before grabbing a bottle of water.

Gracie had reverted back to her cool, distant composure when he rejoined her on deck, and thanked him politely when he handed her the bottle. "I apologize for my temper. I never discuss such matters with a stranger."

The photo in his pocket, the image of the child she had been, felt for a moment as stiff as the line of her back. Drew thought of the bandage on the little arm, the unsmiling old Mexican, and all the bits from the sea Gracie had used to decorate her cottage. When they'd arrived at her childhood home, the way she had hesitated, just for a fraction of a second, before speaking to her father was almost as telling as the cold indifference the old man had shown both of them. Drew knew love and fear, and saw both in Gracie, but there was something more. Something had caused a serious rift between her and her family, and he sensed it had nothing at all to do with her working in the city.

He was also tired of being shut out by whatever it was. "Can you stop the boat?"

She wouldn't look at him. "We should keep going."

"We will, in a minute," he lied.

Gracie throttled down, shutting off the engine before turning to him. "We don't have time for—"

"I'm not a stranger to you. Not since last night." Drew took her hands in his. "Talk to me."

"I have nothing to say." She tried to extract herself from his grip. "I don't know you."

"Wrong." He held on. "I told you my life story. You know me better than my mother. I'm your friend."

"I am not friends with liars or impostors," she flared.

Suddenly Drew understood her aloofness and what she might be hiding behind it. "You don't have anyone, do you? Ever since you left the village, you've been alone."

Gracie paled, and then her shoulders drooped. "There is no time for friends," she said, her voice thin and hurt. "What I do is more important. I protect what I love."

"So do I." The boat rocked a little as he snatched her off her feet and carried her down belowdecks.

"Drew, what are you doing?"

"Guess."

Her expression became alarmed. "*No quiero.* Drew, I don't want—"

"I don't need the translation. I get it." He put her down on her father's bunk, and pinned her there on her back. "I don't want to do caveman things like this. Ever."

Her eyes narrowed. "Then why are you now?"

"One of us has to, and you never will." He tore open his shirt, popping buttons in the process, and pushed her hand flat against his damp chest. "Now tell me I'm a stranger."

Her fingers flexed against his skin. "You're a stranger."

"A stranger you kissed," he reminded her. "Like I was the one you'd been waiting for all your life."

"That was how *you* kissed *me*." She shifted under him. "The only ones who are waiting for you are your friends."

He touched his mouth to a delectable spot beneath her jaw. "So you're saying that I'm not the man of your dreams."

"I have no dreams." Her hand trembled as she ran it up to his neck. "Andrew, please. When you leave, we will never see each other again. Don't do this to me."

"All right." He let go of her and rolled onto his side. He waited for her to get up and hurry away, but when she sat up he put his hand on her shoulder. "I just want you to know one thing."

She looked down at him.

"You will see me again. Once my friends are safe, I'm coming back here." He ran his hand down the length of her back before drawing it away. "For you."

Drew expected Gracie to run off again, not spin around and grab him. Before he could react she was on top of him, her mouth on his, her hands pushing his shirt away from his chest, her legs bracketing his. Astonishment paralyzed him as she poured all her passion into the kiss, her tongue sliding against his, her fingernails scoring his skin as she freed his arms.

Abruptly she sat up, bracing her palms against his chest as she looked down at him, her hair falling around her beautifully flushed face. "So? This is what you want, yes?"

"Oh, yes." He gripped her hips, shifting her so she could feel his pounding erection. "It's yours, sweetheart—but only if *you* want it."

She rubbed herself against him, her eyelids drooping and her lips parting. "I want you."

Drew lifted his hips to take his wallet out of his back pocket. As he flipped it open and reached into the bill-fold, Gracie's expression changed to outrage.

"You dare try to give me—"

"Protection." He took out the two condoms he always carried and placed them in her hand. "But if you want the money, you can have that, too. My credit cards are phony and the car's a rental, and my laptop will self-destruct the minute you try to use it. I don't have anything else to offer." He thought for a moment. "Okay, I'll give you all the *Battlestar Galactica* T-shirts I brought with me. Including my favorite blue 'What the Frak?' one that Katee Sackhoff signed for me at the last SF convention."

She pressed her lips together for a moment. "Starbuck signed your T-shirt?"

"You get the Syfy channel all the way down here?"

She shook her head. "I buy the DVDs from eBay."

"You *are* the perfect woman." He pulled her down, meeting her lips halfway with his while he helped her with her buttons. Under the prim blouse she wore a pale lavender bra edged with dark purple lace. By the time he discovered that her panties matched, he had her under him again, her thighs around his hips and the words she murmured in Spanish rushing in his ears. He left her only long enough to strip down to his skin, and then she rose to her knees behind him, her hands sliding around his waist as she pressed her cheek against his back.

"Be still," she said when he tried to turn around. She already had one of the condoms unwrapped, and deftly rolled it over the head of his penis and down the length of his shaft. Her fingers gently combed through the thatch of red hair before stroking over the aching swell of his sac.

"I should mention," he said, gritting his teeth, "that I'm not made of ice."

"So? You have two condoms. We use the other and start again." She fisted his cock, giving it a delicious squeeze before she climbed off the bunk, winding herself around him so that the bits of satin she wore slid against his hot skin. Before he could tear them off, she hooked her thumbs in the sides of her panties and pushed them down, kicking them off.

"Gracie." He picked her up, bringing her lips to his mouth, and her arms and legs went around him as she lifted her hips and nudged him into place. Drew wanted to go slow, but she was already melting over him, her slick heat parting and engulfing him as she rolled her hips

The bunk was too far away; the floor was too hard. Drew held her against him and walked up on deck, ignoring her startled sound as he carried her back to the bench seat under the stern canopy.

"Someone will see us," she whispered.

"Not unless they point a telescope at us." He caressed her cheek. "Don't you like how it feels?"

She smiled. "Too much."

Seeing her naked in the sunlight was almost as satisfying as laying her out on the cushioned top of the bench. She spread her thighs and pulled him in between as he crouched over her, positioning himself until he lodged just inside her. As he stroked in, he bent down to kiss her, giving her his tongue as well as his cock.

She arched, gripping him as she drew him in, working him into what felt like a hot, wet vise. When their body hair tangled Drew shuddered and groaned, enduring the pulsing tightness in his groin to fend off the urge to come so he could give her what she needed.

She tugged at him with her hands and her body, her voice almost a whimper, her sex so damp now her movements sounded like kisses. "*Ahora, por favor*, Andrew. Please, now."

He cupped her small breasts with his hands, working his palms over her nipples as he drew back and thrust in, watching her through narrowed eyes. Her face bloomed with color and pleasure, her eyes dilating as she arched

up into him, her body shivering. The heat made them
both sweat, but it only intensified the sensations as their
bodies danced. He tossed aside finesse and fucked her,
slow and deep, in and out, building on her response until
she was writhing, out of control, her thighs tightening as
she pushed her breasts into his hands and went rigid.
Drew bent his head to latch onto one tight nipple, scoring it with his teeth, and she came with a wild cry, squeezing him like a wet fist.

Drew pushed in deep, hearing his own groan as he
followed her, coming so hard his ears rang. She caught
his mouth with hers and drank the sounds he made, her
hands smoothing over his wet hair until he drifted down
back to earth.

He lifted his head to see her looking at him with desperate eyes. "Hey." He smoothed back her hair to kiss
her brow. "God, did I hurt you? I couldn't—"

"I feel wonderful. I have never . . ." She glanced up
and abruptly eased out from under him. "We should
go now." She hurried across the deck and disappeared
below.

Drew rubbed a hand over his face and looked up at
the underside of the canopy. The shadow of a seagull
passed over it before the bird landed atop the outboard
motor. It seemed to be watching him. "See anything you
like?"

The seagull opened its beak, uttered a sound like a
bray of shrill laughter, and flew off.

The twelve islanders seemed to defer to the dark-
skinned man with the silver hair as their leader, Samuel
noticed, the men silently looking to him for cues. The
redheaded Caucasian woman standing beside him—the
only female who wasn't showing signs of pregnancy—
also seemed to have some influence over the group, as
most of the women kept watching her.

It took Charlotte a few minutes and a great many
hand gestures to discover why they had come to the

villa, and even then she was not quite clear. "They want to talk to us, but only if we go down to the beach with them. They also can't stay long. I think he's only giving us an hour."

"They must know about the cameras."

She nodded. "I think we should go with them, although I don't know how effectively we can communicate. Colotl doesn't understand what weeks and months are, but it's obvious that they've been on the island for a while, definitely much longer than we have. Maybe they can give us some idea of what this is about."

Samuel had already assessed the other members of the group. None of them was carrying weapons, but all of the men were in prime physical shape. If they attacked en masse, he wouldn't be able to fend off all of them. "Should they decide they want to do more than talk, I want you to run to the house and barricade yourself in."

"They know I'm a medic and you can heal," Charlotte said. "With eleven pregnant women on this island, attacking us would be like trying to shoot two golden geese for dinner. There's also the obviously genetic connection we share."

"You think they're Takyn."

"It's that or we're on the island of Unwanted Multiracial People who all decided to get pregnant at the same time." She glanced at the group's leader. "Colotl is starting to look worried. We should hold off on discussing this in English until later."

The redheaded woman came to Charlotte and touched her arm. As she did, Samuel saw the tattoo of a scarlet spider on the inside of her wrist. *"Me llamo Tlemi. Vámonos, por favor."*

He offered Charlotte his arm, and together they followed the islanders down the path to the beach. The men thrust their torches into the sand, creating a wide circle in which they sat with their respective female companions. Only Colotl and Tlemi positioned themselves in the center, and gestured for the Americans to join them.

Samuel sat down across from them with Charlotte. The circle of flames illuminated their faces, and he realized they were quite young, probably in their early twenties. Following his instincts, he tugged down the collar of his shirt and showed them his tattoo. Charlotte followed suit, turning slightly as she pulled down the shoulder of her wrap to reveal her stylized turtle. She touched it and then reached out to Tlemi, pointing to the spider on her wrist.

Colotl nodded and lifted his braid, turning his head to show the silver scorpion inked on the back of his neck.

All around the circle the other islanders did the same, showing animal tattoos in various colors. Samuel found it interesting that all of the women had been inked on their forearms and the men on their napes.

"Takyn," Charlotte said, touching her ink and then Samuel's before making an encompassing gesture at the islanders. She then said something in slow, simple Spanish, to which Colotl only looked puzzled. "He doesn't understand the words for 'mother' or 'father.' If they were raised in a Mexican orphanage, they'd speak Spanish."

Colotl and Tlemi exchanged a look before he nodded to her. To Charlotte, she said, "I speak little English. Segundo teach me so I know what he say."

Charlotte exchanged a glance with Samuel before she said, "Segundo had us kidnapped from America."

"We from America," Tlemi said quickly, nodding toward the others. "Born America. We babies, master buy us, bring us Mexico."

"That explains why none of them appear to be native Mexican," Charlotte told him. To Tlemi, she said, "Who is this master?"

Tlemi's expression changed from cautious to fearful, and she shook her head. "No talk master."

"If you'll just tell me his name—"

"No," Colotl repeated sternly.

"All right, no talk master." Charlotte held up both

hands palms out in a mollifying gesture. "Why are you here on the island?"

"Send us here, live free, have babies," Tlemi said slowly. "Not free. Never leave. Segundo come—"

Colotl spoke sharply to her, and she snapped back. He glared at Samuel.

"Colotl afraid talk Segundo," Tlemi said, obviously angry. "I no afraid." She turned to Samuel. "You heal with hands. I see you."

"How did you see this?" he asked her.

"Watch you. In your eyes." She pointed to her temple and then to Charlotte's face. "See her heal, in your eyes."

"I think she's admitting that she's the ~~~~~~~~ ~~~~path," Charlotte murmured to him.

"A remote viewer, perhaps." Samuel glanced at Colotl. "Tlemi, how long have you and the others been on the island?"

She conferred briefly with Colotl, who at last nodded. "Here eight moons." She made a circle with her fingers.

Charlotte mimicked the gesture. "Eight moons that look like this?" When the other woman nodded, she dropped her hands and looked at the other women. "Eight months. Sam, most of them must be in their third trimester."

"Where do you live?" Sam asked Tlemi.

She pointed to the villa. "We have house." She moved her hand from one side of the island to the other, and then counted on her fingers before she added, "Six houses. Yours seventh house."

Samuel grew thoughtful. "He must have had one built for each couple. I wonder why he went to so much trouble and expense."

"Because he's a crazy person," Charlotte muttered before she spoke to the other woman. "Tlemi, I hear others in my mind, the way you see them." Charlotte tapped her temple. "Why didn't I hear any of you before tonight?"

Tlemi glanced at Colotl before she said, "Walls."

Samuel frowned. "There are walls on the island?"

"Colotl gift make walls." She turned to speak to her companion, which made him mutter under his breath. "Watch." She nudged him. "He show."

Samuel felt the air grow cool and heavy as a curtain of mist formed between them and the island couple. It swirled for a moment before the fog as well as Colotl and Tlemi faded from sight.

Charlotte reached out, flattening her palm against an invisible surface. "It feels like water, but it's as solid as glass. I can't push my hand through it." She closed her eyes brie-, "I can't sense either of them. They're gone."

"No gone." The unseen curtain dropped, and Tlemi smiled at her. "Good wall, yes?"

"A very good wall." Samuel had the feeling that making things disappear wasn't the only thing Colotl could do with his gift. "Tlemi, how are we being watched? We know it's not only the cameras."

She shifted, visibly uncomfortable. "Master watch. Master know everything you do. Always."

He saw a flicker of alarm in Colotl's eyes, and abruptly changed the subject. "Whom do you need us to heal? Is it Pici?"

The smallest woman blurted out something before clinging to the scowling man beside her.

"Pici small." Tlemi made a circling gesture over her own pelvis. "Baby big."

Charlotte glanced at the fearful woman. "I'll have to examine her, but if I'm understanding her correctly, Pici may be too small to deliver her child vaginally." To Tlemi she said, "Won't Segundo take Pici to a hospital?"

The other woman shook her head. "No leave island."

"Can you perform a C-section, Charlotte?" Samuel asked her.

"It's major surgery, and I'm not an obstetrician. But I've assisted on several, and I know the procedure." A strange look passed over her face. "I think it's my fault that we're here."

Samuel thought of the medical room. "They seemed to be prepared for you."

"I'm a licensed midwife, Sam. I'm just working fire rescue until I can find the right obstetrical practice to join." Her expression turned bleak. "Last month I had to submit all of my personal identification, school transcripts, and professional certifications for state verification. My parents made sure I was legal, and I've always passed every background check, but anyone taking a close look would realize Charlotte Marena didn't exist until she was in first grade."

Tlemi was trying to follow their conversation, Samuel noticed, and he smiled at her. "We can help Pici."

"Don't make them any promises," Charlotte warned. "Aside from the fact that I have only the bare minimum in medical supplies, I have no anesthesiologist, no nurses, and no safe blood for transfusions."

"Blood." Tlemi nodded and extended her arm, pointing to the crease of her elbow. "Segundo take from us."

Charlotte peered at her arm. "She has a fresh needle mark." She looked at the other woman. "Wait a second. Are you telling me that the blood inside the house is yours?"

"Segundo take, moon and half-moon." She showed her the spider tattoo. "Mark on bag."

"My God." Charlotte looked appalled. "That bastard has been stockpiling their blood."

"Samuel." Colotl said his name carefully, and then spoke to Tlemi in their language.

"Colotl say we go," she said. "You help Pici?"

"Yes." Samuel looked directly at the other man and held out his hand. *"Amigo."*

Colotl clasped his hand, and then spoke to the others. The men rose, helping their women to their feet, and after taking their torches began to head in different directions. Only Colotl and Tlemi remained behind.

Once the other islanders were out of sight, Colotl

brought a circle of mist around them and then nodded to Tlemi.

"Segundo watch you," she said quickly. "Tell master everything you do, we do. Colotl, I not know how."

"A man came and watched us last night," Charlotte told her. "Could he be reporting what we do to Segundo?"

"All men watch you. Take turns. Colotl send. Protect. Segundo know other way." She tapped the side of her head. "Like me, like Charlotte."

"He's a telepath?"

"I see in men eyes, but not Segundo. His eyes . . ." Tlemi made a helpless gesture. "Not like us."

"Samuel." Colotl took a folded black cloth from his pocket. He opened it, revealing the surface, which was covered with intricate embroidery.

At first Samuel thought it was only a gift, until Colotl tapped one square on it and pointed to the villa.

"It's a map of the island," he said to Charlotte as he studied it. He pointed to six other squares. *"¿Casas?"*

"Sí." Colotl pointed to a circle in the center of the map. *"Cueva."*

"Cueva means cave," Charlotte told him.

"Samuel. Colotl." Colotl pointed to the circle on the embroidered map and then the moon. *"Aquí mañana por la noche."*

After Charlotte translated, Samuel turned to Tlemi. "Why does Colotl want me to come to the cave tomorrow night?"

"Talk. Plan. Segundo not know cave, not see night." She paused, searching for words. "Charlotte. We leave island, go together, keep secret?"

"I understand," she told Tlemi before she eyed Samuel. "They want us to help them to escape."

Chapter 14

Genaro watched as the last of the Manzanillo police officers were stripped of their uniforms and marched into the holding cell. His own men, now dressed in the confiscated uniforms, silently followed him to the largest of the interrogation rooms, which his team leader, an experienced ex–Army Ranger named Evan Marlow, had converted into a command center.

"We've set up checkpoints on all the roads leading out of the city," Marlow told him as he came in to examine the operation. "The local news station is broadcasting the fugitive serial killer story on the hour. We've set up our own switchboard, and have our interpreters fielding calls from concerned citizens, government officials, and satellite agencies, but I doubt we can hold them off for longer than forty-eight hours."

"Get Delaporte on the phone." Genaro eyed the row of computers his techs were using to trawl for information. "What about Energúmeno?"

"The compound is deserted. We're questioning some of the old women who were left behind, but they claim they know nothing." Marlow nodded toward the satellite images posted on the wall. "All of the vehicles we spotted at the compound yesterday are missing. It could be that the target decided to move to safer ground."

"Run a property search and see what else he owns, then send the chopper for aerial recon." Genaro accepted a mobile phone from one of the techs. "Don? Thank you for the timely rescue."

"Glad you're all right, Mr. Genaro." His security chief sounded as if he hadn't slept all night. "We have a cleanup crew en route, ETA six hours. Dr. Kirchner is under twenty-four-hour guard. With your permission, I'd like to fly down there and supervise operations myself."

"I need you in Atlanta." Genaro walked out of the operations room and down the hall to Carasegas's office, where he sat down in the dead cop's chair. "I also need leverage against Energúmeno."

"He's hiding his assets with dummy corporations and bogus investments, most of them administered by a British expat named Foster Stanton," Delaporte said. "Stanton started out as an academic, but was sliding into the antiquities black market when he dropped off the grid back in the late seventies. He resurfaced a few years ago, about the same time Energúmeno began buying up dozens of land parcels and most of the agricultural and municipal waste disposal companies in central Mexico."

"Waste disposal?" Genaro frowned. "Are they fronts for drug operations?"

"No, they appear to be legitimate. He could be using them for money-laundering purposes, but that's the other thing." The chief sighed. "We haven't been able to connect any drug activity at all to him. No suppliers, pipelines, storage facilities, labs, or a single skirmish with a rival operation. In Mexico that's unheard-of, sir."

"A dummy cartel would be an effective smoke screen for a more lucrative enterprise." He grew thoughtful. "Before Carasegas shot himself, he claimed he wasn't working for Energúmeno, but for God. That order of delusional fanatics you investigated, the ones posing as Catholic priests, what were they called?"

"Les Frères de la Lumière."

"I want everything you already have on them, and see if they're operating in Mexico."

"That order is based in Europe, sir," Delaporte said, sounding doubtful. "We've yet to find any of them operating in America."

"They may be using the churches here as cover." Genaro picked up the crucifix statue Carasegas had on his desk. "This country is obsessed with religion." He tossed the cross into a drawer.

"Yes, sir. I'll call you when I have new information." Delaporte disconnected the line.

Marlow appeared outside the door's window, knocking once before looking in. "The owner of the café across the street is at the front desk. She claims Riordan and a woman had coffee there before leaving together last night. She claims she doesn't know who the woman was, but she's lying."

"Does she speak English?" When Marlow nodded, Genaro stood and took off his jacket. "Bring her to me."

The café owner, an older woman still wearing a flour-dusted apron and hairnet, came in accompanied by Marlow. She glanced around, her expression curious.

"What is this?" she asked. "Where is Chief Carasegas?"

"The chief is out conducting a search of the city." Genaro indicated the chair in front of the desk. "Sit down, please." As soon as she did, he glanced at Marlow, who closed the door and came to stand behind the chair. "You reported that you saw the serial killer bring a woman to your café last night. Who was she?"

The woman shrugged but averted her gaze. "I tell your man, I never see her before."

Genaro weighed the time-saving benefits of having her taken to one of the interrogation rooms and beaten until she talked. However, she had come to the station on her own, and her business was located across the street. For those reasons he would have to use persuasion. "Señora, this man has already murdered three people over the last two days. As soon as he is finished using this young woman, he will kill her, too. Help us save her life."

The café owner looked uncertain. "But she tell me that he is friend."

"I believe she was trying to protect you, ma'am," Marlow put in. "She knew if she asked for your help, you would be in danger."

"Perdóname, mi Madre." She paled and crossed herself. "Her name Agraciana Flores. She come from my husband's village."

"There was a PROFEPA agent named Flores assigned to the Tacal case," Marlow said.

"Sí," the woman said, nodding eagerly. "Agraciana work for people protect islands."

"Did she tell you anything about the man she was with, or where they were going?" Genaro asked.

"No, señor. She have *café* with him, and then drive away together." The woman wrapped her arms around her waist.

"Which direction did they go?" Marlow prompted.

"She take bay road." She gestured in the general direction, and then gave Genaro a stricken look. "Agraciana have beach house there. Maybe he make her take him there."

"We'll call Chief Carasegas and let him know to check on Ms. Flores," Genaro lied. "Thank you for helping us. Marlow, would you show the lady out?"

After the café owner left, Genaro returned to the command center to make several calls, where Marlow joined him a short time later.

"I've put a man on the café to watch for Flores and Riordan," the team leader said. "But they're probably hunkering down at her beach house."

"I doubt Riordan would be that stupid. Flores called her office this morning to request two days off." He paused as one of the techs handed him a sheaf of fax copies of the PROFEPA agent's government personnel file and several police reports.

"She told her supervisor her mother was ill."

Marlow's brows rose. "So she is helping him."

"Given that Flores's mother disappeared ten years ago, and was declared dead by her husband in 2008, that is a reasonable assumption."

Genaro went to one of the computer stations. "I want to see this police report." He handed a fax to the tech, who performed a search and opened the file on the screen, translating the page into English.

Marlow scanned the report. "Looks like she disappeared on her way home from work."

Genaro tapped an address on the screen. "Display this on a map."

The tech brought up a satellite image of the city with one small red balloon.

Marlow glanced at Genaro. "Her mother was working at Energúmeno's compound when she disappeared."

Genaro thought of the old women he had seen in the gardens. "Or she never left."

Charlie silently followed Samuel back to the villa, but as soon as they were inside she stopped and focused. The islanders had spread out in all different directions, their emotions muted, their thoughts intense. "Everything is working now. I can feel all of them out there."

"I think we need a cup of tea." He led her into the kitchen. "Can you hear what they're thinking?"

"Loud and clear, now that Colotl has dispensed with his shields." She pressed her fingertips to her temples. "Only problem is, they're all thinking in that odd language. I can't understand a word of it."

"I'm not a linguist, but what I heard sounded almost archaic," he said as he took out a pan and filled it with water. "If it is an obscure or dead language, this master Tlemi spoke of probably used it as a control measure."

"How would it control them?" She joined him at the stove.

"If any of them escaped his custody, speaking an uncommon language assured they wouldn't be able to easily communicate with outsiders." He glanced at her. "How old were you when you were adopted?"

"I don't know," she admitted. "The Marenas thought I was about five or six."

"I meant your first family."

"No idea. Probably a baby." Charlie went over to the fridge. "Do you want some fruit?"

"No, thank you." He took out two cups and a tin, opening the lid to sniff the contents before spooning some into the cups. "When my parents adopted me, I was about a year old, but I had already learned to speak a few words."

She could imagine what a beautiful baby boy he must have been, and felt a pang of longing. "'Mama' and 'Dada'?"

"My mother told me later that they had no idea what I was saying, but she wrote down in my baby book the words I spoke by how they sounded." He watched her arrange some pineapple slices on a plate. "A few years ago I had the sounds analyzed. It turned out that my cradle language was Chinese."

"Some of the other Takyn mentioned that they spoke odd languages as kids." She sealed the plastic container before returning it to the fridge. "I couldn't speak Spanish when I met the Marenas, and they didn't speak any English, but I understood their thoughts perfectly. I also don't have a problem with any other non–English speaker's thoughts. So why can't I understand the castaways?"

"Perhaps because you've never before been exposed to this particular language." He added hot water from the pan to the cups before he picked them up from the counter. "Why don't we go and talk in the living room?"

"You mean the pit of decadence and depravity?" She grimaced. "All that red makes me nervous."

He seemed surprised. "I thought most women find it romantic."

"Maybe women who don't work in the medical field,"

she said. "All it reminds me of are severe injuries, bio-hazardous material, and blood."

"We should still make use of the room occasionally." He turned his back on the kitchen camera. "If we are going to plan a successful escape, we'll have to keep up appearances." He shifted his eyes up.

That reminded her. "I don't like the idea of your going by yourself to this cave tomorrow night," she said as she followed him to the living room. "We don't know how Segundo is getting his information; they could have an informer among them. And even with Colotl's shields, eventually he will find out about whatever you and the men have planned."

"There will be risks," he agreed. "But, Charlotte, consider the alternative. As much as I would enjoy having a child with you, I will not allow either of us to be bred like animals."

He always came up with something she couldn't argue with, and while he was right, she still felt annoyed. Even the way he remained standing, politely waiting for her to sit down first, got on her nerves.

Deliberately she set the fruit on a table and moved around the room. "Why does someone buy twelve American children of mixed blood, raise them to speak a language no one understands, and then strand them on an island to fend for themselves?"

"He could be attempting to create a gene pool," Samuel said as he sipped his tea. "Or he purchased one that had already been created. Aside from the placement of their tattoos and the racial diversity, the way they interacted with each other gave me the impression they were a unit."

"All but Pici," Charlie pointed out. "She isn't tattooed on the forearm like the other women. She's also younger than the others by at least five years." She idly picked up a red satin pillow and plucked at the corner tassels. "If that's his goal, he's going to need more livestock."

"Seven couples aren't a viable gene pool?" When she

nodded, Samuel asked, "What if every man impregnates every woman and each of their unrelated female offspring?"

"Still not enough. Even if you could convince the couples to play musical beds and breed with the next generation to produce a superhuman population, you have to allow for infertility, stillbirths, genetic anomalies, and diseases," she told him. "Even under ideal circumstances with near-perfect reproduction, you'd have to start with at least two hundred unrelated couples. Otherwise inbreeding is inevitable within a few generations."

Samuel grew thoughtful. "What if he doesn't intend to create a superhuman subspecies?"

She eyed him. "Then what's he going to do with the offspring? Sell them the same way their parents were? Who would want . . ." She stopped as she realized the obvious answer to her own question, and the pillow fell from her hands. "Not GenHance."

"They could be a potential buyer, but to me this operation has all the hallmarks of a long-term investment. Consider our accommodations and our duties." He made a sweeping gesture. "One does not keep livestock pampered in a mansion in order to supply a slaughterhouse."

Samuel was choosing his words too carefully again. "You've figured out why they're here, and you're keeping it from me."

His expression never changed, but a guarded look came into his eyes. "I haven't yet obtained enough facts to make a reasonable hypothesis, Charlotte."

"My ass, you haven't." She came over to him. "I want to know. Now, you can tell me yourself, or I can climb inside your head and stay there until you forget *not* to think about it."

"While you keep your secrets safe from me?" he countered. "Doesn't seem quite fair, does it?"

"What secrets? You know about my job, my ability,

my parents forging my records. When we were chatting online I confided in you about everything. God, I even told you about the men I've dated." Charlie threw up her hands. "What more do you want to know?"

"What happened to you before the Marenas took you in? Who was your first family?" As she began to reply he shook his head. "You've already said that you can't remember, and I know it's not the truth."

All the fight went out of her, and she turned away. "Don't make me go there, Sam. It's not a nice place. I just want to forget about it."

"But you haven't." He came up behind her and put his arms around her. "It's because you've never told anyone."

"I thought about it. The way Aphrodite talked, it sounded like she'd been kicked quite a bit. I thought she might understand. But every time I tried . . ." She hesitated and leaned back against him. "It's always been like a nightmare that I could wake up from and forget for a while. Telling someone else makes it real again."

"Facing it is the only way to get past it," he suggested as he guided her over to the sofa and sat down with her. "It helps to have a friend there when you do."

She rested her forearms on her thighs as she hunched forward. "I was adopted by a couple in California. They were young, beautiful, knew all the right people—like an eighties version of Brad and Angelina—and they had money. Lots of money." She gave him a sideways glance. "Your kind of money."

"It isn't everything, Charlotte," he said gently.

"It was to my parents. You and I probably had very similar childhoods. The big, fancy room filled with toys. The private nanny, the catered birthday parties, the designer clothes, the carefully selected friends." She smiled a little. "For me, it was like being part of a fairy tale. King and queen for parents, me their little princess, all of us living in a castle high up on the hill. It was almost like what they tell us heaven is. Of course, I knew we'd live happily ever after, because that's how my nanny said all fairy tales end."

"Yours didn't," he guessed.

"No." Charlie swallowed against the tightness in her throat and turned toward Samuel. "I didn't understand why my mother was so angry that night; I didn't know what investment scams and fraud were. I didn't even realize my father had strangled her and my nanny that night, just before we left the house. I was six years old, and my daddy was taking me on an adventure. My first." Tears spilled over her lashes. "His last."

Samuel pulled her closer. "That's enough, Charlotte. You don't have to say another word."

"I do. Let me, before I change my mind." Quickly she wiped her eyes and forced herself to go on. "My father drove up to the Golden Gate Bridge and took me on the walkway. When he picked me up and climbed over the railing, I thought he wanted me to see the water. Then he kissed me, and he told me we'd be together forever." She stared at nothing. "He jumped off the bridge with me, Sam."

Samuel muttered something and pulled her onto his lap. She linked her hands behind his neck and pressed her hot face against his cool skin.

"I really don't remember hitting the water, which I know was a blessing. The next thing I knew I was clutching my father's shirt as we floated away in the dark. I couldn't wake him up, and I couldn't swim, so I just held on and cried." She shivered, remembering. "The water was like ice. When we reached the shore my arms and legs were so numb I could barely crawl. Once, I looked back, but my father was gone. The current had taken him away."

He stroked her cheek. "You must have been terrified."

"Enough to hide in the bushes for a day and a half, until I was too hungry to sleep. That's when I heard the first voice in my head, and saw an old woman out walking her poodle. She was tired and annoyed with the dog for peeing on her carpet. I followed her to her house, and when she went inside, I stole some oranges from a tree in her backyard. I crawled behind the lawn mower in her shed to eat them."

"You weren't injured?"

"My back and my head hurt, but after two days I was fine." She sighed. "Just cold. Always cold and hungry."

"How long did you live like that?"

"Probably a couple of weeks. People in that part of the city liked to garden, so I found plenty of fruit and vegetables to steal, and sheds and crawl spaces where I could hide and sleep." She realized that the nausea she normally felt when she thought about her father and the bridge wasn't affecting her now. Samuel had been right; it did feel better to talk about it. "I ran away from everyone who saw me, of course. I didn't understand their thoughts, and I was afraid. I thought they'd know I let my daddy drown, and they'd put me in jail, or take me back to the bridge and throw me off again. Crazy stuff."

"You suffered the unthinkable, honey, and you survived it. That's not crazy at all." He kissed her brow. "What made you decide to stay with your second family?"

"Mama Marena." As always, simply saying her name made a sweet warmth spread through Charlie. "I heard her thoughts as soon as she saw me from the kitchen window. All this love and longing; she thought I was a little lost angel that God had sent to her. When she came out of the house, she had an old quilt in her hands. She sat on the steps and smiled while she waited for me to come to her. When I did, she wrapped me up and carried me inside. She made me warm milk and honey, and sat with me in her rocking chair, singing to me until I fell asleep. I was hers from that day on."

He took her hand in his. "Is she the one who named you Charlotte?"

She smiled. "At first she called me Charlatana, probably out of wishful thinking. When it came time to fill out my papers she got a baby book from the library and looked for an American name that was close to that. Charlotte was the result."

"What does Charlatana mean?"

"Talkative." Her lips twisted. "After Mama found me, I didn't speak or make a sound for months. She assumed I was mute, not that it made a difference to her."

"She sounds like a wonderful woman."

"Mama would say she was nothing special." She looked up at him. "She wasn't beautiful or young, and she'd never gone to school. To make a few bucks every week she sold cookies and cakes to the local bodegas. But she saved my life and my soul, Sam. She took care of me, and cherished me, and protected me until the day she died. I'll never know love like that again."

A strange look came over his face. "Are you so sure of that?"

"I read minds, and I know people rarely love anyone but themselves," she assured him. "They say the words to their husbands and wives while thinking about how much they hate them. They tell their kids they love them while they seethe with resentment over how much work they are, or how young they are, or all the advantages they have. You know what most people really love? Things that make them feel good, or help them stop thinking about how miserable they are. Alcohol. Drugs. Sex. Food."

"You make me feel good, Charlotte." He cupped her chin to tip her face up so that she felt his words on her lips. "Does that make it all right to love you?"

Chapter 15

"It's just sex, Sam." Charlie started to climb out of his lap, but he closed his arms around her to hold her there. "Physical attraction and mutual pleasure are powerful things, and they can seem like love, but they're not."

"As spectacular as it is, I wasn't referring to the sex. I mean *you*, the woman you are, the soul inside this beautiful body." He studied the stubborn set of her jaw. "You don't accept that."

"I think we're in a desperate situation, possibly one that will kill us, and you need hope." She glanced down at his arms. "I'm all you've got to hang on to right now. It doesn't bother me. I'm holding on to you, too."

"For a woman who can know anyone's thoughts and emotions, sometimes you can be remarkably imperceptive." He brought her hand up to his face. "Read me now."

"No point." The problem with her ability was that it pierced through every lie, even the ones people told themselves. If Samuel had to cope with their situation by convincing himself that he had feelings for her, she wouldn't take that away. She patted his cheek. "I'm happy with our being friends with benefits."

"Naturally. You believe I love only money and sex, and you're determined not to let anyone hurt you again." He turned his head and kissed her palm. "If you are correct in your assessment, you should find no surprises in my head. Only you, naked, atop large stacks of thousand-dollar bills."

Maybe it would be best to bring him back to reality, Charlie thought as she slid her hand down to the side of his throat and covered the strong pulse there with her palm. "Okay. Think about me."

Samuel kept his eyes open and locked on hers as she let the barriers drop and reached out to him. Reading someone she was touching at the same time always quickly established a connection, but this time the thought stream came over her, wide and shocking clear and relentless, as if she'd stepped into a waterfall.

Charlotte so bright and quick but so lonely like me waited so long to find us never knew how it would be so complete see me as I am not as I appear we could be so much together I want that I want Charlotte see her shine in the night every night my treasure in the dark

As Samuel's thoughts flooded her, Charlie felt the heat of his passion entwined with something stronger, an emotion she hadn't felt since the day Mama had wrapped her in that old soft quilt. It encircled her and wove through her, that silvery white light, so pure and perfect that it took her breath away. The other sensation it brought was one much older than Mama or that night on the bridge, one she had consciously forgotten on one level but that still lingered in some tiny corner of herself, waiting to be needed again.

The connection between them felt stronger than before, effortless and consuming, and while she no longer needed to touch him to maintain the link, her hands glided around his neck. The steady pulse beneath his skin quickened as she trailed her fingertips along the cords and muscles, following them to his broad shoulders. There was so much of him in her head that she could feel the heavy, rough delight he experienced as he became aroused, the way his blood heated and his muscles coiled while he fought back the urge to respond.

"You want me," she whispered against his cheek.

"With every breath I take." Desperation tinged his thoughts as he caught her hands. "Charlotte, if you keep"—he groaned as she brought his hands to her lips before she pressed them to her breasts—"doing this, we won't be discussing anything."

"You can still use your mouth," she promised as she stripped off her top. Somehow she had gone from cuddling with him to straddling him. A wanton impulse made her shimmy against him, and he responded by squeezing her breasts. From the anxiety that shadowed his thoughts, she knew he worried he was being too rough. "No, it feels good, *mío*. I love the way you touch me."

"Seducing me won't change how I feel about you," he said as he slid his hands down to her waist. "Your body is lovely, and you give more pleasure than I can put into words, but that's not all you are to me, Charlotte."

"It's what we have." She pushed her hips back and forth to rub her crotch against him. "Enjoy it, *mío*."

He pulled her closer. "If I had any pride left, I'd resist your charms and stalk out of here."

"I'll give you a one-minute head start before I chase you down and molest you," she said, smiling. She bent down to touch her lips to his in a lingering kiss as she opened the front of his shorts and slipped her hand inside. "On second thought, no, I won't."

The curl of her fingers around the straining spike of his penis made him shudder, and as she caressed him Charlie watched his eyes. Tiny silver lights, like shards of a mirror, glinted inside the black of his irises, growing brighter with every stroke of her hand. Playing with him made her own sex clench in anticipation, and feeling his desire in her mind fueled her own arousal.

Charlie shifted backward until her feet touched the floor, dragging his shorts over his hips and pulling them down out of her way. When she straightened, his bobbing erection grazed the tip of her breast, and she turned slightly to catch it between the curves of both. She cupped her breasts from the sides and worked them against him, dipping her head to kiss the gleaming dome. As soon as her lips touched the straining head, his mind filled hers with his particular longings.

"You like me to kiss you here." She teased him with a flick of her tongue along the ridge of his glans. "Or maybe you want something more?"

"I want everything you'll give me." He watched her, clenching his teeth as she rubbed her lips back and forth across his cock head. "But more of this particular attention may bring things to a very rapid end."

She smiled against him. "I hope not, *mío*."

As she engulfed him with her mouth, Samuel shuddered, his fists bunching in the cushions beneath him. Charlie sucked lightly, working the flat of her tongue against the tight satin of him, her fingers spreading over his bulging thighs. She closed her eyes as she bobbed her head, sliding her lips down to take more of him, and felt his hands threading through her hair. She drew up, letting him pop out of her mouth and taking a moment to admire the slick bulb before glancing up to see sweat trickling down the sides of his face.

"You don't have to do this," he murmured.

"You like how it looks as much as how it feels." She licked him. "That excites me. So does knowing I have you exactly where I want you."

He offered her a tormented smile. "Then have me, Charlotte."

As Charlie drew him back in, Samuel tried to say something more, but his words dissolved into a low, rumbling purr. He was like some huge predatory feline, sprawled there under her hands, his fingertips kneading her scalp as she sucked him. Being part of a lover's mind had never before tempted Charlie, but now she felt both sides of desire, the bold and wanton brightness of her emotions twining with his darker, primal hungers.

The wet friction and seductive pull of her mouth

made his penis swell even larger, distending the veins beneath his skin and producing creamy pearls of semen that she sipped away. She cupped his testicles as they tightened, sweeping the pad of her thumb over the bulging heat as she took as much of him as she could manage, holding him in her mouth and sealing her lips around his shaft. His hands snarled in her hair, and she heard his purr become a guttural roar as the first pulse jetted out of his cock.

Tasting and teasing him had aroused her more than Charlie realized; when she drank from him it brought her right to the edge. She released him and pressed her cheek against his thigh, her hand slipping down between her own thighs.

Samuel swept her up onto the sofa and pressed her back, pushing her sarong up over her hips before he thrust his hands under her bottom. He brought her up to his mouth, parting her with his tongue to find her clit. He dragged his tongue against it as he thrust two thick fingers into the clenching ellipse of her vagina. His thumb went lower, nudging and then pressing in between the curves of her bottom.

It proved too much for Charlie's self-control. Her hips heaved up as she shattered under his mouth, her body bowing as the wrenching delight put her on the rack and held her shaking and pleading. Samuel rode her through one climax and pushed her to the next, his fingers plunging in and out of her contracting sheath, his tongue working against her clit in a relentless abrasion until the pleasure took her again, hurtling her over the edge into pure bliss.

He moved up over Charlie, taking her in his arms and turning her so that she lay atop him. While her skin cooled, he stroked his hands up and down her back in a soothing motion. Although aftershocks still jittered through her limbs, she couldn't move. She did put up her barriers, slowly, reluctantly.

"You're not in my mind anymore."

"No."

She'd been with enough men to develop a healthy appreciation for sex and all its pleasures, but she'd never read their thoughts in bed. If all men felt the same things Sam had, she'd really been missing out.

Or it's just him, and I'm in real trouble now.

"Being hurt doesn't scare me, you know," she heard herself say. "I don't enjoy pain and suffering, but I know it's unavoidable. What I can't do is give my heart away to anyone who says they love me. The last time I did that, I ended up getting thrown off that goddamn bridge."

His hands stilled on her back. "I'm not your father, Charlotte."

"I know that." She propped herself up on her elbows and looked down at him. "I care about you, Sam, more than I should. You're gorgeous and interesting and kind, and I could fall in love with you so easily. But trust is just as important, and for me that takes a long time. Mama loved me the moment she saw me, and I knew it—I felt it—and still I made her wait a year before I even said one word to her. So if you really want my heart, you're going to have to give me more than just time. You're going to have to earn it."

Samuel took her hand in his. "All right."

Charlie felt that echo of familiarity again, and stared at their joined hands. She could feel the same bewildered emotion coloring his thoughts. "So have you remembered when we met? Was it in a hospital? Emergency room? I was working in D.C. for a while; maybe our paths crossed there."

"I don't think so." He studied the weave of their fingers. "We held hands like this. It was dark. Cold. There was someone there with—"

"—cold hands," she finished his thought, and closed her eyes as his description sent her spiraling into some murky place she had forgotten. "There were needles, too. Monitoring equipment." He'd gone very still. "What is it?"

"Charlotte." His eyes searched her face. "I think we first met in a lab. The place where they changed us."

The Englishman's island appeared deserted, but as Gracie brought the boat to the long, empty floating pier, Drew got the sense that their arrival had not gone unnoticed.

"Where's this guy's boat?" he asked as he stepped off to help her with the mooring lines.

"He keeps it in a cove on the other side of the island." She tested the lines before taking his hand and climbing up onto the pier. Her eyes shifted to three birds circling overhead before she gestured toward the trees. "His house is over here."

Drew tried to hold on to her hand, but Gracie walked away, leaving him to follow. It wasn't until they were following a narrow sandy path through the thick brush and soaring palms that he noticed the steel poles scattered around them. Each had cameras perched atop it on a swivel base, and all of the lenses were moving slowly to follow them.

Drew stopped by one of the devices, and the camera stopped moving. "Gracie, we *are* being watched. Why?"

"The Englishman is obsessed with his birds, so he puts cameras everywhere. They are programmed to track movement." She glanced back at him. "Come, Andrew. If your friends are out here, he'll know."

The lack of expression on her pretty face and the flatness of her voice made him wonder just what was going on in her head.

As she started off again, he called after her, "Are you mad at me because we made love?"

She spun on her heel and strode back to him. "That was private. You will not speak of it to anyone. Ever."

"What do you want me to do?" he demanded. "Act like it never happened?"

"Yes. Please." Her voice broke on the words, and she hurried away.

"Not in a million years, lady." He took off after her, catching up just as Gracie reached the house. His anger faded as he looked up at four stories of what appeared to be a tiered pyramid. "Is this a temple?"

"Yes." She skirted a statue of a reclining primitive figure with a bug-eyed face and an empty bowl in his hands. "Before he came to the islands, the Englishman was an archaeologist. He is an expert on Aztec culture."

"So you gave him his own *pyramid*?" He glanced at the intricate carvings in the stone. "How did you get it here?"

"It's only a replica, Andrew." She moved toward an opening in the center of the lowest level.

He caught her arm before she went inside. "How can he live in something like this? It doesn't even have windows."

"Saves me the annoyance of having to wash them, my boy." A tall, slim man stepped out of the shadowy interior and smiled at Drew. "You'll be Agent Frasier." He extended his arm. "Foster Stanton, at your service."

"Dr. Stanton." He accepted the handshake, which was as guileless as the other man's expression. "This is some place you have here."

"I found myself inspired by the Barceló Karmina Palace hotel. Since that was modeled after a Mayan temple, I felt the Aztecs merited a similar homage." He swept an arm in a theatrical gesture. "Please, I've a lovely tea waiting for us. Do come inside."

Drew couldn't think of anything he wanted to do less than have tea inside the pseudo temple, but Gracie had already disappeared inside, leaving him with the smiling Englishman. Instinctively he scanned the immediate area, his mind reaching out for any copper he could use, but the house and the surrounding grounds seemed completely devoid of it and all other metals.

"If you're a touch claustrophobic, old boy," Stanton said, "we can talk out here."

His polite offer made Drew feel like a paranoid moron. "No, I'm fine."

Stanton showed off his long white teeth. "Then follow me to the best homemade crumpets you'll find this side of Devonshire."

The interior of the structure was a series of high stone corridors illuminated by freestanding halogen lamps fashioned to look like burning torches. Aztec artifacts occupied most of the curved, lighted niches in the walls, but as Drew passed and got a closer look at them, he realized they were too new to be anything but replicas. From the dust patterns in the empty niches it was clear that several had been recently removed.

"Why did you switch from archaeology to bird-watching?" he asked the Englishman.

"I discovered I had an affinity for our feathered friends," Stanton told him. "I wasted much of my youth scrabbling after bits and baubles left behind in forgotten tombs. The only history of any real value is that which we make ourselves."

Drew eyed a tall stone vase from which golden peacock feathers sprouted, and frowned. "How do birds factor into your philosophy?"

"When nearly every other living thing on the Earth became extinct, birds survived by evolving and occupying the skies." The Englishman's voice took on a dreamy softness. "They've become the watchers of time."

"I guess they have." Stanton, Drew decided, had spent too many months behind his binoculars. His attention was diverted as they entered a wide, circular room furnished like the lobby of an exclusive hotel. Gracie stood by a wheeled cart while she filled three delicate porcelain cups with tea from a matching pot. On a low table an assortment of platters held cakes, pastries, and finger sandwiches.

Drew saw another woman walking out of the room: a younger girl dressed in a white blouse and black shirt. Another woman came in a few moments later carrying another plate of fruit. She was older than the first but wore the same garments, as if they were some type of uniform.

"*Gracias, Conchita,*" Stanton said to her. "That will be all."

The woman nodded and left just as silently as the girl had, her movements as slow as if she were walking through water.

"Is that your wife and daughter?" Drew asked.

"God, no. They're part of my staff." Stanton accepted a cup from Gracie and sat down in one of the tapestry-covered chairs. "You really must try the crumpets. They're obscenely appetizing."

When Gracie tried to give him a cup of tea, Drew shook his head. "I thought you were a recluse."

"My studies require a great deal of my time." He sipped from his cup before setting it down. "Surely you don't deny an old man some creature comforts?"

For the first time Drew realized just how young Stanton looked; he couldn't be a day over thirty. "Agent Flores said you've been living in Mexico since the seventies. Did you come here with your parents when you were a kid?"

"Something like that." Stanton sat back. "Do you have any children, Agent Frasier?"

"No, I'm single." Drew glanced at Gracie, who remained waiting by the cart as if she were just another servant. "Dr. Stanton, we came here looking for some Americans who were kidnapped. Have you seen any strange boats in the area?"

"Since my island borders the reserve area around Las Islas Revillagigedo, I don't see many boats at all," Stanton said. "However, my employer recently took a tour of the islands and mentioned seeing a boat docked at one of the islands."

"Which one?" Drew asked.

"He didn't say, now that I think about it. But never fear." The Englishman smiled. "He'll be joining us tonight, and you can ask him yourself."

"I'm sorry, but I can't wait that long." Drew turned to

Gracie. "If we leave now, we should be able to check all of the islands."

"You can't leave before dinner. Conchita," Stanton called out, and when the older woman appeared, he asked, "What are you preparing for the evening meal?"

"Camarones rancheros, señor," the woman said, staring at the floor.

"Ah, shrimp sautéed with vegetables and spices—one of her finest dishes," Stanton said, sounding pleased, and shooed away the servant. "Quite worth the wait, Agent Frasier, I assure you."

As Conchita passed Drew, he saw a mark on the side of her neck: a light brownish yellow bruise surrounding two small round scabs. "Maybe another time, thanks. Agent Flores?"

Gracie gave Stanton a strange look. "We could return in a few hours to have dinner with you."

"Given the amount of agitation Agent Frasier is trying so valiantly to conceal, I think that highly unlikely, my dear. We will have to resort to plan B." The Englishman rose and nodded past Drew, who turned to see two men armed with steel machetes.

Drew finally understood the missing artifacts, and why he couldn't sense any copper around him. Before they arrived, Stanton must have removed everything Drew might use with his ability.

"Why the elaborate charade?" he asked the Englishman. "You could have had her kill me on the boat."

Gracie started to say something, and then shook her head before she spoke to Stanton in rapid Spanish.

"Our dear Agraciana is many things, Mr. Riordan, but she's not an assassin," Stanton told him. "As it happens, she has gone to great lengths to see to it that you live a very long and extremely pleasant life."

"Is that what your boss told you?" Drew demanded. "Genaro lied. He only wants revenge, and my DNA. He'll cut my throat the minute you turn me over to him, and then kill the rest of you to cover his tracks."

"Fortunately for all of us we don't work for Jonah Genaro. But we'll discuss that later, over dinner." Stanton nodded to the men who flanked Drew. "Take him downstairs and lock him up."

The gleam of the sharp machete blades and the confident grip of the hands holding them convinced Drew that making a break for it was not an option. That left Gracie, who accompanied them to a stairwell in the outer corridor.

"Whatever fairy tale Stanton told you is bullshit," he said as she climbed down the steps in front of him. "I know too much about your operation now. He can't afford to let me live."

Gracie didn't reply, and once they reached the bottom of the stairs she switched on a light, illuminating a damp stone cellar and a row of human-size cages.

"Nice," Drew said, eyeing some irregular dark stains on the stone floors inside the steel cages. From them he sensed minute traces of copper mixed with another metal, and guessed they were blood. "What's next on the agenda? Interrogation? A beating? Both?"

Gracie unlocked the center cage and held the barred door open. "Inside. Now."

He moved into the cell, watching as she locked him in and spoke to the guards, who retreated back upstairs. "Does *Papi* know you use his boat to do Stanton's dirty work, or do you lie to him, too?"

"My father knows." She turned her back on him. "If you cooperate, you will not be hurt."

"Too late for that." He paced around the small space, trailing his fingers across the bars. "I appreciate the meaningless sex, though. Every guy should have one last decent bang before he's executed and cut up for spare parts. Is there a bonus involved, or was fucking me expected as part of services rendered?"

Drew expected Gracie to shout, or laugh at him, or leave him to rot. Instead she came over to his cage, gripping the bars as she pressed her brow against them; her eyes closed.

"I was six years old when they took my mother," she said, her voice barely above a whisper. "She went to work one morning and I never saw her again. When I was old enough to be useful, Stanton came to see *Papi*. He showed him pictures of Mama. She was older, but we recognized her. She was taking care of some American children. He said as long as we did what we were told, Mama would be safe." She opened her eyes. "I did not marry Eduardo. I went away to school, and earned my degree, and took a job in the city."

His anger wavered. "So they forced you to become a civil servant and protect the environment. Any particular reason why?"

"Stanton promised me all I would have to do was protect the islands and the other children." Her hands slipped down the bars. "As soon as you told me what you were, I had no choice. No one can lie to our master. He looks into our minds. He knows everything the children think."

"What children are you talking about?"

"You. Your friends. The others like you." Slowly she pulled up her sleeve and turned her forearm over, using her nails to dig into and then peel away a layer of flesh-colored latex. Beneath it was an old tattoo of a stylized dolphin. "And me."

Chapter 16

"You've been at this all day," Samuel said from the doorway of the treatment room. "You should stop for the night and go to bed."

"While you run off by yourself to meet the boys at the mystery cave?" Charlotte placed some rolled bandages on a shelf according to size. "Yeah, I should sleep like a baby."

"I won't be long." He noticed the towels she had folded and placed on the counter next to an instrument tray. "What *are* you doing in here?"

"There are eleven, possibly twelve, pregnant women on this island, Sam. Any or all of them could require medical treatment at any moment." She closed the cabinet. "Since I'm the only one who can do that, I have to be ready."

She had been on edge ever since last night, when he had suggested their first meeting had been at the lab where as infants they had been genetically altered. Samuel knew the shared memories had disturbed her, but when he'd tried to discuss them, she'd told him she was too tired. When he'd woken up to a half-empty bed, he'd found her using the lab equipment in the treatment room.

Now he glanced at the slides and vials she had placed in a rack beside the microscope. Each was stained dark red. "You've been testing blood."

"I took a sample from each of the bags." She picked

up a clipboard. "All of it is human, disease-free, and type O negative."

His brows rose. "We all share the same blood type?"

"Don't worry; that's all we have in common." She gestured toward a complicated-looking piece of equipment. "That uses microfluidics and nanotechnology to pull DNA from a blood sample and type the sequences. None of us are related."

"Us?"

"I drew some blood samples from you the first night we were here," she admitted. "After what we remembered last night, I'm very glad that I did."

Now he understood why she had been so distant. "You thought we might be siblings. Charlotte, we look nothing alike."

She shrugged. "Brothers and sisters don't always resemble one another, and considering we're both larger than average, I had to be sure."

"Do you feel better now that you know?"

"Not really." She tossed the clipboard on the counter and headed for the door. "Do you want to eat before you leave? I can throw together a salad or something."

"I'm not hungry." He moved into her path. "What else is bothering you?"

"Nothing." She came up short. "Do you mind?"

"I won't leave you alone like this," he told her. "I'll skip going to the cave and instead follow you around the villa and harass you unmercifully for the remainder of the night."

"Of course you will. I had to get stuck on Pregnancy Island with the only man in the world who wants to talk about my feelings." She shoved him aside and stalked down the hall to the master suite.

Samuel followed her, and watched from the doorway as she began tearing apart the bed. "Am I sleeping on the couch?"

She ignored him as she tossed aside the coverlet and

sheets. When he came over to her, she glared at him. "Will you just stop? Please?"

"Let me help you." He removed the fitted sheet to reveal the bloodstained mattress.

Charlotte's expression changed, and she climbed onto the mattress, stretching out in the center and looking down at one particular stain. She sat up quickly. "That son of a bitch." She stood up, walking off the mattress.

Samuel glanced at the stain, which was located halfway down the left side of the mattress. He could touch it and discover exactly whose it was and how it had gotten there, but Charlotte appeared to already know. He went to stand beside her at the glass wall, where she was staring out into the night.

"I always check myself twice a week," she said in a hollow voice. "I forgot until this morning, and when I felt for the strings they weren't there. So I ran an ultrasound on myself, and my uterus was empty. It's gone. Under the circumstances I should have expected it, but things have been so insane that I didn't think."

"I'm sorry, but what's gone?"

"My IUD." She gave him an ironic look. "They must have removed it here while I was unconscious. That's my blood on the left side of the mattress."

Samuel slipped his arm around her waist, and after a moment she rested her head against his shoulder. "How much time do we have before you could conceive?"

"None. It's not like the pill," she added. "Once it's out, I'm unprotected."

"So you could be pregnant now."

"If I am, I won't test positive for a couple more days. And if we keep having sex . . ." She shook her head.

Samuel knew beneath the anger she was frightened, enough that she might consider taking desperate measures. "Honey, listen to me. If you discover that you are carrying my child, I want to know. Before you decide to do anything about it, please talk to me."

She looked puzzled for a moment, and then her expression filled with disgust. "My God. You think I'd abort our baby without telling you? What kind of woman do you think I am?"

The tightness in his chest eased. "I didn't mean—"

"No one has the right to force us to have a child," she snapped. "By doing this they've violated both of us. But if there is going to be a baby, Sam—and there probably will be—then it belongs to us, not them. We have the responsibility, and we decide what to do about it, together."

He didn't mean to say it, but the words spilled from him. "I want our child to live."

"So do I." She gave him a tired smile. "Now go talk to the friendly natives, and find a way to get us the hell off this island."

Drew sat in one corner of the cage and watched a beetle creeping down one of the bars. Dusty threads from an old spider's web clung to its legs and wound around its dark green carapace, hampering its movements. He reached out as it slipped and caught it in the palm of his hand.

"Nothing to eat down here, pal," he said, and he gently freed it from the webbing. "Not yet, anyway."

With no windows, the only light in the room came from the single bulb hanging overhead, but Drew's Takyn abilities included an acute sense of night and day, and told him the sun would be setting in a few minutes. His imagination kept bouncing between two images: the dolphin tattooed on Gracie's forearm, and the bruised wounds on Conchita's neck.

Dinnertime.

To build even a small replica of an Aztec temple required serious money, as did collecting artifacts made from pure gold and kidnapping Americans right off the street. Gracie had called the mystery man "the master," and claimed he could read her mind. It all added up to one big, ugly reality that Drew wasn't sure he wanted to face.

"If you see Samuel, tell him I'm sorry I screwed up," he told the beetle as he set it on the floor. "But don't mention it was because of a girl. That'll make me look like a real chump."

"Andrew, it's time."

He looked up to see Gracie unlocking the door to his cage. Her face appeared pale and drawn, but there were no marks on her neck. But then, why did he care if there were? "For what?"

"The master is here." She opened the door. "He wishes to see you."

He eyed the two armed men standing behind her. "And if I refuse?"

"Then they will hit you and drag you upstairs," she said flatly.

He stood and stepped out, recoiling a little as she took hold of his arm. "I'm not going to make a run for it," he lied.

"The master would never let you escape." She pressed her forearm against his and curled her fingers over his palm, and that was when he felt the length of the blade under her sleeve, and the tingle that told him it was made of solid copper. "You must accept this if you want to live."

Drew moved closer, using his body to hide her arm from the guards. "So it's do or die, huh?"

"You will have only one chance to do the right thing." She fiddled with her hair, dropping her hand long enough to slip the copper dagger from her sleeve to his before she moved ahead of him. "I hope you will."

Drew dropped his arm to his side as he used his ability to reshape the copper blade into a cuff of metal wrapped around his wrist. The leather-and-wood hilt he slipped into his pocket as they made their way into a wide, dark room lit by burning torches.

Stanton had installed a shallow indoor pool in the

center of the room and edged it with a deck of tiny, brightly colored tiles that formed an intricate mosaic of a flowering garden. Reflected on the surface of the pool was a wall made up of curved, shallow recesses. Only a dozen or so were illuminated by built-in lights, but those held small, primitive ceramic statues of male and female figures, each with the head of an animal.

Drew saw Stanton behind a sheer curtain at the other end of the pool, where he was handing an ornate goblet to a large, shadowy figure sitting on an odd-looking bench. The Englishman spoke in a low voice to the shadow before he emerged and dismissed the guards.

"Mr. Riordan." Stanton offered him a chilly smile. "Our most gracious master has decided to forgive you for your transgressions against him, and will permit you to rejoin your brothers and sisters. From this day he expects you to serve him with the love and the loyalty of a devoted son."

"He does." Drew glanced at the curtain. "Maybe you should tell him that I'm an only child, I already have a terrific father, and . . . oh, yeah. I don't serve bloodsucking monsters."

Stanton scowled, but before he could speak, a deep, rasping laugh echoed around the room.

"This one has a bold heart," the laughing voice said in heavily accented English. The figure lumbered to his feet, sweeping aside the curtain with a flick of his hand. "Come closer, boy. See what the beautiful path makes of a god."

At first Drew thought the flickering of the torches made the peculiar patterns of light and shadow on the towering body approaching him. The man appeared to have painted his skin white and black, and bedecked himself with so much heavy jewelry that his movements sounded metallic. Then Drew saw that his skin wasn't painted, and the gold on his body wasn't jewelry.

The gold *was* his body.

What might have once been human stood nearly

seven feet tall and wore an open white linen robe over a
black loincloth. His legs and arms were partly covered in
pale, dead-looking flesh that had turned black around
the rough gold that formed his joints and most of his
muscle. From collarbones to waist no skin was visible;
his torso appeared to be solid metal. Gold also slashed
across his face, covering one eye and bisecting his nose
and one corner of his mouth. The hair growing from his
scalp fell around his ghastly face in long, two-toned
strands that were black hair at the roots and then became thin gold wire.

Drew expected to smell decay from the exposed
dead tissue, but the only scent that came from the master was hot and acrid, the way metal smelled when it
overheated.

Suddenly the copper Gracie had slipped him felt too
tight around his wrist. "How did this happen to you?"

"Not easily." The bottom half of the master's ravaged
face split to show two rows of golden teeth. "You are not
afraid? Most men cower when they look upon me."

"I can cringe and whimper with the best of them,"
Drew said, "but I'm more interested in finding out
what's happened to my friends. Did you abduct them?
Are they here?"

"Mr. Taske and Ms. Marena have joined the master's
other children," Stanton said. "We've seen to it that they
now have a very happy and comfortable life together.
Don't you agree, Agraciana?"

"Yes." Gracie, who stood pale and silent beside Drew,
looked at the floor. "The master is very good to us."

"So good he has to kidnap people to get them to join
the family?" Drew looked into the golden eye of the living statue. "What's really going on? Are you keeping
them somewhere so you can feed on their blood? Is that
how you're able to live in this condition?"

The master laughed again. "I am a god, boy. When
Cortés realized he could not end my life, he had his men
dig deep beneath the temple, and there put me in the

ground. Five hundred years I lay trapped in the earth, waiting for my children to come for me. But I was forgotten."

"I found him under a temple some workers uncovered in Mexico City," Stanton said, his voice filled with pride. "It was my blood that brought the master back to life."

Drew had never been much of a history buff, but even he remembered the name Cortés. "So you were an Aztec."

Gracie drew in a quick breath, and the master's smile faded.

"This is the last king of the Aztecs, Mr. Riordan." Stanton gave Drew a pitying look. "This is Motecuhzoma."

"That was the past," the master said, making a dismissive gesture. "Now I am Energúmeno, returned to life and restored to my people. I have found my children, and saved them from the dogs who would butcher them. With my protection and care they will be safe, and in return, they will give me back my House of Eagles."

"The Eagles were once the king's warriors," Stanton explained. "They devoted their lives to battle in his name."

Drew's stomach turned. "Harvesting their DNA to make your Eagle soldiers is a waste of time. My ex-boss has been trying to do the same thing for years, and he still isn't able to make it work."

"We're not cutting them up the way Mr. Genaro does, Mr. Riordan," Stanton said. "We're allowing them to reproduce naturally. This guarantees that their offspring will inherit their unique attributes."

Drew's jaw dropped. "Are you saying that you're *breeding* them? Like farm animals?"

The Englishman shrugged. "In a few weeks the first child will be born, at which time it will be brought to the master to be trained as its parents were. As soon as the rest of the women give birth, we will take their children, switch their partners, and begin again. Within fifty years we will rebuild the House of Eagles with an army of superhuman warriors, ready to fight."

"To fight for what?"

"My kingdom," Energúmeno said.

"Our warriors will take back the land stolen by Cortés and those who came after him," Stanton said. "When Mexico has been purged of outsiders and interlopers, then he who was Motecuhzoma will resume his rule. Your sons and daughters will be among those who restore our king to his throne, Mr. Riordan. They will change history."

Digging up the rotting Aztec vampire had probably driven Stanton crazy, Drew decided, and abandoned the idea of reasoning with him. "Look, Your Majesty," he said to Energúmeno, "I'm sorry about what was done to you. No one should be made to suffer. . . ." He gestured toward the vampire's grotesque body. "But this happened hundreds of years ago, and the men who invaded your kingdom are all dead. The world has changed and moved on. We're civilized now. No one goes around conquering other countries."

"Indeed." Energúmeno seemed amused. "I have been watching man since I was set free, and it seems that very little has changed since my first rule. You have better weapons and larger armies, but you still battle over land and power. You invade distant lands and kill those who oppose you. I have watched these wars being fought on your television. CNN."

Drew felt frustrated. "It's more complicated than that."

"No, boy. When it comes to war, it is always very simple. What you take belongs to you." He made a sweeping gesture. "This land and its people are mine."

"No matter who you were, the Mexican government won't hand their country over to you," Drew warned. "They have their own military, and they can call on the American government for help. Your 'children' may have powerful abilities, but they're no match for the kind of weaponry used today. Don't start a war you can never win."

"We've already begun, and we are winning," Stanton said smugly. "The master has brought all of the major drug traffickers in Mexico under his control, and is using them to eliminate their smaller competitors and take over key territories. Doubtless you've seen the news reports about how vicious the street fighting has become over the last few years. The effectiveness of our campaign has convinced authorities on both sides of the border to virtually abandon these regions. Once the police and the foreigners retreat, our patrols see to it that they don't return."

"You can live the life of a prince, boy," Energúmeno said. "Or I can feed on you until your veins run dry. How will it be?"

The thought of Mexico being gradually turned back into the Aztec empire seemed as improbable as America handing its states back to the British. But an hour ago Drew would never have believed anyone, human or otherwise, could survive being buried alive for five centuries. Stanton couldn't pull off this war on his own; without Energúmeno, he would be powerless. And while Drew had never used his talent to kill, he knew he couldn't permit the vampire to force the Takyn to breed his new army.

"Answer the master," the Englishman snapped.

The dark kyn are difficult, but not impossible, to destroy, Matthias had once told him. *Some of the old texts claim that a dark metal is poisonous to them, and that complete decapitation will kill them.*

"I wouldn't mind being treated like a prince." The copper band around Drew's wrist grew warm as he used his ability to fold it over and over, increasing the metal's density as much as he could before stretching it out into a razor-edged, foot-long blade. "Do I get to pick out my own princess?"

Gracie turned and slapped his face, at the same time giving him a desperate look. He nodded slightly and let her shove him away from her. As he pretended to stumble toward Energúmeno, the copper blade tore through his sleeve before whirling across the space between them.

The Aztec shouted as he threw up his arm and the blade buried itself in a section of decaying flesh. Yellow-streaked blood poured from the wound as Drew pulled the blade back and brought it around, this time sending it toward the vampire's neck.

As Stanton shouted and lunged at Drew, Energúmeno moved in a blur of motion, seizing Gracie and using her body as a shield for his own.

"Drop the blade." Golden knuckles bulged as the vampire clamped his hand over Gracie's mouth. "Or I will tear off her head."

Drew knew that if he didn't act now, he would probably never get another chance. He also knew he wasn't fast enough to take off Energúmeno's head before the vampire did the same to Gracie.

Logic dictated his choice, but love made it for him.

The copper blade hung motionless for a moment before Drew released it from his control and it fell to the stone floor.

Energúmeno heaved Gracie at Stanton, who ripped the scarf from her throat and stuffed it into her mouth. As he pinned her arms behind her he said, "I will kill them for you, master. You can watch as I drain their blood and feed their carcasses to the fish."

"This wasn't Agraciana's idea," Drew said. "I used my ability and forced her to do it."

Gracie uttered a muffled shriek as the vampire grabbed the front of Drew's shirt, lifting him off his feet and spattering the front of his shirt with the odd-colored blood dripping from his wound.

"This one has value to me," Energúmeno said. "His sons will become my personal guard, and his daughters will serve as my concubines." He glanced at Gracie. "Since he has already chosen his woman, she can bear them for me." He threw Drew to the ground and stepped over him. "Take them to the island."

Samuel slipped out of the villa just after sunset to meet with the other men, and while Charlie was tempted to follow him, she knew she had to keep up an act for the security cameras. So she tidied their bedroom, cleaned and sterilized the test materials she had used in the treatment room, and then moved down to the kitchen to start making a vegetable stew for their evening meal.

Giving herself busywork didn't stop her from brooding over the possibility that she was pregnant. Some women claimed they knew the moment they conceived, but Charlie didn't feel any different from the way she had before they were abducted. It was also the wrong time of month for her to be fertile; her MC always ran like clockwork. According to her mental calendar she wouldn't ovulate for another week.

I should have told him that, she thought as she added some chopped tomato to the pot of boiling water. *But then I wouldn't know how he felt about having a baby with me.*

Children had always been in her plans for the future, but only as part of her professional career. Ob-gyn had always been Charlie's calling, and she had spent all of her spare time studying and acquiring the certifications and licensing she needed to go into practice as a midwife. Seeing patients through the long, uncomfortable months of pregnancy and helping them bring their babies into the world was the kind of work she had wanted to do since the very first infant she had delivered.

Sharing in those small miracles would also make up for the fact that there would never be any of her own.

The experiments performed on Charlie had saddled

her with an unwanted ability and an irreversible genetic taint; she had always considered it a moral imperative to ensure that she remained childless. Being Takyn had also ruled out the possibility of adoption; as long as there were men like Genaro eager to exploit her gift, any child she brought into her home would never be safe.

Making those decisions had been wrenching, but had also given Charlie a sense of security. Now Segundo had stolen that from her.

That was what Samuel could never understand: just how deeply violated Charlie felt. Assuming she was still protected had made becoming Samuel's lover a little easier for her; discovering her IUD had been removed had brought everything crashing down on her head. If she hadn't already conceived, every time they had sex the odds that she would become pregnant would multiply exponentially.

And we will be having sex, she reminded herself viciously. *Every day, or Segundo hands me over to the guards.*

A hissing sound brought her back to the reality of her stew boiling over the sides of the pot. Quickly she turned down the heat and reached for the paper towels. Her hand faltered as fear and despair spread through her thoughts, as black as a cloud of ink in clear water.

She couldn't have a baby on this island. Not against her will. Not knowing that the moment it was born Segundo would take it away from her. Nor could she abort her own baby, or kill it after it was born.

Charlie walked slowly out of the kitchen, blindly following the wordless thought stream in her head. It dragged her feet across the glass floor and into the red living room, where she went to the largest of the windows and opened it.

The sound and smell of the sea came rushing in with the night breeze, cooling her hot face and the stinging tears beading on her lashes. The only place she had ever felt safe was in the water, where nothing mattered but time and tide. The problems that seemed so enormous on land melted away in the sea, which did not care about them or her. To the water she was something to be swept away, filled and taken apart, until her bones sank and buried themselves in the rich silt.

She heard a low, almost monotonous keening sound coming from her throat as she wrapped her arms around her waist and rocked, heel to toe.

Charlie immersed herself in the overwhelming bleakness, allowing it to settle over her so that it dissolved away the ravenous fear that had been tearing at her heart for months. Her hand crept to her belly, and while she didn't understand why it was flat instead of swollen, she could feel the life kicking inside her. She couldn't go on like this; it had to end as it should have, in the darkness of the sea she loved, where she would walk into the waves and swim out into the night, away from the island and everyone on it, until she was too tired to turn around and make it back to shore. . . .

But I hate the water.

It was seeing her hand on the doorknob that wrenched her out of the thought stream, and Charlie staggered back, one hand over her mouth as bile surged in her throat. Her shoulders struck the wall, and she slid down, pressing the heels of her palms to her eyes until the last echo of the other, suicidal mind dissipated.

"Oh, God, no." She struggled to her feet. "Pici."

Chapter 17

The trek to the cave gave Samuel a tour of the island's flora, although he had yet to encounter any animals other than birds. Insects and reptiles were also noticeably absent, as were any signs of previous occupation. While the brush and trees grew in thick profusion, enough so that they regularly hampered his progress, the layer of decaying vegetation on the ground seemed remarkably thin.

He stopped in a gap between some palmetto plants and knelt down, gathering up a handful of the browned, fan-shaped leaves they had shed. Beneath them he found no ants, maggots, or other insects; only bits of twig and crushed shells speckled the brown dirt. On impulse he tossed aside the leaves and dug his fingers into the soil, scooping away a handful. The new layer he exposed appeared comprised of small, light brown leaves and larger chunks of silvery wood, with hardly any soil at all.

Not soil, but mulch.

Samuel kept digging down, finding a layer of gray-white gravel under the mulch. Beneath that his fingers uncovered black powder mixed with dark gray ash.

He brought a pinch of it to his nose. "Charcoal?"

The walls of the small hole he'd dug grew wet and began to collapse in a puddle of dark brown mud. He thrust his hand in one last time, feeling for the next layer and grabbing a handful of it. When he brought his hand out of the tannin-tinted water, he saw that he held a chunk of thin, tightly compacted rotting paper.

The newspaper pages were falling apart into a pulpy sludge, but he could still make out some of the print, and a date: *29 Septiembre 1989.*

Samuel sat down beside the hole, dropping the decomposing newspaper onto the ground as he looked around him again. It took thousands, perhaps millions, of years for the Earth to form an island, usually from the eruption of an underwater volcano or the accumulation of seashells deposited on shallow-water reefs, where they were cemented together by coral.

This island was neither.

"Samuel."

He looked up at Colotl's dark, frowning face, and watched as Tlemi emerged from behind him. Both of the islanders carried bags made of net and filled with folded cloth.

"Why you dig ground?" Tlemi asked. "We wait; we think you not find cave."

"I found something else." He stood and brushed off his hands. "The master made this island, didn't he? It's some kind of artificial habitat."

Tlemi looked helpless as she shook her head, obviously not understanding him.

Colotl's eyes shifted to the hole in the ground, and he muttered as he bent to fill it back in and cover the spot with a palmetto leaf.

"No dig holes in island, Samuel," Tlemi said. She pointed to the ground and then pinched her nose as she grimaced. "Bring bad smell, make us sick."

He turned to Colotl and made a broad gesture. "The whole island"—he pointed to the covered hole—"is like this?"

Colotl hesitated, and then nodded.

The implications made his stomach turn. "Christ."

Tlemi touched his arm. "We go to cave, talk safe there."

He nodded and followed the islanders through the

brush until they reached a densely wooded thicket of
pine. In the center of it a twenty-foot-tall, grass- and
vine-covered mound rose, and it looked impenetrable
until Colotl took hold of a section of dead vines that
turned out to be woven over a bamboo frame. Behind it
a narrow opening led into the mound.

Samuel saw flickering light and stepped inside. The
gap was so narrow he had to turn sideways to fit through,
but after several feet it opened out into a wide area of
rough stone surrounding a bubbling spring.

The water here was clear and smelled sweet. Samuel
nodded to the other men standing around it as he knelt
down and looked at his reflection. Beneath the surface a
series of white PVC pipes fed streams of fast-moving
water into the pool.

None of it made any sense to him. "Why did the master make this cave?"

"Liniz, Colotl make," Tlemi said as she took a napkin
from her bag. "Clean water to drink."

She opened the napkin, which had been embroidered
with an outline of the island, inside which were a dozen
circles around specific symbols. The circle representing
the cave had three wavy lines inside it; others held different geometric shapes.

Tlemi pointed to the wavy lines. "Water." She moved
her fingertip to the others. "Food, cloth, blade, club, arrow, spear. We make, hide. Save for leave island."

Samuel tapped the symbol she had identified as
"blade." "How many of these did you hide here?"

"I not know number words. Every moon make two.
Now have this many." She held up all her fingers, curled
them over, and extended five on one hand and one on
the other.

Sixteen blades would arm everyone on the island, but
they wouldn't be enough to overcome Segundo's guns.
"How many of the other weapons did you make?"

One of the men said something to Colotl, who went
over to speak in a low voice to him.

"Same as blades. Make two, every moon." She took out another napkin and opened it to show the island embroidered again, but this time with a network of lines that indicated the topographical features. At three points around the island, stitched lines radiated out, ending in small crescents.

"Segundo boats." Tlemi pointed to the crescent shapes, and then traced the stitched lines over to the outer edge of the island. "Come this way." She tapped a ridge of lines on the island parallel to the approach. "Wait, watch here. Segundo come, use arrow, fire." She made an arc with her finger from the ridge to the crescent.

Samuel shook his head. "We can't burn the boat; we'll need it to get everyone off the island."

Colotl rejoined them. "Samuel." He turned and spoke quickly to Tlemi, who argued with him before heaving a sigh.

"Liniz, Ihiyo worry." She touched her lips. "You open mouth, show teeth."

"The men want to look at my teeth?" he asked, just to be sure. When she nodded, he stepped forward into the light, turning to Colotl as he opened his mouth.

The islander bent his head to look inside, and then gestured for Liniz and Ihiyo, who came over and did the same before Ihiyo muttered something.

Colotl drew the blade from his belt, but instead of attacking Samuel he slashed it across his palm and held the bleeding wound up in front of Ihiyo's face.

Samuel held still. "What is he doing, Tlemi?"

"Showing Ihiyo blood not make you change." She gave him a hesitant look. "You no want drink?"

"I'm afraid I don't drink blood." And why would Ihiyo and Liniz think he would?

Before Samuel could ask, scuffling footsteps came from the outer passage. Instantly the men spread out while Colotl pushed Tlemi behind him.

Charlotte emerged into the cave, her hair a wild tangle, her face shiny with sweat. "Thank God." She hurried over to Tlemi. "Where is Pici?"

Her question caused Ihiyo to surge forward, but Colotl caught his arm.

"Pici sleep," Tlemi said.

Charlotte shook her head. "No, she's wide-awake." She turned to Samuel. "Someone has to take me to her, right now."

"Why, Charlotte?"

"My thought stream crossed hers, and I felt everything she was feeling," she said. "Pici is going to kill herself. Tonight."

As soon as Charlotte uttered Pici's name, Ihiyo shoved his way past them and ran out of the cave.

"Wait," she called after him, and then turned to Samuel. "She's not inside. She's walking on the beach. I don't know where."

Her voice trembled, and Samuel realized Pici's decision to drown herself must have brought back memories of her adoptive father and the horror he had put her through on the bridge. "We'll find her in time," he promised.

Once they left the cave, Samuel scanned the surrounding area. Even if they all scattered, the island was too large for them to search every inch of shoreline. "Charlotte, did she think of a particular place when she left the house? A favorite swimming spot, or a cove, or something?"

She shook her head. "She just kept walking and looking at the water." Her eyes shifted up. "She could see the moon, but that doesn't help." She closed her eyes and concentrated. "Driftwood. She had to walk around piles of it."

Tlemi spoke quickly to Colotl, and then said to Samuel, "We know where she is." She pointed to the west side of the island. "Colotl will guide us there."

"If you'll hold on to me," Charlotte said as they followed the islanders into the brush, "I can try to reconnect to her."

"No." When she gave Samuel a surprised look, he added, "There are some things you should never have to feel again, honey, and this is one of them."

She bit her lip before she nodded. "It's not her fault. She's so young, and she's afraid for the baby."

Colotl guided them along a barely perceptible trail through several thickets and groves before the vegetation began to thin and Samuel could hear waves washing up on the sand. As they emerged into the open, Samuel saw Ihiyo running ahead of them toward the water. He was shouting Pici's name.

"We're too late," Charlotte whispered.

"No, we're not." Samuel kicked off his shoes and took off after Ihiyo.

Colotl and some of the other men followed him in, but as soon as Samuel dived into the waves he shot ahead of them, cleaving through the rough water with broad, powerful strokes. He passed Ihiyo, who was still shouting, and turned his head from side to side until he spotted her. She was already a hundred yards offshore and swimming steadily away from the island.

Samuel didn't waste his breath trying to call her back, but headed directly for her, crossing the distance between them as quickly as he could. Pici looked back, and when she saw him she stopped swimming and sank beneath the surface.

Water closed over Samuel's head as he submerged to go after her. Moonbeams filtered down around him, silvering the silhouette of an awkward shape. Bubbles poured from Pici's mouth as she rapidly sank toward the dark bottom.

Pressure became a vise around Samuel as he swam down after her, reaching out and snatching the drifting material of her robe and using it to pull her limp body into his arms. He kicked with all his strength, driving both of them rapidly toward the moonlight.

As his head broke the surface he dragged in oxygen, turning Pici so that her back was pressed to his chest.

She didn't move for several moments, and then she coughed out some water and began breathing.

"Be still," he told her when she made a weak attempt to push away his arm. Once he was sure he had a good grip on her, he used his free arm and his legs to propel them back toward the beach.

Colotl met him halfway to the shore and flanked Pici, helping to support her. He spoke sharply to her, but when she didn't respond he looked over her head at Samuel.

"She's all right," he told the islander, nodding at the same time. "Charlotte will look after her."

Ihiyo and the rest of the men converged on them as they reached the shallows, and Pici's distraught partner let out a terrible wail as he saw her condition.

"Tlemi," Samuel called. "Tell him she's alive. Charlotte."

"Here." She pushed her way through the men and placed her hand on Pici's throat. "Let's get her out of the water."

Samuel carried her up onto the sand, where several of the women had spread out some palm fronds. Remembering the recovery position Charlotte had used on Findley, he lowered Pici down gently onto her side.

Charlotte knelt beside her and checked her pulse, then put her ear to the other woman's chest and listened. "Her lungs are clear." She placed her hands on the sides of Pici's distended belly, moving them slowly over the mound until she felt something. "The baby's active."

Ihiyo fell to the sand on the other side of Pici, his face stricken with fear.

"We need to get her warm and dry," Charlotte said to Tlemi. "Whose house is nearest to here?"

"Yours," Tlemi told her, pointing past the driftwood piles.

Colotl helped Ihiyo to his feet while Samuel lifted Pici. The other islanders walked ahead, lighting their path with torches as they made their way down the beach.

Charlotte paced Samuel as she kept an eye on Pici's face. "This is not over yet," she murmured to him. "I need to give her a complete examination and then monitor her for the rest of the night."

"What are your concerns?"

"Aside from the fact that she's suicidal, trauma like this often results in premature delivery." She glanced out at the water. "If she has the baby tonight, by tomorrow morning they'll know, and they'll come to take it."

Samuel looked down at Pici's young, pale face. "Not if we convince them that she drowned herself tonight."

Charlotte stopped in her tracks and closed her eyes briefly before she turned to him. "It's too late."

"They could have given me superstrength." Drew crawled across the bottom of the hold. "Or eyes that shoot laser beams. Yeah, that would be better; I'd just have to wear sunglasses all the time. I look good in shades."

The nylon cords they'd used to bind his wrists and ankles had been knotted so tightly they cut into his flesh with every move he made, but he ignored the discomfort as he inched across the rough planks toward the shape huddled in one corner. Gracie hadn't moved or spoken since the guards had tossed her below with him, but he was pretty sure she was conscious.

"I bet you got a cool ability," he continued, wincing as his knee rammed into a nail head protruding from the deck. "Like you can walk on water, or breathe it, or something like that, right?"

Gracie uttered a muffled sob.

"It's okay," he assured her. "You don't have to tell me anything right now. Unless you're a mermaid." He reached her, and shuffled around until he cradled her body with his. "If my kids are going to have fins or scales, I should know that now. I mean, after I figure a way to get that gag off you."

Gracie made a choking sound as she turned and pressed her face against his chest as she wept.

"Don't cry, sweetheart." He rubbed his cheek against her hair. "I'll get us out of this. I swear."

He kept talking to her, soothing her as best he could until she calmed and quieted. At last she lifted her face, working her jaw until the gag slipped down over her chin.

"Good girl." Drew caught an edge of the scarf still stuffed in her mouth and tugged until it fell to the deck, and Gracie released a long, shuddering breath.

"Better?"

"They're taking us to the island." Her voice rasped out the words.

"Is this the same island where they dumped Samuel and Charlotte?" He felt her nod. "Good."

She stiffened. "No, Andrew, it is not good. It is the end of our freedom. We'll be kept there as prisoners, having children for the master until we die."

"I promise you, that rotting piece of shit can't make us do anything." He pressed his lips to her forehead. "Do you trust me?"

"What do you think?" She hiccuped a laugh. "I gave up my life for you."

"No, I think you decided to take it back." He strained at the cords around his wrists again, and felt them loosen a little. "Samuel Taske is one of the smartest men I know, and I'm no slouch, either. So, tell me about the others like us. How many are on the island with my friends now?"

"Twelve," she said slowly. "They lived with the master until a year ago, but he kept them secluded. I saw them a few times when I went to his estate at night. They are strange."

Drew had been counting on recruiting some of the former orphans. "How strange?"

"They speak an old language—he would not let them learn Spanish—but it is how they walk and move and work. They do everything together, perfectly." She hesitated. "At first I thought they were like machines, but it is more than that. They act as a group, not as individual people."

"Did the master train them to do that?"

"I don't think so. Seeing them always made me think of a herd of wild horses running together, or a pack of wolves hunting down prey." She sighed. "Stanton said that I was supposed to be one of them, but something went wrong with me."

He almost had one hand freed. "There is nothing wrong with you, sweetheart."

"They think I can't do anything like the others. That I am defective." Her voice dropped to a whisper. "But they're wrong." She made a low, keening sound.

Drew went still as he heard a heavy thump on the outside of the hull. "Gracie, what are you doing?"

"*Los delfines* saved me when the men threw me away." As several other thuds sounded, she tucked her head under his chin. "Now they always come when I call them."

He heard what sounded like high-pitched, chattering squeals, and remembered the tat on her forearm. "Are you talking about dolphins?" He felt her nod. "You can communicate with them?"

"I can bring them to me, and make them do what I wish." She lifted her head. "They will ram the boat until it sinks. They will drown Segundo and the others. All I have to do is think it."

"That means I'll die, too."

She shook her head. "I won't let them harm you. They will take us back to shore."

Drew yanked his hand out of the cords and touched her cheek. "We have to get to the island and free the others. Your ability can help them escape."

"The others, they hate me because I am different, and because I have been serving the master," she said slowly. "When they see me, they kill me."

He pulled the cords from his other wrist before he put his arms around her. "That walking corpse forced you to work for him. If they don't understand that, I'll be happy to explain it to them."

"We're almost there." Gracie let out another, lower sound, and the thuds on the hull stopped. "When I'm on land I can't call them, Andrew. It only works when I'm in the water, or on it."

Drew heard the boat's engines throttling down. "Then if things don't go well on the island, we'll go for a swim."

Light shone down on them as the door to the hold opened, and Drew put his hands behind his back, winding the cord between them.

"Stay behind me if you can," he muttered.

The machete twins had been sent down to retrieve them, and, after cutting the cords around their ankles, they hauled them up and gestured for them to go above.

Burning torches held by Segundo and the men illuminated the deck, which had been stripped of everything but the pilot's helm and a giant, ornate chair where Energúmeno sat covered in a cloak of gilded white feathers.

The boat had been docked at a narrow, dark pier. Drew could see a ribbon of glittering sand and the silhouettes of palm trees. A bamboo-covered ridge rose some twenty feet above the shore, mostly covering some kind of dark structure, but there were no signs of light or life.

The vampire rose from his chair and walked to the stern. "My children do not come to greet me. Where are they?"

"We never come at night, master," Stanton said. "They are probably sleeping."

"I feel them near. They do not sleep." Energúmeno climbed out onto the deck and bellowed something in his native language, and then waited as if expecting a response.

Nothing moved or made a sound, but Gracie suddenly pushed Drew down on the deck.

Something hissed over Drew's head, and he saw a
flaming arrow slam into the chest of one guard and
knock him over the side. The night air became streaks of
flame as more arrows appeared, some sizzling out in the
water but others hitting the deck, the side of the boat,
and the vampire's feathered cape.

Drew grabbed Gracie and dragged her behind the
chair, looking around it as Energúmeno tore off the
flaming cloak and threw it in the water.

The pier began to rock wildly, the posts lifting as if
trying to pull themselves out of the water.

"Take off your shoes," he said as he pulled his off, and
shrugged off his jacket.

Another guard fell to the deck, his clothes on fire, his
hands clutching the arrow buried in his neck.

"Time for a swim." Drew pulled Gracie behind the
burning man and jumped over the side with her.

The shock of the cool seawater dissipated almost at
once, and he put his arm around Gracie as he swam away
from the boat. She kept pace with him, only tugging at his
arm to steer him toward shore. Once they reached the
shallows, he planted his feet and looked back to see Stanton using a fire extinguisher to put out the flaming deck,
and the vampire striding across the undulating pier toward the shore, where a group of men carrying spears
and clubs rushed out of the trees and surrounded him.

"You dare attack me?" Energúmeno shouted, outraged. "I am your father."

The biggest of the men stepped forward and said in a
calm voice, "We are your captives, not your children."

"That's Samuel." As Drew slogged the rest of the way
through the water to the beach, he peered at the giant
confronting the vampire. The man sounded like Samuel,
but his beard was gone and so was his slow, limping gait.
"I think."

The vampire gestured all around them. "I created this
paradise so that you might live long and happy lives
here. Is this not what a loving father provides?"

"You imprisoned us here. You've treated us like animals," Samuel countered as he moved closer. "That is not love, but enslavement of the worst kind."

Energúmeno scanned the faces of the other men, and spoke to them in his strange language. A dark-skinned man came to stand beside Samuel, and leveled the spear in his hands at the vampire's chest.

"This ends," Samuel said, "tonight."

Whatever they had planned to do went awry as another man rushed past them, shouting furiously. Before he could club the vampire, Energúmeno moved his hands through the air, and the man was flung backward onto the sand.

Drew started toward the group, but Gracie yanked him back. "You can't go near the master when he's like this."

"Why not?"

Her lower lip trembled as she looked away. "You will see."

The group converged on the vampire, only to be knocked away by some invisible force. Whatever the vampire used, it was fast and effective. In less than a minute Samuel was the only man left standing.

"You are stronger than the others." Energúmeno sounded almost proud. "It will not save you. You are still mortal."

"You were the same, once," Samuel said.

"Perhaps I was. But no more." The vampire made one last gesture, a mere flick of his fingers, and Samuel's shirt seemed to explode, falling in tatters on the sand around him.

The big man staggered back, but somehow remained standing.

"This is what happens when you displease me," Energúmeno said in a louder voice. "I will no longer provide for you and receive nothing in exchange. If you do not wish to starve, then you will give me one child on each night of the full moon. If no child is brought to the

boat, then no food or comforts will be given to you." He
looked at Samuel. "And you . . . you are never to come
into my sight again. If I ever see you again, I will take
you and your woman apart, inch by inch."

Drew watched Energúmeno's regal stride as he returned to the boat, where Stanton started the engines
and headed out to sea. As Samuel bent to check the first
man the vampire had cut down, more figures came hur-
rying out of the shadows. One, a dark-haired woman
carrying a case, dropped on her knees beside Samuel.

"Stay here," Drew told Gracie.

Drew ran to the injured, stopping a few feet away
when two of the men who saw him coming brandished
their clubs. "Samuel."

The big man turned. "Andrew?" His gaze shifted to
the men. "No, he's a friend."

"I got it." Drew quickly tore off his shirt and turned
his back to show them his ink. As the men lowered their
clubs, he joined Samuel. "Sorry. I intended this to be a
rescue, but the bloodsucker shanghaied . . ." His voice
died away as he saw the gashes and cuts on Samuel and
the other men, who looked as if they'd been run through
a meat grinder. He glanced at the unconscious form on
the ground, whose torso had lacerations so deep and
wide Drew could see some of his internal organs. "Jesus
Christ."

"You can pray later. Start helping the wounded up to
the house."

The dark-haired woman, whom Drew recognized
from news photos as Charlotte Marena, reached out to
Taske. "Sam, I need you to help me with Ihiyo, right now,
or he's going bleed to death."

PART FOUR

Burning Dawn

Chapter 18

September 29, 1987
Malibu, California

Emily woke to the sound of a heavy thump, and rubbed her eyes, which were still sticky from crying. Before she called for her nanny, she listened for the voices of the fairies who told her everything, but for once they were silent.

The door to her bedroom opened, but instead of her nanny it was Daddy. The fairies told her how happy he was to see her, and that everything was going to be all right now.

"You're supposed to be asleep, you little minx," her daddy teased as he sat down next to her.

Emily hugged him. "Is Mommy still mad?" The fairies had told her terrible things about her mother, that she was going to hurt Daddy and make Emily go away, but Emily didn't believe them.

"No, baby. She'll never be mad at you again. I promise." Her father picked her up. "How would you like to go for a car ride?"

Daddy's mouth was smiling, but he felt so sad about Mommy that the fairies started crying in Emily's ears. "Why is Mommy sleeping on the floor downstairs?"

He gave her an odd look before he said, "She's very tired."

Daddy carried her out into her nanny's room, where Emily saw her nanny was also sleeping on the floor. "So is Miss Mary," he whispered in her ear.

Emily smelled something bad and wrinkled her nose. "Did Nanny mess in her bed?"

Daddy didn't answer her, and neither did the fairies, who were still crying. He carried her down to the garage, where he put her in the front seat of his car.

Emily, who was never allowed to sit in the front, looked all around her. Daddy's car was beautiful, and Mommy said she must never touch, but she couldn't help stroking the polished wood in front of her. As soon as Daddy got in she snatched her hand back.

"Where are we going, Daddy?"

He smiled at her. "Someplace wonderful."

Daddy drove through the city toward the park where Nanny sometimes took her to play, but he didn't stop there. He went past it toward the big water.

The fairies were sobbing so much that Emily had to press her hands against her ears to talk. "Can't we go back to the park, Daddy? I want to go on the slide."

"You like sliding, don't you?"

She nodded. "It makes me feel like a bird." Sometimes she flapped her arms on the way down, hoping she would rise in the air and soar over her nanny's head, but that never happened.

Daddy drove into a little parking place by the water and stopped the car.

When he came around to open her door and help her out, he said, "I need you to hold my hand now, Emily, and don't let go."

She looked at the big red bridge. "Are we going up there?"

He nodded. "We'll see the whole city."

Emily skipped alongside her father as he led her to the entrance of the walkway. He had to boost her over the little gate, which was locked, and then he jumped over it, pretending to fall and making her laugh.

"Good thing I don't have to do that every day," he joked, dusting off his trousers before he took her hand again. He pointed toward one of the big towers. "Let's walk up there."

Emily would have told him how much she liked going out at night and walking on the bridge, but the fairies wouldn't shut up. They were yelling in her ears so loudly that her head began to ache, and her footsteps dragged.

Daddy noticed. "Don't be afraid, Emily."

"I'm not; it's just . . ." Mommy had said the fairies weren't real, and she didn't want to make her father angry, not when they were having so much fun. She lifted her arms. "Pick me up?"

Her father bent and hoisted her up in his arms, holding her close. "Better?"

She nodded.

Daddy carried her all the way to the tower, and then turned to look back at the city. It was so much prettier at night, with all the lights sparkling like jewels.

"Put your arms around my neck and hold on tight." When she did, her father climbed up on top of the railing.

Emily glanced down at the dark water far below. There was nothing for her father to hold on to, and if he slipped, they would fall. "Daddy."

"It's okay, Emily. We're going to be together now." He kissed her forehead. "Together forever."

The fairies began to scream.

Chapter 19

"All right." Charlotte stripped off her bloody gloves and dropped them in the trash bin beside the table before she moved back and leaned against the wall. "That's all I can do for now."

Samuel had spent the last hour working with her on Ihiyo's internal injuries. They had discovered that while his healing ability could heal minor wounds, it would not repair damaged arteries or organs. "Will he make it?"

"I don't know. I'm not a surgeon." Her head drooped. "Half of what I did I've only read about in books. But he's stable, for now."

"I will watch Ihiyo, Charlotte," Tlemi, who had been assisting her, said. "You should go see to the men."

Samuel caught her arm as she headed for the door. "If you need to monitor him, I can check on the others."

"No, it's okay." She looked at Tlemi, and pointed to the monitor beside the table. "If the numbers on there start changing, yell for me."

Samuel accompanied Charlotte downstairs to the living room, which they had converted into a makeshift infirmary. Nearly all of the islander men had been wounded by the bizarre creature who had brought Drew to the island, but most of the injuries had proved non-life-threatening.

Charlotte went first to Colotl, who despite dozens of wounds remained conscious, and whose chest and arms were swathed in bandages. After checking his pulse and temperature, she lifted one edge of his chest dressing.

"This looks a lot better." Knowing he didn't understand her, she gave him a smile and a nod before meeting Samuel's gaze. "The edges of his wounds are starting to pink up and close."

"They heal like we do," Sam's red-haired friend said as he approached Charlotte and held out his hand. "I didn't get a chance to introduce myself during the bloodbath. I'm Drew Riordan."

"Charlie Marena." She ignored his hand and gave him a hug. "Sorry I snapped at you on the beach. What that thing did freaked me out."

"Same here, sister." He patted her back before drawing away. "If you have everything under control here, I've got to go and get my woman. She's still hiding out down by the beach."

Samuel frowned. "You brought one of the other Takyn with you?"

"No, but I found one when I came here. Long story." He glanced at Charlotte. "I'll be back in a few minutes."

Samuel noticed Liniz's woman, Xochi, giving Drew a troubled look as he left. "Charlotte, did you see the woman on the beach?"

"I saw Drew jump off the boat with someone." She closed her eyes for a moment, and surprise and something like pain flickered across her face. "I can't read her. Ah." She rubbed one of her ears.

"What's wrong?"

"She doesn't think like a human being." She shook her head a little, as if to clear it. "All I get from her are these piercing sounds. Kind of like what bats make, I think."

Xochi appeared beside her. "Agraciana." She pointed in the direction of the beach, and then covered her ears and shook her head.

Charlotte smiled at her. "Honey, I have no idea what you're trying to tell me."

"We'll figure it out when Drew returns." Samuel rested a hand on her shoulder, and then reached out to touch Xochi's arm. As soon as his palm touched her skin, he felt her voice inside his head, this time speaking flawless English.

—must tell Tlemi that the outcast is here so she can warn them about her—

Charlotte flinched under his hand. "Sam, this woman is dangerous. She's some kind of—"

"Outcast, I know. I can hear Xochi's thoughts." He noticed the island woman's astonished face. "And I think she can hear ours as well."

Yes, Samuel. Your mouths are speaking your language, but I hear you in mine. Xochi's thoughts grew frantic. *The woman who came to the island with your friend is not one of us. She serves the master.*

Charlotte's mouth flattened. "What exactly does she do for this bastard?"

"I obeyed him," a cool voice said.

Samuel turned around to see Drew with a petite dark-haired woman. Although her clothes were damp and her hair disordered, she projected an aura of calm disdain.

The islanders all reacted in sync to her presence, the men struggling to get to their feet while the women formed a protective line in front of them.

"What are you doing?" Charlotte demanded.

A flood of voices answered her inside Samuel's head, their replies terse and angry.

"You must be Agraciana," Samuel said.

The woman ignored him and turned to Drew. "We have to leave. If I stay here, they will kill me."

"Samuel." Colotl staggered over to him, grabbing his arm as his legs gave way. Charlotte caught him from the other side, and as soon as she touched him his voice echoed inside Samuel's mind. *Agraciana's voice is her weapon. She can seduce or kill with it. You must silence her before she uses it on us.*

"Oh, for God's sake, shut up." Charlotte's blunt order silenced Colotl and the other thought streams. "Now, look. I don't care what Circe here can do; I didn't spend the last three hours patching you guys up just so you could turn into pigs."

"I agree with my lady. There has been enough violence for one night, my friend." Samuel gestured for the other islanders to stay where they were before he spoke to Agraciana. "Why did you obey the vampire?"

Drew's expression darkened. "Well, for one thing, he's been holding her mother hostage since Gracie was a kid—"

"You don't have to tell them anything." Agraciana folded her arms. "I can defend myself."

Samuel watched as she scanned the room, focusing on a bowl of figs. A strange aqua light flickered in her dark eyes as she uttered a short, high sound, and the bowl shattered, spilling smashed figs onto the table.

Colotl surged forward, fighting Samuel's grip.

"Let him go," Agraciana said. She tilted her head, studying his face, and then laughed. "No, *hermano*, Energúmeno never made me. This is what I am." She yanked up her sleeve, exposing the tattoo of a blue dolphin.

"She's Takyn," Charlotte said.

Colotl muttered something ugly.

"I am the same as him. As all of them." Agraciana flicked her fingers at the islanders. "We were made in pairs. But the boy made for me died, and I had no more value for them. I was discarded, and when I was brought here, I was alone. I had no one to be with me. To help me." To Colotl, she said, "I tried to tell you, but you were a coward, and you blocked me out. So I did what I had to do, so that I could live." She lowered her arm. "Just as you did."

Doubt flickered through Colotl's thoughts, and the rest of the islanders exchanged puzzled looks.

"I can feel all of them now, buzzing back and forth

with their thoughts and emotions," Charlotte murmured. "They can connect with one another as a group."

We never told her or Energúmeno that we could do this, Charlotte, Colotl thought. *It was the only way we could protect ourselves against him.*

"I always knew what you were thinking to one another," Agraciana said. "Even when you blocked my thoughts, I could still hear yours. And I never told the master." She turned and walked out of the room.

"Nice going," Drew said to Colotl. "Just for the record, Gracie was dumped here with me because she tried to help me kill Energúmeno tonight. What we did probably cost her parents, the only people who have ever cared for her, their lives." He took off after her.

"Come on," Charlotte said. "We need to get them settled down before they start bleeding again."

Samuel helped Colotl back to the sofa, where the islander rested for a moment before he spoke to the others in a low voice. When he finished, he held out his hands to Samuel and Charlotte.

Unless she attacks one of us, we will not harm the outcast. Colotl's thoughts were sluggish with exhaustion. *Perhaps you can persuade her not to leave the island. She knows much about the master and his men.*

"How can she leave?" Samuel asked.

"She's thinking of dolphins," Charlotte answered before Colotl could. "She can control them with her voice. Be nice if she could call enough to take all of us back to the mainland."

"We can't run away from this," Samuel told her. "We have to find a way to stop the master before he hurts anyone else."

You are the way. Colotl pointed to his chest, where the gashes the master had inflicted on him had vanished. *He gave you his blood, hoping to change you. You did not turn, but it has made you as strong as he is. That is why he commanded you never to come near him again. He fears you, Samuel.*

"What do you mean, 'he didn't turn'?" Charlotte demanded.

Energúmeno wishes to make more of his kind to serve him and rule over his people, Colotl thought. *So he makes the biggest and the strongest of us who are found drink from a goblet of his own blood. Until now no one has survived this except Samuel. We know he has not turned you because he did not become like the master. He did not grow fangs or try to drink your blood after you were beaten.*

Samuel's stomach surged. "I think that transfusion you gave me after they left us here saved more than my life, Charlotte."

Charlotte released their hands and stalked out.

Without her, Samuel couldn't read Colotl's thoughts, but the islander must have absorbed some of his language, for he said in thick English, "Charlotte afraid. Go, talk."

Drew spotted Gracie sitting on the end of the pier, her hair dancing with the breeze, her legs dangling in the water. As he approached he noticed she had her hands braced on the edge, as if ready to push herself in.

"If you want to go skinny-dipping," he said, "first you have to take off your clothes."

She looked up at him. "You should go back and be with your friend."

"You're prettier than he is." He sat down beside her. Sleek, dark shapes moved beneath the surface of the water, disrupting the waves with almost imperceptible circular wakes. "I'm sorry about what happened in there. You didn't deserve that."

"They are right to despise me for what I've done. I never killed anyone, but I brought men to Energúmeno whom I knew he would torture and murder. I even arranged everything so that Tacal could kidnap your friend. I did whatever he told me to, no matter what it was." Her shoulders hunched. "For that, I should die."

"I worked for Jonah Genaro for a couple of years," he told her, nodding as her eyes widened. "I ran his tech department, and while I never killed anyone personally, some of the work my technicians did resulted in several kidnappings and murders of people like us."

"I don't believe you."

He shrugged. "I can give you all their names, once I add your mother and father to the list."

"You are not to blame for their deaths, if they are dead." Her voice grew dull. "The master doesn't kill right away. He will hurt them, and feed on them, for several days." Tears slid down her cheeks. "He likes to take his time."

"Energúmeno can't do anything to them if he's deceased." Drew turned her to face him. "The others want to make that happen, and while they didn't win the battle tonight, the war is still on. If we stay and help them, I think we can figure out a way to put this bloodsucking bastard back in the ground for good."

"They don't want my help, Andrew. They hate me, and if I stay, they will kill me." Her voice broke. "And I will let them."

"Sweetheart, at this moment, you are the most valuable asset they have." He pressed a finger to her lips. "Not because of this, but this." He tapped her temple. "You've been watching the vampire for years. You know what he wants, how he does things, his strengths, his weaknesses. . . . You're practically an Energúmeno encyclopedia."

A glimmer of hope flashed over her face. "None of the children have seen him more than a few times, and even then he always kept his distance." She gave him a startled look. "I thought it was his disdain for mortals; he truly does believe he is a god. But now I think . . . he may be afraid of them."

"If he wasn't before tonight, he is now." He put his arms around her. "So, can you send the dolphins off into the wet blue yonder?"

She uttered a piercing sound, and the dark shapes changed direction and headed out to sea. "I should go and talk to Samuel."

Drew caught a glimpse of the big man following a tall, lean figure stalking down the beach. "I think maybe that has to wait for now."

Charlie knew she should go upstairs, check on Ihiyo's condition, and tell Tlemi that Colotl was recovering. As the only medical care provider, she had a duty to put her patients first, and she had never let anything interfere with her responsibilities: not her personal life, not her emotions, and certainly not the current bizarre circumstances in which she was being held captive.

She left the villa and walked down to the beach, staring out at the horizon. Clouds had swallowed the moon, and now nothing separated the blackness of the sky from the dark depths of the sea.

What Brent Collins had done had given Charlie an abiding hatred of suicide; she considered it the most selfish act a human being could commit. Yet standing here, knowing now that she might have to live with Samuel for the rest of her life, she understood what drove people to the brink of it.

I was afraid I'd die with him, she thought, wrapping her arms tightly around her waist. *Now I'm afraid I won't.*

She felt Samuel coming toward her, felt it on her skin and in her bones, and her despair deepened. She had loved her father with all the purity and trust of a child, and he had tried to drag her into death with him. Now Samuel had her heart in his hands: Samuel who was handsome and rich and kind, just like Brent. Once more she felt small and dark and ugly, a changeling cast as a princess, entirely dependent on him. If they managed to confront the vampire again, would they escape certain death? Or would he die as her father had, leaving her to crawl away, broken and alone?

"I can't take any more." Her voice sounded harsh against the soft rush and ebb of the waves.

"We've all had a rough night. Tomorrow things won't seem quite so hopeless." He came to stand beside her, but when he tried to put his arm around her she moved out of reach. "Charlotte?"

"As soon as Ihiyo is stable, I'm moving out. Let Segundo come and find me."

He frowned. "You can't. There is nowhere else for you to go."

"It's a big island." She gestured vaguely inland. "I'll live in one of the other houses, or with Pici at the cave."

Samuel came around her, peering down at her face. "Is this because the vampire supposedly gave me his blood? Obviously I'm not going to turn into one or infect you. The texts say—"

"I don't give a damn about the texts."

He straightened. "Then why are you leaving me?"

"I'm not your wife." Shouting that made her feel like a bitch, but she couldn't take another second of his endless kindness and compassion. "I'm not your girlfriend, your lover, or even your occasional roll in the hay. We're strangers who had sex to save me from another beating. I'm grateful, and the sex is good, but it's meaningless. In real life you and I would never have gotten together. So whatever you think we have here is a fantasy. It doesn't exist. I can't leave you, Sam, because I was never *with* you in the first place."

He gave her the once-over. "Are you finished?"

The politeness was icy now, but still firmly in place. She could yell at him until she gave herself laryngitis, Charlie thought, and it wouldn't make a difference.

"Yeah." All the fight went out of her, and she trudged off, determined to get away from him before she made a bigger fool of herself.

A massive arm scooped her off her feet and deposited her over a broad, stiff shoulder. Charlie was so sur-

prised she hung there without struggling as he carried
her off the beach.

"Hey. *Hey.*" She twisted, but his hold simply tightened. "You can't do this."

"Yet I'm doing it."

His voice sounded odd, and when she reached out
with her mind she slammed into an impenetrable wall,
so much like her own mental barriers that it dumb-
founded her. "How did you—"

"I don't know." He edged his way between the rough,
ringed bark of two coconut palms. "I don't care."

Charlie turned her head, trying to see where he was
heading. "Is this supposed to impress me or intimidate
me? Because it's not working. I know you won't hurt me."

Samuel remained silent as he waded through the
brush and stepped out into a small open area, where he
deposited her on her feet.

Charlie eyed the blanket on the ground, on which a
covered basket sat. All around the edges of the grass a
hedge of scarlet hibiscus bloomed. "What is this?"

"My sad attempt at a romantic midnight feast." He
bent down and moved the basket to one side of the
blanket. "I intended to surprise you."

"When did you—" All the air jolted out of her lungs
as Samuel seized her, dropping to his knees and laying
her out on the blanket. Before she could breathe again he
had her pinned under him, his mouth an inch from hers.
"I don't want to make love."

"That's convenient." He reached down and tore her
shirt from collar to hem, shoving the pieces aside before
using his arm to lift her and rub her upper body against
his chest. "Neither do I."

"Sam. Please." Charlie felt her entire body flush with
heat. "We can't do this."

"Why not?" He covered one breast with his hand,
kneading it urgently. "It means nothing, remember?"

He bent his head, not to kiss her but to put his mouth
to her throat, dragging his teeth across her skin before

he laved her with his tongue. The erotic abrasion sent a shock wave of lust through her head, demolishing her resolve and knotting in between her thighs.

When Charlie tried to touch him, he dragged her arms over her head, holding them there with one big hand while he hooked the other in the waistband of her shorts. She heard the button pop and the zipper come apart, and then he was sliding down over her, pushing her legs apart to make room, his breath hot and fast against her sex.

His tongue pushed into her, wet and forceful, going deep, fucking in and out of her before he lashed it over her clit. The heat and ache exploded inside her as she came against his mouth, her hands twisting bunches of the blanket as he penetrated her with his fingers, working them into the liquid contractions of her sheath, pushing her through the delight and into another realm where the world dissolved along with her.

Catching her breath was impossible; he was on top of her a heartbeat later, his big body hard, his muscles bunching as he shifted her legs to his arms and his cock to her folds, pressing in so thick and hard she shuddered, almost sure this time he would split her in half. But her body had been made for a man like him, and it flowered around him, taking him in and clasping him in the most intimate embrace, stroking the impaling shaft, stretching and contracting to grip the broad base.

She felt the weight of his testicles, heavy and tight, caught between the press of their bodies, and a ferocious need came over her. She wanted to feel his semen pumping into her more than she wanted to breathe.

"Look at me." When she did, he drew out with a slow, torturous movement, leaving just the head of his penis tucked between the slick ellipse of her labia. "Now you tell me this isn't real." He released her wrists, cradling her face between his hands as he stroked into her and once more held himself there. "Walk away from this."

The merging of their sexes had her shaking with need;

blindly she struck at him with one fist, wanting the blow to hurt her as much as him. "I can't." She opened her throbbing fingers to press them to his lips. "I can't give you what you want. I can't love you if you're going to leave me."

"Then be with me, Charlotte." He kissed her fingers, her palm, her wrist. "Be with me and love me, because I will never leave you."

She felt his mind touch hers, his thoughts filling her with the strength and heat of his emotions. As their bodies moved together, his gliding and stroking in and out, hers holding and caressing, Charlie felt the last wall crumbling. He was all over her, inside and out, and there was no part of her he did not possess. She felt all that he was spreading through her, warm and delicious, twining around the surges of desire, enveloping her like water, illuminating the dark corners of her heart. She felt no fear as the pleasure broke over them, and wrapped her arms around him, taking the thick, heavy pulses of his semen into her core, immersing herself in the primal satisfaction of being a woman, his woman.

Sweat dripped from his face onto her shoulder as he sagged, his breath rushing against her ear, his fingers tangling with hers. When he tried to roll away from her Charlie held him, unwilling to release him from the clasp of her flesh.

"I didn't know," she whispered.

"That I love you?" He lifted his head. "Good God, woman. I've all but tattooed the words on my forehead."

"No, I meant us. This. That we could be like this together. It was good before, but this." She closed her eyes. "I can't even describe it. You were everywhere inside me."

"The dark kyn seem to practice a form of emotional bonding. The texts describe it as evil and perverse, a deliberate corruption of matrimony, but I think it's their form of love."

"What do the vampires have to do with us?"

"We have abilities similar to theirs, and we already know that we're drawn to each other." He brushed some hair back from her cheek. "Perhaps we can create the same kind of bond." He started to say something more, and then fell silent as he rolled away from her and sat up.

"Tell me."

"None of us have birth records other than what was issued to our adoptive parents, which were forged. We know we were genetically altered and tattooed as infants before we were adopted out. We have powerful and diverse psychic gifts, we heal rapidly, and we've all survived injuries and illnesses that should have killed us. Agreed?" When she nodded, he glanced back at her and asked, "So why did they do it? What was the purpose?"

"Probably just to see if they could." She propped herself up on her elbow, tugging him down beside her. "They must have thought they failed, or they wouldn't have placed us for adoption."

He nodded. "Before we were brought here, I believed the same thing."

She slid her hand across his chest, tracing her fingers in small circles over his heart. "So what's your new theory?"

"Charlotte, I think the scientists were trying to do the same thing as this Energúmeno, but in their case they actually succeeded." When he saw her expression, he added, "We were created to be an army. One that kills vampires."

Chapter 20

"We're still conducting the street search, but all of the leads we've received have turned out to be dead ends," Marlow said. "Nothing turned up on any of Energúmeno's properties. The company that owns the cellular transmission tower outside the city sent a repair crew; they're in custody now, but when they don't report in, there will be inquiries. We don't have much time left, sir."

Jonah Genaro set aside the front page of the *New York Times* and drank the last of his coffee. "Did you question Delgado?"

He nodded. "The warden didn't offer anything of value, although if you need any leverage on local politicians—"

Genaro glanced up. "What I need, Mr. Marlow, are Riordan, Taske, and Marena. Stop making excuses and find them."

"Yes, Mr. Genaro." Marlow turned on his heel and left.

The presidential suite at the Barceló Karmina Palace was as secure as it was sumptuous, but Genaro felt caged. Back in Atlanta he could have retreated to the vault beneath his enormous home, where he kept his extensive collection of antiquities. The only time he ever relaxed was when he was surrounded by the forgotten glory of his Roman ancestor, Genarius, who had clawed his way up from nothing to become one of the most important and influential men of his time. While Genaro didn't believe in reincarnation, he had often felt as if his ancient ancestor watched over him, reaching an invisible hand across the millennia to guide him along the path to power.

Genarius wouldn't have sat in a hotel suite, waiting like some indolent fool.

When Genaro stepped outside into the hall, two armed men turned toward him, their expressions blank, their eyes watchful.

"I'm going out for a few hours," he told them as he went to the elevator.

In the lobby, he had the concierge send for his car, and directed his driver to take him to Energúmeno's compound. Along the way he used the car phone to check in with Delaporte back in Atlanta.

"We've linked Les Frères de la Lumière to a European arson-for-hire ring," his chief of security said. "They're burning down properties and taking a cut of the insurance from the owners via charitable donations to the order. It's all strictly across the pond, sir; we've confirmed that they're not operating anywhere in Mexico."

An inventive insurance scam, but not one that interested Genaro. "What about Energúmeno's assets? Have you found anything new?"

"He's contributed to some campaign funds of local and state officials involved in environmental protection. Looks like a PR move to tie in with his waste-disposal holdings."

Genaro looked out at the marina the car was passing, and saw a deckhand casting off a bowline from a charter boat. Two tourists were seated behind the captain, already drinking beer. The casting perch above the helm was shrouded with a fitted canvas cover that looked mildewed around the seams, as if it hadn't been removed in some time. They'd be drunk by the time they went around the restricted zone to waters where they could fish without getting arrested. . . .

"Don, check into these the campaign donations," Genaro said. "I want the officials' names, titles, job descriptions, and any legislation they've been involved in."

"What are you looking for?"

"Protected habitats, wildlife reserves, or any area with restricted access. Anyplace Energúmeno could operate from with impunity." He leaned forward to tap on the glass divider, and when the driver lowered it, he said, "Take me to the police station downtown."

"We'll need some time to do the research, sir," Delaporte was saying.

"We're out of time. Put everyone you have on this, and get it to me before the end of the day." He ended the call and sat back, mentally reviewing the maps he had seen of the city. As the driver stopped in front of the station, he glanced out to see a woman sitting alone in the shadowy courtyard of the café across the street. Although he couldn't see her features, the scarlet poppy she wore tucked in the hair above her left ear drew his gaze.

You should have tried the wine. . . . Energúmeno does not allow us to leave the compound. . . . As soon as you walk through the gates, you will forget me.

"Wait here." He got out of the car and watched the girl as he crossed the street. She didn't try to run, only offering him a gap-toothed smile as he approached.

Genaro pulled out a chair and sat down. "Did he send you, or leave you behind with the other useless women?"

She sipped from a glass of red wine, licking a drop from her upper lip. "You have an interesting mind, señor. No other man has ever remembered me after I compelled him to forget."

"*Compelled?* You drugged me."

She set down the glass. "You must leave Mexico now."

"Tossing me in a prison didn't work," he told her. "Neither will threats from your employer."

She studied him for a long moment. "My master could have killed you from the moment you arrived in Manzanillo. You do not interest him anymore. Go back to America, señor."

When she rose, he stood and seized her wrist. "I'm not finished with you. Where is he? What has he done with the Kyndred?"

Instead of looking frightened, she chuckled. "If only my master had given me permission to compel you to go." She lifted her hand.

Genaro grabbed her wrist, but instead of gouging her nails into his neck, she rested her hand against it. A terrible longing devoured his anger as he gazed into her beautiful eyes and remembered her lovely name.

"Forgive me for shouting, Quinequia," he said, bringing her wrist to his lips. "It's because I want you."

"I will tell you a secret, *amigo*. When I touch them, all men want me." She leaned closer, resting her luscious curves against him. "You are cold and vicious, and care for nothing but power, but I could make you my lapdog. At least for a little while."

"Yes." He nodded, eager to please her. "Take me with you. Let me care for you. I can't lose you."

Her breath, sweet with wine, touched his lips just before she kissed him. Genaro enfolded her in his arms, avidly working his mouth over hers, delirious with desire.

"Very nice for such a nasty man." Quinequia pulled back and looked down. "Now you will release me."

His arms fell to his sides, and panic made him blurt out, "Don't send me away again."

"No, unfortunately, I cannot do that." She gripped his throat with both hands. "Listen to me, Jonah Genaro, and obey me. You will not search the islands. The man you seek is not there."

"Not there," he agreed, his voice dull.

"*Bueno.*" Quinequia's eyes burned into his. "You will forget our meeting, and when I leave here, you will never think of me again."

"Forget." The word tore at him, but the pain ebbed almost immediately as her face blurred. "Never again."

She led him back to the table, helping him to sit in the chair. "Good-bye, señor." She took her hands away, turned her back, and walked across the street to his car.

Genaro sat and looked at the empty wineglass across the table until a man touched his shoulder. He glared up at his driver. "What is it?"

"You've been sitting here for a while, sir," the man said, his expression uneasy. "I just thought I'd see if you were all right." He tugged at his collar, as if it felt too tight.

"I'm fine." He stood, inhaling deeply to clear his head. "Wait for me in the car."

He watched the driver retreat, and then turned to pick up the wineglass. A faint red imprint on the rim indicated a woman had been drinking from it, but the courtyard was empty. The last thing he remembered was being in the back of the car as it pulled up to the police station, and checking his watch.

He turned his wrist to look at his Rolex. Twenty-three minutes had passed, and he couldn't remember a single moment of them.

Genaro took out a handkerchief, wrapping it around his hand before he picked up the wineglass and carried it across the street with him.

Inside the station he went to the command center and called one of the research techs over. "I want this analyzed," Genaro said, handing him the glass. "Use the saliva for DNA typing and run the prints. Cross-reference both against our acquisition database in Atlanta."

"Do you have any details to narrow the search field, sir?" the tech asked.

"Just one." Genaro's collar had grown damp with sweat, and he reached up to loosen his tie. "She's female."

*   *   *

By morning most of the islanders had recovered enough to return to their homes, where Charlotte suggested through Tlemi that they stay.

"Pici's contractions have stopped, and Ihiyo is stable," she assured them. "If anything changes, I'll send word."

Xochi glanced at the other women and then replied in her language.

"She say, you no need," Tlemi translated, and tapped the side of her head. "We know."

Colotl issued some instructions as well, but stayed behind with Tlemi as the other islanders left.

The women looked after their patients while Colotl took Samuel down to the beach to show him his hook-and-line method of fishing. Although they couldn't communicate without Charlotte or Tlemi, simple sign language sufficed, and they caught breakfast in a few minutes. Then Colotl gave him another, less enjoyable tutorial on how to gut and clean their catch.

"How delightful," he muttered, pausing for a moment to shake off the scales clinging to his hands and forearms. "With all the fish I eat, I must remember to give Morehouse a raise." As he applied the knife again, it slipped and sliced across the skin between his thumb and forefinger. "Damn it." He pulled off the strip of rag he'd used to hold back his hair and wound it around the gash.

Colotl frowned and reached into the pouch he carried, taking out the long pointed leaf of a succulent plant, and gesturing for Samuel to apply it to the wound.

"Don't tell Charlotte, or she'll break out the suture kit," he joked as he unwrapped his hand. The rag had no blood on it, he saw, because the cut had closed before it could begin bleeding. For a long moment he stared at it, and then, as a chill ran down the length of his spine, he brought his fingers up to his mouth, touching the edge of his teeth. None of them had turned into fangs.

"Samuel." Colotl gestured toward his mouth, tipping his head back and pushing a finger behind his front teeth, moving it from side to side.

He imitated the motion, but felt only the roof of his mouth. He removed his fingers and shook his head.

Colotl released a breath, looking as relieved as Samuel felt.

"You guys went fishing and didn't tell me?"

Samuel glanced over at Drew, who was crossing the sand. "I thought I'd let you and Agraciana sleep in."

"I appreciate that." Drew gave Colotl a wary look before crouching down to examine their catch. "Nice. I haven't had fresh fish in years. Samuel, we've got a problem."

"Is this new or preexisting?"

"New. Earlier I took a walk around the house and the grounds. There isn't any copper within five miles of this spot. Which is basically the entire island."

Without copper, Drew couldn't use his ability, which allowed him to manipulate the metal into any form he wished.

"They're running the houses off methane-fueled generators."

"Yeah, I already checked them out. They're solid steel, and all the wiring is fiber-optic." Drew kicked over a shell in the sand. "According to Gracie, copper is poisonous to the vampire. Figures he'd make sure the natives couldn't get their hands on any." He frowned down at the sand.

"Samuel." Colotl picked up the cleaned fish that he had strung together, and pointed to the villa. "*Niccuiz*. I take." He gestured toward the sun as if moving it to the center of the sky. "*Tiyazque oztotl*. Cave." He pointed to them and himself.

"We meet at the cave at noon."

Samuel exchanged a nod with him, and after the islander strode up the beach he turned to Drew, who was kneeling and sifting sand through his fingers over a small mound of the same. "Now is not the time to build sand castles, Andrew."

"I'd make millions if I did." Drew stood and surveyed the rest of the shore. "Is it all like this? The whole island?"

"I haven't walked the entire perimeter, but I assume so." Samuel eyed the sparkling sand. "Is it artificial?"

"Yeah." Drew uttered a pained laugh. "It's also riddled with gold."

"Surely you mean pyrite, or mica."

"Samuel, besides computers, the only thing I'm an expert on is metal." He bent and scooped up a handful of the sand, stirring it with his fingertip. "Everything that glitters here is the real deal. At least one-sixth of the beach is twenty-four karat." He poured it out of his hand. "Cagey bastard. He hid it in the one place Cortés's descendants and the historians would never think to look." He glanced up. "The vampire is—was—Motecuhzoma. Last king of the Aztecs."

Samuel listened as Drew related what the master and Stanton had told him. When his friend finished the bizarre tale, he grew thoughtful. "That explains the artifacts in the villa. I thought they were reproductions, but they're simply newly made."

"You really think he's the big M?"

"It's possible," Samuel said. "Early explorers always brought disease to the Americas. It's not a broad leap to imagine one of them was dark kyn. He must have turned the Aztec, who viewed his transformation as the process of becoming a god."

"Maybe that's what let him survive what he's been through."

Drew shook his head. "He's gone loony tunes, but he's still smart. He's been taking over the drug cartels, and he can control anyone else he needs. If he does build this army and uses it to take over Mexico, Motecuhzoma's revenge is going to have a whole new meaning."

Of all the objects in the villa, the only ones Samuel

had not been able to touch-read had been the strange clubs hung high on the first-floor entry wall. "Come back up to the house. There's something I need to do."

Samuel intended to drape the security camera with a cloth to obscure the lens; instead he found the equipment smashed and dangling from a frayed wire. Drew reached up, pulling down the ruined unit and running his fingers along the wires.

"More fiber optics." He inspected the camera. "Looks like it exploded."

Colotl joined them and grimaced at the twisted mass of metal. "Charlotte." He mimed striking something with a club, and then swept his hand toward the rest of the villa.

Drew whistled. "Your lady has a bad temper."

"She doesn't want them to know Pici is close to delivering." Samuel led the men into the living room, where he began taking apart the modules making up the conversation pit. "Grab one of these and bring them out into the hall."

By stacking the modules, Samuel was able to fashion a small tower beneath the display of the clubs. "You'd better climb it," he told Drew. "It won't hold my weight."

"Just catch me if I fall," Drew joked as he started up.

With Colotl's help, Samuel was able to hold the modules steady, and Drew worked one of the clubs free of the hooks holding it to the wall. Colotl reached up to take it from him before he climbed back down.

"Xitlachia," Colotl said, his expression sobering as he passed it to Samuel. *"Micoani yaotlatquitl."*

"Sounds like he's trying to say 'handle with care,'" Drew said, only half joking.

Samuel hefted the surprisingly heavy weapon. Carved from a single piece of teak, the four-foot-long business end had been fashioned like a squared blade, with deep notches on both sides. Single rows of black, prismatic stone blades had been fitted inside the notches, their rectangular shape as puzzling as the razor sharpness of their exposed edges.

"It's not a club," Samuel murmured, turning it over. "It's a *macuahuitl*." At Drew's blank look, he added, "An Aztec sword."

Drew's expression turned skeptical. "Sorry, but in every movie I've seen, swords are made of forged steel or iron. That's just a big wooden stick with some black rocks stuck in it."

"According to the historical accounts I've read, these were very effective in battle. One Aztec warrior used his to decapitate a horse." Samuel closed his eyes briefly, drawing on his ability, which now provided only a glimpse of a powerful hand streaked with gold fashioning the weapon. "The vampire made these himself. I wonder why."

Drew made a rude sound. "Maybe he's into arts and crafts."

"This isn't a decoration." Samuel took a test swing, pitting the stone-blade edge against one of the suspended animal masks. The blade cut through the jaguar's clay-and-hide visage as if it were made of paper, sending half of it to smash on the glass floor.

"Oh, yeah." Drew blew out a breath. "That's a sword."

"You break that floor, boys," a tired voice said, "and you'll be mopping it up for weeks."

Samuel looked up as Charlotte came down the staircase. "How are the patients?"

"Ihiyo is in and out, but no fever, no signs of sepsis. That's my good news." She rubbed a hand over the back of her neck. "Bad news is that Pici's contractions have started again. They're sporadic, and I've given her a mild sedative, but if her water breaks, I have no choice but to deliver the baby. As small as she is, that's probably going to be by C-section." She eyed the *macuahuitl*. "Just what are you planning to do with that thing?"

"Use them to hurt the bad guys," Drew said.

"We'll take down the others from the wall," Samuel

decided. "There aren't enough to go around, but with Colotl's help I believe I can make more."

"Can I have a word with you in private?" Charlotte asked, her voice tight.

Samuel led her into the kitchen. "I know you don't like violence, but we need more weapons."

"Why? So I can turn this place into a hospital?" She leaned back against the counter and folded her arms. "Why don't you guys build a boat instead?"

"We couldn't finish it before they come back for Pici's baby," he reminded her.

"The vampire could come back with them, too." Her lips thinned. "Last night he didn't even touch you, and he still cut you guys down like you were paper dolls. Even if you make a hundred of those sword things, none of you could get close enough to . . ." She stopped and stared at him. "No."

"My ability to heal means I am the only one who has a real chance of withstanding the vampire's ability," he said quickly. "If we can lure him back to the island, and I alone attack him, I could survive his assault long enough to decapitate him—"

"You're talking about cutting off the head of an immortal monster using a weapon that will probably bounce off him. At which point, he dismembers you with a single thought." She pushed herself away from the counter. "I've got to get back upstairs."

He caught her hand, tugging her back to him. "He's not invulnerable, and I know once we talk to Agraciana we'll figure out how to get to him. I'm not going to die on you. I keep my promises, honey."

"You'd better." She curled her arms around his neck, resting her cheek against his chest. "All right, I'm in. What do you need from me? I can spare you some scalpels if you want to use the blades."

"I'll send Drew up to have a look at your equipment and see what he can use. He needs some copper to work with," he added as she gave him a quizzical look, "but

Energúmeno seems to have stripped all of it from the island."

She pulled back and frowned. "How much does Drew need?"

"I can't say."

"As much as you've got." Drew came around the side of the doorway. "Sorry; I was eavesdropping. Leftover habit from my scary life as a GenHance mole."

Charlotte lifted her head. "Vulcan?"

"My Internet fame precedes me." He grinned before he glowered at Samuel. "Hey. You didn't say she was one of ours." He tilted his head as he studied Charlotte. "You're not Sapphira; she's Canadian. I've met Aphrodite and Jezebel, and I know Delilah's safely hidden away in the Rockies."

"What, am I the only one who doesn't get invited to these Takyn get-togethers?" Charlotte demanded before she sighed and held out her hand. "I'm Magdalene."

"Maggie? No shit?" Drew whooped and grabbed her in a bear hug before he held her at arm's length to inspect her again. "And you're a medic. Damn, girl, the way you shoot I thought for sure you were a Green Beret or something."

Samuel raised his brows. "She shoots?"

"Yeah, and she scores. Majorly." Drew tucked his arm through hers. "So, okay, you played through to the end of three, right? Is he still alive? Is the war over or not?"

"They made a hundred and seventy million dollars in one day on three," Charlotte chided. "Trust me; he's in cryo until they release four." She glanced at Samuel. "We've played some online games together a few times."

Samuel followed them upstairs, only half listening to their conversation about gaming together. Drew's mention of Delilah had sent a fresh wave of guilt through him; he had yet to tell Charlotte how badly he had treated their Takyn friend. Fortunately it was daylight, or she might have plucked the shameful memories straight from his mind.

"I feel a little tingle," he heard Drew say, and looked in as his friend walked around the treatment room. "Wherever it is, it's not much. Maybe some wire fragments inside one of these units."

"I don't want to take anything apart if I can help it," Charlotte told him. "I might have to run some other tests on Ihiyo or Pici."

Drew nodded. "I can search for it without destroying anything. Although we'd have it made if one of us could mind-forge gold." He described his discovery on the beach.

She seemed skeptical. "The entire island can't be made out of it. I read an article once that said if you put together all the gold ever mined in the world throughout time, it wouldn't fill two Olympic-size swimming pools."

"Gold that we know of," Drew corrected. "The Aztecs hid what they had from the conquistadors. Mixing it with beach sand and building an island out of it is pure genius."

"The island is not made of gold." Agraciana came in and went to Drew, who put his arm around her. "The master did recover his gold from where he hid it five hundred years ago, but it is only a small part of what he used to create the island. Most of it was built atop waste brought here on barges."

"He made an island out of trash?" Charlotte shook her head. "I don't think that's possible. This place is too big."

"It is the truth." Agraciana smiled a little. "I helped him finish it."

Samuel listened as she detailed how Energúmeno had spent the last twenty years shipping tons of waste to a lifeless atoll, where the barges were then deliberately wrecked to form a six-mile-wide foundation.

"It took almost a decade for him to collect enough waste to completely cover the barges and begin terraforming it," Agraciana said. "Native coral formed to cement the ships together beneath the surface, while the elements of methane containment and topsoil layered atop the decaying waste shaped the landmass. Once the garbage had been sealed off, methane generators were installed, and the landscaping and building began."

Samuel saw that Drew and Charlotte didn't quite believe her claims. "What she says is true. I dug a hole near the cave, and I've seen the layers."

"So we're basically trapped on a floating landfill." Charlotte sighed. "Marvelous."

"The master intends to build more islands like this, once we solve one significant problem that prevents him from doing as he wishes," Agraciana told her.

Drew snorted. "What more does he want?"

She made a horizontal movement with her hand. "If weather conditions or other hazards make it necessary, he wishes to be able to move them."

A thought occurred to Samuel, one that was so dangerous it might kill them all. It also might be their only way to escape. "Agent Flores, were you here on the island when the villas were built?"

"For most of the construction, yes." She looked puzzled. "What do you need to know about them?"

He picked up Charlotte's notepad and a pen. "Everything you can tell me about the piping."

Chapter 21

A god did not require sleep, only rest and seclusion from the burning rays of the sun. The immortal who had once been Sokojotsin accepted this, as he had so many distasteful aspects of his existence. He did not count the hours he spent in his dark chamber; compared to the centuries he had endured in the earth, they were nothing.

As soon as night darkened the air, Energúmeno rose from the ornate dais that served as his bed. He would not waste another second of his reign on his back.

A woman stepped out of the shadows. "Master."

Energúmeno held out his arm, and Quinequia came to him, her pretty hands soft against his ruined flesh, her lips smiling and softening her unfortunate countenance as she tipped her head to one side, offering him her throat.

The metal of his fangs emerged, and he lowered his head, piercing her thin skin. Her blood sweetened his mouth and drove away some of the pain that racked his limbs, but after a few moments he set her aside.

The euphoria she felt evaporated just as quickly. "Do I displease you?"

"No," he lied.

In the time of his first rule he would not have permitted such a creature within his sight; a king was entitled to be surrounded by beauty in all things. But while

Quinequia's form would never deserve his attention, she was the only one of his children who did not cringe at his touch, and whom he could feed upon regularly without losing himself to blood madness. She also had other, equally valuable uses when it came to dealing with mortals.

He could smell one of them on her now. "Why have you been with Genaro?"

"He still searches for you. I thought I would persuade him to fail." She stroked her fingers over the gold protruding from his chest. "He remembered me."

"He cannot." Energúmeno frowned. "He is mortal."

"His greed for power consumes him. It controls him so much I do not think even I could bind him to me permanently." She moved her shoulders. "He is well guarded now, but I can lure him away from his men. Do you wish me to kill him, master?"

"No. I have other work for you." He set her aside as other servants came in carrying linens and pots. "The first of my warriors will soon be born. Go to the House of Eagles and ensure all is in readiness for him."

"It will be." Quinequia bowed to kiss the back of his hand before she withdrew.

Energúmeno tolerated the tentative touch of his body servants, who scoured away as much blackened, rotted flesh as they could before rubbing his limbs and torso with the sweet-smelling floral unguents he had taught them to make. The fresh blood he was obliged to drink to sustain his beleaguered flesh had not yet fully restored his body, another annoyance, but his steward had sworn to him that in time it would. After all the centuries and so little change, however, he sometimes wondered if he would ever be healed. Dressed in newly made garments, he made his way from his private chamber to his reception room, where Stanton awaited him.

His steward's nervous pacing reminded Energúmeno of the foolish rebellion staged by his children. Even now he regretted not unleashing the thousand blades on

Samuel Taske; the American deserved a lengthy, lei-
surely death for instigating the others to violence.

Something admirable about the manner in which
Taske had faced him, however, had stayed the immortal's
hand. As calm and steady as an Eagle warrior, the American had not feared him. More than he wanted the man's
heart in his hand, beating its last beneath the clench of
his fingers, he wanted that courage.

Taske knew now there was no escaping his duty, and
in time would pass along the gifts bestowed by Energúmeno's blood to the many fierce, powerful sons he would
sire to serve the new kingdom.

Segundo stood waiting by his throne, a goblet in his
hands. In the old tongue he greeted him with, "You fill
my eyes with beauty and terror, my king," and bowed
low before presenting the drink.

The scent of the blood mixed into the wine brought
forth Energúmeno's fangs, but Segundo had not yet
changed his garments, which still stank of seawater and
smoke. Energúmeno struck out with his hand, the gold
striping it clanging against the silver goblet as he
knocked it away.

"Do you never bathe?" he demanded.

"Forgive me, master." Segundo dropped to his knees,
his eyes on the floor. "I was obliged to attend to less
important tasks, and time escaped me. With your permission, I will go and tidy myself now."

"You will remain." The immortal gestured for another waiting servant. "Bring more of my wine." To
Stanton he said, "What of my children?"

"All but four have returned to their homes. Ghost required medical treatment, and remains with his woman
and the Americans. Scorpion and his woman have also
stayed behind." Segundo stared at the blooded wine
splashed across the tiles, and swallowed before he added,
"We observed the children through the cameras in the
seventh house, until Turtle destroyed them."

Taske's woman would have to be punished, but as always Segundo would see to it. "Where is the daily report?"

"The birds have returned, but they brought nothing with them."

It had been his servant's idea to use birds as messengers. Trained to fly out to the island by day and return at night, they carried reports on the children's activities in tiny capsules attached to their legs. "So our eye on the island has closed."

"It would seem so, master." Segundo stood slowly. "They have not yet touched the other cameras, if you wish to observe them."

Such tasks Energúmeno left to Segundo and his other servants, as he considered it beneath him to personally spy on his children. Yet after the ugly events of the previous night he would be gratified to see them once more obedient.

He rose from his throne. "Show them to me."

His servant led the way to the rooms he had filled with his strange machines and the rows of glass squares that showed black-and-white images from all of the houses on the island. Those that showed the interior of the seventh house had gone black, but the others displayed every room in the other six dwellings. However, none of his children appeared on any of the squares. "Where are they?"

"They should be sleeping now." Frowning, Segundo went to one of the machines and began to press its buttons, which moved the images. "The American did this."

"My children obey me," he reminded his steward.

"So they do, master, but this man is an instigator. I believe now that he will never accept your authority over him." Segundo gestured toward the glass squares. "After the events of last night, I know he is responsible for this. Even now he has probably lured the children from their homes to plot against you."

Energúmeno's annoyance grew. "An army needs generals. Taske's sons will have the wisdom and the spine to lead my children to victory."

Segundo shook his head, his voice growing shrill. "We will have no army if he poisons the others, which he will if you do not kill him now—"

"Silence." Energúmeno gave him a clout that knocked him to the ground. "I am their father. I decide who lives for my glory, and who dies under my heel. Not you."

Segundo licked the blood from the gash on his mouth. "I tell you this out of my love for you, master. Without you I am nothing."

Weary of his steward's eternal mewling, he gazed at the images of the empty rooms. Little flickers of white light appeared along the bottom edge of one square, and then seemed to leap to another. "What is that?"

"I don't know." Segundo got to his feet and returned to the console, adjusting the knobs to make the images larger.

The lights crawled across the glass squares until they appeared in each one, and seemed to shoot up. It was only when gray clouds appeared with the lights that Energúmeno realized what was happening. "They do this to destroy the other cameras?"

"Not only the cameras, master." Segundo straightened, his expression almost smug. "They have set fires in all the rooms. They are burning down the houses."

"They will come soon, Charlotte."

Tlemi's voice halted Charlie's nervous pacing, but did nothing to dispel her anxiety. "I should have gone with them."

Samuel and the other men had left almost an hour ago to finish setting fire to the other houses; they might not make it back before the boats arrived. At which point Charlie and the women would have to hold off Segundo, and quite possibly the vampire, by themselves.

Charlie surveyed the faces of the other women, most of whom had the good sense to look frightened. Samuel's plan to burn down all the houses was insanely risky, especially if Energúmeno decided not to send anyone to rescue them. "All right, we need to get ready. Tlemi, what can the others do?"

"Xochi move plants." She turned and spoke in Nahautl to the other woman, who nodded and touched one of the bamboo canes. The long, straight length began to coil like a spiral, at the same time sprouting new shoots that grew at an astonishing rate.

"Good. If any of the master's men come up from the beach, she needs to trap them in the bamboo." Charlie waited for Tlemi to translate that for Xochi before she noticed Pici struggling to get up from the makeshift stretcher they'd used to bring her down to the beach. "No, sweetie, you don't have to do anything."

Pici fell back, and then said something to Tlemi.

"She want to help," Tlemi explained.

"You're pregnant," Charlie told her, and rested her hand on the mound of her belly. "You just take care of this little guy for now."

Pici snapped something, and a seagull darted into their hiding place, landing on Charlotte's arm and giving the back of her hand an ungentle peck.

"Ouch." She shook off the bird, and then went still as six others landed in front of her, glaring up at her with angry black eyes. "What the hell?"

Tlemi made a face. "She use birds."

Charlie pushed the memory of a Hitchcock movie out of her thoughts. "Okay, Pici, you can help." When the pregnant woman reached for her hand, she assumed she wanted only some reassurance, but then Charlie felt her press something small and cylindrical against her palm. She looked into the other woman's eyes, and while she didn't understand her thoughts, she could feel the urgency of her emotions.

"I'm going to walk down and see how much room there is under the pier. Stay here," she told Tlemi.

As soon as Charlie ducked beneath the pier, she

opened her hand and examined the object Pici had passed to her. The small plastic cylinder had a cap on one end, and contained a tiny roll of paper. She opened it and removed the note, unrolling it to reveal a hand-written message.

"What did she give you?" Tlemi asked from behind her.

"I'm not sure." Charlie turned and held out the paper. "But you won't have to translate it. It's written in beautiful English."

The pale hand trembled as it took the paper. "I can explain."

"You don't have to." Charlotte seized her by the throat. "You lying bitch."

"Please. You don't understand." Tears streaked Tlemi's face. "I had to do this."

"You had to use your ability to spy on us, and tell them whenever we didn't follow the rules?" Charlie tightened her hand. "You're right; I don't get it. How could you?" She shook her. "Did you enjoy watching through Sam's eyes while they beat me? Did you?"

"Segundo said if I didn't," Tlemi said, her voice stran-gled by the pressure of Charlie's hand, "he would kill Colotl."

"You idiot." Charlie shoved her away.

"I stopped a long time ago. I've been lying to them about everything, ever since they murdered Mocaya." The younger woman coughed and rubbed her neck. "I only told them the truth about you because I thought the master had turned Samuel. I was afraid he would attack us for our blood."

"Even if he was a vampire, Sam would never hurt anyone." Charlie felt the sincerity of Tlemi's emotions echoing in her words, and the shame that filled her thoughts. "If you try to help them tonight, I will kill you myself."

"I won't. Not ever again." The other woman glanced over her shoulder. "Are you going to tell the others?"

"If I did, *they'd* probably kill you." Grimly she looked

around, measuring the available space. "We need to move the women away from here." She felt a wave of rage slam into her mind and staggered backward, shuddering as Tlemi caught her.

No language came through the thought stream, only gruesome images of Energúmeno standing over Samuel's body, holding a still-beating heart in his hand. What he imagined doing next made her double over and vomit.

"Charlotte."

"I'm all right." Charlotte wiped her mouth and straightened. "Get the other women and go. Stay out of sight." She managed to raise a mental barrier against the murderous thoughts barraging her mind before she hurried out.

"What are you doing?" Tlemi called after her.

Charlotte didn't look back. "I have to warn Samuel."

"That's the last one." Samuel stood back with Drew and watched as flames rose against the windows inside the house.

Colotl and the other islanders joined them, each carrying the torches they had used to set the fires.

"Beautiful work," Drew said. "If you ever want to go into the arson business, take me as your partner."

Capping off all the gas pipes before they set fire to the villas ensured that the structures would burn instead of explode, which bought them more time. According to Tlemi, Segundo and his men lived on one of the protected islands in the vicinity; it would take at least an hour for them to arrive. Assuming they would come to rescue them.

"They will come," Agraciana said, accurately guessing his thoughts. "The master needs us too much to let all of us die."

"But he'd have no problem killing a couple of us to serve as examples," Drew guessed.

"That is Energúmeno's way." She gave Samuel a

troubled look. "If we cannot prevail, I will summon my dolphins, but . . . I cannot control more than four. That means only three can come with me."

Samuel glanced at Drew. "This time, we'll win."

"Samuel." Colotl pointed to a figure running toward them. "Charlotte."

He ran to meet her, catching her in his arms as she stumbled and gasped for breath. "What are you doing here?"

"Energúmeno." She clutched his shoulders. "He's coming. You have to go the cave and hide. Now." She tried to pull him in that direction. "Sam, please. I've seen what he's planning to do to you, and you can't stop him. He's too strong, too angry."

"Drew. Colotl." When the men joined them, Samuel quickly issued instructions for them to rejoin the women and take up defensive positions, and then added, "I need the weapons."

Charlotte stiffened. "Didn't you hear me? He's going to stick his hand in your chest and pull out your heart and eat it. You can't heal from that. This time, you *will* die."

Samuel looked at the other men. "Give us a minute, please." When they moved away, he cradled her face between his hands. "Honey, we don't have a lot of time left, so I need you to listen to me now. We've talked to Agraciana about Energúmeno's powers. He can hurt me from a distance, but to kill me he has to make physical contact. I'm not going to let that happen."

"You can't stop him." She gave Agraciana a desperate look. "She can control dolphins, right? Have her call one to take you off the island before he gets here. When you get to the mainland, you can get help—"

"I'm not leaving you, Charlotte." He brought her hand up and pressed it to his heart. "As for this, he can't have it. It belongs to you."

With her fists she gripped the front of his shirt, and pressed her brow against his chest. When she lifted her head again, her expression was one of complete calm. "You aren't leaving me, Sam. If he kills you, he kills me, too."

"Honey, you can't—"

"You won't be here to stop me." She took a scalpel from her pocket and held it up between them. "You know how I feel about suicide, but I'd rather end my life than live without you. So if you die, I die."

He could take the scalpel from her, and warn the men about her intentions. But with her medical knowledge and training, how long would they be able to prevent her from following him into death? Suddenly he realized the other reason she had made her ghastly threat. "When you read his mind and thought of me dying, this is how it felt for you."

She nodded. "That, and I threw up. You don't have to do that, though."

Samuel laughed as he wrapped his arms around her, lifting her off her feet until their eyes were level. "I love you, Charlotte Marena, and I'm not going to die tonight. I'm going to live for you. I'm going to live with you. And when we're very old, and ready for the next place, then we'll go together."

She closed her eyes. "Please, God, yes."

"Samuel," Drew called. "Time to move."

As they joined the others, Agraciana moved to flank Charlotte. "You read the master's mind tonight, yes?"

"I picked his thoughts." Her hand tightened on Samuel's. "They were as ugly as he is."

Agraciana's voice became tentative. "Can you tell me, was he thinking of anything else besides coming here?"

"You don't want to know," Charlotte muttered before she saw the other woman's expression. "He wasn't deciding how he wanted to kill you, if that's what you mean."

"But did he think about my parents?" Before Charlotte could answer, she said quickly, "I don't know what my mother looks like now, but my father is an old man, with white hair and a scar on his neck here." She touched a place on her throat.

Charlotte shook her head. "I'm sorry, but I didn't see anyone like that in his thoughts."

Instead of showing disappointment, Agraciana smiled a little. "Then there is still some hope. Thank you."

By the time they reached the seventh house, the fire inside had caused the windows to burst and belch columns of black smoke into the sky. While Colotl directed the other men to take up defensive positions along the tree line, Tlemi came to speak in a low voice to Charlotte, who returned a few minutes later.

"We have another problem," she told him. "Pici's contractions have started again. The stress of this is just too much for her and the baby."

Samuel had taken the precaution of removing everything Charlotte might need for the delivery from the treatment room before setting fire to the house. "We'll have to move her away from here."

"Tlemi and I are going to carry her down the beach until we're out of sight." She eyed the tree line. "Ihiyo should go with us. He'll help keep her calm." She turned to him. "And no, don't suggest I stay with her. She's not ready to deliver yet, and you need me here." She stalked off toward the pier.

"You had to get mixed up with a telepath." Drew slapped the back of Samuel's shoulder. "You know, you'll never be able to throw that woman a surprise birthday party. Or make her think you were working late at the office."

"It doesn't matter." He eyed his friend. "And I'm not mixed-up. I'm in love with her. Come on."

They went to retrieve the weapons they had stashed beneath the sea grape bushes.

"Yours." Drew handed him two *macuahuitl* before hefting the bundle with the others they had made. "If you want to change your mind, we can all rush him."

"If this doesn't work, I need you in reserve." He glanced over at the women. "Whatever happens, I'm depending on you to get the islanders back to the States. Matthias will help you resettle them."

Drew uttered a sour chuckle. "I think he'll need to buy a maternity hospital."

"If I don't make it, he'll be able to purchase several." Samuel smiled. "As my long-lost brother, he inherits the bulk of my estate."

"You mean you didn't leave me anything in the will?" Drew mocked.

He grinned. "Other than my shares in Intel and Microsoft, which I believe are presently worth a few million, no."

"Maybe you should stop worrying about the vampire and start worrying about me." Drew turned his head, his eyes shifting past Samuel. His smile faded. "Oh, shit."

Chapter 22

Energúmeno had never loved her. Quinequia had accepted that as soon as she had been taken from the streets in Mexico City and brought to Manzanillo to be presented to him. That day, she had discovered that her ability couldn't overpower his ancient mind or the rage that had sustained it for so long. Contrary creature that she was, she adored him for it, and served him with loyalty so fierce she even defied him now and then in order to protect him.

Her love had brought her to this cantina, where she sat and drank cheap wine while she waited. She didn't know for whom or what, only that she had to be here.

A man sat down in the chair across from her, his smile lighting up an unremarkable face. "Hello, little sister."

Quinequia eyed him. "You are mistaken, señor. I have no brothers." The whore who had given birth to her had bled to death after a botched abortion when Quinequia was five; she had huddled against her mother's rotting body for two days before the stench and hunger had driven her out on the streets.

The man reached across the table and covered her hand with his. *"È una cosa importante da ricordare."*

Quinequia had never spoken Italian, but she knew instantly what he was saying. *It is an important thing to remember.* And she remembered him, her mentor, the man who had saved her.

No one knew about him. They had met when Quinequia had lived on the streets of Mexico City; he'd found her one day holding court among the other ragged, filthy orphans. He had laughed at her confusion when her ability had failed to enslave him.

"Your charms are not irresistible, my dear," he'd chided in flawless Spanish. "I can teach you what to do when they fail you, and much more."

Quinequia had never gone to school; that was for children with homes and families. But street life had taught her that no one did anything for free. "Why would you do that?"

He had pulled up the sleeve of his shirt to show her a strange picture just above his elbow. It had been made part of his skin, just like the gray bird on the back of her hand. "Because we are family."

He had taken her with him that day, first to the beautiful rooms in one of the big hotels, where maids had washed her and dressed her in clothes so clean and soft the touch of them felt like angel's wings. A butler had brought a cart with so much lovely food she had not dared do anything but stare at it, at least until her mentor told her it was all for her. Then she had thrown herself at him instead of the food, clutching him as she sobbed like a baby.

He had stroked her hair and let her cry until she hiccuped. "I am going to take care of you now, little sister."

So he had, from that night on. During the next three years he had taken her all over the world with him, teaching her everything he knew, training her how to better control and use her gift, and then finally explaining her purpose. By the time they returned to Mexico, Quinequia was nine years old, and more than ready to begin the work.

"You look like a proper street urchin now," her mentor had said as he surveyed the ragged, filthy garments she wore.

Quinequia eyed another brother who came into the room; a silent and watchful teacher whom she had met in England. "I will never tell anyone about us."

"You can be made to tell, little sister. So you must be made to forget." Her mentor rubbed a little more dirt on her cheek, and then pushed the hair he had deliberately snarled back from her eyes. "If you need us, we will know. If there is time, we will come for you. If there is not, you must protect us."

She nodded, and when the other brother had come to lay his hands on her neck, she had not resisted.

Memories flooded her as she looked across the table at her mentor. The words he had spoken to her had lifted the mask over her memory placed in her mind the night he had brought her back to Mexico and returned her to her life on the streets.

"You have come back for me."

He nodded. "Your work here is finished."

Now that she recalled everything, she felt confused. The only reason he would come personally was to take her away with him. "Am I being replaced? Is that why you are here?"

"No, my dear." He stood and offered her his hand as she rose from her chair. "You are being recalled."

Her lower lip trembled as she fought back her tears. "Then I have failed you."

"You are wrong." He put his arm around her. "Now, come. We have one more task to perform."

Charlie stopped beneath a coconut palm and surveyed the area before she looked at Tlemi. "Tell him to put her down here."

Ihiyo, who had insisted on carrying the other end of the stretcher, nodded as Tlemi translated. In sync with Charlie's movements, he carefully lowered Pici to the ground, then came around to kneel beside the stretcher. The pregnant girl sighed as her lover took her hands in his and spoke to her in a soft, low voice.

Tlemi gestured for Charlotte, and she followed her out of the secluded spot down to the beach. "I must tell you something."

Charlie held up one hand. "If you've done anything else for the master, I don't want to know about it."

"No, it is about Pici." She glanced over at the grove. "When she was a little girl, the master had her taken from her family in America. Her parents' names are Jill and Robert Colfax, and they lived in Houston, Texas. Jill was a teacher, and Robert sold insurance."

"Why are you telling me this?"

"It is our hope that if the master defeats us, you may still escape him someday. If you do, she wishes you to find her family and tell them that she is dead."

"She's not dead." Charlie suddenly understood. "If he wins, she's not leaving the island."

"No." She gave her a sad smile. "This time, Ihiyo will go into the water with her. So will the rest of us."

Charlie saw the grim logic of it; if they couldn't win against the vampire in life, they would do it in death. "If he kills Samuel, I'll be joining the party."

"I thought you might." Tlemi held up a well-wrapped plastic container. "Since we came to the island, I have been writing about Energúmeno and what he has done with us and our country. When you and Samuel came, I wrote about you. If we must go into the water, I will give this to the waves. It will be our voice to the world."

"Assuming it washes up on the right beach." A flash of bright light distracted Charlie, and she turned her head to see what appeared to be three full moons in the distance, each bouncing like balls on the surface of the water. "Are those searchlights?"

"Yes." Tlemi inhaled sharply. "The master has brought all three boats, and all of Segundo's men."

Charlotte squinted, trying to scan for thoughts. The blankness she felt meant Colotl had already created a shield between them and the sea. "How many men does he have?"

Tlemi gave her a helpless look. "Sixty. Maybe more."

Samuel had been counting on one boat with Segundo and his guards, not an army that outnumbered them three to one. "I've got to go and warn him."

Tlemi nodded. "I will stay with Pici and Ihiyo."

Charlie took off down the beach, running along the fringe of the waves where the water had packed down the sand. When she got within earshot she began shouting for Samuel, whom she finally spotted standing on the island side of the pier. He was watching the approaching boats, two rock-studded clubs in his hands, until he heard her voice and turned.

"Charlotte?"

She didn't wait for him to come to her, but sprinted to the pier. "There are at least sixty men on those boats," she said when she reached him, dragging in air and swallowing before she added, "If we run now, we can wait until they land and then swim out to the boats. We can strand *them* here."

"That's not the plan, honey." He put an arm around her and kissed her brow. "Go and take cover."

She wanted to take one of the clubs and beat him over the head with it, until her thought stream twined with his, and she saw what he had planned. "You're crazy. He won't do that."

"He believes he's our father and our king." His mouth hitched. "He'll do it." He gave her a gentle push toward the trees. "Wait for me up there, Charlie."

It was the first time he had called her by her nickname, and it made her eyes sting. "My name is Charlotte," she told him before she turned and hurried away.

Drew came out of the trees, holding out an arm and then pulling her along with him into the bamboo thicket. "You were supposed to stay with the pregnant chick."

"You knew about this challenge thing?" she demanded.

"Yeah. I even helped him modify the *macuahuitl* blades." He shoved her behind him.

"Modify them with what?"

"The human body stores a few milligrams of copper, mostly in the liver," Drew said in a conversational tone. "It's used by the body to produce energy, protect against free-radical cell damage, and keep the neurotransmitters firing, and even helps us metabolize iron."

She tried to see past him. "I don't need a hematology refresher."

"Then you know you can find traces of it elsewhere, like bound to proteins floating around in your veins." He glanced over his shoulder. "By the way, you weren't planning on using any of that bagged blood you had chilling in the upstairs fridge, right?"

Before Charlie could answer, the first of the boats reached the end of the pier, and she saw several armed men jump off to form two lines. The weight of the towering figure who followed them caused the entire pier to shake.

Charlie froze, her eyes widening as she saw the enormous golden daggers in the vampire's hands. "Drew. I don't think he's going to use his power."

"Energúmeno," Samuel called out before he crossed the *macuahuitl* over his head. "You have claimed to be Motecuhzoma, last king of the Aztecs. You have called us your children, and yourself our father. Is this what you believe?"

"It is what is," the vampire said. "I gave you this life, and now I will have it back."

"Perhaps you will," Samuel said. "I challenge your rule."

Energúmeno abruptly stopped and stared at him. "You cannot take my throne from me. You are mortal."

"I was, before you brought me here." Samuel lowered his arms. "Now your blood runs through my veins. You remember. I'm told you fed it to me yourself."

Segundo came up beside the vampire. "It is a trick, master. He has not turned. Kill him now."

Energúmeno swept one of his daggers to one side,

slitting the steward's throat with one motion before he kicked his body from the pier. Segundo fell into the water with a splash, his body quickly sinking out of sight.

The vampire advanced several paces, halting just out of Samuel's reach. "Cortés poured boiling gold down my throat, and that did not kill me. Nor could five hundred years entombed in the earth. Put down your weapons now, warrior, and I will see to it that you die quickly and cleanly."

"A warrior doesn't kneel before death." Samuel tossed one of the *macuahuitl* at the vampire's feet. "He fights to it."

Energúmeno tossed away one of his daggers before he bent and seized the hilt of the Aztec sword. "So you will." He flipped the heavy blade around his hand so fast it whistled through the air.

Charlotte surged forward, stopped only by Drew's arm.

"Oh, no, you don't." He pointed to the men wading through the shallows up to the beach. "How are they going to attack?"

"I don't care." She wanted only to get to Samuel.

Colotl came up on her other side and caught her hand, holding his other out to Drew. As soon as he took it the islander's thoughts streamed into her mind. *Charlotte, we must know what they mean to do. Help us.*

"God damn it, Maggie." Drew dragged her around. "Tell me what they're thinking before they get to us."

She threw down her barriers, gathering up all the thought streams careening around her. "They know where we're hiding. They're going to drop. Throw grenades. Gas us. Knock us out. Carry us back to the boats."

Colotl closed his eyes briefly. *I have told the others. We must scatter before they use the gas. We will circle around behind them.*

The islanders began moving out through the brush as Charlotte looked down at the pier. Samuel and the vampire were circling each other and trading blows,

throwing titanic shadows onto the sand. Wood splin-
tered and flew as their swords met, while the planks of
the pier groaned and cracked. Blackened flesh hung
like rags from the vampire's body, while blood ran
freely from terrible gashes on her lover's arms and abdomen.

She grabbed Drew's sleeve, tearing the shoulder
seam. "He can't keep this up. He'll bleed out before he
can heal." Her eyes shifted as the women came out from
under the pier. "Jesus Christ, what are they still doing
down there?"

"They're part of the plan." As the women tossed
burning torches onto the pier behind the vampire, Drew
grabbed her. "That's my cue. Stay put."

Charlie ran after him toward the pier, her eyes fixed
on Samuel, who was staggering backward, his free hand
covering his left eye. Energúmeno advanced slowly, the
fire from the burning pier illuminating the golden fili-
gree around the gaping black wounds in his decayed
flesh.

Dolphins shot out of the water, distracting Charlotte
as they slammed their bodies into some of the men wading toward the shore. Gulls screeched as they hurtled
down from the sky, tearing at the men's faces. As the islanders emerged from the brush they formed a line and
marched toward the beach, each using his or her abilities to attack in unison. One seemed to pull a stream of
fire from the burning villa and directed it like a blow-
torch at a pair of men stumbling onto the sand, while
another flicked his hand at a dune, causing it to rise up
like a wave and then collapse on the burning bodies,
burying them.

Bamboo shot across the beach, undulating and curling as it encircled ankles and wrists before tightening
into green manacles. As the vampire's men struggled to
free themselves, some began shooting at the islanders.
The fire thrower set some of the bamboo alight to form
a high barrier of flames between the men and the island-

ers, while the sand mover created an enormous crater behind the twisting bodies. An invisible force pushed the trapped men close together while the bamboo formed a cagelike sphere. Charlotte glanced over to see Colotl's tattoo glowing as he focused on the writhing limbs of the vampire's helpless men. A moment later the bamboo sphere dropped into the massive hole in the beach, and another dune stretched out, filling in the hole until the men vanished from sight.

Charlie looked back at Samuel, who had dropped to his knees, and shrieked his name, only to find herself on her hands and knees in the sand. After shoving her down, Drew sprinted past her toward the water.

"No." She pushed herself up, struggling to her feet. "Sam, no."

"Now your heart is mine." Energúmeno held his sword to one side, raising the golden claw of his hand above Samuel's chest.

Charlotte screamed.

A misty figure appeared out of thin air between the vampire and Samuel, solidifying into Ihiyo's body.

"For Mocaya," Charlotte heard him say just before he jumped at Energúmeno.

White ice instantly encased the vampire's body, freezing him in place. A moment later something came whirling through the air from the water like a giant boomerang. Just before it struck the vampire's back, she saw it was another *macuahuitl*, this one covered with blades on all sides.

Samuel shot to his feet, his massive arm sweeping his sword up in a slashing blow.

Stone screeched against frozen metal, sending an explosion of ice crystals into the night air. Energúmeno stared at Samuel in disbelief, ice cracking and shedding in chunks from his arm as he brought his golden hand up to his face. Ice-coated gold began to fall away from the vampire's body, thudding onto the damp sand. Energúmeno looked down as his right arm dropped, and then his legs collapsed outward. He opened his mouth as if to speak, the horizontal gash extending across his face and disappearing into his frozen hair. His golden eye remained open as most of his head slid onto his shoulder and rolled away.

Charlotte felt one last wave of thoughts from the immortal, and caught her breath.

Samuel stood over him to make one final blow, the stone blades of his *macuahuitl* cutting cleanly through the vampire's neck. When the decapitated torso toppled over, he dropped the sword, turning away and starting toward Charlie.

She could hear the shouts of Energúmeno's men as the islanders surrounded them and attacked. Their frantic thoughts and emotions hammered against her mind, but suddenly Samuel was there, too, pushing them away and protecting her.

He stopped a short distance from her, his bloodied hands at his sides as he looked over at the islanders, who were finishing off the last of Energúmeno's men. "You weren't supposed to be here."

"None of us were." She closed the gap between them and touched his battered face, then surveyed the rest of him. Despite the blood loss most of his wounds had already begun to close, but she could feel the rawness of his emotions. "You okay?"

"I am now." He bent his head, resting his brow against hers.

"He was like you were before we came here," she said softly. "Pain filled every moment of his life, and he suffered it for so long he forgot what it is to be whole and well and sane. His last thought was how wonderful it felt to finally be free of it."

Drew came to them, his trousers soaked to the thighs. "You two okay?" As Samuel nodded, he glanced at the vampire's remains. "Can we get off this fucking island now?"

"Yes." Samuel looked out at the bodies on the sand,

and the tired faces of the islanders walking toward them. "Let's do that."

"We didn't find a match for the woman's fingerprints, but the DNA from her saliva tested positive for three alteration markers." Marlow handed Genaro the lab reports.

Genaro flipped through the pages. "There should be six markers." He glanced at the screen of his laptop, which displayed a video call screen. "You'll have to re-test the sample, Eliot."

"I don't think that's necessary, sir," his geneticist said. "She would show three only if one of her parents were human. My guess is she's second-generation Kyndred."

"Test the sample and make sure." Genaro rubbed his tired eyes as he ended the video call and handed the reports back to Marlow. "Has Delaporte faxed the results of the property searches?"

"No, sir, but our background check on Foster Stanton turned up something interesting. He's been receiving a large annual grant from the U.K. to study bird migration patterns." Marlow went to the wall map. "The site where he's supposedly conducting these studies is an island here, about two hundred miles out." He tapped the spot, and then moved his fingertip a short distance to a tiny cluster of islands nearby. "PROFEPA backed legislation to establish a protected area. No boat is allowed within six nautical miles of these islands."

It appeared to be the perfect place to conceal the Kyndred, but he wasn't convinced. "Get me satellite images."

Marlow left, and returned a short time later with a sheaf of printouts. "These were the last images recorded by our satellite before it moved out of range about twelve hours ago. There's a large structure that looks like some sort of religious temple on Stanton's island." He put one image on the desk, and then placed another atop it. "The satellite also picked up a fifth island that doesn't appear on any of the maps, but appears to be inhabited." He pointed to the seven large structures forming a ring around the island.

"That's it." Genaro closed the laptop and got to his feet. "Call our pilots at the airport and have them prepare the helicopters. We'll be leaving as soon as they're ready to take off."

"How many choppers will we need, sir?"

He wasn't letting the drug lord escape him again. "All of them."

On the way to the airport, Genaro placed a video call to Delaporte to tell him they were relocating. "I don't know how many we'll be able to recover from these islands, but have the lab in Los Angeles make arrangements for a dozen new acquisitions. Also, have them prepare interrogation rooms for Taske, Riordan, Flores, and Marena."

"Sir, I checked satellite images of those islands last night," his security chief said. "There's nothing on them but some palm trees and birds. You're wasting your time going out there."

Delaporte didn't know that Marlow had pulled the satellite images, or that he had just betrayed himself.

Fury erupted inside Genaro, but he kept his expression bland. "Well, then you've saved me a long and uncomfortable flight. Good work, Don."

His security chief looked satisfied. "I'll continue with the property searches, and get back to you as soon as we find anything of interest, sir."

"You do that." Genaro ended the call and immediately dialed Eliot Kirchner's private line. "Don Delaporte just tried to divert me away from the Kyndred. You were right. He's a traitor."

"I'm sorry to hear that, Jonah." The geneticist sighed. "I'll take care of him personally."

"Keep him sedated in isolation until I return," Genaro told him. "No one is to have access to him but you and me."

At the airport Marlow directed all of his men into the waiting transport carriers before joining Genaro. "We'll have to move quickly. I just got word that the Mexican army is on its way down here to take back the city."

More of Delaporte's handiwork, Genaro guessed. "Once we have the acquisitions secured, we'll fly directly back to the States."

In the air, ten minutes away from the islands, Genaro saw black smears, too dark to be clouds, marring the bright blue sky. He put on the headset that allowed him to talk to the helicopter pilot. "Is smoke coming from a ship?"

"No, sir." The pilot pointed toward the horizon. "It's coming from that landmass over there."

Beside him, Marlow checked the map, and then swore. "It's the unmapped island," he shouted over the noise of the rotors.

"Don't try to land," Genaro instructed the pilot. "Make a low pass so I can see what's down there."

"Yes, sir."

The helicopter descended to fly through the drifting smoke, dissipating enough of it to provide a partial view. The remains of the structures still smoldered, but from the amount of scorched rubble it was clear they had been burned to the ground. Unmoving bodies littered the beach in front of one of the houses, and smaller fires had broken out over the remainder of the island.

As the pilot completed his final pass, something exploded behind them, sending a shock wave through the helicopter. Genaro looked back to watch a small mushroom cloud of fire and smoke billow into the air.

"The survivors may have retreated to Stanton's island," Marlow shouted.

Genaro nodded, and told the pilot to change course, but from what he had seen he knew they were too late. Whatever battle had been fought was finished, and the victors were long gone.

Several hours later Marlow emerged from the Aztec temple on Stanton's island and confirmed Genaro's suspicions. "They left everything behind: money, drugs, artifacts, and enough weapons to outfit an army division. The Mexican government is sending a couple of navy ships out to investigate the source of the fires."

The sounds of three more distant explosions made Genaro glance out at the sea. "Recall your men. We're leaving."

Marlow nodded and gave the order over his hand-held.

On the flight back to California, Genaro brooded over the events of the day. The complete failure of the mission had created a substantial setback, but had also resulted in exposing the most dangerous spy in his organization.

Delaporte's military training wouldn't protect him from the barrage of drugs and torture Genaro planned to use on him. Given his level of access to GenHance's operations, the lengthy time he had spent working for the company, and the number of crimes he had personally committed, his security chief was not working for the government or the authorities. Instead Genaro felt sure that Delaporte reported directly to a competitor interested in stealing the transerum; as soon as Kirchner came up with a successful formula, Delaporte probably would have taken it and the geneticist. But if that were the case, why was he trying to prevent the Kyndred from being captured?

After landing at one of the secluded airstrips GenHance maintained, Marlow escorted Genaro from the helicopter to the limousine waiting at the edge of the runway.

"I've got to debrief the men, sir," he said. "I'll fly back to Atlanta tonight."

"Report to my office first thing in the morning," Genaro told him before he climbed into the back of the limo. He would need someone to replace Delaporte, and

Marlow had proven to be reliable, if somewhat unimaginative.

Marlow gave him a casual salute and trotted off toward the hangars.

Genaro waited for the car to move, and when it didn't, he pressed the intercom button. "Take me to LAX." When no reply came over the speaker, he reached for the button to lower the divider. "I said—" He fell silent as he saw the empty driver's seat.

Delaporte's familiar voice came over the walkie-talkie strapped to the small bundle of gray bricks and wires sitting on the center console. "Good-bye, Jonah."

Genaro turned and grabbed the door handle.

As the limo exploded, flying shrapnel forced Marlow to drop to the ground and cover his head. He waited until the rain of twisted metal and glass ended before he raised his head to look back and get to his feet. Men started running out of the hangars, shouting as they hurried toward the burning vehicle.

He took out the satellite phone he had used only once in Mexico, and pressed redial.

The voice that answered was not the one he expected, and its dark beauty sent a trickle of cold sweat down Marlow's spine. "Is it done?"

"Yes, my lord." He looked once more at the burning wreckage that had become Jonah Genaro's funeral pyre before he gave Richard Tremayne a final assurance. "He's dead."

Chapter 23

Agraciana had suggested going to her village after discovering the boat engines contained only enough fuel to take them back to the mainland. "We can take shelter in my father's house while I arrange transportation for you back to America."

They had arrived just before dawn, and at first the dock appeared empty. It was only when Agraciana stepped off that an elderly man emerged from the shadows and called her name.

"Papi?" She ran to him, halting only when she saw the silver-haired woman standing beside him. All the color drained out of her face. "Mama?"

The woman nodded, her eyes bright with tears as she held out her arms.

Charlie tensed as more people walked down the dock, until she saw the flashlights and blankets they were carrying.

"I think we're among friends," Sam told her.

The islanders remained on the boats, almost huddling together as they watched the villagers. Their odd behavior reminded Charlie of the near-complete isolation they had lived in for most of their lives.

"Tlemi." She smiled at the redhead. "It's okay. Come with me and Sam and meet Agraciana's friends."

Colotl took her hand, helping her off the boat and

walking beside her down the dock. He appeared braced for another battle, but did nothing as the excited villagers surrounded them. Everyone talked all at once as kind hands draped blankets over the islanders' shoulders. Another woman brought a tray of brightly colored ceramic mugs filled with a steaming brew that smelled spicy-sweet, and began handing them out as the other islanders cautiously approached.

Colotl took a sip from his cup, met Charlie's gaze, and grinned like a boy.

Drew left Agraciana with her parents and came over to Charlie and Samuel. "Gracie says they've got food and cots for everyone over at the church. The men of the village will keep watch so we can get some sleep."

Charlie frowned. "How did they know we'd come here?"

"A man and a woman stopped by here an hour ago," he said. "They knew everything that happened to us. They also brought Gracie's mother home."

"Who were they?" Samuel asked.

Drew shrugged. "No one recognized them, but Gracie's father said the woman wore a red flower in her hair. She also had a tattoo on the back of her hand." His mouth hitched. "A dove."

"Sam." Charlie watched the sun glisten along the gleaming white hull of the vessel sailing into the bay. It had been three days since they'd escaped the island, and while the villagers had taken good care of them, she was more than ready to go home. "Is that our ride back to the States out there?"

Samuel shaded his eyes for a moment to have a look before he continued reeling in his line. "I believe it is."

"That's not a boat."

"It's not?" He peered again. "How odd. It bears a striking resemblance to one."

"It's a yacht." She turned to him and planted her hands on her hips. "You chartered a *yacht*."

"We're smuggling thirteen people into the United States," he reminded her.

"Thirteen American citizens who were experimented on by mad scientists before they were sold to a vampire," she corrected.

He nodded. "Whatever you want to call them, honey, they're still not going to fit on a rubber raft."

Agraciana appeared at the other end of the dock and waved. "Come to the church," she called to them. "Dinner's ready."

Samuel secured the hook to the fishing pole before shouldering it and pulling out of the water the string of fish he'd already caught. He surveyed them with satisfaction. "I'm going to miss this."

Charlie picked up his bait bucket, wrinkling her nose at the contents. "I'm not."

They walked down the dock and through the dunes to the shell-lined path leading to the church that had served not only as their hotel but as the village's command center. Over the last seventy-two hours Agraciana's family and neighbors had gone into action, bringing a seamstress with piles of garments she altered to replace the islanders' worn clothing, a cobbler to fit them with shoes, and a hairdresser to trim their shaggy manes. A lovely old red velvet lounger had been brought over specifically for Pici's use, as well as a stereo, a television set, and a DVD player.

Charlie had chuckled at the islanders' reaction the first time the television had been switched on. At first it frightened them, until Samuel changed the station to one that showed cartoons, which soon fascinated them. While they couldn't understand the Spanish dubbing, none of them seemed to tire of watching the antics of Tom and Jerry.

The aroma of delicious food met them at the doors to

the church, and Charlie and Samuel paused there to admire the sight of the picnic tables they had been using for meals, now laden with so many platters, bowls, and baskets the tops were completely concealed.

The generosity made Charlie's heart ache. "Every cupboard in this town must be bare by now."

"Not for long," Samuel said. "Tomorrow Drew and Agraciana will make sure everyone is amply repaid for their efforts."

She glanced at him. "They're staying behind?"

"For a few weeks, so Agraciana can have some time with her mother." He put his arm around her shoulders. "Charlotte, as soon as we return, Matthias will take charge of relocating the islanders. You and I have other business to attend to."

Charlie knew Matthias had a network of safe houses and properties, but the islanders didn't know him. "We can go with them, make sure they're okay."

"Unless you want to change your identity, we have to make a public appearance. Give the media a happy ending." Before she could say anything he added, "All it will take is one press conference. I've already arranged it and the cover story about our rescue."

So it had begun; she had expected it, but not so soon. Everything would be so easy for him; he'd make a call, transfer some money, talk into some microphones, and his world would be just as it was before they were taken. Because Charlie had been on the job when she'd been kidnapped, she knew she was facing a six-week administrative leave and a mandatory psych evaluation. She had four hundred dollars and change in her checking account; not enough to cover even her rent for a month. Although under the circumstances, she wouldn't be surprised to discover that her landlord had sublet her apartment and put her belongings up for auction on eBay.

"Charlotte?"

She gave him a blind smile. "Sure, I can do a press conference. We both want our lives back; we should do whatever it takes."

Samuel closed the door to the church. "Forgive me, but I don't want to be a lonely cripple again, or talk to you on a computer, or lie awake at night wondering where you are and what you're doing. I want you with me."

"You think you do." She tried to choose her next words carefully. "Sam, when we were on the island, you thought you were going to die. So did I. We said a lot of crazy things. We needed something good, and it was. It was wonderful. But it's over now."

His hands dropped away. "I meant every word I said to you."

"I'm sure you did, *mío*." She turned away. "But we're safe now, so I'm letting you off the hook. You can go back to Boston or wherever and sell your antiques and manage your millions. I'll be fine."

"You're a brave woman." He put his hands on her shoulders. "You're also a terrible liar. I didn't know that."

The only thing she could use as her last defense was the truth. "You don't need me anymore."

Samuel turned her around. "I love you, Charlotte Marena. Without you I have no life, so please." He touched his lips to hers. "Don't leave me."

She couldn't read his thoughts until the sun set, but she didn't have to. Everything he felt for her was in his voice, in his eyes, and in the heart beating against hers. "I won't. At least, not until we're very old, and gray haired, and ready to go to the next place."

Samuel kissed her until the church door opened and Drew stepped out.

"Sorry to interrupt, but Gracie needs to talk to you." He gestured inside.

Charlie and Samuel followed him into the church, past the tables where everyone was still enjoying the food, and into the hall where the cots had been set up.

Agraciana stood in front of the television, which was showing a funeral of someone important, judging by the hundreds of mourners in attendance. When she saw them she reached over and shut it off.

"Is something wrong?" Charlie asked.

"I am not certain." She reached into her pocket and took out a business card. "The man and woman who brought my mother home left this with her. In all the excitement she forgot about it." She offered it to Samuel. "They asked her to give it to you."

He glanced at the card and showed it to Charlie, who read the two lines printed on it.

"Michael Cyprien. I don't know that name, but he has an international phone number." She looked up at him, but he only shook his head.

"Should we call it?" Drew asked.

"No." Samuel pocketed the card. "We should go have dinner with our friends."

The media wanted much more than one press conference, but Samuel's small army of attorneys and security guards as well as sympathetic city officials kept them at bay as they left the mayor's conference room. After a brief trip to Charlie's apartment to collect what she needed, their police escort drove them directly to the airport, where Samuel's private plane waited.

Charlie, who had never flown anything but economy class, tried not to gawk at everything while Samuel spoke to the pilot. After turning down the drink offered by the pretty flight attendant, Charlie sank back in the sumptuous cushions of her seat and closed her eyes.

A big hand reached across her to buckle her seat belt and adjust the back of her seat to a reclining position.

"I'm not sleeping through my first flight on the Concord."

"It's not the Concord, honey." Samuel tucked a weightless, prewarmed blanket around her. "It's only a Learjet."

"Oh." She pursed her lips and pretended to look around. "Well, this isn't bad, for a compact." She yawned. "Probably gets better gas mileage, too."

"I'll have to consult my mechanic." He lifted the arm between her seat and the other two beside it, and adjusted those so they reclined at the same angle. By the time he took off his jacket and sat down beside her, Charlotte was asleep.

The flight attendant silently offered him another blanket, but Samuel shook his head. She nodded and retreated to the front of the cabin.

Samuel could sleep whenever he wanted, but as he had discovered on the island, he no longer needed to. It seemed to be the final gift of his transformation, one that worried him until he'd discussed it privately with Matthias when he had met them on the yacht.

"It is the same for me, Samuel." The former Roman soldier, who had survived two thousand years buried in an icy grave, looked out over the water. "After I came down from the mountain, I did not sleep for months. Lifting weights before you retire helps quiet the mind." His expression softened. "So does lovemaking."

Samuel took out the card Agraciana had given him and handed it to him. "This was left for us in Mexico. The number is unregistered. Michael Cyprien is the name of a reclusive, mysterious billionaire who apparently owns enough of the U.S. to secede from the union and form his own country, and yet has never once been interviewed or even photographed."

Matthias read the print. "I think this is an invitation to talk." He returned it. "Are you going to accept?"

"I don't know." He tucked the card away and glanced at the islanders, who had gathered in one of their circles on deck to silently commune with one another.

"The time ahead will not be easy for them," Matthias said. "To avoid unwanted attention, we must separate and settle them in different locations. From what Charlotte has told me, they have never before lived apart from one another."

His comment made Samuel consider an alternative. "Perhaps they don't have to."

Still yawning from the ridiculously long nap she'd taken on the jet, Charlie stepped out of the terminal and surveyed the waiting limo and the uniformed chauffeur. "Looks like we're right back where we started, Sam." As they walked over, she peered at the smiling face of the driver. "Hey, I know you. James, right? How's the lung?"

"Working perfectly, thanks to your care, ma'am." He touched the rim of his cap before his expression sobered and he regarded Taske. "Sir, I can't tell you how sorry I am for what happened on the bridge that morning. If you want my resignation—"

"Not in this lifetime, Findley, or any other." Taske pulled the driver into a careful bear hug before resting a hand on his shoulder. "You still look pale. Are you certain that you're well enough to drive?"

"I won't be running any marathons for a while, sir," Findley admitted ruefully, "but I can manage the drive home."

Once they were on the road, Charlie felt a fresh surge of apprehension. "You never told me exactly where home is."

"I own several properties here and abroad, but I spend most of my time at Tannerbridge." He picked up her hand and frowned. "You're cold."

She nodded. "I'm a little clammy, too. Nerves."

"You've survived a sniper attack, an abduction, the island, and the American media," he reminded her. "All with the courage and fortitude of a tigress. I'm sure you can manage a visit to my humble abode."

"If the abode were humble, which it's not," she guessed. "No one names a duplex or a town house or a double-wide trailer."

"My parents were sentimental." He rubbed her hand between his. "Don't be afraid. If you hate it, we'll leave and find a nice, quiet hotel."

She hmphed. "Now you're trying to distract me with sex."

A groove appeared in his cheek. "Is it working?"

"Could be." The foot of space between them became unbearable, and Charlie unbuckled her seat belt to shift herself over onto his lap. Once she had her arms looped around his neck and her face tucked under his chin, she sighed. "Tell me about your bed."

"It's a custom-built double king." He bent his head to whisper, "With silk sheets and a down feather duvet. They smell like sunshine."

"Okay." She closed her eyes. "Forget the hotel."

Findley drove for more than an hour, leaving behind the city for the back roads through the country, where the forests seemed to march on forever. Now and then she would see a private road leading off through a gate, most crowned with a curving sign proclaiming the property's name in elegant letters: Emerald Acres, Hudson's Folly, Feathersound.

"Feathers don't make any sound," she grumbled to Samuel as Findley turned and brought the limo to a halt before a towering pair of gates fashioned out of wrought iron to resemble a bridge.

For a moment she felt a spike of terror, until she saw the forms of the diminutive couple walking hand in hand over it.

"My parents met on Tanner Bridge," Samuel said, tightening his arms around her. "But I'll have it taken down today, if you like."

"No, that's okay. Not everything that happens on a bridge is bad." As the gates opened and Findley drove through, she glanced back before meeting Samuel's worried gaze. "We found each other on one, remember?"

The drive stretched another two miles before they reached the main house on the estate. Charlie eyed the stately brick structure, which was too large to be called anything but a mansion. A slim man stood waiting by a gigantic, merrily splashing bronze fountain, its pool-size basin edged with dozens of petite red rosebushes. As soon as the car stopped he came to open the door.

"Welcome home, sir." He turned to Charlie. "I'm Morehouse, Miss Marena. It's a pleasure to meet you."

His British accent made her scowl. "I bet you're the guy who came up with those evil chocolate-cherry scones that Sam e-mailed the recipe for."

"I'm afraid I am." Morehouse looked a little flustered. "I'm sorry if you didn't enjoy them."

"You see this?" Charlie patted her hip. "At least ten pounds of this is your fault." She grinned. "So, you got any more stashed away in there?"

Morehouse suppressed a smile. "I'll serve them with your tea this afternoon, madam."

"I know you want to give me a tour and all," Charlie murmured as they followed the house manager inside, "but I need a shower, and you to scrub my back. And my front. And anything else you feel like scrubbing."

Samuel's eyes darkened. "I would be delighted, but I do have something to show you first."

She sidled up against him. "Is this a fast something?"

"If we stay inside," he said.

While Morehouse took their cases up to the master suite, Samuel led Charlie through a bewildering labyrinth of magnificent rooms to a long, wide atrium. Glass skylights provided sunny light and glimpses of the sky, while a wall of French doors offered a panoramic view of the gardens beyond the main house. "Wow." Charlie stopped and smiled as she looked out at the maze of flowers, arbors, and trees, and the ring of picturesque cottages in the distance. "This is gorgeous." Her eyes shifted as a man and woman came walking out of a bower of sweet peas, their arms around each other. "Uh, your gardeners are really friendly."

"They are." He sounded amused.

As the couple walked into the sunlight, the woman's neatly trimmed red hair blazed, and the man's dark skin glowed like melting chocolate.

"Tlemi and Colotl." Charlie turned to stare at him. "What are they doing here? I thought Matthias was going to take them to his farm in Tennessee."

"I persuaded him to bring them here." He gestured toward the cottages. "As you can see, I have more than enough space, and they'll have the time they need to adjust to our culture, learn English, and decide what they want to do with their lives."

"That's really great." Charlie saw Pici and Ihiyo joining the other couple. "Wait. How many of them did he bring?"

Samuel smiled. "All of them."

"So you've basically adopted twelve grown-up kids." She tucked her arm through his. "It's going to be a lot of work, and probably cost you a large fortune."

"Luckily I've made several." His smile slipped. "If my wealth is still an issue, I'll give it all away tomorrow. I have everything I need now."

"You are a crazy man." She squeezed his hand. "But there might be others like them out there. We can't help them if we're living in a one-room apartment on my salary."

"What about you?"

"You mean, do I want to live in the mansion or the one-room apartment?" She pretended to think. "You know, I really need to see this bed."

He bent his head and kissed her before guiding her around. "Right this way, madam."

Epilogue

Anyone hoping to get a table at the most popular French restaurant in Manhattan usually had to make reservations six months in advance. The food at D'Anges, however, was rumored to be well worth the wait. So it was odd that on the night of September 29, passersby noticed that the front of the restaurant remained dark, and every table stood empty. The only explanation had been taped to the front door: a small white sign that simply read, CLOSED 9/29 FOR PRIVATE FUNCTION.

"They're late." In the restaurant's kitchen, Rowan Dansant-Meriden glanced at her watch. "The snapper bisque won't be fit to eat soon."

"Then we will serve it chilled." Jean-Marc, the owner and head chef of D'Anges, as well as one of her lovers, took off his apron before he ran a soothing hand along her tense back. "You do not have to do this."

"What, leave Samuel alone in their clutches while I hide in the kitchen like a girl?" She made a rude sound. "I don't think so." She glanced over at Charlotte Marena, who was having a laughing discussion in Spanish with their pastry chef. "Hey, Maggie, stop distracting the kid from his work. He's got to finish those champagne éclairs."

"*Lo siento,*" Charlotte said, bumping shoulders with Enrique before joining Rowan and Jean-Marc and glancing at the clock over the sous-chef's station. "They're late."

"Come on." Rowan linked arms with her. "We'll go keep the boys company." She looked back over her shoulder. "If you feel the urge to change, I left some clothes for you upstairs."

Jean-Marc chuckled and blew her a kiss.

The women left the kitchen and went around the corner to the private room reserved for the chef's table, a weekly event that Manhattan's most devoted foodies would do anything to attend. Tonight only two men sat at the long glass table, and both were completely engrossed in a laptop showing a football game.

"Who's winning?" Rowan asked.

"Green Bay," Drew said absently. "Rodgers is merciless tonight."

"For now. The Patriots will have no difficulty coming from behind," Samuel assured him before he smiled up at Charlotte. "They're late."

She sat down beside him and helped herself to one of Rowan's delicious *amuse bouches*. "Second thoughts, maybe?"

"Payback," Drew said. "We made them wait first. For months." The sound of the front doorbell made him straighten. "At least they don't hold a grudge." He switched off the laptop and stowed it under his chair before he shrugged into his jacket.

"I'll show them in." Rowan sauntered out.

Samuel took Charlotte's hand in his. "Genaro is dead, Kirchner is in prison, and Delaporte has destroyed everything that might expose us."

She smiled a little. "You mean, stop worrying about something as simple and easy as meeting the vampires whose DNA was used to change us into superhumans."

"We were created to hunt them down and kill them," Samuel said softly. "I think we can hold our own."

They both looked up as Rowan returned with three strangers. One, a broad, scarred-faced man with light eyes and an impassive expression, surveyed the room before stepping to one side. Behind him a petite, chestnut-haired woman stood beside a man who could have been Jean-Marc Dansant's twin brother.

Samuel rose to his feet. "Welcome, Mr. Cyprien, Dr. Keller, Mr. Navarre."

"Monsieur." Cyprien inclined his head, and then studied Charlotte and Drew for a moment. "We are happy that you finally agreed to this meeting."

"It's Alexandra," the woman said to Samuel. "And we're not that happy. You wouldn't even tell us your names."

"I believe you already knew some of them." Samuel gestured toward the empty chairs at the other end of the table. "Please join us."

"We assume you can't eat food," Rowan said as she brought a bottle of wine to the table. "Can you handle a little overpriced merlot?"

"Thank you, no." Cyprien took the seat directly opposite Samuel's, but lifted his hands from the table an instant after touching it. "This is made of copper."

"Yes, it is." Drew took a penny from his pocket and flipped it into the air, where it hung suspended as it stretched out and became a miniature dagger. "So are most of the fixtures in this room. Which, by the way, I will not hesitate to use to skewer your immortal asses"— the little dagger flew across the room and buried itself in the wall behind Cyprien's head—"should you try to help yourselves to some takeout."

Alexandra burst out laughing. "God, you guys are smart."

"We are not interested in feeding on any of you, monsieur." Cyprien held up his palms in a gesture of surrender. "We wished only to meet our progeny."

Charlotte scowled. "We are *not* your children."

"Technically, no, you're not," Alexandra agreed. "We can't have kids."

Everyone looked over as Jean-Marc entered the

room. "Ah, you have arrived. I must go soon, but I thought . . . I would . . ." He trailed off as he stared at Cyprien's face. *"Mon Dieu."*

"Guess whose DNA you got," Rowan drawled.

Cyprien rose and slowly extended his hand. After a moment, Jean-Marc took it in his own and began speaking to him in their native language.

"Does he fuss at you for leaving your clothes on the floor?" Alexandra asked Rowan, who nodded. "Some things *are* genetic." To Cyprien she said, "Quit talking in French. It's rude to the English speakers, which is everyone else but Phillipe."

Both men glanced at her and apologized at the same time before uttering identical chuckles.

"This is incredible." Cyprien regarded his twin. "Are there others among you who are . . . like the two of us?"

"We don't know," Samuel said. "But it's safe to assume there will be some Kyndred who were altered to be body doubles." As Cyprien met his gaze, he added, "So they could assume your identities after you were killed."

Cyprien sat back down. "We have no quarrel with you, monsieur. I wish you to understand that. We chose to intervene on your behalf in Mexico to protect you."

"He's telling the truth," Charlotte murmured to Samuel.

"So you must be a mind reader. I have a similar problem, just with killers." Alexandra's expression turned wry. "And yes, we do have excellent hearing. If you don't want us to hear what you whisper, you need to be about a block away."

"What we want, Doctor, are some answers," Charlotte said. "Why are you protecting us? Why offer to meet us? What do you really want?"

"Well, primarily we'd like to establish diplomatic relations so you don't end up being used by our enemies as weapons against us." Alexandra ignored the sharp sound Cyprien made. "Trust me; I have the inside track on this. I was one of you before I grew fangs."

"*You* were Kyndred." Rowan looked skeptical.

"If you don't believe me, I'll give you before and after blood samples." Alexandra tapped the inside of her forcarm. "For the 'after,' you'll need the master of small change here to coat a syringe with copper. Nothing else penetrates our immortal asses."

"I think any exchanges of blood should be avoided for right now," Samuel said. "We accept that you have wanted only to protect us, but you murdered Jonah Genaro. We can't condone or support that kind of violence."

"Oh, so we should have just let him go on kidnapping you, and dissecting you, and using your DNA to make monsters?" Alexandra asked sweetly. She blinked as Drew slid a thick file across the table at her. "What's this? A petition?"

"Evidence," Drew said flatly. "Some of us have spent years compiling it. We had put together almost enough to shut down GenHance and put Genaro in prison for the rest of his life."

Cyprien picked up the file and skimmed through it. "So you believe you do not need our protection."

"I am saying that we never asked for it," Samuel said softly.

Cyprien closed the folder. "Genaro's death does not guarantee a safe future for the Kyndred or the Darkyn. For that, monsieur, we must work together."

"Like a team?" Drew asked.

Phillipe muttered something, and Alexandra grinned. "No, pal. Like a family." Her eyes strayed to Jean-Marc, who was shaking and groping for a chair. "Is he okay?"

Rowan swore under her breath as she went to him and helped him to sit. "He will be in a second." She knelt beside him, holding his hands as he hunched over.

Alexandra's eyes widened as Jean-Marc's body began to grow larger and his long black hair receded into his skull, and she knocked over her chair getting to her feet. She reached the chef at the same moment Charlotte did.

"It's okay," Charlotte told her. "He doesn't take long to change."

"To change into what?"

"My other boyfriend," Rowan said, sighing as the transformation ended, and a big blond man lifted his head. "Say hi, honey."

"Hi, honey." The big man pulled her close and gave her a lingering kiss before he looked around the room. "They the vampires?" he asked, his deep voice just as startling as his appearance.

"That's us." Alexandra sat back on her heels. "So he can cook and shape-shift. I'll be damned."

"We have a great deal to learn from one another," Cyprien said. "Perhaps that is the best place for us to begin." He rose and walked over to Samuel, and held out his hand. "In hope that our people may someday become friends, monsieur."

Samuel looked at Charlotte, who nodded, as did Rowan and Drew, before he took Cyprien's hand. "You can call me Paracelsus."

Turn the page for an excerpt from

Nightborn
Lords of the Darkyn

Coming from Signet Select in March 2012

Korvel knew the brief battles in which he had engaged had not harmed him greatly, but the poisonous effect of the copper lodged in his flesh had rendered him weak and listless. In another time he would have fought his way back to life and his place in it, but his current apathy made it a difficult thing to desire. Why leave the dull gray void in which he lay suspended, only to return to a world that no longer held any interest for him?

His dismal thoughts conjured images of the young nun with the angelic face. She had been tormented and nearly raped; she remained alone on the other side. He suspected he hadn't killed all of the men who had attacked the château, and if they came upon her while he was helpless . . .

Korvel reached for consciousness, and at once the void dragged at him, becoming a sea of muck through which he waded, one infuriatingly slow step at a time. He was much weaker than he had guessed, dangerously so; if he were to awaken, it would have to be by will alone.

Once more he thought of the green-eyed angel who had tended to his wound. Whatever faith had compelled her to abandon life and serve an uncaring God, she was still an innocent. As such she needed—no, deserved—his assistance. *I will go to her, and keep her safe.*

He could feel her, close to him now, her presence like a muted caress. Even through the gnashing teeth of fresh pain, she calmed him. His weakness grew as his sense of her faded, and he reached out blindly, capturing her warmth and enfolding it against him. There she remained, unresisting and silent, until his thoughts dwindled and he entered a darker corner of the void to rest and heal.

Sometime later, the setting of the sun roused Korvel to consciousness. He sensed this time that he had more strength to draw on, and crossed the emptiness with only a brief effort. He felt her warmth slipping away, and opened his eyes.

Cracked hand-carved moldings framed a rough plaster ceiling spotted with small water stains and draped in one corner with the dusty remains of some long-dead spider's trap. The soft amber light illuminating it came from fat beeswax candles set in crystal goblets half-filled with pretty pebbles and shells that had been spaced like treasures across a stone shelf. A muslin pinafore hung from the knob of a bolted door, over which a plain wooden cross had been nailed. A basket with balled wool and knitting needles sat beside a shabby tapestry chair; a chipped blue stoneware jug sat inside a matching basin in an iron stand.

He turned his head to see a small shrine built atop an old secretary: flowers and votive candles in punched-tin holders surrounding a diminutive statue of the Virgin Mary in her blue robes and white headdress. A rosary of gray stone beads and blackened silver lay draped around the base of the statue.

If this were the cloistered cell it appeared to be, then the nun had brought him to her convent. If this were a jail cell, the French police had greatly improved the living conditions within their prisons.

A flutter of fabric drew his attention to the foot of the pallet, where the nun stood with her back toward him. She was in the process of undressing, and while Korvel knew he should look away, he couldn't stop watching her. She tugged the bloodstained gray habit over her head to reveal the long line of her spine. She tugged at the drawstring of her only undergarment, a pair of loose cotton drawers, before sliding them down her legs.

Now naked, she went to the basin stand, where she poured water from the jug into the bowl and began to wash the blood from her body.

The tightening of his muscles didn't distract Korvel from watching her, but the knotting in his groin did. His shaft hardened and swelled.

Carnal desire racked him, demanding relief, and it stunned him. It had been so long since he had wanted any mortal female that his arousal seemed utterly alien, as if some unseen predator had burrowed under his skin.

The nun's body beckoned to him, an oasis of pleasures yet to be had, but he could resist her by thinking of her innocence. She belonged to God, not him. It was when she took down her braids and unraveled them, combing through the long, bright strands with her fingers, that he crumpled the bed linens in his fists. Once free, her hair fell in luminous waves all the way to her hips, glinting like fiery gold in the candlelight.

Korvel had not seen a woman with such hair in centuries, not since mortal females had lived out their entire lives without once cutting a single hair from their heads.

He frowned as he saw that the light had also chased the shadows from her skin and revealed a collection of odd, pale marks all over her. The random positions of the marks and the fact that she was a nun made it highly unlikely that they were tan lines. The marks themselves formed a variety of shapes; on her left hip one narrow stripe curled like a lock of hair, but a few inches above it a broader, straight slash bisected her shoulder blade.

Only when she dried herself and went to kneel before the shrine did she come close enough for him to see the faint ridges of the marks, which made Korvel realize at last what they were.

Scar tissue. Someone had grievously abused the nun, so harshly and often that they had left her scarred from her nape to her knees.

Lust ebbed, scoured away by shock, shame, and an empathy he had never felt for a mortal of the modern world. As she took down the rosary and began murmuring her prayers, Korvel recalled the years of punishment he had once endured, the dismal human life he had never been able to forget. Small wonder she had turned her back on the world to cloister herself. Perhaps, like him, she had never received a single kindness from her birth family.

As Korvel pushed himself into a sitting position, the nun glanced over her shoulder and then kissed the rosary before replacing it. Instead of scurrying for clothing to cover her nakedness, she came to the pallet, climbing up onto it and pushing him back against the pillows.

Shocked anew, Korvel stared at her. "What are you doing?"

"Attending you." She pushed her hair over her shoulders and produced a small folding knife, opening it and plying it against her forearm. Her body heat combined with the blood scent and slammed into him, as merciless as it was enticing.

Korvel managed to turn his head away as she brought her arm to his mouth. "No."

"Take it." She pressed against his cheek with her free hand, guiding his mouth along her thin skin until his lips parted.

As hot as it was luscious, her blood coursed inside him as if it were molten copper, eating away at his coldness and flaring in every shadowy corner of his soul. He wanted nothing more than to roll her beneath him and take her completely, his teeth piercing her throat, his body pushing into hers, drinking from her and moving inside her until she knew and wanted nothing but him.

He was descending into the thrall of bloodlust, which seemed as bizarre as his sudden desire for this mortal. Never had he been tempted to drain a human upon whom he fed, for he knew the act that would send them both into the nightlands. There she would die, and he would be trapped, senseless and unmoving, for days. Now at last he understood the terrible temptation of that thrall and rapture, and how it destroyed all reasoning, all will.

Korvel wrenched his mouth from her, and for an instant it was as if he tore the heart from his own chest. "Stop."

A line formed between her brows. "Am I not to your liking?"

Her taste had nearly reduced him to a beast, not that he would frighten her by saying so. "You have given enough to restore me. That is all I can ask of you." Because his voice sounded so harsh, he caught her hand and brought it to his lips. "I am grateful for your kindness."

"Kindness." She seemed bemused, and ran her fingertip across the tight line of his mouth, wiping away a trace of her blood. "You have a very strange way of speaking, Englishman."

"Korvel." He wanted to hear his name on her lips.

She tilted her head, spilling a cascade of rose-streaked gold over her bare shoulder. "I am obliged to call you 'my lord,' or, at the very least, 'Captain.' "

He couldn't keep his hand from brushing back the fine flax of her tresses, or from curling around her nape. "Call me any damn thing you wish," he murmured as he brought her face down to his.

New York Times bestselling author

LYNN VIEHL

The Novels of the Kyndred

Shadowlight

With just one touch, Jessa Bellamy can see anyone's darkest secrets.
What she doesn't know is that a biotech company has discovered her
talent and intends to kill her and harvest her priceless DNA. Gaven
Matthias is forced to abduct Jessa so he can protect her, but she has a
hard time believing the one man whose secrets she can't read. As a
monstrous assassin closes in, Jessa will have to find another way to
know if Matthias is her greatest ally—or her deadliest enemy.

Dreamveil

Rowan Dietrich grew up on the streets. Now she's out to start anew,
find a job—and keep her identity as a Kyndred secret, as well as her
ability to "dreamveil" herself into the object of others' desires. But
Rowan isn't using her gift when world-class chef Jean-Marc Dansant is
stricken by her beauty and strength. And when dark secrets from her
past threaten her new life and love, she realizes she can't run forever...

Frostfire

As one of the genetically enhanced Kyndred, Lilah's mind-reading
powers make her vulnerable to a mysterious biotech company willing
to murder to acquire her superhuman DNA. But her true fear may
come from her own Kyndred brethren...

**Available wherever books are sold or at
penguin.com**